D027742
34143 0028 1399

The Tides of Peace

DENISE ROBERTSON

The Tides of Peace

WARRINGTON BOROUGH COUNCIL	
34143100291309	
Bertrams	11/03/2010
AF	£7.99
BUR	

Published in the United Kingdom in 2010 by Little Books Ltd,
Notting Hill, London W11 3QW

10 9 8 7 6 5 4 3 2 1

Text copyright © 2010 by Denise Robertson
Design and layout copyright © by Little Books Ltd

All rights reserved. No part of this work may be reproduced or utilized
in any form or by any means, electronic or mechanical, including
photocopying, recording or by any information storage and retrieval system,
without the prior written permission of the publisher.

A CIP catalogue record for this book is available from the British Library.

ISBN 978 1 906264 13 0

Every attempt has been made to trace any copyright holders. The author and
publisher will be grateful for any information that will assist them in keeping
future editions up to date. Although all reasonable care has been taken in the
preparation of this book, neither the publisher, editors nor the author can accept
any liability for any consequences arising from the use thereof, or the information
contained therein.

Printed and bound by CPI Bookmarque, Croydon.

BOOK 1

Chapter One

June 1945

SARAH HAD SET THE BACK door ajar and lowered the blinds, in an effort to make the kitchen cooler, but still Catherine could feel sweat pooling in the crevices of her body, even in her eyelids. She thought longingly of a cool bath, but getting in and out was so difficult now that bathing had lost much of its charm. Her baby was due in seven weeks. Seven weeks!

She came alert suddenly, aware that both Sarah and Hannah Chaffey were looking at her questioningly.

'Sorry? I didn't quite hear . . .'

'You were dropping off,' Hannah said, but her tone was indulgent. Everyone was being so nice to her nowadays, Catherine thought. She was bringing a fatherless baby into the world, and as such she was an object of pity. 'Should I be sorry for myself?' she wondered, as she accepted more tea and sympathy. Last night Sarah had told her that she had had a hard life. It was said in such kindly tones that Catherine had wanted to laugh out loud. In her opinion, Sarah had suffered far more at the hands of an abusive husband. At least she herself had been loved – even if her lover had been a man whose ultimate duty lay in returning to his wife and children. If Max knew she was carrying his baby, her heart told her, then he would come to her. But even as she thought it she acknowledged that her head knew better. Max had gone back to New York to pick up the life that World War Two had rudely interrupted, and she would never hear from him again.

'Hannah was saying it doesn't seem four weeks since VE night. More like five minutes.' Sarah was pouring again, and pushing Catherine's tea-cup towards her. 'Drink up. You need your fluids on a day like this.'

'We were talking about the Russians,' Hannah said ominously. 'I was saying they'll rule the world before they're finished. You mark my words: they won't be content with half of Germany. That'll be just the start of it.'

Catherine sipped her tea, and then replaced her cup in the saucer. 'You could be right, Hannah. David Callingham was talking about it last night. He says they're forcing the Americans to withdraw to westwards, and our troops, too. Their desire to dominate Germany is understandable, given what they've suffered. But Churchill won't let them take over anywhere else. Nor will the Americans.'

Hannah's smile was a masterpiece of irony. 'Well, if Sir David says so it must be true. Me, I think they'll gobble us all up. And Churchill won't be able to do a blind thing about it. Still, I can't sit here as if I had corn growing.' And with that she gathered up dusters and polish, and went off to battle with whatever speck of dust dared to lurk.

'You really don't need to put up with her.' Sarah was looking at Catherine with anxious eyes. 'I can do everything here, you know that. I did it before.'

Catherine was silent for a moment, remembering the time when Sarah had been housekeeper here, and she herself had been at the hospital working with Max Detweiler, he as a surgeon expert in repairing the ravaged faces of servicemen, she as a lowly Red Cross nurse. Winning the war had been the only thing that mattered. An end in itself. Catherine had not allowed herself to think of the moment when the war would be over, and Max would go back to his wife and children, but that moment had duly come.

As for Sarah, the end of the war had seen her fleeing a violently abusive husband – a man who at any moment might erupt back into her life. Into both their lives. She smiled at the woman who had once been her servant and was now her friend. 'It doesn't feel like peace-time, does it? All this talk of armies and demarcation lines.'

'See!' Sarah was rising from her seat. 'Hannah has upset you with her chatter, and you nearly ready to drop.'

'Finish your tea,' Catherine said. 'It'll take more than Hannah to upset you and me, considering what we've been through. Now, I fancy a night at the pictures if we can find someone to watch the children. What do you want to see?'

⸻

It was quiet in the colliery yard as David Callingham drove in. Since the war in Europe had ended, people did not feel the same urge to work for victory. Unless they had men in the forces that were still ranged against the Japanese, most people regarded their task as accomplished. Besides, as the prospect of nationalising the mines loomed nearer, there was a growing mood of resentment towards coal-owners. He saw it in the men's eyes. They still deferred to him as owner of the colliery in which they laboured, but there was a new air about them, a sense of growing power.

'Surely Churchill won't go down,' Alistair Groom, David's agent, said, when David mentioned the impending election and the nationalisation that would surely follow. The coalition government that had governed Britain throughout the war had resigned ten days after the war in Europe had ended. Churchill had asked that the coalition should remain in place until the Japanese were defeated, but Labour had refused. They wanted an election, and they wanted it now.

'Labour mean business,' David said now. 'They're in good shape. Better shape than the Tories, in my opinion. Churchill is a popular figure, but this country's been turned upside down in the past five years. Anything could happen.'

'If Labour did win they'd nationalise, I suppose,' the agent said. 'They've talked about it long enough. But it's a far cry from threatening to actually doing it. I wouldn't worry.'

They got on with day-to day-business then. It wouldn't do for him to tell Alistair the truth, David thought – that he could hardly wait to have the burden of running the colliery lifted from him. Instead they hammered out the detail of running a pit with a workforce of hundreds; and then, over a dram, discussed more pleasant things.

'We've set the date,' David said. 'Valerie expects to be demobbed in August, and if she is we'll probably marry in the autumn. Quite quietly, we're both agreed on that. My sister has raised no objection . . . unusually for her.' The two men looked at one another, half-smiling. India, David's sister, was not known for her sunny disposition.

'That's nice,' Alistair said drily.

David nodded. 'Long may it last.' His tone was fervent and they both laughed.

It was a relief when the buzzer blew, and the noise of the lathes died away. 'Come on, Pammy, I need to cadge a tab.' Joyce linked her arm through Pamela's and urged her towards the canteen. The women settled around tables, cups in hands and cigarettes dangling from their lips. The talk nowadays was all of peace-time, when the men came home and the women took up their rightful role as homemakers.

'May God strike me dead if I ever work again,' one woman said. Metal curlers glinted beneath the scarf wound turban-wise about her head. 'I'm going to do my chores each morning, peel the spuds for him coming home, and then sit with my bloody feet up the rest of the day.'

'You'll die of boredom, Freda,' someone said, but Freda was adamant.

'Can't wait to be bored, pet. Bring it on.'

There was general merriment, everyone competing to be more outrageous in their plans for peace. Pamela stayed silent, hugging her thoughts to herself. She would have to work for a while, while Michael studied. After that there would be babies and holidays and making a perfect home. She would be like her sister, Catherine, glowing with a baby in her belly – but unlike poor Catherine she would have a man to protect her. When Catherine had married into the Callingham family, Pamela had envied her. All that wealth! But she hadn't been married five minutes before her young husband, Sir Henry Callingham, had been shot down, and now she had been left in the lurch by that American. Max had been attractive in an American sort of way, but she herself would never have fancied him, Pamela thought. And he was Jewish. Even if he had been free, that would have been a problem.

'I'm so lucky,' Pamela thought. She felt contentment well up in her, until she noticed that one woman had not spoken yet. 'Any news, Edith?' Her son was a prisoner in Japanese hands, and she had had no news for months.

Edith shook her head. 'Not yet. Next week, maybe.'

'Yes, bound to be soon,' Pamela said, but the crowd had gone silent. They had forgotten about Edith in their jubilation at their own freedom, and now they felt guilty. There was no sign of Japanese resolve weakening, Pamela thought. The Americans had been locked in combat for months, trying to recapture the island of Okinawa. American losses were said to be in excess of 10,000; the Japanese death-count even higher. '*They'll never give in,*' Michael had said when he was last on leave. '*Not while they've a man standing.*'

'Come on, everyone,' Joyce said, sensing the change in mood. 'Let's get back before the buzzer goes, and give the bloody foreman a heart attack from the surprise.'

───────

Hannah had brought in the post when she swept out the lobby. Sarah saw it lying on the hall table, and the familiar terror flowed over her. It was nearly two months since she had made her escape from Hamish, and since then there had been not a sign that he had noticed her leaving, let alone wanted her back. But though the bruises on her body had faded, the fear remained. She knew her husband too well to think he would give up so easily.

And yet it had been so different when they met. He had taken pity on her, a young war widow working as a barmaid to feed her baby son, Joe. Hamish had been warm then, diffident and gentle, making her feel safe. And then he had gone to fight in France, and had come home wounded in mind as well as body, a different man. She shivered, remembering the years spent with him in the lonely Scottish croft that was his home. She had borne him a child, but that had made no difference.

She riffled through the letters. Nothing addressed to her, nor anything for Cathy that had a Scottish postmark. It was always possible Hamish would write to Catherine, if he didn't have an address for her. Had war really changed him, or had it simply stripped away the veneer to show what lay beneath? It came to the same thing.

She put the post on the kitchen table for Cathy and went in search of her children. She could hear them shouting in the back garden, and her heart lifted at the sound. On that early morning when they escaped from the Scottish croft, Joe had been silent, almost mute. Now he, at least, was recovered.

She opened the back door and went, smiling, into the sunshine.

Catherine opened the letter with shaking fingers. She had recognised the handwriting immediately – she had seen it often enough on hospital case-notes, as well as in the few letters Max had written to her when they were apart.

When she had extracted the folded sheets. she held them in her hand without opening them. She needed to sit down before she saw what was written there. Just that very day she had been thinking that she would never again hear from him. Perhaps he had had a change of heart? Perhaps his return to his wife had not gone smoothly? Perhaps he had heard that she, Catherine, was carrying his child? Except that only Sarah and David knew whose child it was, and neither of them would have betrayed her.

Max and she had been lovers for three years, while bombs rained down upon them, and men, the patients they were treating, had suffered and died. And then he had gone back to his wife and children, as they had both always known he would. Now he was writing her a letter. Slowly she opened the pages.

He began formally with '*Dear Catherine*', so it was not a love letter. She read on.

'*So it is over, at least for Europe. Except that it is not over, and perhaps it never will be. I am in Lower Saxony in north-western Germany, near the town of Bergen. It's the site of Belsen concentration camp. They say 50,000 Russian prisoners of war, and a further 50,000 inmates, died here, latterly of typhus, a few months before we reached them. We, or rather our lot, have been here for two months now. I only arrived three days ago, but we are still struggling to cope. The British 11th Armoured Division got here first, finding 60,000 seriously ill prisoners inside and another 13,000 corpses unburied. Some of the troops are still here, young boys, their faces grey with the horror of what they have seen. They have had to bury bodies en masse, Catherine.*

'But some we will save . . . each day I remind myself of that. And it is over. That is what matters, bringing an end to it. There are children here, mostly boys under 14, parents' whereabouts unknown. We fed them on milk at first, all they could take, but it was hard to come by. This country is devastated, Catherine. A huge charnel-house. I can feel my own humanity slipping from me with each terrible detail that comes to life.

'And this was not the worst place. At Buchenwald they tell me there was a portable scaffold for public hangings that they forced the prisoners to watch. The commandant's wife had a lampshade made from human skin. It had a particularly good tattoo. I will skim over the worst of the cruelty, but nothing, for me, compares with what members of my own profession have done. They have used human beings as guinea pigs, operating on them without anaesthetic. You know what my faith meant to me, but how can I believe in God, in anything, when this has happened in the world?

'I try to force myself to remember Archie McIndoe, and the work we did in England – the men we gave back not only a face but a personality. That was rebuilding. All I see here is destruction. Forgive me, Catherine, for telling you these things, but I always found it easy to open my heart to you. Now I fear I abuse that privilege.

'I spent two weeks at home before I came to Europe. It was wonderful to see Aaron again. Quite a young man now, or thinks he is. And Ruth is like Miriam, her mother, quiet and calm and loving. Oh Catherine, I wondered whether or not to write this letter, but I can speak to you as I can speak to no one else. Is it wrong of me to do this, when we agreed we would not keep in contact? I just wanted to share the exhilaration of victory with you . . . or perhaps to warm my hands at your exhilaration. For me, there can be no triumph in all this horror.'

Catherine read on until tears made it impossible to read further, and all she could do was hold the pages tightly in both hands.

The bus was crowded, and Pamela had to stand most of the way. When a seat became vacant she slipped into it gratefully, leaned her head back against the seat, and closed her eyes. If only there were an end in sight, and Michael could come home. She lived with the constant fear that he would be sent to the campaign in the Far East, but he had assured her this would not happen. It was the constant muttering about the Japs fighting to the last man that got her down. There were millions of Japanese: that was why they had invaded China, because their own islands could no longer contain them. The war might go on forever, and she and Michael never get a home. Then they would just have to get married, anyway, and to hell with waiting for demob. She undid the knot of her headscarf and tightened it under her chin to emphasise her determination. It would work out because she would make it work out.

There was a good smell coming from the kitchen when she reached home. Her mother had pulled herself together now that her father had a job. It didn't pay much, but somehow it made things seem more respectable, and that meant everything to someone as conventional as her mother. 'How did she have me and Catherine?' Pamela wondered, not for the first time. 'She frets if she has a hair out of place, while we don't care what anyone thinks.'

'There's a letter for you,' her mother called, as Pamela took off her coat and hung it on the hallstand. She ran upstairs, clutching the flimsy envelope, because she liked to read Mike's letters in private. It began in its usual cheery way.

'*Hello, Pamela, otherwise known as Buggerlugs. A few lines to tell you that I miss you like crazy, as our American allies would say. And not just because I am bored here, twiddling my thumbs. To think I used to long for an end to ops, and now I'd do anything for just one more scrap. That was really living, Pam!*

11

Still, we are getting regular lectures here about re-integration into civilian life. All the lecturers are Left-wingers – Communists, according to Chalky. But as he is dyed-in-the-wool Tory that's to be taken with a pinch of salt. What matters, my darling, is that I will be home some time. That is all that matters.'

Pamela folded the letter when she had read to the end, and tucked it inside her bra. She liked to keep his latest letter there, close to her heart. It wasn't exactly comfortable, but it reminded her that sooner or later he was coming home.

They ate at opposite ends of the dining-table, seldom exchanging words unless about the quality of the meal.

'I want to listen to Churchill,' Rupert said, wiping his mouth with his napkin and rising from the table. India clucked in irritation, but she carried coffee through to the living-room and poured a cup for her husband.

'I saw Catherine Allerton today.' She said. 'She's grotesquely huge, so her baby must be . . .'

'Ssh!' Rupert's admonition was harsh, and India felt her cheeks flush. Churchill's voice was booming out, warning the nation of the dire consequences of voting Labour in the coming election. He was accusing Clement Attlee of seeking to behave as a dictator. Labour would not be able to afford the British public free expression, he was saying. 'They would have to fall back on some form of Gestapo.'

Rupert stirred in his chair at that, but India pricked up her ears. At least the old man was not mincing his words. Labour, Churchill continued, 'finds a free Parliament odious.'

'How true!' India said. For the first time that day she began to feel relaxed. Her period was two days late, and she was living in constant fear that it would begin, and disappoint her once more. For a moment she contemplated letting Rupert into the secret, but why should she? Let him stew. The sight of Catherine Allerton today had reminded her of painful things. The little hussy's marriage to her brother Henry had been the start of all their bad luck. India was convinced now that it had precipitated her father's death. The marriage had made Catherine Lady Callingham when Henry inherited the title – a girl whose father was in trade . . . and not even that, since he had been made bankrupt. A bankrupt in the Callingham family, even if it was only by marriage!

Thankfully, Henry had died before there had been issue, so the chit had been out on her ear; but Henry's death had given the estate and the title to David. Even without a leg withered by polio, he would not have been up to running the estate; and now he too was marrying an empty-headed little fool. It was too much.

'I've found out that the Allerton girl is pregnant by a Jew . . . an American Jew. A doctor. And I gather he's left her . . .' But Rupert was shushing her again, not taking in a word she'd said. When the speech finished, he switched off the wireless and shook his head.

'I thought that was splendid,' India said. 'Now drink your coffee.'

Rupert picked up his cup, but he did not raise it to his lips. 'The old man's lost his touch,' he said. 'He thinks we're still fighting a war, but this nation wants peace, wants it desperately. He'll come to regret that speech.'

———

David had put aside his evening paper to listen to the Prime Minister. Now he picked it up again, trying to forget how his unease had mounted as Churchill spoke. More rumours of the Russians taking over Germany as well as Poland. It might not be true, but when something was mooted constantly it had a habit of coming to pass. At least the Japanese were retreating on Okinawa. Okinawa! He rolled the name round in his mind. Half of Britain knew of the savage fighting for that tiny island. Without the war they would never have heard it mentioned. At least Hitler had done wonders for the knowledge of geography.

The war was practically over, but too many good men had died in it. If his wasted leg had not kept him at home, he might have died too, so the polio which had struck him down as a child had been a lifesaver in the end.

He poured himself a scotch and sat down again. It was too warm for fires, but on these lonely nights he missed the comfort of a blaze. He would have loved to discuss the speech with Catherine, but it wouldn't do to ring at this time of night. Churchill had gone too far. The electorate didn't want to be reminded of the Gestapo, much less be threatened with it.

He was still ruminating when the phone rang. 'Valerie! How lovely to hear from you.' As they talked he felt himself relax. This was not the woman he loved, but it was the woman he was going to marry, and moreover it was a woman he liked and admired. She would be demobbed soon, and then his loneliness would be at an end.

They talked on until they were both weary. 'I love you,' she said. David longed to say, 'I love you too,' but all he could manage was 'Me too. Sleep tight.'

Afterwards he sat on, unwilling to switch on lamps around the room. The only woman he had ever loved was Catherine, his dead brother's widow. Now she was carrying another man's baby, and he himself was marrying someone else. The war had swept them all up in its wake, and now they must get on with it. 'I must do well by Valerie,' he said aloud, remembering the night she had given herself to him freely, and eased his heartache over Catherine. He sat for a moment contemplating the intricacies, the sheer bloodiness, of life, and then he levered himself up and limped to refill his glass.

Chapter Two

July 1945

'IT'S UNBELIEVABLE AFTER ALL HE'S done!' Shock still registered on Catherine's face. She held the newspaper in one hand, the other resting on her swollen belly. In a Labour landslide, the voters had rejected Winston Churchill, the man they had cheered to the echo a few short weeks before. 'Labour's got a majority of 150!' she said, her voice displaying her disbelief.

Privately, Sarah was not as shocked as her friend. She had heard mutterings in shops and as she waited for the bus. Everyone was agreed that Churchill had been the man for war, but few saw him as a man to win the peace. 'Bloody warmonger!' one woman had defiantly said of him, although another woman had then called her an ungrateful bitch. But the Gestapo allegation he had made against his political opponents had rankled with everyone. All the same, without him, Hitler might well have had his way with Britain. Already Sarah was regretting her own protest vote. She had not dreamed it would be part of a landslide.

'It's no good you upsetting yourself,' she told Catherine now. 'Not with you nearly nine months gone.'

David skipped over the front pages. The result had sickened him; no point in wallowing in the details. Instead he concentrated on news that the navy was attacking Tokyo. 'A powerful task force', it was called. It had joined the US Third Fleet in dawn raids on the Japanese capital as bombers attacked major cities. What did that mean? Which major cities?

He turned back to the front page. Impossible as it was to believe, it was the Labour leader, the seemingly nondescript Clement Attlee, who would now head the British delegation at Potsdam where the course of post-war Europe was to be charted. A year ago it would have been the triumvirate, Churchill, Roosevelt, and Stalin; of those, only the Russian leader was now left. How would Attlee handle the war in the Far East? Not in a Churchillian way, that was certain.

As soon as possible after the war's end, he and Valerie would be married. He put the newspaper aside and tried to analyse his feelings. Part of him was looking forward to her return: he liked her company, admired all her qualities. She would be a good and dutiful wife, and he must match her and be the husband she deserved. But he would always love Catherine. Had loved her from that first moment when she had come to Kynaston in her white tennis dress, a ribbon holding back her hair and an almost comic look of determination on her face. She had been 14 or 15 then, and he the same. She had never flinched at his wasted leg, never congratulated him on his game in the patronising way most people did, because they couldn't conceive of a cripple playing at all.

Catherine had never done that, just as he had never questioned that it was his brother Henry who would win her. Henry was not only handsome and able-bodied, he was possessed of an enormous charm and strength of character. After their mother died, he had been the only person who could stand up to India. Of course, Catherine was going to say yes when Henry made one of those whirlwind proposals that the onset of war had encouraged, before going off to join the RAF. In the moment when he heard that Henry's plane had gone down David had had one brief flash of exultation: now, at last, Catherine could be his. But reality had returned almost instantly. She would never be his, but that didn't stop him loving her. Valerie was reality, and he would cherish her, but the ache for Catherine remained.

He picked up his paper and returned to the news of the day.

———

'Of course, I'm not surprised. The stupidity and ingratitude of the average man and woman never ceases to amaze me. He saves their neck, and now they wash their hands of him.' India tried hard not to sound smug, but Rupert's abject misery was almost too much to bear. It was only an election. The country was in a mess that the Socialists would make worse, but let them flounder for a while. In three or four years, when the worst was over, Anthony Eden could take over. Churchill would be too old. Eden was a gentleman, which was more than could be said for some politicians. All in all, it had not turned out too badly.

Now she tried to change the subject. 'I see they've lifted the ban on our men fraternising with German women. Not that a ban would have stopped them, but at least the principle was there. The sooner we get them all home the better. We might get back to normal then.'

Rupert had stayed buried in his paper. Now he lowered it. 'Have you any idea of the mess that exists in Europe, India? It will be years before we're free of our responsibilities there. There are thousands of displaced people, half of them starving. We'll be lucky to escape a plague. There'll certainly be unrest, even bloodshed.'

'Thanks for the lecture,' she said tartly. She wouldn't tell him her news now. Well, her almost news. Her period was four days late. Still time for another disappointment, but four days was four days. She wouldn't tell him, either, that she had married him only so that he could give her children. Sons to inherit Kynaston. David might be in possession of it now, but it would be hers one day, she could feel it in her bones. It would only be fair, because she was the one who loved the house, every mellow brick, every shining window of it.

'More tea?' she said as sweetly as she could, and lifted the tea kettle from its silver stand. Lately it was sometimes hard to work Rupert out. In the beginning he had fawned around her like a love-sick calf. Now, sometimes, she thought he looked at her oddly: half-angry, half-amused. She still found him as boring as she always had, but if she really was pregnant everything would be different. She would forgive him for being a bore if he gave her a son.

And it would be a boy, she was sure. Valerie Graham-Poole would have girls. That milkmaid type always gave birth to girls, and the fact that the estate was entailed meant her boy would be David's heir. Rupert's silly name, Lindsay-Hogg, was a nuisance, but that could be dealt with when the time came.

She looked up and saw Rupert's eyes on her. Cool. Cold, even. And definitely different. Below the level of the tablecloth her hand dropped to her belly. A child – if there was a child in there it would make all the difference.

———

Catherine put down the paper, and pushed her breakfast tray aside. She had done her best to eat everything Sarah had prepared, but it had been a struggle. What with reading details of what was still being uncovered in the camps, and the toll of Allied dead in the Pacific, it felt as though victory in Europe had made no impact. There wasn't a shred of brightness anywhere.

She contemplated the rest of the day. There wasn't a lot you could do when you couldn't see your feet. It was worth it, though. In a few weeks she would have Max's child. It would be a boy –

somehow she knew it would be a boy, although a girl would be just as welcome. He was bound to have black hair. Hers was dark enough, and Max . . . where the silver did not glint, his hair had been jet black and curled tight. She had teased him about his hair, declaring it a mop, and sometimes, when they made love, winding her fingers in it until he squealed with mock-pain. And suddenly she wanted him here beside her, wanted him desperately.

She put down her head and wept, but only for a moment. Max was the past; the baby was the future. She mustn't upset her baby. When she had dried her eyes she got up and dressed. She would go shopping, if she could find anything to buy. She would have a bite of lunch at the Grand Hotel, and then take a taxi home. It was hard to be enthusiastic about such an expedition, but she did her best.

And she quelled, too, those uncomfortable thoughts that would keep on surfacing. She had never loved Henry Callingham. Had liked him certainly, but never loved him. She had married him because she was pregnant with another man's child, and that man, Joe, was already dead in France. 'I was too cowardly to face the world,' she thought. 'I stole a cover for my own sin.' Then Joe's baby had been stillborn, and now she was Lady Callingham, and was living in a fair degree of splendour on the money Henry had left her.

'I won't think about it now,' she told herself resolutely. If it hadn't been for the war, none of it would have happened. And she had tried to atone, throwing herself into nursing, comforting suffering men, and men afraid of what fate had in store for them. But that, too, was an area which it was uncomfortable to remember. She pinned her hat firmly in place, and went off to find solace in shopping.

Pamela had woken early, and then remembered that she had a precious day off. She had rolled over and luxuriated in the lack of need to get up. When the war was really over, she would never again have an alarm clock in the house. Smells of frying drifted up from downstairs. They had used their bacon ration a week ago, so heaven only knew what was in the pan. Lately her mother had been obtaining something called white puddings – where from, she was reluctant to say. They were huge greyish sausages that oozed fat in the pan, and tasted like heavily seasoned wet bread.

It didn't matter, because nothing could spoil her mood. Michael would be home tonight for seven whole days. He would have to spend some of it with his parents, but she would have him to herself for at least five days. His last letter had said so. She rolled the words around in her head. *'I just want to be with you, Pammy. Just hold you and smell you and touch you and know that nothing will ever separate us again.'*

It would be hard at first, particularly finding a place of their own. They couldn't afford to buy, and rented accommodation was scarce. 'But we'll manage,' Pamela thought confidently, and spent a happy half-hour mentally furnishing their first home. At last she leapt out of bed and made her way downstairs. She mustn't waste the day.

The pavement was warm beneath her feet as she moved from shop window to shop window along the High Street. If she saw something nice she would buy it, and to hell with saving up, Michael deserved that she looked her best. She was turning away from a shoe shop when she caught sight of India Callingham, who was now India Lindsay-Hogg – except that she used the Callingham name whenever she could. 'When I marry Michael, I'll be proud to be Pamela Hamilton,' Pamela vowed.

It was only then that she realised India had just emerged from Risdon's, which catered only for babies and children. She had a Risdon's carrier in her hand, so she must have bought something. Perhaps it was for Catherine's baby's layette. India was sort of its aunt, in a way, or would have been if Henry had not died.

Henry had been RAF, as Michael was, but now he was dead. And Michael was alive and coming home. Truly, she had a lot to be thankful for.

Catherine's legs were aching intolerably, and there was a dull pain in the small of her back. For a moment she wondered if this could be the onset of labour, but no, she was simply tired, and the thought of the journey home in the crowded bus was not appealing. As soon as the baby was safely here she would learn to drive and buy a car. An Austin, or a little Ford, perhaps. She was musing about colour and make when she heard her name. 'Catherine!' It was David, his face wreathed in smiles.

'Catherine, let me.' He was taking her parcels from her, holding her elbow, guiding her through the crowds on the pavement. They paused on the corner and he looked at his watch. 'Have you had tea? They may still be serving at the Grand . . .'

Catherine was shaking her head as he went on talking. 'Better still, dinner. Let me give you an early dinner and catch up on your news.'

She hesitated, thinking longingly of home with her maternity corset loosened and her feet up. It was long enough for David to play his trump card. 'If you say no, I'll have to eat alone – or throw myself on India's mercy. You wouldn't do that to a chap, would you?'

She was still smiling as he swept her through the doors of the hotel and into the ornate dining-room.

Over dinner they talked of the election. 'Churchill came across as weary on the stump,' David said. 'When we were at war, he was fuelled by a determination to win at all costs.'

'He knew how much depended on it,' Catherine said.

'For all of us. But his party political broadcasts were lacklustre. Not by most standards, possibly, but certainly by his own. And some people think him too old – he's 70, after all. But it was that Gestapo speech that did it for him. I knew it as soon as I heard him utter the words. It made him seem vicious, a war-monger.'

'And then there was that dreadful front page in the *Mirror*,' Catherine offered.

'True, "*Whose finger on the trigger?*", and all that. People are weary of war, Catherine. Men and women, they're ready for peace.'

The train was five minutes late, and every minute seemed to Pamela like an hour. But at last Michael was there, stepping down, looking so handsome in his uniform with the new insignia on the cuffs.

'Let's get a drink,' he said, when they had kissed and clung in the middle of the crowded platform. The Station Hotel was smoky and crowded, but squirreled away in a corner booth they were unconscious of the other drinkers.

'It can't be long now. They're already letting people go. Chalky White says they're demobbing thousands every month. From munitions too – so you'll get your freedom.'

'I'll have to work, though, at something. If I get a chance to stay on at the factory, I will. Till you get home, anyway. The money's good, and I'm used to it now.'

He reached for her hands. 'Poor little hands, all rough and coarse with work.'

'Pig!' she said, and would have drawn her scarred hands away except that he was raising them to his lips.

'I'm worried about finding a place to live,' she said at last. 'Mummy says we're welcome to live with them, but it wouldn't be the same.'

'They'll be building houses, soon. Chalky says anyone with house-building experience is being fast tracked for demob. Half a million homes have been destroyed . . . and that's not counting the ones too damaged to live in.'

'There'll be prefabs. I saw a picture of one in the *Express*. They've got everything, even cookers and refrigerators.'

'Refrigerators! You want luxury!'

They were laughing and then suddenly Michael was rising to his feet. 'Let's get out of here. I need to make love to you. Now!'

~~~

Sarah listened to the evening news bulletin. It was all about Potsdam. Funny to think of her country's future being settled in a foreign country. And Germany, at that.

It was still broad daylight outside, and Catherine should be home before dark. She had rung from the Grand Hotel to say she was eating with Sir David, and not to prepare supper, but she would not be late home. 'I'm tired,' she had said, and Sarah had clucked sympathetically, remembering the long, hard days of late pregnancy. Even if Cathy wasn't home by dark, the street lamps would be lit. Street lighting had been restored for a month now, and Sarah still got pleasure from seeing the lamps spring to life.

She was feeling quite safe and settled when the phone rang. She lifted the receiver, half-expecting to hear Catherine's voice. But there was only silence.

'Hello?' she said. And then again, 'Hello?'

Nothing. She stood, holding her breath, wanting to put down the receiver, and yet desperate to know who was on the other end. And suddenly she was back in that croft beside the loch, with no one and nothing within earshot. Only a terrible shouting, and blows raining down upon her head.

It had been so very different in the beginning. Gerard Foxton, her first husband, had died early in the war, before little Joe was even born. Her war widow's pension of 32 shillings for

23

her and 11 shillings for the baby had been just enough while she was living with her dad, but the house was tiny and crowded, and she had wanted a place of her own. To rent – there would have been no hope of a colliery house without a man to go down the hole for it. So she had taken a job in the pub, and once she had learned how to pull a pint and get the change right, she had quite enjoyed it. The customers were mostly men from the camp, tie-less and bare-headed, their battle-dress jackets loosened at the neck. Miners, whose pub it had once been by right, stayed in the corner, keeping themselves to themselves. The soldiers looked down on the miners, thinking them shirkers. That was because they didn't know the pit.

She had never noticed Hamish Carlyle until the night her brother Jim had come to tell her Molly, his girl, was pregnant. '*She'll have to come to us,*' he'd said, and her heart had sunk into her boots at the thought of one more body in her father's crowded house. And then one man, a soldier, had caught hold of her hand. '*How about a bit of the other, Sally? Come on, I know you're up for it.*' She had heard a voice, then, deep and Scottish: '*Is he bothering you, miss?*' It belonged to a tall man with reddish hair, and stripes on his arm, and the other man had shrunk away. '*Only a bit of fun, Sarge.*'

She had said, 'Thank you,' and turned away to hide her flushed cheeks. And that had been the start of it.

David locked up the house when he returned to Kynaston. He was in for the night, now, although it was still light outside. The dogs had come to greet him, tails wagging in anticipation of a walk. Well, perhaps he might relent before bed-time, but now he wanted a drink and a chance to reflect on the evening. Catherine's face was rounded and she had the glow of pregnancy about her. He had heard it spoken of, but never seen it for himself until now. It increased her beauty: war and loss had given her pretty face added character.

He was still thinking of her when the bell chimed in the great hall. He pulled back the bolts and opened it to find Valerie on the step.

'I've got 48 hours, David! No time to ring – I scrounged a lift and just came. Isn't it dreadful about Churchill and the election?'

Her arms were around his neck, her lips soft on his cheek, his mouth. He liked her so much, had liked her ever since he sat next to her at dinner in Kynaston, the night India had set her cap at Rupert. Everyone had been discussing the difficulties the Allies were facing, fighting in Europe and the Far East at the same time, when the girl on his right had put her hand on his arm. 'They tell me you're in the Home Guard?' she had said, and he had noted that she was small and dark with kind eyes. Rather like Catherine, in fact.

He had said, 'Actually I'm a captain, and in charge because I'm the only man fit enough to climb over fences.' She had laughed, then, a genuine laugh, and he had suddenly relaxed. And now he was going to marry her. He tried to close his mind to his muddled thoughts, and make his fiancée welcome.

When she had divested herself of her day clothes and was comfortable in nightgown and robe, Catherine settled in a chair in the morning-room and took Max's letter from its hiding-place. She could hear Sarah in the kitchen. If she came in, she would hide the letter in the pages of the evening paper. It wouldn't do to revive the idea of Max in Sarah's mind. She had a suspicion that Sarah didn't approve of Max's leaving her, even though she had tried to explain that that had been agreed from the beginning. Besides, it was just a letter. He had ended it by saying there would not be another. '*I will not write again, dear Catherine, unless, perhaps, the world turns on its axis.'* What did that mean?

She turned back to the first page and reread it, but it was the second page that reduced her to tears. *'They are making German civilians visit the camps to see for themselves where people were burned to death in ovens, for some of them were still alive when they were thrown in. We have men acting as guides, pointing out the piles of hair shorn from women, toys taken from children before they were gassed. Even torture equipment some of the guards took pleasure in. They had a "sound machine" to hide the noise of the screaming.*

'I don't know why I tell you this, Catherine, except that if I don't tell someone I will go mad and you were always so wise, so comforting.'

Catherine put a hand on her belly. The baby had been quiet today. For a moment she contemplated taking out a sheet of writing-paper and penning a reply: 'Max, take heart. You have a child on the way. New life, a fresh start.' Except that his letter bore no return address.

She folded the letter at last, and put it back in its envelope. At least German civilians were being made to see what had been done in their name. Some broke down and cried at the sights before them, the letter said, but others appeared indifferent, even disbelieving. She heard the wireless crackle to life in the room next door. Sarah hung on news broadcasts, but she herself could rouse little interest in them. Her war was over. She must think of the baby now, and their future.

David had been so sweet today, driving her back to Mellows and almost lifting her over the threshold. She was lucky to have him in her life, and she would make sure Valerie felt welcome when they married. India would do all she could to shut Valerie out, but David was more than a match for her. And, from what David had told her, so was his bride-to-be.

She concentrated on thoughts of their wedding, in an effort to beat out the horror of what she had just read.

Chapter Three

August 1945

'IT'S GETTING WORSE.' HER MOTHER'S voice was dispirited, and the cause of her misery was the dried-egg omelette on her plate. Pamela looked up from spreading margarine thinly on her toast. 'Cheer up, Mummy. The war's nearly over, and then we'll have real eggs. And bananas. And joints instead of sausages. And . . .'

'Don't go on. It may be funny to you, darling, but if you had to provide meals . . . they think women can do miracles.'

'Loaves and fishes!' That last was her father, behind his paper. 'The Yanks are not doing badly. It says here they're about to end petrol rationing.'

'They're sitting on oil wells, Daddy. That's the difference. Anyway, can't stay – going to be late if I miss the bus.'

Pamela felt a curious happiness as she let herself out of the house. She had her parents back as nice, normal people again. Her mother moaned a bit, and her father was more taciturn than before the war, but compared with the shattered people they had been after the business went bust, they were wonderful.

On the bus she thought about the day the bailiffs had come. She had wailed and cried, because she felt she was losing everything. 'I was a spoiled little brat,' she thought, and then smiled to herself. Big Sheila wouldn't have said 'spoiled brat', she'd have said 'spoiled bitch'. 'I've changed with the war,' Pamela reflected. 'And I've widened my vocabulary, into the bargain.'

She had still been in her nightdress when the bailiffs came. She had peeped from the landing and seen two men in shabby raincoats arguing with her mother, who was weeping. The second man was moving from one piece of furniture to another. '*Who are you?*' she had asked, and, when he returned the question in an insolent way, she had said: '*I'm Pamela Allerton, and this is my parents' house.*' He had waved a piece of paper. '*Court order. We're here to distrain on your father's goods.*' And until that moment she had thought they were rich, and safe. She had called for her father, then: '*Daddy! I'm frightened, Daddy.*' But he would not come out of his study.

It was David Callingham who had saved the day, paying off the men because Catherine was his sister-in-law and this was her family. Catherine had stood in the hall, wringing her hands. 'And all I could see was her huge diamond engagement ring,' Pamela recalled, looking down at her own tiny solitaire. 'What an empty little fool I was then!'

'More tea?' India tried not to sound irritated, but Rupert was buried behind his newspaper as usual. It was almost as though he were trying to shut her out. 'I asked if you wanted more tea, Rupert?'

Her husband lowered the paper and pushed his cup towards her. 'Yes, please. It says here that there's a growing fear of unemployment once the war ends. Materials are in such short supply that they can't see a return to manufacturing – not on any scale, at least.'

'People are never satisfied,' India declared. 'They seem to want – to positively want – to wallow in misery. All this going on about Belsen and Auschwitz. It was unfortunate, but it's over now . . .'

The paper had been raised again, but now it was lowered. 'Unfortunate? Sometimes, India, you take away my breath. Have you forgotten that Dimbleby report – what was it he called it? "The most horrible day of my life". The man's a seasoned war journalist, and he was sickened, India. Sickened. I'm told people are stumbling out of cinemas where they're showing newsreels of Belsen. Then vomiting in the gutters. And all you can say is "unfortunate".'

India felt her cheeks burn. He was always putting her down, trying to make her feel ashamed. Well, realism was nothing to be ashamed of, and she wouldn't be. Instead she would drop the bombshell she had been keeping until dinner tonight and a celebratory drink.

'I'm pregnant,' she said baldly. 'Officially. I saw the doctor yesterday. It's due on the first of March.'

She had expected Rupert's eyes to fill. She had expected him at least to thank her. But all he said was, 'Well done. We'll have to make sure you take things easy, then.'

She felt disappointment burn in her throat. It was not enough.

The papers were still full of Potsdam. The desire to defeat the enemy had turned Russia, America, and Britain into a cohesive whole that was falling apart with peace, Catherine thought. There was disagreement about where Germany's frontiers should be drawn. America and Britain were fighting the Polish move to seize huge tracts of German soil, and expel the German population, but Russia was on Poland's side. Who would win?

In her heart, Catherine could hardly blame Poland. Of all the occupied countries, it had suffered most. Now it wanted its pound of flesh. The Poles had paid dearly for victory. She remembered the Polish pilots they had had in the hospital, fierce little men whose only aim was to be back in the air again and killing Germans. One of them, told his burned eyes were beyond repair, had beaten his pillow with his clenched fists. And still Poland was not free. Stalin was also against free elections in the East European countries.

Stalin, Stalin – everything seemed Stalin, nowadays. Had the world swapped the menace of Hitler for the menace of Stalin? And would it have been different if it had been Churchill at Potsdam instead of the mild-mannered Attlee? Neither he nor the new American President, Harry Truman, looked as though they could say boo to a goose. It was all very unsettling.

When she had laid aside the paper she felt no better. For the moment she must concentrate on getting her baby safely into the world, but what then? And what of Sarah? She too must have a future. The pittance Catherine paid her to look after the house was not enough, but it was all she would accept. Today she had taken the children to visit her father down in the village, but she had no place in her old home, now that her brother Jim's Molly was queening it over the household.

'I must do something for her,' Catherine thought. 'And for myself, and for the children. All the children. Especially the children.' But what was she equipped to do? Change dressings on burned faces; write letters for men whose fingers had been burned to the bone; spoon liquid into the slit that was all that remained of a mouth? Thank God those skills were no longer needed, even if they were the only skills she had.

Sarah felt odd as she walked through the village. Once she had known every cobblestone, the colour of every front door, the shop signs, the pattern of the church railings. Now, there was a subtle difference. The church was still there, and the shops – so the change must be in me, she thought, and hurried on.

Even inside her father's house, she felt odd. Once, she had

been mistress here, but now it was her sister-in-law Molly's domain. Hannah had filled in the shift times for her, so her visit was timed for when both her father and brother Jim were at home. Only Terry was missing. For a moment Sarah felt her throat constrict at the memory of her younger brother, dead in the pit aged 17.

But only for a moment. Her father was rising from his chair, holding out arms to his grandchildren. 'Get yourself in, lass. By, that's a fine lad there, little Alexander. And is this our Joe? He's grown an inch, I'll bet.'

'It's only a week since you saw him, Dad.' Molly was shifting her own son from one arm to the other, and there was a bite to her words even though they were said with a smile. Molly had two children now. Meg was almost four, and the little boy was 18 months. 'I'll have to be careful,' Sarah thought. 'There's jealousy here.' Molly seemed different now, but Sarah couldn't quite say how. Perhaps it was the fact of being a mother: that certainly made you feel more grown up. But there was a defiance, almost a brassiness about Molly that she hadn't seen before.

She was being ushered towards the fire which roared up the chimney despite the summer's day outside. 'All right?' That was Jim, newly washed from the pit, but still with tell-tale black rimming his eyelids.

Sarah nodded, but Jim was leaning forward. 'You'll come to me if you hear from yon Scotsman? Remember, we're your family. I'm not easy about you two women alone up at Mellows, and this is still your home, Sarah.'

That was too much for Molly. 'Don't be daft, Jim. Why would she move back here from a posh house like Mellows? Besides, there wouldn't be room. Honestly, sometimes I think you leave off your brain with your pit boots.'

It was a relief when Hannah Chaffey, who was her father's neighbour, erupted into the room, full of the latest village gossip, and ready, much to Molly's disgust, to ooh and aah over Sarah's children.

They met in the gentlemen's club. 'Can't say the food's improved with victory,' Rupert said, eyeing the menu.

David merely smiled. He had spent the morning visiting some of the returned servicemen, all of them recovered wounded, and still in the bright blue uniforms that marked out men injured in combat. 'What'll I do, Sir David?' one had asked piteously, holding out the stump of his arm. 'I was a fitter and turner. I won't turn much with that.' Behind him his wife had bitten her lip in anguish and looked at David as though she was expecting him to provide an answer.

He had cleared his throat and launched into an explanation of the measures that would ensure a decent future for returning servicemen, but he had an uneasy feeling that, whatever the measures were, they would prove inadequate. Not that the Government could solve everything. Too many men had come home to find their dream of an idyllic reunion turn to ashes. Last year a man called Patmore, a Fusilier, had stabbed his heavily pregnant wife to death because the child she was carrying was that of an Italian prisoner of war. Patmore had pleaded provocation, and had escaped what could have been a death sentence, He had been given five years' penal servitude instead. That was not the only case of murder in similar circumstances. Each time a case was presented to him, his heart was in his mouth in case he could not effect some decent solution, and it would end in tragedy.

Now he ordered corned-beef pie, with apple charlotte to finish, and soup to start. He folded the menu and handed it back to the waiter. 'Splendid news about the baby, old chap. India telephoned this morning.' Privately, he felt sorry for any child of India's – though Rupert was a decent enough stick, so it would probably be all right.

But the father-to-be was not exactly glowing at the prospect. 'Yes, splendid news. It's what India has always wanted. And you must be making plans, too. It's to be a spring wedding, rather than an autumn one, India says?'

'We can't be sure of that, even. Valerie expects to be free before long, since they're letting a lot of ATS go. But there's no knowing, not while Japan holds on.'

'The Japs will fight tooth and nail,' Rupert said. 'You know their code: "No surrender". Still. . .' He raised his glass. 'Here's to a double celebration.' He drank, and then put down his glass. 'Now, I wanted to talk to you about the future.'

David's eyebrows rose a little. 'That sounds portentous.'

'We're worried, David. By "we", I mean the Conservative Association. This war has involved years of disruption to family life, with the attendant consequences. Soon we'll be swamped with returning servicemen, not all of them able to find work. The rise in prostitution in the cities is staggering, and street crime has boomed in London – how long before it comes here? I'm told the country is awash with guns, most of them American army issue. £25 for a handgun, they say. The black market during the war has created an army of men and women who live on their wits. A lot of them are deserters, so you can imagine their moral standards. We have acres of bomb-damaged and urban wasteland. . .'

David could be silent no longer. 'Steady on, old boy. I don't recognise the England you're describing. Rather the contrary: I see a weary country, tired and weakened, but proud of all it has achieved.'

'All true, David. But so is the picture I painted. Our task is to make sure that your version of Britain is one that prevails.'

'This is nice,' Catherine said, setting down the tea-tray. She was always pleased to see David. Today, though his brow was furrowed. 'You look tired,' she said as she passed him his cup.

'Not tired, Catherine. Pole-axed better describes it. I've just had the most extraordinary conversation with Rupert.'

'About India?'

'I wish it had been. No, about politics. He wants me to stand for this parliamentary seat at the next election. George Harris is standing down then, apparently.'

'I think that's a wonderful idea. I can just see you in your robes.' Catherine was laughing but still half-serious.

'MPs don't have robes, Catherine. And anyone less qualified than I to run a country . . . I have to have my hand held to manage the estate.'

'Don't be silly. You've done a marvellous job since Henry died. And you know that, in your heart of hearts.'

David was shaking his head, and Catherine would have remonstrated with him, but a pain had started low down in her abdomen.

'Catherine?' He was setting down his cup. 'What's the matter?'

For a moment she couldn't speak, and then the pain was subsiding and she could respond. 'I'm not sure, but I think the baby is coming.'

―――――

The walk back from the village was slightly uphill, and little Joe's legs were protesting. Sarah picked him up and set him on the pram. 'There now, not much longer and we'll be home.'

She had enjoyed the visit to her father and Jim. And Molly was all right underneath. She'd been spiteful, though, about the poor Bevin boy. It was hardly his fault that Ernest Bevin had drafted him into the pits when he'd probably wanted to join the

RAF or the Royal Navy. No one who hadn't been brought up to it wanted to go down the pit, and, as coal was essential to the war effort, the Government had made them do it. Each pit now had its quota of quite posh young men, who were known as Bevin boys. After all, a posh accent was not a crime.

The boy had come trudging up the street as she was leaving, and Hannah had called him over. His name was Hartley Walters, but Molly referred to him as 'the bloody nancy boy'. He had held out his hand when Hannah introduced him – and, yes, his hands were soft, and a bit girlish. But his eyes had been kind, and he had been nice with the bairns.

Sarah was almost at the entrance to the drive when she saw the doctor's car turn in at the gate. He wasn't due for a visit, he'd been the day before yesterday. She quickened her pace and began to run.

———

India went upstairs as soon as she reached the house, and changed out of her clothes. She felt hot and irritated. People were so stupid, or most of them.

In the bathroom she looked at her body critically. Good, firm flesh. It would thicken and sag with pregnancy, but a little self-discipline would remedy that. And a child brought activity into your life. She wouldn't be a passive mother, she would run with her son, and teach him to straddle a horse, and ride with him over land that would be his one day.

When she had changed, she stood at the window and looked out, but the sight of the other roofs annoyed her further. Suburbia, that was what she had been reduced to. Houses huddled together with what they pathetically described as gardens in between them.

She turned away, and reached for hand-cream. Sun could do terrible damage to hands. Even as a child in India she had seen friends of her mother with hands that were positively gnarled by the sun. The women's conversation had been banal, too, as stilted as the conversation here, but something about the atmosphere of the Raj had made it bearable. Grandeur, she thought. That was what made the difference . . . grandeur.

Even when she had performed the creaming of her hands to her satisfaction, she felt unsettled. It would be hours until dinner, and then only more boring conversation. Boring, boring, boring! The newspapers were no better, boring and full of silly gossip about inconsequential people. Perhaps this evening Rupert would show a little more enthusiasm over the baby than he had when she first told him.

She went back to the window, but there was no solace there. At last she went downstairs and took a bottle of wine from the rack in Rupert's study. The wine at Kynaston had always come cool from the cellar. This was positively lukewarm. Nevertheless, it helped.

She downed the first glass, and poured herself another.

Through a haze of pain and sweat, Catherine tried to concentrate, and time her pushing to the midwife's commands. The doctor was in the background, as was Sarah, looking anxious. Once, she had heard David's voice on the landing. 'Where's David?' she had said, and Sarah had told her he was watching the bairns.

'Watching the bairns?' She had heard her own voice repeating the words, and then came a wave of pain more agonising than the ones before. 'What time is it?'

It was 9 o'clock. She tried to think. Was this the first day? Nine o'clock on the first day, or had she been here for days and days? They were talking about Japan, and something about birds dying in the air. 'Is it the war?' she asked. 'Is it the Japanese?'

But the nurse was shushing her, and then the pain was engulfing her, and finally Sarah was beaming above her, and wiping her face with a flannel. 'It's a boy, Catherine. A beautiful little boy. Perfect he is, perfect.'

'Are you sure?'

'Well, if she's not, I am. You have a son.' That was the doctor. And then someone, Sarah, was putting the baby into her arms.

'He looks so wise,' she said. The baby's eyes were searching her face.

'He can't focus yet,' the doctor said. 'But he knows you're his mother.'

And then David was by the bed, putting a tentative hand to the blanket that swaddled the baby. 'He's beautiful, Catherine. And you're all right. Thank God.'

Pamela appeared then, looking flustered. 'I came as soon as I heard. Oh, Cathy, Cathy, he's gorgeous.'

Catherine felt overwhelmingly weary, but she couldn't close her eyes. Not when she had visitors.

'I think she needs sleep now.' The nurse was ushering everyone away and Catherine could feel her lids drooping. She had wanted to ask why David had tears in his eyes, but it was too late now. She would have to ask him tomorrow.

Chapter Four

August 1945

IT WAS QUIET IN THE agent's office, but the clamour of the pit could be heard outside. The Alistair Groom's voice was grave. 'I don't like the mood at the moment. The men are excited, but it's a vengeful kind of excitement. You would think they'd be all sweetness and light with the war over. With so much class hatred and prejudice, it makes you wonder how we ever won the war.'

David shook his head. 'Remember what Orwell wrote at the beginning of the war? I think I can remember the words, after a fashion: "England is the most class-ridden country under the sun. It is a land of snobbery and privilege . . . but in any calculation you must take into account its emotional unity, the tendency of all its inhabitants to feel alike and act alike and together in moments of extreme crisis." Well, the crisis is over now, and so is the unity. We'll just have to do our best to cope.'

It was two weeks since the second atom bomb had fallen, this time obliterating Nagasaki, Japan's shipbuilding city. Within hours the death toll had stood at 70,000, and the American President had promised 'a rain of ruin from the air'. Five days later, Japan had surrendered unconditionally. The myth of their fighting to the last man was exposed as so much hot air, and American forces, under General MacArthur, took over the Japanese mainland.

David was still remembering that feeling of absolute victory when Alistair spoke again.

'Absenteeism is up, and that makes things difficult. It's almost as though the men are marking time until nationalisation. I don't know why the Government doesn't concentrate on the railways. The rolling-stock is half of it Victorian; its bridges and tunnels are decrepit; and the signalling systems are downright dangerous. Compared with them, the mining industry is super-efficient. And still they want to take us over. I had to discipline a man the other day – an overman, as it happens – and he said it straight out. "We'll be your masters before long. See how you like that."'

David made sympathetic noises. In truth, he could hardly wait for nationalisation. He lived in mortal dread of a death in the pit that his family owned. The death there of Terry McGuire a few years back had brought home to him the price of coal – and there had been two more deaths since then.

Now he steered the conversation back to matters of today's business, and, when he could, he made his escape. Valerie was due home this afternoon, and if he was quick there might just be time to call in at Mellows and see how the baby was faring.

———

The women were sinking wearily into canteen chairs and lighting up their tabs. 'Does anyone else feel flat?' That was Sheila.

Pamela patted her stomach. 'Reasonably flat.'

'Don't be narky, Pam. You know what I mean. Flat, like . . .' She was seeking for the right word.

'Bloody miserable?' suggested another woman.

'It's anticlimax,' Pamela said. 'We were all geared up to win the war, and now we've done it the point's gone.'

'Not for me. My man's in Burma. The war may be over, but he's still stuck there. And when he writes he's never happy. He was called up before he finished his apprenticeship. Now he thinks he won't get back into his trade when he comes out.'

'They'll make sure troops don't get disadvantaged.' That was posh Virginia. 'Surely they'll do that?'

'Virginia, pet, what your posh school didn't teach you about was real life. Now the war is over, politicians won't give a toss for squaddies. They won't be necessary any more. Don't have a job? Hard lines. My mam's told me about ex-soldiers going from door to door selling stuff after the last war. Begging in the gutter, some of them.'

Pamela had her own dim memories of a man who used to come to the door selling socks. Her mother always bought a pair, although her father's socks came from the men's outfitter's in town. '*He was a soldier,*' had been the explanation, given in the hushed tones that might have been used for an unmentionable disease. Surely it wouldn't happen this time? Not to people like Michael, who had risked their lives for freedom.

Lizzie was talking now. She was a woman who seldom spoke, so she had their full attention. 'It's not just the high-ups letting them down. It's their own folk, in some cases. Those they should be able to depend on. My brother was away three years – three years! He came home to find a note on the kitchen table: '*Make a cup of cocoa if you like and there's a tin of pilchards in the larder if you feel peckish. Joan.*' Pilchards! A man gives up three years of his life and he comes home to pilchards.'

Ordinarily there was always someone with a wisecrack when a story ended, but this time no one spoke. It was a relief when the buzzer sounded, and they could go back to their benches.

'There, now.' Sarah was nodding approvingly. 'You've got it off to a T.' At first she had carried out the bathing ritual, but gradually Catherine had taken over from the experienced mother, and today she had done the whole thing herself for the first time.

Once the clean and sweet-smelling baby was back in its pram and out in the fresh air, the two women sank gratefully into chairs, each clutching a coffee cup.

'Are you still going to the school today?' Catherine asked.

Sarah nodded. 'Yes, best get Joe's name down for next term. He say's he's looking forward to it, but we'll have to see. He's a clingy little lad.'

'Understandably.' Catherine was quick to little Joe's defence. 'He's had a lot to cope with.'

They were both silent for a while, remembering the bleakness of those Scottish days, and the unspoken menace that neither of them could be unaware of for a second.

'What are we eating today?' Catherine asked, at last.

Sarah sighed. 'When the time comes, I'm going to dice up our ration books and force feed them to that butcher. He's drunk with power – and the best stuff's under the counter.'

'And yet we haven't really suffered. We're all healthy, and the children are sturdy. It's a great tribute to the British housewife's ingenuity.'

'Ingenuity? Desperation, more like. Marzipan made out of haricot beans and almond essence . . .'

'That was disgusting,' Catherine interrupted.

'Mashed parsnip for mashed banana.' Sarah continued. 'Carrot jam.'

'Baked bean pie! We used to get that at the hospital. We could only get it down if we drank gallons of water with it. It was dry as dust.'

They reminisced happily for a while, and then Sarah changed the subject. 'I met Hannah's Bevin boy the other day. Strange chap. Like a girl. Well, you know. . .'

'Sensitive?' Catherine queried.

'Soft, according to our Jim. But he does his share of the work – no one's got a bad word to say about him. And he can put up with Hannah, who's his landlady.'

'Which makes him a saint,' Catherine said fervently.

They were agreeing that Hannah meant well when Catherine caught sight of David in the garden.

'I hope he doesn't wake the bairn.' Sarah was alarmed.

'He won't. Look, he's just peeping in.'

'You would think it was his bairn,' Sarah said, and then, as if she had gone too far, 'Well he's always been good with our Joe and Alexander.'

'He's a nice man,' Catherine said, and made for the garden door to welcome the visitor.

'I suppose you have references?' India had not asked the girl or the mother who accompanied her to sit down. It didn't do to give wrong impressions at the outset.

'She's got a letter from the headmistress,' the mother said, digging the girl beside her with an elbow.

'Let her speak for herself. I presume she can speak?' The girl was looking at her as a rabbit might regard a stoat.

India sighed. If this was the calibre of worker on offer, getting staff again might not be the boon it had seemed when wartime was making it impossible. 'Speak up, girl. You won't always have your mother to do your talking. Cat got your tongue?'

This was proving enjoyable. India turned to the mother. 'Is she backward? I need someone of average intelligence, at least.'

The mother put out a hand to steady herself. She was licking her lips as though seeking words.

'Well?' India tapped her foot to show her irritation, and the girl suddenly came to life.

'I was in the top four in the class, and Miss Vincent always said my needlework . . .'

'You can sew?' India perked up at this. There were so many tedious tasks that involved needle and thread. Rupert took a positive delight in shedding buttons.

She was about to show a more gracious side to them, but the mother had gathered her coat together at her throat, and was putting her free hand on her daughter's arm.

'She can sew very well, as it happens, but she won't be doing it for you.'

'What do you mean?' India felt a sense of panic and then, swiftly, anger.

'I mean I'd rather see her scrubbing pavements than working here. Come on, Betty, pet. We're going home.'

Of course she was well rid of them, India consoled herself as she shut the door. The last thing you needed in servants was impertinence. And the girl had been mentally defective, that much was plain. There would be someone else along tomorrow, and a queue once the armaments industry closed down. The servant class had had its moment in the sun. Now it would have to resume its proper place, and she could hardly wait.

But however fine a staff she acquired for this house, it would never equal the old days at Kynaston. India thought back to the time when her mother had presided over a great house, and everything had run on oiled wheels. 'I want it back,' she told herself. 'I want what I had then: the knowledge that I lived in a great house, that I belonged to a family of importance, that I mattered.'

Joe had been impressed with the school. The headmistress had given him a sweet, and shown him a toy telephone box and a whole row of books. He could have access to both she had told him, once he was a big boy and came to school. She had cooed over Alexander, and set to rest all Sarah's doubts about entrusting her precious son to strangers. 'Is his daddy in the services?' she had asked, and when Sarah said, 'He was. We're not together now,' the other woman had merely nodded sympathetically.

All in all, Sarah felt good as they crossed the playground and emerged from the gate. It was then that she saw the Bevin boy. He had two books under his arm, so he must have been to the library.

'Wait on, Joe,' she said, and shrank back inside the gate. It wasn't that she didn't like the man. There was nothing about him to dislike. But, if she had acknowledged him, he might have fallen into step beside her, or even taken the pram and pushed it. It was what Hamish had done on that first fateful meeting away from the pub. She never wanted to walk alongside a man again. There was nothing came out of it but trouble. She had learned that the hard way.

She glanced down at her son. He was looking troubled. 'It's just a game, Joe,' she said. 'It's just a little game.'

———

Michael was there when she came out of the factory gates, looking unbelievably handsome in his blue uniform.

'Darling, is it really you?'

She was flying across the space between them when she heard the catcalls behind her. 'Ooh, it's Scarlett and Rhett!' 'Hollywood!' 'Look at our Pam's bit of all right.' 'You go for it, Pammy.' She felt her cheeks flush. What would he think?

But he was sweeping off his peaked hat and waving it aloft, then folding her into his arms and bending her back before giving her a long slow kiss. 'How's that ladies?' he said when they straightened. 'You wanted Hollywood – we gave it to you.'

The women were laughing and crowding round, and Sheila

was whispering in her ear, 'You've got a good one there, Pammy. Watch your Ps and Qs, and don't let anything spoil it.'

She murmured a promise not to do anything like that, all the while thinking that she was the happiest – and the luckiest – girl in the world.

———

'I saw Archie Parker today, India.'

'Really,' she said as non-committally as she could. There was a note in Rupert's voice which didn't augur well.

'He said he'd bumped into you in town.'

'Yes, I believe we did meet. More cauliflower?' Across the table he was looking at her with that horrid glare he wore so often now.

'No, thank you. You didn't mention meeting him.'

'Didn't I?' She noticed that a picture was hanging slightly awry on the wall behind him. Dare she go and alter it? She decided not to. Instead, she said, 'I can't tell you about every single person I meet, Rupert. It would be too boring – for both of us.'

'He says you spoke to him about David?' So Archie had blabbed. Men were so stupid.

'I may have done.'

Rupert threw down his napkin and leaned back in his chair. He was going to sit in judgement on her. He did it all the time now, and it was too much to tolerate.

'You *may* have done? Don't tell me you could forget telling the chairman of our local Conservative Party that your brother was a complete idiot, a man who – what was your phrase? – couldn't manage a whelk-stall, let alone govern a country, and was therefore totally unfitted to be a parliamentary candidate?'

'I don't know that I did say that, but what if I did? It's true. And if you're going to be horrid I'm going to simply close my ears.'

'He's your brother, for God's sake. Your flesh and blood.'

'That doesn't affect my judgement, not about something so important. He's not up to being an MP, Rupert. Apart from anything else he has a disability. He is . . .'

'. . . less than perfect? Is that it? Well, in my opinion he's a fine man, a man of integrity and judgement. If I have my way, and if I can persuade him, he'll be the next member for this constituency.'

In the kitchen, India took the blancmange from the meat safe with trembling hands. If Rupert had known Henry . . . if Henry hadn't died . . . if he were there, at Kynaston now . . . Henry had been perfect, and he was the one she had lost.

But before she went back to the dining-room she brushed the tears from her cheeks. No one had ever seen her cry, and no one ever would.

≈

Mrs Earnshaw had left them a casserole. Now David opened a bottle still dusty from the cellar, and they sat either side of the long table to share their meal.

'We must talk about what you want to do with this place,' David said, as Valerie served. 'It hasn't been refurbished for years. It's been repaired, but the curtains and furnishings have been here since time immemorial. It's time for a change.'

'I don't know that I want to change anything. It's all rather splendid. Besides . . .'

She hesitated and then grinned, and David nodded understanding. 'India wouldn't like it?'

'That, David darling, is somewhat of an understatement. I'll do what needs to be done, don't think I won't, but I'm not going to go mad and try to change a marvellous house. I don't intend to be intimidated by India, easy as that would be – but let's not start with unpleasantness.' Her eyes were dancing but her chin was up.

'She will be a match for my sister,' David thought, and liked the idea.

They talked of the future of the nation, then. 'It won't be easy for anyone,' David said. 'Demobilisation won't be the overnight business that everyone is expecting. The world's in a ferment. India – the country, I mean, although now I think of it, it fits my sister, too – is a hotbed of unrest. The Government will need to keep men out there.'

'And Russia, I don't trust the Russian Bear. It means to swallow up Europe.'

'Do you think so?' David was surprised at the vehemence of her tone.

'I do. You watch. Stalin won't be content with his own borders. We'll have to decide how far we'll let him go . . . and there's no Mr Churchill to stand firm.'

'I like the look of the new Prime Minister, though.'

Valerie was nodding now. 'Yes. Though I hated the scenes in the House.' The shrunken Tory ranks had sung 'For he's a jolly good fellow' when Churchill, no longer Prime Minister, had taken his seat on the first day of the new Parliament. The massed ranks of Labour, not to be outdone, had roared out 'The Red Flag', and, from all reports, it had not been a light-hearted duet.

'Attlee is warning of hard times ahead,' David said. 'It was in *The Times* this morning. America ending Land Lease means we're in serious financial trouble. We owe the Yanks billions –'

'But they're letting us off most of it,' Valerie interrupted.

'We'll still have to export every damn thing we make, which means shortages will continue. However speaking of Parliament, I had an unusual invitation this week.'

'Yes?' Valerie was leaning forward.

'Rupert wants me to stand as an MP.' He watched her carefully, half-expecting that she might recoil at the idea.

But her eyes were brightening, her hand reaching for his. 'What a marvellous idea! You'd be bound to win, and you'd be perfect, David.'

'She loves me,' he thought. 'And what's more, she admires me.' He felt something stir within him – a feeling of satisfaction, or was it pride? Whatever it was, it was not unpleasant.

The baby had ceased to draw on her nipple now, and Catherine eased the sleepy head away from her breast. 'There now, little one.' She rose to her feet, swaying a bit with weariness. Or was she just awash with contentment? Whatever it was, it was rather a nice sensation. She had called the baby Benjamin. Ben Callingham – it was a good name. But there was a better one: Benjamin David Callingham. Yes, and David would be godfather if he agreed.

A shaft of guilt shot through Catherine then. She had originally stolen the name of Callingham, marrying Henry when she was carrying another man's baby, a baby that had died before birth. Now she was bestowing it on another outsider. I would not now do what I did then, she thought. I would be braver and stand alone. She had been 18, and now, with the wisdom of hindsight, she could see that she had been a young 18. She had fallen in love with a village boy, Sarah's brother Joe, and he had gone off to war. News of his death in action had come at the moment she realised she was pregnant. Henry Callingham's proposal, made on the eve of his departure on active service, had seemed a miraculous escape from her problem.

She had been married before she realised that the deception she had perpetrated was sinful. Her baby's death before birth had seemed to her like retribution, and then Henry himself had died before she could make up to him for what she had done. But what was done *was* done, and she could no more un-name herself now than fly. So she would just have to get on with it, and make what amends she could.

When the baby was safe in the crib, she crossed to the window. The sky was clear with stars, pale but present. Somewhere under that sky her baby's father was doing his best to mend broken lives.

'God bless you, Max,' she thought. 'And thank you for my son. Our son.' She was still smiling as she climbed into bed.

~~~

'You're insatiable,' Pamela whispered when Michael reached for her again – but she wanted more, too. She could never get enough of him. Inside her, above her, around her. When they reached a climax together, she tried hard not to make a noise. Her parents must know Michael had crossed the landing, but it wasn't fair to rub their noses in it.

'You know something?' Michael said, as they settled for sleep at last. 'One day, one night, we'll spend all our nights together, and never have to be apart again.'

'You'll get bored with me,' she said, knowing that he never would.

'Silly girl,' he said sleepily, and that was that.

Chapter Five

October 1945

THE MORNING PAPER MADE GRIM reading. Six thousand troops were unloading food ships in British ports as the dockers' strike deepened. Ships were queuing outside ports, the food that was desperately needed rotting in their holds. The strikers, 43,000 of them, were holding out for a minimum wage of 25 shillings a day.

David had expected workers to rally behind a Labour government, but the dockers were not the only workers to be restive. Munching his toast, he thought about the Government. Attlee he liked, especially if the tales swapped in the clubs were true. Apparently the Prime Minister had no time for political pleasantries, nor was he an intellectual like Stafford Cripps. Before the war he had steered his party away from the pacifism that might have done for Britain. During the war he had served the coalition faithfully, allowing Churchill to be charismatic while he got on with the work.

Cripps was less likeable, though, in truth, it was probably that thin, ascetic face that put people off him. Hugh Dalton he had little room for, and Herbert Morrison he actively disliked. The jewel of them all was Bevin – Ernest Bevin, orphaned at eight and rising to be the most powerful of the trade-union leaders. 'I would trust him with my life,' David thought, and smiled to himself as he realised that Bevin would probably regard him as an oppressor of the poor and not fit to wipe his boots on.

He turned the page. Two traitors to their country had been executed: Pierre Laval in France and Quisling in Norway. Both men had deserved their fate, but it was a grim reminder of war. More cheerful was an item about demobilisation: a million servicemen and -women were to be released in time for Christmas, and a further million released from munitions work. But Manny Shinwell, the minister of fuel and power, wanted coal production increased by 18 million tons annually. He was calling for 'the utmost effort' from miners and managers.

'I wish him luck,' David thought, recalling the mood at the pit these days. However, Shinwell's words had their effect on him. It was time to put his newspaper aside and get to work. 'Utmost effort,' he reminded himself, as he limped out of the house.

'So your due date is March 1st,' the doctor confirmed. 'That's a good time. The winter's spent, and the baby will have the benefit of summer.'

Long after the doctor's car had sped down the drive, India savoured the thought of her son in the pram in the garden. Decent prams were unobtainable now, but Henry's pram was stored in the attic at Kynaston. David had used it after Henry, but it was still Henry's pram. She would have it brought down, and refurbished. There would be other things in the attic too, items with history, much better than the cheap utility stuff available now.

What wouldn't be there, though, was anything fashionable, and she was longing for some new clothes. Wartime garments had been designed to save material. Even turn-ups on men's trousers had been banned, and pockets strictly rationed. As if the war could be won or lost on the strength of a few inches of material! The Government had ploughed money into campaigns on how to reshape old clothes. But poor people's clothes barely lasted one wearing, never mind being made over. India had had many of her own couture items altered, and that had worked well; but she was tired of the drab colours of wartime – the greys and blacks and dark browns.

She sat with her feet up, contemplating a brilliant fashion future until the clock told her it was time for the nap she gave herself each day. This pregnancy was important, and you couldn't be too cautious.

~~

It had been a lovely christening. Benjamin had cried at the cold water, but it was just a thin little wail and quickly subdued. David had been grave throughout, taking his duties as godfather seriously. Pamela, as godmother, had held Ben, and her father had stood in for Michael, the other godfather, who couldn't get leave for the day. The vows had been taken in all seriousness, the promises to bring Ben up in the Christian faith made in firm voices.

Cathy had wrestled with her conscience over the question of baptism. Ben was half a Jew, – except that Jews held that Jewishness came down through the female line, so perhaps a Christian baptism was correct? In any event, it was all she could manage, so she had gone ahead. The vicar obviously knew all about her, for he never questioned the absence of a father. What would he have said if she had told him that the father was Jewish? Anyway, it was done now, and Max would never know – so who would be hurt? Perhaps Ben, if she was depriving him of his heritage; but she couldn't worry about that now.

She laid him in his pram when he was dressed, and then

pushed the pram into the porch, which was as near to fresh air as she could manage at this time of year. Above the Otterburn blanket his dark hair fanned on the pillow, the black lashes were fluttering as he tried to ward off sleep. So young, and already determined. 'You would be proud of him, Max,' Catherine said, but only under her breath.

━━━

Pamela glanced at the clock. It was 11, and still she had no urge to get up. Days off work were too precious to be wasted on rushing around. Soon, though, she would have plenty of days off. The factory was reducing production, and rumours of lay-offs abounded. She was ready to go. Her zest for work had gone with the VJ celebrations. She would miss the money, though. They were going to need another job between them, and would do until Michael finished college. That's why they were being careful about contraception. A baby would be a disaster at this stage.

Except that babies were bliss. When she held little Ben in her arms she felt possessed by an emotion more powerful than anything she had known before. If she were to get pregnant, Catherine would not see her stuck. 'Except that I wouldn't ask her,' Pamela thought. Memories of her former self crowded in again. She had expected everyone and everything to do her bidding, give her whatever she wanted. But everyone had been selfish before the war. Selfish and stuck-up. She remembered the odious Roger with all his silly pretensions, and heard her own voice: '*What will Roger think when I bring him home?*' As if it had mattered a damn that they had lost their big house and were living in a small, borrowed one.

Roger had skedaddled when he realised there were no concealed riches, and the thought of the lucky escape she had had chilled her. 'We are better people now,' she thought – and better people didn't lie in bed all day, dreaming! She swung her legs to the floor and embraced the day.

———

David had to stoop in the doorway to enter the room. A strange smell, antiseptic yet sickly, came from the bandaged leg of the man in the chair by the fireplace. He was one of the few Japanese prisoners of war who had been fit enough to come home after a short hospitalisation. Most of them were so diseased and starved that they would be lucky to see their homes after Christmas, if indeed they ever saw them again. An inquiry was already under way in Australia, and a dreadful litany of cannibalism, torture, and unspeakable atrocities was unfolding. This man had been captured late in the war, luckily for him.

All the same, the atmosphere in the house was tense. 'How is he?' David asked.

The woman must be no more than 30, but she looked older. 'He's been a bit upset.'

David moved to the fireside, but the man didn't look up at him. 'How are you, Martin?' No reaction but a shake of the head.

'It was this that started him off.' His wife was pointing at a tin on the table beside the chair. 'It was full of odds and ends, rubbish, really.' She picked up a tattered paper. 'To *all Allied Prisoners of War,*' it read. '*The Japanese forces have surrendered unconditionally, and the war is over. We will get supplies to you as soon as is humanly possible and will make arrangements to get you out, but, owing to the distances involved, it may be some time before we can achieve this. If you have been starved or underfed for long periods, do not eat large quantities of solid food, fruit or vegetables at first. For those who are seriously ill or very weak, fluids such as broth and soup, making use of the water in which rice and other foods have been boiled, are much the best.*'

David folded it carefully, and put it on the table. 'You're

home now, Martin. Here with Elizabeth and your children. And I promise you, I promise you, nothing like that will ever happen again . . . to you or to anyone else.'

Limping out into the fresh air, he felt tears sting his eyes, but his mind was made up. Men like the one he had just left deserved a decent country to live in. A decent world. When he got back to the office, he would ring Rupert and say he was ready at least to talk about throwing his hat into the ring.

Ben was sucking vigorously now. 'Greedy boy,' Catherine murmured, warm in the comforting fug of feeding-time. As she sat there, she looked around the room. When David had given Mellows to her, it had been furnished, with carpets and curtains. Since then she had replaced nothing, and the only things she had bought had been for the baby. It would be nice to have some new furniture in the house, but she would have to be careful with money. Henry had left her more than comfortable, but she couldn't splurge. And she must be careful what she said to David, because he would press money upon her at the drop of a hat, and he had already been generous enough.

Anyway, there were precious few goods in the shops, even if you had the money, so she would have to content herself for now. 'I'm lucky,' she told herself, 'I have more than I deserve.' Perhaps she would buy some new clothes instead. Yes, a new dress. A suit, even. Red – it would be heaven to have something red!

She let out a chuckle, and then looked down to find her son's eyes on her, round and dark and questioning. He couldn't be focusing yet, could he? Except that he was truly an exceptional child, so anything was possible.

Sarah loved the moment when Joe emerged from the school gate and came towards her, beaming at the sight of his mother and brother. 'So what did you do this afternoon?' They had done something magical with used matchsticks, but she couldn't quite make out what. And he had done a drawing of a cat, and the teacher had given it a four out of five.

They were deep in conversation when Hannah hailed her from behind. Hannah was still weak from a night at the pictures, where she had seen *Brief Encounter*. 'That Trevor Howard, he's not handsome but ooh . . .' The way the 'ooh' emerged from her lips was as near an obscenity as Sarah could imagine.

'You're daft, Hannah,' she said. 'It's only a film.'

'No.' Hannah was adamant. 'It's that touching . . . she goes back to her man, and he never knows, and the loveliest music's playing, and she's remembering. My eyes were like puddings. I'm going again at the week-end.'

They parted on the pork-shop corner. 'By the way, Hartley was on about you. Said he saw you at the school.'

Hartley was the Bevin boy. 'Oh yes,' Sarah said, furious with herself that her cheeks had grown hot.

'He'll be leaving Belgate soon,' Hannah called after her. 'Better get a move on.'

Sarah had to restrain herself from breaking into a run, so anxious was she to distance herself from gossip. Why did people make something out of nothing all the time?

She was still fretting when she got home and started on the tea.

'I've been thinking about new clothes,' Catherine said as they sat at the table, Joe and Alexander munching happily between them and Ben asleep on Catherine's knee. 'I want a red dress. Quite a straight skirt. Polka dot would be nice. A little collar, one of those stand-up Chinese ones. Short sleeves – no, three-quarters. And a red patent-leather belt. Quite narrow.'

'Is that all?' Sarah's voice was heavy with sarcasm.

'It's quite a simple dress, nothing flashy.'

'No, except that it doesn't exist. Short of taking yourself off to London or Paris, I don't think you'll find it.'

'I'll make it, then,' Catherine said defiantly.

'I didn't know you could sew?'

'I can't, but there's dressmakers!'

They were deep in discussion about coupons and material when the phone rang.

'I'll get it. Don't disturb the bairn.' Sarah crossed the hall, her head full of paper patterns and tacking stitches. 'Belgate 494,' she said.

There was no reply. Only silence and the faint sound of breathing.

'The doctor called today,' India said when they were settled in the drawing-room with coffee on a tray between them.

'Oh yes? Everything OK?' Rupert didn't look up from the cup he was stirring.

'Yes. My ankles are a little swollen, but that's not significant, according to him.'

'Good. Have you had sugar?'

'No. Thank you. Aren't you interested in what he had to say?' A little knot of discomfort had formed inside her chest. He was still punishing her for telling the truth about David. It wasn't fair.

'I'm sure you'll tell me if it's important.'

'He says it'll be born on the first of March.'

'You've told me that. Good job it isn't the first of April. All Fools' Day.'

'Is that all you can say? About the day on which your son

will be born?'

'India, it could be a girl.'

'It's a boy.'

'Because you will it to be a boy? My dear, not even your will is strong enough to decide a matter like that. Anyway, I'm glad to hear about the date. We can make plans. Oh, and I heard from David today. He will stand for Parliament when Harris stands down. So that's two pieces of good news in one day.'

She wouldn't dignify him with a reply. He was deliberately baiting her, but she wouldn't rise. Instead she said, 'They say the film on at the Odeon is very good. Trevor Howard and Celia Johnson in *Brief Encounter*. It's from a play of Noel Coward's, so it should be worth seeing.'

'I miss you, too, but it won't be long now.'

'Will you get leave at Christmas?' Pamela changed the receiver to her other hand because her arm was aching with its weight.

'Of course I will.' That was what she loved about Michael – he was always hopeful. 'I've told you, darling, it's not last in, first out. It's the reverse. And I've been in since early 1940, so I'm sure to get an early slot. That means I can start my college course next summer. The time will fly, you'll see.'

'I can come and work wherever you're studying,' she said. 'So I'll be there to feed you and look after you.'

'And distract me. I know you, little minx.'

'But I can still come, if I'm good?'

'Of course you can come. I couldn't do without you for three whole years.'

When she put down the phone, she was crying, but they were happy tears.

When Valerie rang off David poured himself a glass of whisky and sought out a chair in the morning-room. He virtually lived in one room now, would sleep there if he could. Kynaston had been built for a large family, a family with an army of servants, not for one man living alone. One day it would ring with children's voices, as it had done when he and Henry were young. He smiled, remembering childhood battles re-enacted on the great stairs, with Henry always the shining knight and he the trusty squire.

If Ben had been Henry's child . . . if there had been no war . . . Ben would be growing up at Kynaston. Tonight, in the bath, he had gurgled and kicked his feet. Catherine seemed not to mind that he popped in at bath times. Mustn't make himself a nuisance, though. All the same, he was Ben's godfather, which made a difference.

When she woke, Sarah was screaming. Or had she imagined that? If she really had screamed, Catherine would have come to her, Joe would have woken up, Alexander cried . . . but the house was still. Sarah lay back, sweat moist on her face. She had been dreaming she was back at the croft, and Hamish towering above her. She had told him not to worry if he couldn't find work, she would get a job. He had knocked her out of the chair, then. She had put her hand on her belly to protect the baby inside it as he had shouted and raged. '*Why? Why do you shame me? Why do you remind me I'm a useless hulk?*' He had hit her again, and she had closed her eyes as he continued, '*You do this. Whore! Slut! Bitch! You make a show of me to my neighbours.*'

Now she sat up in the darkened room and pulled up the eider-down to ease her shivering. 'He will come for me one day,' she thought. 'Sooner or later, he will come for me and his child. For Alexander. And there is nothing and no one who will stop him.'

Chapter Six

December 1945

BEN ENJOYED HIS BATH NOW that Catherine had moved it to morning. He was wide awake as opposed to sleepy, and was kicking his legs vigorously. Sometimes she told herself he was forward for his age. David certainly thought so. She smiled, then, thinking of the first time she had let David help with the bathing. He had looked like a worshipper at a shrine, a knight of the realm with a towel over his shoulder and another across his knee. Which was only fitting for the world's best baby.

She was lifting the slippery little body to her towel-draped knee when she heard Sarah's voice in the hall. Then a man's voice and laughter. Intrigued, she swaddled the baby and carried him to look out of the door. David was there again, a woollen scarf wound around his neck beneath a face reddened with exertion. 'What is that?' she said, in tones of disbelief.

'It's a Christmas tree,' David answered, and then, 'well, we always had one at Kynaston, remember? There's no point this year, with no one there but me, so I thought . . .'

He was looking crestfallen and Catherine moved forward. 'Look, Ben,' she said, holding the baby aloft, 'your very first Christmas tree!'

David's face relaxed, and Sarah bustled away in search of a pot.

'I know it's big,' he said apologetically. 'I suppose I got carried away a bit, remembering Kynaston.'

'Big is fine,' Catherine said firmly. 'But we'll need to borrow your toys and tinsel.' Their eyes met, and each knew that the other was remembering that past Christmas. There had been a tree in the hall at Kynaston, and carol singers at the door, as the news came that Henry was missing, believed killed.

'I know, David. I know. Henry loved Christmas – so let's do him justice with this tree.'

'He'd've liked that,' David said, and started to rewind his scarf. 'You don't need me, do you? I thought I'd just pop down to the village.'

'No,' Catherine said. 'No, we can manage perfectly well on our own.'

<hr />

'Anyone in?' Sarah pushed at the half-open door, expecting to see Hannah Chaffey in her chair by the fire. But it was not Hannah. It was the Bevin boy, who had been toasting his stockinged feet at the fire. He was obviously newly home from the pit for he had the pallor of a man just come off night-shift. Now, though, his cheeks were reddening, and he was leaping to his feet, the picture of confusion.

'She's not in. I mean, Mrs Chaffey . . . she's not in.'

Sarah was turning to go, trying not to smile at the sight of him adjusting shirt buttons and scrabbling for his shoes, when he spoke again. 'She won't be long. Well, unless –' He reddened further.

'Unless she meets someone and stops for a chat?' Sarah finished for him.

'Well,' he was smiling, 'something like that. I've just made tea if you'd like a cup?'

It seemed churlish to refuse, so she put the brake on the

pram, and sat down on the opposite side of the fire, drawing Joe to stand at her knee. Alexander was engaged in his favourite activity, exploring. She would have to keep an eye on him. The Bevin boy – for the life of her she couldn't remember his name – returned with a cup and saucer, trying hard not to let the tea slop into the saucer. He brought something else, chocolate finger-biscuits. He held one out to Joe, but her son wouldn't touch it until she urged him to take it.

'He's shy,' Sarah said – but Joe was not shy. He was afraid of men. All men. Alexander had no hesitation in taking the biscuit and biting down on it with obvious pleasure.

'It must be strange for you here,' she went on, trying to make conversation.

'It was at first, but I've settled. I missed home at first. My mother sends me parcels to cheer me up.'

'So that's where the biscuits came from?' He nodded, and she continued. 'I couldn't tie Hannah in with chocolate fingers, somehow. Anyway, where is home?'

He came from Twickenham, which was part of London. 'I wanted to join the RAF, but my name came out of a hat, and here I am. And it's OK. The men were wary of me at first. I was a townee . . .'

'I expect they said bloody townee,' Sarah said, and they both laughed.

'My dad and my brother are pitmen,' she said. 'Well, of course you know Jim . . .'

The ice was broken, and they talked freely. They were deep in conversation about the forthcoming Nuremberg trials of Goering, Hess and the other Nazi leaders, and whether or not William Joyce, the Britain whose nightly broadcasts from Germany had had an effect on morale, was a traitor, when Hannah appeared in the doorway. She took in the scene at a glance.

'Don't get up,' she said. 'I'll just put these sausages in the meat-safe, and I'll join you in a cuppa.'

Sarah's heart sank. Hannah was bound to make a thing of her and the Bevin boy. He was certainly good-looking, in a Leslie Howard kind of way – but handsome is as handsome does. She had had her fill of men.

The tea was hot and sweet, too sweet, but David forced himself to drink it. Opposite him, the other man and woman were raising cups to their lips but the woman's hands were trembling.

'So you've been out of the army for six weeks, and you've been here, living with your in-laws, and no prospect of a house?' Nine people were living in a three-bedroomed colliery house. The man had served since the early days of the war. Before that he had been a grocer's boy. Now that grocers were staffed by women, his chances of re-employment there were slender, if not non-existent. 'How do you manage?'

The woman's cheeks reddened. 'Me mam and dad have one bedroom, me sisters are in another, and we have the third one.' David nodded his understanding.

'With your children? All three of them?'

The woman nodded. David looked at the man. 'That must be difficult?'

The man agreed. 'Sometimes we come and sleep down here.' David knew what he meant: when they needed to make love, they tiptoed furtively down to the communal room. What a reward for five years of blood and toil!

'I can't promise, but I'll see what I can do,' he said.

As he drove away, he contrasted the man's circumstances with his own. Soon he and Valerie would marry, and Kynaston would come to life again. Twenty-seven rooms, each big enough to house a family. He had escaped the war – unless you counted the loss of a brother – and his peace would be a much easier affair than the peace of this returning soldier. 'It isn't fair,' he thought. 'It's damned unfair.'

The only thing that consoled him was the thought that one day he might get a chance to redress the balance.

<hr>

'But you have no experience of proper childcare?' India said. It was a statement, not a question. The girl sitting saucer-eyed in front of her was 15 years old, the eldest of seven children, and sure that bringing up six younger siblings was qualification enough.

'Well,' India said again, 'do you or don't you have experience?'

'I used to bath the bairns for me Mam when she took bad.'

'No, I mean in a proper household?' This was obviously too much for the girl to cope with. She just gaped.

'I'll keep your name in mind,' India said. 'Shut the door on your way out.'

The next applicant was a novice in her 40s. Where were all the 20- and 30-year-olds, India wondered – and then supplied the answer. Their heads had been turned by high wages in wartime factories. No nannying for them. She studied the woman in front of her: pale face, rings round her eyes, work-worn hands clutching a shabby handbag.

'I see you're a widow?'

The woman nodded. 'Yes. He was killed at Arnhem.'

'Hmm,' India deliberated. 'He must have been quite old. Was he regular army?' Again the woman nodded. 'And you had no children?'

'We had a boy died at birth. And I lost a little girl – diphtheria.'

India struggled to suppress a giggle. 'I see,' she said. 'Not a particular recommendation for a role in childcare, is it?'

She was about to continue when Rupert's voice cut through the room. 'I think my wife means that she's looking for a particular type of person for this job.'

India had not realised he had come into the room. The woman rose to her feet and was clutching her coat together. 'However,' Rupert was advancing upon her, holding out a hand to take her elbow, 'I think I might know of the right position for you.' He picked up a pen from the desk and scribbled something on a notepad. 'Tomorrow I want you to take this to my offices on the Broad Chare. Give it to my secretary, Miss Adamson. I'll have spoken to her by then, and we'll see what we can do.'

He ushered the woman out, and it was a few moments before he returned.

'I hadn't finished the interview,' India said, crossly.

'I'm sure you hadn't. There were probably quite a few moments of torment left, but I, my dear, had heard enough.'

'So you listen outside doors now?' Inside her, discomfort that was almost fear was forming. He behaved so oddly nowadays.

'Only when I must,' Rupert said wearily. 'Only when I must.'

<hr />

They had sipped rum and orange at their break, and the foreman had turned a blind eye. For 12 women this was their last day, and Pamela was one of them. 'Gee, it'll be strange in here without you lot.' Joyce had a streamer round her neck and a paper hat on her head, but her tone was doleful.

'We won't lose touch,' Pamela said.

'You will. Renee'll go off with her Welshman when he gets out. Welsh Wales she'll be in. You'll be the same, Pammy. Folk always say they won't lose touch, but it's life, pet. It kind of carries you away.'

It was true Pamela thought, as she returned to her bench. Right now she couldn't imagine life without these women, but her life would move on. Michael would come home, her life would be brimming, with a home to build, and children . . . well, children eventually.

She was deep in thought when Joyce spoke from behind her. 'But we shared some times, didn't we?'

The two women looked at one another for a moment, remembering the tears, the sweat, singing 'Land of Hope and Glory' when news came of victory in Europe, the moment Pamela had been summoned to the foreman's office to hear that Michael's plane had come down, and a hundred other moments.

'Yes,' she said quietly. 'We shared some times.'

David had looked at the clock as they went into dinner. Seven-thirty. He could decently leave at ten. Two and a half hours. He tried dividing the evening into courses. Three, then port and cheese, and coffee. Five, and small talk after. Six. Dessert would be the half-way mark. Half-way through the entrée would be a quarter. Suddenly India's voice penetrated his musing: 'I said, "Does Valerie know when she'll be released yet?"'

He said they had no idea of a date yet, abandoned silly sums, and entered into the conversation.

Rupert was in serious mood. 'They say 55 million will be the ultimate casualty figure.'

'Surely not.' India sounded patronising, as though she were reproving a child. 'How does he stand her?' David wondered. Even pregnancy had not softened his sister.

'The death toll is not the only worry,' he said. 'I saw a man today . . . he's had five years of war, and now he and his family are living in the three-roomed house of his in-laws. Six adults and three children in three bedrooms. No privacy, no space, and no hope of a house in the near future. I felt ashamed talking to him.'

Rupert nodded. 'And Britain is not the only country affected.'

A servant was putting pâté before them, and David smiled his thanks. 'Why do you say that, Rupert?'

'We've lost about 6.5 per cent of our housing stock. In some areas of Europe where there was fighting, the whole lot's gone.'

'America is doing its best, though.' An International Monetary Fund and an International Bank had been set up to regulate the world economy, and last week the Commons had voted to accept a £1,100 million loan.

Rupert was nodding but his tone was rueful. 'Beware the Yanks bearing gifts, David. We'll repay that money, you can be sure.'

'Pay for it, never mind repay it.' India was on to one of her hobby horses now. 'They'll expect us to kow-tow to them. They think they won the war single-handed. That's what infuriates me.'

'We couldn't have done it without them.' The men spoke in unison.

'Oh yes, stick together, men always do. But Beaverbrook was against taking their money, and Churchill abstained.'

'Which proves why he couldn't continue as Prime Minister,' David said. 'This country can no longer stand alone, India. You'd better get used to that sad fact.'

Catherine had fed Ben and settled him in his crib. Now she undressed, and then went to the bathroom. A weariness came upon her at bedtime these days. When she was a girl, it had sometimes been hard to sleep, and going to bed a waste of time. But she longed for her bed now.

She was cleaning her teeth when she heard the knocking at the door. She had left her watch on the bedside table but it must be at least 11 o'clock. Sarah was still up, and listening to the wireless in the morning-room, but she couldn't leave her to answer the door on her own at this time of night. By the time she had rinsed away the toothpaste and refastened her dressing gown, she could hear that Sarah was crossing the hall.

Catherine reached the landing, and looked down, past the branches of the huge Christmas tree to the door. 'Wait!' she called out – but it was too late. Sarah had opened it, and the figure on the step was advancing into the hall. It was Hamish. Shrouded in a coat and muffler, raindrops glistening in his hair, but recognisably Sarah's husband.

By the time Catherine reached the hall, Sarah had shrunk back against the oak hallstand and was staring at her tormentor as though mesmerised.

'I've come to see my wee-un.' Hamish's voice was slurred, his eyes bloodshot and unfocused.

'You can't see him now. He's asleep.' Catherine tried to keep her voice steady.

'I've come to see my wee-un!' he said again, only more aggressively than before.

'And so you shall,' Catherine said. 'In the morning.' She tried to wheedle. 'You wouldn't wake a baby at this time of night, would you?'

He shook his head as though trying to dispel cobwebs from his brain. 'I've come . . .' It was then that he started to cry.

Neither of the women had expected this. Sarah lifted her arms. 'Any moment now, she'll embrace him,' Catherine thought, 'and if she does, she'll be doomed.'

She moved quickly between man and wife, and flashed a warning glance at her friend.

'Sarah, telephone for a taxi. The number is on the table there. We want to go to the Mason's Arms in Belgate.' She turned to Hamish. 'You need a night's rest, and tomorrow you can see your boy.' Would he take this from her? She was buying time to think of a plan. 'They'll let you have a room at the pub. I'll give you the money . . .'

It was the wrong thing to say. His voice when he spoke was a roar. 'I have my own money. You and your money! You took my wife and bairn away from me – bitch!' For a moment she feared he would strike her.

She could hear Sarah behind her, speaking urgently into the phone, then putting it down. 'They're coming,' she said. 'Five minutes.'

'Would you like a cup of tea?' Catherine asked Hamish desperately.

He shook his head. 'I need a drink.'

'Sarah, there's a malt whisky in the sideboard.'

She saw Sarah hesitate, and again signalled with her eyes. She had no intention of moving as long as she was the only thing that stood between Hamish and the sleeping child upstairs. Sleeping children, rather – for there were her own baby and little Joe to consider, too. Joe would be traumatised by coming face to face with Hamish again. So how would they manage tomorrow? She banished that worry from her mind and concentrated on how she would get Hamish over the step and out of her house.

When Sarah came back with the whisky, she handed it to him, and urged him to drink. He had drained the glass when they heard the welcome sound of Belgate's ancient taxi outside. 'We'll see you tomorrow,' she said as they bundled him into the back seat; and then 'Mason's Arms,' she told the driver.

It was not until she and Sarah were back inside, with the hall door bolted, that they could look at one another and give way to the fear that possessed them.

⁓

As she lay in the bath, Pamela thought back over the day. It had been sad to say goodbye, but if you wanted to move on goodbyes were sometimes inevitable. Soon Michael would be home, and they could get married. A house – well, a flat – even rooms – would be hard to come by. Half the country seemed to be house-hunting, and demand would grow as more men returned. But Michael would have a gratuity, and she had her nest-egg – £302 in the bank, every penny scrimped and saved from her wages. It wasn't much, and yet it was a fortune. All the difference between one room and a house.

She was exulting when she put out the bathroom light, and crossed the landing. It was late, but a light still shone below. She had expected her parents to be long tucked up and asleep. She went downstairs, tying her dressing-gown as she went. 'Dad? What are you doing up?'

He was sitting at the table, a cup of tea in front of him. 'I'm thinking, Pamela. Just thinking.'

'That sounds serious.' She sat down opposite him.

'I want to go back into business. Work for myself. I have this idea. Everyone is sick of utility furniture – everything plain, everything the same. I couldn't afford to manufacture furniture from scratch, as I used to do. But I'm thinking about conversion. Buying utility stuff, and adding that extra touch.'

'Decoration, you mean? Embellishment?'

'Something like that. It would work, Pammy. I know it would work. I'd start slowly at first, with as little outlay as possible. I wondered – do you think – would Catherine lend me some money? I wouldn't need much. A couple of hundred should do it.'

Pamela looked at his face – trusting, hopeful, wanting to restore all he had lost. She remembered the day the bailiffs had come and he had locked himself in his study while she pounded on the door in tears. He had lost everything: the factory, his pride, even his home. But now he was ready to try again. She thought of her nest-egg. She could wait for a house; a room would do. 'Well,' she said, 'if she won't, I will.'

Chapter Seven

December 1945

SARAH HAD BEEN AWAKE SINCE before daybreak. The children were quiet, but the house was alive with noises, and she jumped at every creak and shivered at every crack. Hamish would be back. She had expected his arrival every day since she had left Scotland and returned to Durham. The fact that it had taken seven months for him to turn up was a source of amazement to her. But he had been like that, liking to play cat and mouse, watch his prey before he pounced.

She struggled to remember why she had loved him. Had she ever loved him? Or had she simply wanted someone to plug the hole that Gerard's death had left in her life? Hamish had been kind in the beginning. And then he had gone to war, and come back injured, and a monster.

She would have to go back to him: Alexander was his child, and he would never let him go. But she would not subject Joe to the hell he had endured at the croft. Perhaps Catherine would keep him at Mellows? She was kind enough to do it, but now that she had a child of her own would she be willing to take on another?

Eventually, as it began to grow light, she fell into an uneasy sleep, but only to dream again of the Hamish of recent memory. Somewhere, far off, Joe was crying, and Hamish was pinning her arms until she cried out: '*I want to go to him!*' She was wasting her words. And he was shouting, '*Why do you do this to me? Why do you shame me? Why, why, why?*' She could hear herself screaming. When she woke, it was minutes before she realised she was at Mellows, and safe – at least for a little while.

═══

Catherine's call had come at seven-thirty: 'Please get here when you can, David. I don't know what to do.'

He was dressed and behind the wheel of the car within minutes. It was still dark as he turned in at the Mellows drive. Catherine was waiting in the doorway. Her hair roamed untidily on to her shoulders, and a red dressing-gown was pulled around her, but he had never seen her look more beautiful. 'Now,' he said, limping towards her, 'I'm here and, whatever it is, we can sort it out.' His arms closed around her, and she clung for a moment. Then she was drawing him over the step and towards the warm kitchen.

'So you packed him off to the Mason's?' he said, when she had stammered out the story.

'I was so afraid, David. He wasn't normal . . . he might have been drunk, but it was more as though he was possessed.'

'Did he threaten you?'

'No. He was threatening, but at the time I never felt afraid. If I'm honest, I felt sorry for him. Alexander is his child, after all, and I think his war injuries still trouble him. But Sarah can't go back to him, David. That's not an option.'

He took another drink of his tea, and then replaced the cup in the saucer. 'I'll go and see him now. Leave it to me. I'm not quite sure how I'll sort this, but you can be sure I shall.'

She was moving towards him again, smiling up at him. 'David, what would I do without you? You are so good to me.'

She kissed his cheek, not knowing that the touch of her lips on his skin was also a dagger in his heart.

'I can't really believe it, but Daddy means to make it happen.'
Pamela smiled at her mother's euphoria. All the same, they
would all have to be sensible. 'It's wonderful, Mummy, but we
have to wait and see if he can do it. It won't be easy to start
again, with everything in such short supply.'

'But that's just it.' Her mother was pouring tea and pushing
forward the toast. 'Eat up, dear, It's the shortages that that will
make it work. People are hungry for colour again. It's been sad
a drab war. Everyone in uniform, everything camouflaged, and
such dreadful clothes and furnishings. Daddy will produce indi-
vidual things – well, not produce them but refurbish them, you
know what I mean. Do you think Catherine will help him?'

'I don't know, Mummy. I don't really know anything about
her financial situation. But I have my house money. I've told
Daddy he can use that if he needs it.'

Her mother's face clouded. 'You can't do that, dear. That's
for you and Michael, and I know how difficult it was to save it.
You've worked so hard.'

'I'll get it back,' Pamela said bravely. 'You never know, we
might all be millionaires eventually. And Mike and I will
manage.'

'Oh Pammy, you were such a headache once, and now
you're such a comfort.' Her mother's arms came round her, and
Pamela felt her eyes prick. If she was truthful, the thought of
parting with her nest-egg was painful. But she had seen the light
back in her father's eyes last night. And lights like that should
never be extinguished.

The doctor was washing his hands at the sink as India struggled back into her clothes. 'It's all going according to plan,' he said when he returned to his desk. 'Are you making sure to rest?'

India shrugged. 'I try. But women's work is never done. We've managed to get a woman to help, but it's not the same. We trained our staff in the old days – they came into the kitchen, and if they did well there, they'd proved themselves fit to work in the house. The people you can get now are the dregs.'

The doctor was nodding sympathetically. 'My wife says the same. She bemoans the days gone when servants were servants. She calls them the ruling class, nowadays. Well, they can pick and choose jobs now, of course.'

India hardly thought a doctor's wife would really understand the servant problem, but it didn't do to show it. 'I know. And nursery maids . . . This poor little boy is not going to be surrendered to inexpert hands, I can promise you.'

'So you've decided it's a boy!' The doctor was smiling indulgently.

'I know it's a boy,' India said confidently.

As she came out into the street, she could see him in her mind's eye. Tall and straight; dark like Henry – in fact, like Henry in every way. She and Henry had shared the Callingham genes; David had always been his mother's child.

As she walked back to the car, she saw that a Christmas tree was being erected on the bombsite at the corner. What a silly waste of public money! She must speak to someone about it. But the sight of the tree reminded her of Christmases past, and Kynaston, when the future stretched ahead safe and sunlit; and the memory made her sad. War was a scourge. If Halifax had been allowed to make peace with Hitler, it would have been so different. Henry would have been installed at Kynaston with a fitting wife, not a fool like Catherine Allerton. She let out a yelp of anguish as the side of her cheek was caught between her clenching teeth.

Once in the car, she turned on the ignition. Somehow, in some way, she must make everything right again, for herself, for Kynaston, and for her son.

'Don't look so astonished, Catherine. I checked. Hamish never arrived at the Mason's Arms. The owner looked at me as though I was completely crazy. So I went to see Crozier, the man who runs the taxi firm. He says that Hamish changed the destination, and told the driver to take him into Durham.'

'What did he want there? Sit down, David, I'm making coffee.' Winter sun was streaming into the room and now he could see the strain of the night before written on Catherine's face.

'You look tired,' he said.

'I didn't sleep much,' she admitted. 'I thought Hamish would be back, and I didn't really see a way out. Do you think we could buy him off? Pay him to stay out of Sarah's life?'

'I hardly know the man, but I doubt it.'

Sarah came in then, apprehension on her face.

'It's all right,' Catherine said quickly. 'It appears he's gone.'

'Gone? Back to Scotland?'

'We don't know that,' David said carefully. 'Come and sit down and have some coffee.'

For a moment or two they drank quietly and then Sarah put down her cup. 'If he's gone – if he has gone – he'll be back. He won't give up. On Alexander, that is. He doesn't want me, but he won't give up on his son.'

'You can't go back to him,' Catherine said flatly. 'You know how he brutalised you. How long would it have been before the children suffered too?'

Sarah looked as though she were about to speak, but then changed her mind. It was David who spoke. 'No one's going anywhere, except into Sunderland or Durham to see a lawyer. This is still Britain, and no one's going anywhere against their will.'

———

'There'll be problems,' David said, as they settled at their table.

'That's an understatement, dear boy.' Rupert was grimacing. 'We're getting all the details from Central Office, and it makes grim reading. There are more than 5,000 child evacuees still in their billets. Some of them have been orphaned by the war, but most are simply not wanted at home, or there's no home left standing for them to return to.'

'That's dreadful.'

'Hopefully, there'll be some sort of resolution. We just have to step up the production of building materials, and get more men out of the services and into work.'

'What will happen to the children if there isn't?' David asked.

'They'll cease to be evacuees, and will become the responsibility of the local authority to which they were sent. And this is just one tiny problem. I wouldn't like to be Attlee, I tell you. If you ask me, Winston has had a lucky escape. Do you know what he said when the election results came through?'

David shook his head. 'He said, "I won the race and now they have warned me off the turf." Lonsdale told me. He got it from the old man's secretary.'

'The way the electorate turned against him was astonishing.' David's tone was rueful.

'Yes, but look on the bright side. Attlee has the all the problems of cleaning up, and the Tories will get back at the next election. That's when you can play your part.'

'I want to do something now, Rupert. I'm making a point of seeing men as they come home, and most of them are in a sorry state. Wounded, or former prisoners. I feel guilty and useless when I listen to their stories.'

'They've been planning demobilisation for years, as soon as the tide turned when the Yanks came in. Those who've served longest will be released first . . . well, almost. The first wave to come out will be men with urgently needed skills, house-building in particular. But they'll only get out on condition they return to their trade. If not, they'll be drafted back in. They hope that a third of all forces will be out by Christmas.'

David let out a low whistle. 'That many?'

'We're in a mess, David, you know that. We are battered, exhausted, and broke. We owe America a fortune – over £5 billion, they say, and they want repaying. Everything we make will have to be for export, so shortages and rationing here will continue. But the real need is for houses. If we can't offer returning men a roof over their heads, I fear there'll be trouble.'

Their meal was served then, and as they ate the conversation turned to less grim matters.

'What about this wedding of yours?'

'I'm glad you asked,' David said, smiling. 'I was wondering: will you be my best man?'

They drank a toast to Valerie and the wedding day, and then got on with eating. 'I like Rupert,' David told himself. 'I had reservations about him at first, but they've gone. He cares about his country. And if he can put up with India, he must be akin to a saint.'

Sarah had thought twice about going shopping. What if Hamish were lurking there? David had assured her he must have gone back to Lochearnhead, but she was still apprehensive.

She had been to the grocer's and the butcher's, and posted some letters for Catherine, and was beginning to relax when she became aware of a figure looming up behind her. To her relief, it was only the Bevin boy.

'Are you all right?' he asked anxiously, falling into step beside her. She nodded.

'Why do you ask?' she said, but she knew very well why he was asking. Hannah had been gossiping – though how she had found out heaven only knew.

'Hannah told me there'd been trouble last night. Your husband . . .'

'How did she know?' Sarah asked, but it was a foolish question. Not a leaf fell in Belgate but Hannah knew about it. 'I'm all right. He's gone back home. Well, we think he's gone back.'

'Hannah told me you'd had a hard time with him.'

'It wasn't his fault,' Sarah said quickly. 'It was the war. It turned him funny.'

Hartley nodded, 'I know. It's happened to a lot of men. But it must have been hard for you – and the children.'

'That's why I left him,' she said. 'For the sake of the children.'

They were reaching the corner now. 'Would you like a cup of tea?' he asked. 'The British Restaurant's just round the corner. We could get the children some orange juice.'

For a moment she hesitated, remembering another man who had fallen into step beside her on this same street. But this boy was different, hardly more than a child. 'Well, just one cup,' she said and turned the pram for the restaurant door.

'So they say it'll be about four weeks.' Michael's voice was excited.

Pamela changed the receiver to her other ear. 'Four weeks! I can hardly believe it.'

'Yes, nor can I. I get two choices of suit, apparently: dark blue or brown, both pinstripe. A bit spivvy, but a suit's a suit. Oh, and it can be single or double-breasted. Black shoes or brown. White shirts – two, I think. And a blue or brown tie, and a hat or a cap. A raincoat. Some people say you get under-wear, but I'm not sure about that.'

'What will you choose?'

'Well, I fancy a trilby. I never wore a cap before I went into uniform, but I do fancy a trilby. Anyway, they say you can sell the lot – there are touts outside every demob centre, waving notes in your face.'

'You wouldn't sell them! You'll need clothes.'

'I don't know. Cash would be nice. We'll need every penny if we're to get a place of our own – and, oh, I'm dying to be alone with you, Pam. To shut our own door on the world. Still, we'll have my gratuity and my savings, such as they are, and your savings too. We should be all right.'

Inside Pamela's chest a pounding started. Should she say she might have nothing to contribute? Would he understand?

In the end she said nothing, except for vows of love and promises to speed the day when they could be together.

⁓

'Well, I think his asking you is inappropriate. Surely he has friends?'

'I rather thought I was his friend. And I'll be honoured to be his best man,' Rupert said. They had left the dinner table and gone into the library to await their coffee. The woman who brought it in looked apprehensive.

'I've forgotten the sugar,' she said. 'I'll just nip back for it.'

'I should think you will,' India said. 'Honestly, you have the attention span of a gnat. Hurry up! The coffee will be cold before we can drink it, if you're not careful.'

Rupert waited until the woman had left the room, and then he leaned forward. 'Must you be so offensive, India? I thought you prided yourself on good manners. Does that only apply to your own class?'

'You have to be hard on servants nowadays, Rupert, otherwise they'll run rings round you. It was different at Kynaston. Servants there knew how to behave.'

'She seems perfectly civil to me.' He had taken up a stance by the fire, one foot on the fender.

'Do sit down, Rupert. You make the place look untidy. Yes, she's perfectly civil. She's also perfectly stupid. That's the trouble.'

He went up to bed as soon as he had drunk his coffee. India, following a little while later, found him already in bed and only the bedside light on her side illuminated. She undressed and slipped into bed beside him.

'Rupert?' There was a muffled reply, and she tried again. 'Rupert? You can love me a little, if you like. It will be all right if we're careful.'

He didn't answer, so she put out a hand and touched him. There was no response, until at last he spoke. 'Go to sleep, India. I'm tired, if you're not.'

In the darkness, her cheeks burned. She had never wanted him, but his not wanting her was another matter. How dare he reject her? How dare he?

———

Sarah had helped Catherine put the lights on the tree when the children were in bed – a strangely subdued Sarah, who had taken herself off to bed as soon as the tree was finished. Now Catherine put out the light, leaving the tree to illuminate the hall. It was four years since that first Christmas with Max in 1941– four years, and yet a lifetime. She had invited him to

Mellows to recover from the injuries they had both sustained when the hospital they worked in had been bombed. He had arrived bearing gifts, tinned fruit and ham, candied fruit and butter, caviar, and brandy, and a plum pudding. She had asked where such riches had come from, and he had tapped his nose and told her Americans were resourceful. They had made love that night for the first time.

Now Max was somewhere in Europe, and she was here, at Mellows, with his son. How strange life was, especially in wartime! She sat down on the stairs, remembering the girl she had been. If anyone had told her then the shape her life would take, she would have run screaming into the night. And yet she had survived. But survivors could still cry. She leaned her head against the banister and tried to hold back the tears. As she blinked, the lights on the tree shimmered and winked. They must make a good Christmas for the children.

At least her children were safe. Papers were still full of stories of the camps. Max would be at one of those camps now, or at least dealing with the remnants of the horror that had happened there. A newspaper account had told of women hiding their babies in their clothes before they went into the gas chambers, hoping that the attendants, prisoners like themselves, would find the child and take it to safety. But the guards were wise to the ruse, and would root out the babies and throw them over their mother's heads into the killing chamber.

Catherine closed her eyes, trying to banish the image. Upstairs her baby was sleeping. Tomorrow night they would light the tree again, and lift the sleepy children to view its splendour. "The world will heal," she told herself. It had no choice.

She sat on for a moment and then she got to her feet, switched off the lights, and went upstairs to bed.

Chapter Eight

January 1946

'NEW CARS ARE SCARCER THAN hen's teeth,' David had told Catherine when she announced her intention of buying a car and learning to drive. So they were looking at an Austin Seven that David said had 'seen better days'. To Catherine, it looked wonderful.

'I don't want to spend a lot of money,' she had said at the outset, but she knew that, unless she stood firm, David would want to buy her something better. 'I owe him so much,' she had told Sarah last night. 'I can't let him interfere with this.'

'Very moderate mileage,' the salesman said helpfully. He'd already explained that everyone had yard-long waiting lists for new cars, when they began to roll off the assembly lines. 'Factories were all tooled up to make military vehicles,' he'd said apologetically. 'There hasn't been a new model since before the war, and it will be a while before we see one. In the mean time, reliable models like this one are at a premium.'

It was a 1937 Austin Seven, with leather seats in a nice shade of green. In the end she paid £650 for it, which David called extortionate, and which the salesman said was half of what he could get on the open market. As a bonus, the salesman drove it to Mellows for her.

'Lesson one tomorrow,' David said when he called round,

and Catherine felt her heart sink. It had seemed like a good idea, but now, as she contemplated the size of her purchase, it seemed a terrifying proposition.

But she wasn't going to look like a coward. 'Tomorrow,' she said. 'I can hardly wait.'

Sarah knew when she picked the envelope up from the mat that it was trouble. She never got letters. Who would write to her? No one official – and it was a very official-looking envelope. She sat down at the kitchen table to read it. '*Dear Mrs Carlyle,*' it began. '*We are commanded by our client, Hamish Carlyle of The Brough, Ardbeg, Lochearnhead, to inform you of his intention to apply for custody of his son, Alexander Carlyle. He is also instituting proceeding for divorce on the grounds of desertion . . .*'

There was more, but Sarah had read enough. She would have to go back to him. If she didn't, he would take Alexander from her. Courts favoured fathers and, to the outward eye, she was the one who had offended by leaving the marriage. She would have to go back, and if she did he would kill her. She remembered that last time: the sound of his fist connecting with her temple, and the dizzying pain that had followed. She would be better dead than going back to that.

India had gone to bed as soon as the doctor had mentioned hypertension. There had been other words – pre-eclampsia, and something that sounded like endothelial dysfunction. 'You need to rest and follow a low-salt diet,' he had said. He had not needed to say more, although he had gone on and on. She must not, could not, lose her son.

So she sat up in bed, a frilly bed-jacket tied at her neck, magazines and grapes to hand, and a bell to summon the daily help.

'We must get more staff,' she told Rupert. 'I need a nursery-maid, and I need her now, to train well before she has to take charge.'

Rupert had looked suitably harassed and anxious to please, and had promised to interview within the week.

Now she leafed through the newspaper that Rupert had brought up with her breakfast tray. It was full of reports of the new United Nations General Assembly that was soon to have its inaugural session in London. The King and the Prime Minister were both to speak at it. Her lip curled at the prospect of a stammerer and a nondescript representing England. At least Churchill would have been impressive at the lectern. Fifty-one nations were to be present – she hadn't realised there were 51 nations. They must have invited pip-squeaks such as Lichtenstein and Lapland. The Assembly was simply the old League of Nations in a new guise, and everyone knew how ineffective the League had been.

News of riots in Paris and Rouen over a bread shortage annoyed her. All the sacrifices she and others had made to free the French, and still they weren't satisfied! Her face lit up when she saw that coal-owners were protesting at Labour's plans to nationalise the coal-mines. Sadly, her brother wouldn't be one of the protesters: he seemed positively gleeful at the prospect of losing the estate's major source of income.

The next item, however, filled her with fury. GI brides were to sail to America on the *Queen Mary*. Whores and illiterates, most of them, and sailing on a luxury liner. It was too much to bear. Not that the Americans didn't know exactly what they were getting. The brides were to be sent to transit camps in Hampshire to be prepared for their American future: the first batch would include 344 women, the youngest a mere 16 – along with their 116 children. All those children, nasty little types, probably, aboard a queen of ships! Truly the war had a lot to answer for.

She threw the paper to the floor, and rang her bell to summon help with her pillows.

The office was really a cubby-hole at the end of the work-shed, but once installed there Pamela felt a rising excitement. It had all happened so suddenly. Daddy had spoken to Catherine, and she had spoken to David Callingham, and he had come up with a yard and shed, part of the estate and now vacant. It was theirs for a year at a peppercorn rent, to be renegotiated later if things went well. Catherine had put up £1,000, and she had put in £100, a third of her savings.

However, her father was paying her £1.15s a week, which was more than she had earned at the factory, and she was to get ten per cent of any profit on top of that. Two men were working outside in the yard, and her father was out securing orders, taking with him the first of the embellished furniture as samples.

'It could work,' Michael had said when she told him about it, and he hadn't seemed to mind that she had dipped into their nest-egg. 'It's going to be all right,' she told herself, as she started to write up the first of the brand-new account books that her father had patiently explained to her last night.

Sarah had no sooner sat down in the tea-shop than Hartley saw something was wrong. They met regularly now, but only ever for tea. It was funny really, how easily she could talk to him, because they had nothing in common. He was a townee, and lived in a detached house called The Lodge, which sounded very posh. Soon he would be off – he was starting university in September, and she would never see him again. So where was the harm?

Today he had on a velvet jacket, corduroy velvet. Not the

rough, grooved velvet that some men wore as trousers: this was a finer material altogether, and the jacket had leather patches on the elbow. His hair was long – long for a man, anyway – and flopped on his brow. That brow was furrowed.

'What's wrong? I know there's something upsetting you, so you might as well tell me.'

She told him of the letter, then, and his brow darkened further. 'You can't go back, Sarah. You make excuses for him, you say it was the war, but Hannah has told me the truth. You shan't go back. It's intolerable.'

Sarah put out a hand to stem the flow of words. 'It's all right. Catherine is getting me a solicitor. She says the same as you.'

Indeed Catherine's reaction to news of the letter had been just as fiery. '*Over my dead body!*' she had said, and had gone straight to the phone.

'I'm lucky,' Sarah thought now. She was suddenly glad that she had put curlers in her hair last night. They had been painful to sleep in, but the result was worth the discomfort. Hartley was looking at her with a little smile on his lips, and she felt her own lips curl in sympathy. He had taken Joe on to his knee and the boy was content there.

'We're like a family,' she thought. 'Him with Joe and me with Alexander.' But Hamish had also seemed like a family man, and look where that had wound up. This couldn't do any harm, though, because, in a month or two he would be gone.

———

'Darling!' Valerie was almost tumbling out of the train in her eagerness to get to him.

Out of the corner of his eye, David saw Pamela Allerton on the station platform, looking remarkably pretty, and also searching the train with her eyes. She must be meeting Michael.

And then Valerie's arms were around his neck, and her lips

were cutting off his breath. 'Steady on,' he said, when she at last drew back, but he said it indulgently. It was nice to be loved. He knew that he could get used to it, with time.

⁓

They had cut out the pieces carefully, first tacking the tissue pattern to the material, and then cutting slowly around it. 'It's lovely stuff,' Sarah said enviously.

'Yes.' Catherine sat back on her heels and surveyed the various pieces. 'I was lucky to get it. Let's hope we don't go wrong somewhere, and ruin it.'

'We won't,' Sarah said confidently.

'I'm glad you're sure. I only hope you know what you're doing because I don't. And you're not to worry about that lawyer's letter: it's as I told you, you didn't desert him . . . well, technically you did, but it will be classed as constructive desertion, according to David, because Hamish's behaviour drove you to it.'

'How do I prove it though? I never told anyone.'

'The doctor knew. You said he saw your bruises one time.'

'That doesn't mean he'd say it.'

'He'd have to, if he was in court. And anyway, I saw, and I'll tell. Now, pass that tape measure, and trust in me, and don't talk of going away. You're not going anywhere – not till you've stitched this dress, anyway.'

⁓

They had made love slowly, savouring each moment. Now they lay entwined, happy just to talk. 'Your parents must know,' Michael said.

'Know what?'

'What we're doing. Which bed I'm in. You know.'

'No,' Pamela said firmly. 'My parents' capacity not to see

what's under their noses is unlimited. Anyway, Daddy is so taken up with his new factory that he wouldn't notice us doing it on the mat in front of him.'

'Bets!' Michael said, and reached for her. 'Have you realised', he said as he entered her, 'that we will never need to be apart again?'

'We will,' Pamela said, pulling back to look into his face. 'We can't be together on the night before the wedding. It's simply not done.'

***

'Do you love me?' Valerie and David were lying side by side, satisfied but still glowing with the exertion of their lovemaking.

'Yes,' David said, 'of course, I do.' But his conscience smote him. Did he love her? Or, did he love her enough? He liked her, loved her smiles, her ways, her inability to hurt anyone or anything. But did he truly love her? Even when they came down the great staircase and went into the dining-room for the cold supper laid out for them, he was still pondering the question.

'Now,' Valerie said, as they took their seats at the table, 'Mummy is making noises about dates, and prophesying doom if we don't get a move on and fix something. I thought April?'

'Sounds good to me.'

'What about India? Will she be up and about by then?'

'Heaven knows. She's taken to her bed like a duck to water. She lies there like Elizabeth the First, issuing orders, sending everyone here and there on errands. She's in paradise!'

'You can be cruel, sometimes! Perhaps I shouldn't marry you, after all.'

David smiled at the mock reproof. 'You couldn't resist marrying me,' he said. Behind her, the portraits of his ancestors looked down in a disinterested way.

Valerie was silent for a moment, and when she spoke she sounded almost sad. 'You're right,' she said. 'I couldn't resist marrying you, even if I wanted to.'

For a moment he was troubled again. Did she know how he felt – or, rather, what he didn't feel? But his doubt was momentary. He had been careful. There was no way she could know that everything was not as it seemed: two people embarking on a lifetime together, with all the enthusiasm in the world.

India lay for a while, staring up at the ceiling. It had come as a surprise, and she was even more surprised at how unwelcome that surprise had been. '*I'm going to move into the guest-room, India,*' Rupert had said. '*I've been thinking about it for a while. We'll both be more comfortable. And I'm just along the landing. You have your bell if you need me.*' She had shrugged, and said, '*As you please,*' because she didn't know what else to say. Would he have stayed if she had asked him to? Not that she ever would have asked: Callinghams didn't beg.

Besides, it would be good to have the bed to herself again. No ugly grunting and fumbling in the night. Procreation was truly disgusting, in humans as well as animals. Now she could have the bedside lamp on all night if she chose, she could read, she could have a wireless installed and listen to light music from a foreign station at 2 a. m. He had set her free. So the upset she was feeling was purely hormonal, and because of her condition.

She turned on her side and drew up her knees as far as she could to accommodate her swollen belly. In a few weeks she would have her son for comfort. She would keep him close by – no night nursery for him. Not at first, anyway. She would have her son, and all would be well. She decided to let her tears be absorbed by the pillow. It was only weakness because of her condition.

In the end, though, she wiped her eyes with the corner of the sheet, and then, mercifully, she slept.

Chapter Nine

February 1946

'You're doing very well. Try to keep her steady.'
It was cold outside, even frosty, but inside the car Catherine felt boiling hot. Driving was much harder than she had imagined. The slightest touch on the wheel, and the car lurched to one side or another. And she had never really realised how huge cars were, even small cars like this one. She had been a passenger in dozens of big cars, and had never felt they were too big for the road. Now she felt as though she were driving a tank.

'Did you see *The Times* this morning?' David asked. They were coming up to a crossroads, her tongue was touching her upper lip in trepidation, and he was asking about newspapers! She didn't answer.

'It said bread will be darker, because there's a shortage of wheat. And they're cutting rations of butter, margarine and lard. I'm beginning to wonder whether we won the war.'

She slowed down for the crossroads, trying desperately to work out who had right of way.

'It's all right, you're doing well. Just take it easy. According to *The Times*, it's because famine looms in Germany, where there's no agriculture left – so we have to share. What do you make of that?'

A horn was hooting behind her, urging her to move on.

'David, what do I do? I couldn't care less about Germany, they can have the lot! Just get me out of here!'

≈

Sarah clutched at her handbag. It was the only way to keep her hands from shaking. The man sitting opposite her was pleasant, even kind, but she was still afraid. He was reading the brief that she and Catherine had prepared together.

At last he looked up. 'You say your husband was in the habit of assaulting you?'

Sarah nodded.

'Did you report any of this to the police, or to independent witnesses?' Sarah shook her head. Didn't he realise that you tried to hide the bruises, because to be rejected, not to be loved and cherished, was a shameful thing. A badge of failure.

The solicitor's brow wrinkled. 'Did you go to a hospital?'

Again she shook her head. He was getting desperate now. 'You must have seen your doctor for something?'

'Yes,' Sarah said. It came out as a croak, and she cleared her throat. 'Yes, I did see a doctor once.'

'And he saw the bruises? Is that why you went to him?'

Sarah tried desperately to recall why she had gone. She could clearly visualise the look on his face when he had seen the bruises, but that wasn't why she had gone there? Or was it? 'I can't remember,' she said.

Afterwards, she would pinpoint that as the moment when the solicitor gave in. 'We'll do our best,' he said as she left, but they both knew it was a waste of time.

≈

'. . . and when Catherine got out of the car she said "Never again!"' Across the desk, Alistair Groom laughed, and David joined in.

'Women!' the agent said fervently.

'Still, it will make all the difference for Catherine when she can move under her own steam.'

'You're very good to her.'

'It's what my brother would have done if the position had been reversed.' But even as he spoke, David knew it was not brotherly love that kept him at Catherine's side. It was something far less noble.

They talked of the pit, then. 'They say the takeover's timed for the turn of the year. And there'll be a National Coal Board to run the industry nationwide.'

David nodded. 'I heard that. Fifteen hundred collieries under one management – they'll have their work cut out. And think of the housing stock. Who'll manage that?'

'And a five-day week for the men, from the outset.' The agent shook a gloomy head. 'Coal exports are dwindling already, and so are the stocks at home. They say London has less than a week's supply left – and they propose losing a day's production? Madness!'

'If all I hear around the House is true, it will be the ports and railways nationalised next. Well, I wish them well. But I mean to see that good people, of whom you're one, don't suffer. I hope you'll stay on with the rest of the estate, such as it will be. For my own part I can hardly wait.'

As if he had picked up David thoughts of India's fury at the pit's going, Alistair suddenly asked: 'How is your sister?'

'My sister is in her element. She's distraught about the nationalisation, of course, but her pregnant state is paramount at the moment. She lies in bed like a beached whale, running everyone ragged. She's enjoying being pregnant so much, I fear she'll want to do it again and again.'

Rupert had insisted on half-carrying her to a chaise-longue newly installed in the morning-room. 'It's not good for you to stay in one room all day. Besides, the daily needs to clean the room and let in some fresh air.'

'So it will be freezing when I go back up then. Thank you, Rupert.'

'We'll build up the fire. Now, settle yourself, and I'll get you a paper.'

'I don't want a paper. I can't be bothered to read it, or even turn the pages.'

'Then I'll read it to you.'

He was trying to be reasonable, to humour the invalid. For some reason this made India so angry that her fingernails ground into her palms. 'If you must.'

There was silence except for the rustle of newsprint, and then he began. 'Heathrow is open at last. To certain flights, that is. It's going to take £20 million to develop it properly, according to this. The first flight was to Buenos Aires, via Lisbon. We might use it next year, when it's fully operational.'

India didn't bother replying. Outside the window the sky was leaden, and she could see rooftops in the distance. At Kynaston, you could look out from every window, and the only rooftops you saw would be part of the estate.

'It says that airmen are on strike in India, Ceylon, and Singapore. Protesting at how long it's taking to ship them home.'

'Back to their crowded little hovels? I expect they can hardly wait.'

'It's a natural instinct to want to come home.' Rupert said it idly, but it set India's teeth on edge.

'What a profound truth! I long to be back at Kynaston every day.'

She expected him to be hurt, even affronted at the insult to the home they shared, but he simply went on talking. 'Not surprising they want to get out of India – it says here that they're expecting widespread riots. The Indian navy has mutinied at Bombay; a man was killed; and there's been bloody rioting in a number of cities already. Sixty dead in Bombay. They want the British out, that's the trouble.'

'More fool them, then. The Raj made India.'

'Hardly made, my dear. Exploited perhaps.'

She decided to ignore him. What could he know of the magic of India. She closed her eyes, remembering Delhi, the scents and the sounds of it. And dear Ayah. If only she had Ayah now, to care for this baby. But Ayah was long dead, asleep in the churchyard. India would have to watch over her son herself.

─────

Pamela was coming to love her cubby-hole, and the hum of activity from the shed outside. If only they could make it work. If they couldn't, her father would be broken-hearted. Two failures would be too much for any man.

But she was beginning to understand the intricacies of book-keeping and filing, and she would work her fingers to the bone if need be. 'I need this job,' she thought. Once or twice she had heard from women who had left the factory. *'There's no jobs, Pammy. Ten of us chasing every vacancy. They think women should just go back to the kitchen sink.'* It was understandable that men who had faced danger and missed home should want everything to return to the safe old ways, but pretending the war hadn't happened was foolish. Women had changed, and men would have to accept it. No doubt some women would be happy enough to retire gracefully, but it had to be a matter of choice.

Besides, she needed to earn while Michael studied, and the need not to get pregnant was equally important. If only making love with Michael were not so sweet. 'We will make it work,' she vowed and, glancing at the clock, saw it was time to put on the kettle and brew up for the men's bait-time.

***

Up on the screen, Margaret Rutherford was giving the performance of her life as Madame Arcati in the film of Noel Coward's *Blithe Spirit*. Rex Harrison was a proper gent, and Constance Cummings lovely, even if she was American. But it was the ghost who fascinated Sarah: she had a most peculiar voice, but peculiar in a nice way.

Hartley had bought her a bar of Fry's chocolate. She had nibbled a bit of it to show willing, and then tucked it away as a treat for the children. Half-way through, though, the remembrance of that sweet, chocolate taste was too much for her. She took it out and had another guilty nibble.

'Nice?' Hartley whispered in the darkness, and she heard him chuckling quietly to himself.

For a moment she gave herself up to thinking how she would indulge her sweet tooth when sweets came off the ration, but gradually worry intruded: she was coming to depend on these outings with Hartley, depend on them too much. But she consoled herself with the thought that soon he would be gone. He would meet some pretty young girl without children or a shameful past, and he would never think of her again. Hannah might try to hide her feelings, but she would see Sarah as a reject, an object of pity. That would be hard to take.

But I've come through worse, she decided, and gave herself up to Rex Harrison and Margaret Rutherford on the screen.

***

'I know what Attlee's up to. He's deliberately delaying their demobilisation because he wants to keep a British force in

India. There'll be trouble when Partition comes,' David said. 'Hindus and Muslims . . . it'll be a hell of a clash.'

'They've lived happily enough together up to now.' Valerie was regarding him over the rim of her glass. They had finished dinner but were both content to sit mulling over the news of the day.

'Under British rule, Valerie, under British rule. Now they scent independence. They want to test their strength.'

'Does it seem to you that an awful lot is happening all at once? All this talk of the people taking over industry, of independence for India, and other things – I feel as though the world is changing too quickly for my liking. I'm not against change, you know that, and I know you'll be happy to be free of mining, but all the same . . ."

'If it ever happens. The Cabinet hasn't agreed to it yet.'

'Daddy says they will. He says Attlee will give away the Empire piece by piece.'

'It's hardly "giving away" to hand people back their own countries.'

'Ohh!' Valerie was pursing her lips in mock-disapproval. 'I always knew you were a Socialist at heart.'

'Perhaps I am, if Socialism is wanting things to be fair. I like feeling my country belongs to me. So why should your average Hindu feel any differently?'

'Well, I still think everything is moving too fast. We haven't finished with the war yet, not while we're still trying Nazis for war crimes.'

'Yes, it's grim reading day after day.' He thought of the grey, nervous figures in the dock at Nuremberg. Little more than a year ago they had been strutting the world's stage, spreading death and destruction. And now they were being made to answer for their crimes.

'I have to go home shortly,' Valerie said. 'So could you please stop looking gloomy and refill my glass? Better still, you could take me upstairs and show me the view from your bedroom window.'

'It's dark outside. You wouldn't see a thing,' he said sternly.

'I can see in the dark,' was her reply.

She took his hand and led him up to bed. 'I do love her,' he told himself. 'I must do, because I want her. So it is a kind of love.'

'But surely the solicitor could see that you're in the right?' Catherine was genuinely perplexed at what Sarah had told her. 'Perhaps he isn't the right man for the job. David said he was the best, but maybe we need someone else?'

'No,' Sarah said desperately. To go through it all again with another solicitor would be unbearable. Today, in that stuffy office, she had had to roll up her sleeve to show the mark on her arm where the scalding water from the kettle Hamish had thrown had landed. The skin was still mottled and shrivelled, and rough to the touch, but the pain, the searing pain, was long gone. All pain went with time. You just had to hang on long enough.

'It'll be all right, Cathy, you'll see. Now, where's this new pattern?' A moment later they were deep in discussion of fabric and thread, and whether or not button-holes should be double-stitched or bound. That, at least, was a safe place to be.

They had not even undressed, simply sat on the edge of the bed to contemplate the grimness of their future.

'We have to face it, Pammy. Even before the war there was a housing problem, unless you came from money. Most cities had slum areas and overcrowding. Hitler kindly destroyed a lot of decent homes, more than a million they say. McGregor – you remember McGregor? – came from Clydebank. He told me that after a two-night blitz there in '41, only seven houses out of a total of 12,000 were left intact. Even if he was exaggerating, and he wasn't that kind of chap, there's a huge problem.'

'But the Government know that,' Pamela said, seeking a glimmer of hope. 'They've promised to rebuild.'

Michael was nodding. 'It's in their manifesto – "Labour will proceed with a housing programme with the maximum practical speed until every family in the island has a good standard of accommodation." I've got it off by heart. But it will take years, decades even.'

'I could ask Catherine . . . or David.'

'I won't start out on handouts, Pam. We have to start on our own two feet or not at all.'

'We might get a prefab. Everyone says they're wonderful, and not cramped once you get inside. Separate kitchens, bedrooms, and a living-room, with gas and electric power, hot and cold water, an indoor toilet in a bathroom. I could live like that.'

'Yes, if we got one we could manage. But they'll house the homeless first, and then the overcrowded. If we live here, the authorities will regard us as well off, in a house this size. And remember, there'll be a rush of marriages now – people like us who want to be together. So the housing demand will grow, and I can't see supply outstripping it . . . not for years.'

'What about the new towns they're planning?'

'They'll be pretty soulless places, Pam, at least at first. No, we have to solve our problem ourselves.'

'Let's set a wedding date, and hope something's turned up by then,' she said.

'No.' She was beginning to find that Michael had a stubborn side. 'No, I'm not starting out living-in, asking permission to breathe in someone else's house.'

'My parents are not like that,' she said, stung to their defence.

'I know, I know.' He was contrite now. 'They've been wonderful. But it's the principle, darling. This isn't what I was promised.'

She put consoling arms around his neck. 'As soon as things settle down at the workshop, I'll ask Daddy for a day off, and I'll simply walk and walk until I find us a place of our own.'

Chapter Ten

March 1946

'SHE NEVER DID!'

'I'm telling you! They called her Dorothy, Dorothy Shipley or something like that, and her mam had told her so much about bananas that when they got some she stuffed herself and died.'

'Only three years old?'

'Three,' Hannah said dramatically, 'and stone dead! Bridlington, it happened. The first bananas since 1939, and a bairn dead.'

'They're queuing six deep at Chalk's,' Sarah said, clutching Alexander to her. 'How terrible to rear a child and then lose it to a banana.'

'Four bananas,' Hannah interjected 'It was four. They must have more money than sense to give a bairn four at one go.'

Sarah suppressed a smile. It would be ten bananas by night-fall. Aloud she said, 'People are desperate for anything to eat though, Hannah. Have you heard that the Food Ministry's sending out a leaflet for squirrel pie. Squirrels! Tree-rats, Dad calls them. I'd sooner go hungry.'

'Well, you likely will, because according to Lauder's lass, her that's in the Land Army, they're running out of feed for cows and chickens. So it'll be squirrels first, and then dogs and cats.'

'Oh hush, I can feel my stomach lifting. As long as I can feed the bairns – that's what worries me.'

Hannah refilled their cups. 'We didn't bargain for it getting worse, did we? Beat Jerry, and the land'll flow with milk and honey, that's what they told us. Peace and plenty. Peace and plenty of headaches, that's what we got. Anyroad, to change the subject, Hartley's on back shift – that's why he's not here.'

Sarah raised her eyebrows in what she hoped was a show of total indifference. 'Oh,' she said. 'I hadn't noticed.'

'He's soft on you.' Hannah folded her arms under her breasts as though prepared for an argument.

'Honestly, Hannah, where you get your ideas from I do not know. He's just a boy –'

'When they're big enough they're old enough,' Hannah said. 'That's all I'm going to say.'

─────

'Steady on,' David said as the car approached the main road. 'I'd quite like to be alive for my lunch with Rupert.' But his tone was indulgent, and Catherine knew he was pleased with her. She enjoyed driving now. 'You're actually rather good,' he said.

She took her eyes off the road long enough to smile at him. He was good-looking, even in profile, but, better than that, he was the best friend in the world. 'I've had a good teacher,' she said.

He would be happy with Valerie, who was warm and sweet and would turn Kynaston into a home. 'But he'll always be my friend,' she thought and smiled at the prospect.

Last night they had walked in one of the meadows below Kynaston, and he had pointed out birds swooping low in a last burst of freedom before nightfall. They had stood for a long time, just drinking in the sight. It wasn't everyone you could be at peace with like that, but she and David understood one another.

＝＝＝＝

'Labour won't call an election before 1949,' Rupert said.

'They could hang on till 1950, if they chose,' David countered.

'Unless they make a mess of it. They're taking a lot on – they could overreach themselves. If you do win the seat, how will you feel about living in London half the week?'

'I've haven't thought much about it. I like London – but I've never been there for longer than a day or two a week at the most.'

'And Valerie?'

'Valerie is more adventurous than me. She'd make a home anywhere.'

'Not much longer – a few weeks.'

'That's right. It's a sober thought: me a married man.'

'You'll be all right,' Rupert said. There was an emphasis on the 'you' and a note almost of envy in his voice.

David looked at him searchingly. 'Everything all right with India?'

'It will be better when the baby is here.' It was said with less than certainty, and Rupert then engineered a fairly obvious change of subject. 'They're getting very excited about these Olympic Games.'

'Yes,' David said, relieved. The International Olympic Committee had met in Paris and decreed that the first post-war Olympic Games would be held in London. 'It's a nice thank-you to Britain, but I suppose most other places are too damaged to host them. Most places in Europe, anyway.'

'They could have gone to America. The USA saved the world –'

'– according to Errol Flynn.'

They both laughed. Around them the club rumbled with gossip, and cigar smoke scented the air.

'Where's the money going to come from?' Rupert asked,

suddenly serious. 'Taxes I suppose.'

'My agent told me today that wages are 80 per cent higher now than they were in 1938.'

'You don't surprise me. And women are taking a share. They'll never go back to the kitchen now.'

'You can't blame them,' David said.

Rupert shrugged. 'Everything will be done by robots eventually. Did you see that item in *The Times* about an "electronic brain"? Some boffins in Pennsylvania have made a computer with a memory. They say it can be programmed to do anything you want it to do, even payrolls. It seems there's no limit to it. Sprang out of wartime research, apparently.'

'Very H. G. Wells.' David sounded rueful. 'Man's a genius.'

'Speaking of payrolls, Central Office tells me that there's a proposal to set MPs' salaries at £1,000 a year. So you'll be sitting pretty once you take your seat.'

'A fortune,' David said laughing. But he couldn't help thinking that a thousand a year certainly was a fortune to most working men. Was it right for someone like him, with a private income, to draw a wage that could go to someone else?

'Sorry, love. It went before I put in the advert. Well, the girl in the shop knew someone who was looking. We put it up, anyway, but really, it was already taken.'

'Do you know of anything else?' Pamela knew she was sounding desperate, but she was past caring. This was the seventh advertisement she had followed up, and every door had been shut in her face.

The woman at the door was shaking her head. 'I don't, love. I'd tell you if I did, 'cos I can see it means a lot.' She put her head on one side, and thought for a moment. 'Tell you what, I did hear there was a woman in Nelson Street might be going to let off her upper floor. You could try there.'

'Do you know the number?'

'I don't, but she's a well-built woman. Nicely dressed. Someone'll know her round there.'

Nelson Street was on the way to the railway station, and Pamela's heart beat faster as she neared it. She stopped two people in the street, but both of them told her the street was full of well-built women. 'You'll have to do better than that, pet, if you want a name.'

———

The pain had started low down in her back, and then blossomed until now it seemed to possess her whole body. The stupid midwife had appeared, beaming all over her fat, ugly face as though she was coming to a picnic.

'If only I could do it without them,' India thought. That was her way, to act alone. The thought that soon they would all be poking and prodding at her, invading her innermost privacy, was unbearable.

As for Rupert, the moment his face appeared in the doorway of the bedroom, she was ready for him, 'Go away, Rupert! This is nothing to do with you.'

'Not long now,' the midwife said. She had rolled up the sleeves of her blue dress and slipped frilly white bands on to hold them in place. Beneath the frills her arms bulged.

'You have arms like Popeye,' India said, and then went into peals of incredulous laughter. She hadn't realised she knew the cartoon figure, but the woman's arms were identical to his. Any moment she would produce a can of spinach.

The woman wasn't laughing. That was the trouble with these people: they lacked a sense of humour.

And then the pain was coming again, and she had to cling to the fat, white arm to stop the scream that must never be allowed to pass her lips. Callinghams knew how to behave in front of lesser people.

~~~

Sarah had decided to knit Hartley a pullover as a parting gift. The wool was green marl, which would look good against his blondness, and the woman in the wool shop had let her off with the coupons.

As she cast on, she thought about the coupons she had saved. They would come in handy, now everything was in short supply. She would be heartily glad when eventually hardship ended – although when that would be was anyone's guess. Every day there was something unobtainable, and a bit of daft Government advice about replacing it, which only rubbed the shortage in. Last week it had been shampoo you couldn't get, and the woman in the chemist's had told her the Government suggested rubbing dirty hair with a dry towel, or steaming it over a kettle. As if you would do that to your bairns!

Still, at least she'd got the wool for Hartley. It was fair enough to give him a gift, for he had been kind to the children. It was from them, really. She was contemplating how and when she would hand it over to him when the phone rang. There was no one there, or at least no one who spoke.

'I know it's you, Hamish,' she said at last. There was no answer. She hadn't expected one.

~~~

The dress was a masterpiece, there was no doubt about it. Together she and Sarah had tugged and pulled at the pattern until now it hardly resembled the dress on the cover. 'It's couture,' Catherine thought, and grinned to herself. Who would have thought Sarah had such skilful fingers? And she herself had come up with some really good ideas.

She rose to her feet and went to check on the crib. Ben was sleeping contentedly, his mouth still pursed where she had detached it from the nipple. She loved feeding him, but she would have to think about giving him more solids for her milk was beginning to dry up. She went back to the desk and picked up a pen. If they made another dress, she would like more rounded shoulders, and perhaps a nipped-in waist and a fuller skirt. Something more feminine. The war was over after all.

Suddenly she thought of the future. Years and years stretched ahead of her, and what was she going to do with them? Ben would grow up and leave her one day. She would want him to. University and then marriage and a family of his own. Perhaps he would be a surgeon like his father. And the thought of Ben grown up was frightening, not only for the void that he would leave in her life, but for the questions that one day she would have to answer.

'I'm glad we chose aquamarine for the bridesmaids.' Mrs Graham-Poole said. Across the table David nodded his head, but Valerie was less in agreement.

'"We" didn't choose any such thing, Mummy. You decreed aquamarine. I think it quite wrong to have hordes of children I hardly know follow me down the aisle at great expense of money and coupons. A simple wedding would be quite enough. I'd have one bridesmaid, who would be Stephanie, my second-in-command for the past three years. It's quite appropriate that she should follow me one last time. After all, David just has one best man. Why do I need seven bridesmaids? It's lunacy.'

'Yes, dear,' her mother said placidly, which meant she didn't intend to change her plans.

'Daddy?' Valerie turned to her father for support.

'Don't involve me, darling. I never argue with Mummy, it doesn't pay. David and I will take our brandy into the study, and you and Mummy can fight it out on your own.'

The men settled in deep leather armchairs, and Graham-Poole let out a sigh of relief. 'Sooner it's over the better, eh?'

David agreed.

'Interesting speech of Winston's last night,' the older man said. Churchill had been addressing an audience in Fulton, Missouri, and his words about Russia had sped around the world. *'From Stettin in the Baltic to Trieste in the Adriatic, an iron curtain has descended across the continent. The dark ages may return on the gleaming wings of science. Beware, I say. Time may be short.'*

'Good phrase, the "iron curtain". But what did he mean by the return of the dark ages?'

Graham-Poole shook his head. 'He's referring to Nazism, of course, and suggesting Stalin could be as bad or worse.'

'Is he right?'

'Who knows? That's the trouble with Russia, it's an enigmatic nation. What was it Winston said in 1939? "Russia is a riddle, wrapped in a mystery, inside an enigma."'

'There can't be another war. Surely the world has learned its lesson by now?'

'You know your Kipling, I suppose. "The burned fool's bandaged finger . . ."'

'"Goes wobbling back to the fire,"' David finished. 'I know that poem well. Too well.'

———

They had been telling her to push for hours, but India was tired. 'I want to sleep,' she said, but the pain prevented sleep. Only the thought of the boy-child struggling to emerge kept her sane. She would never go through this again – but once would be enough. She would call him Gervase for her father, and Henry for her brother, who had died a hero. 'You have good blood,' she would tell the boy, and make him proud.

The fat white Popeye arms were intruding again. Suddenly she felt a slither, a downward movement. 'One more push . . . good girl!"

And then a cry, the most magical sound India had ever heard. She felt her body sink back, duty done.

'It's a girl, Mrs Lindsay-Hogg. A beautiful, beautiful little girl!'

And Rupert's great moon face was looming over her, disfigured by delight. She might have known it would be a girl. That was her lot in life, to be disappointed.

They were tugging and pulling at her now, doing vile things, but it didn't matter. It had all been for nothing. She closed her eyes and turned her face to the wall.

———

Michael had crept along the landing to her room once everyone was in their bedrooms, but neither of them felt like making love.

'I'll be tiptoeing along this landing until I'm old and grey,' he said, putting his arm around her as they lay together like spoons. For once Pamela didn't try to cheer him.

'It was awful today. I practically got doors shut in my face. There are 20 people chasing every let, that's the problem.'

'God, it makes you wonder why we risked our lives. Not for a land fit for heroes, that's certain. I heard today that some people are saying that Dresden was a war crime!'

'Like Coventry – or Guernica, come to that?' Pamela was indignant. 'The Germans taught us how to bomb cities. It's them we can thank for our present parlous state.'

'I keep thinking about these so-called new towns. Twenty of

them at the cost of £380 million, according to your father's paper. That should free up a few houses. We might be lucky.'

'It'll never happen. If they concentrated on repairing war damage, it would make more sense. I saw heaps of perfectly good houses today – without roofs, but well-built underneath.'

They were silent for a while and then Pamela spoke. 'I still think we could ask Catherine to ask David.'

'No!' Michael stiffened. 'I've told you, I am not starting out as a poor relation. I still have some pride left.'

'All right, all right. Don't fly off the deep end.'

'Well it makes me angry. Labour promised us change, change for the better. We voted for change. Now it seems none of it meant anything. We were going to have free medicine, no one afraid of doctor's bills. And now the British Medical Association has launched a million-pound fighting fund to stop the Bill. So much for the brave new world.'

'Never mind.' Pamela wriggled round to face him. 'Do you want to?'

'Not, much. Not tonight.'

'Good,' she said 'Let's go to sleep. It'll all seem better in the morning.'

BOOK 2

Chapter Eleven

June 1947

'I CAN'T TAKE MUCH MORE. First we were all nearly frozen to death . . .'

'. . . it wasn't that bad,' Sarah interrupted. 'The children loved the snow.'

'Snow?' Hannah's voice rose. 'Blizzards, you mean! First time in my life I've sat in candlelight. The one consolation was the King and Queen were doing it too. Buckingham Palace lit by candlelight – I mean!'

'All right, it was a bitter winter. But it's summer now – well, almost. Why are you harking back?'

They were seated in the kitchen at Mellows, tea on the table between them. Sarah had carried coffee to Catherine in the morning-room, but here there was a good strong pot of tea.

'I'm not harking back, I'm only saying it was grim, and then just when we're getting pulled back together the Government sticks the knife in.'

'It's hardly that,' Sarah protested mildly. She had read the morning paper: food rations were to be cut again; newspapers reduced to the wartime size of four pages; a cut in tobacco and petrol imports; and the slogan to be "Export or Die".

'They're cutting the tinned meat ration to twopence worth a week. Twopence worth! Try feeding a man on that. There'll be

113

a revolution, you mark my words. Working men won't stand for empty bellies. It's all right when there's a war to win, but somebody should tell that Parliament lot it's peace-time now.'

'It's dollars,' Sarah said. 'Do you want another cup? There's a dollar shortage.'

'Why should that affect us? We use pounds here.'

Sarah thought of the impossibility of explaining world finance to Hannah as Catherine had explained it to her the previous day, and changed the subject. 'I had a letter from Hartley yesterday.'

Hannah's cup wobbled back to its saucer. 'Well?' she said.

'Well what? He's getting on all right. Working hard.' Sarah paused, wondering how much to reveal. 'Anyway, he'll tell you himself. He's coming back here in the summer holidays.'

'I told you.' Hannah beamed with satisfaction at being proved right yet again. 'He's soft on you. I hope you keep your hand on your ha'penny while he's here.'

Sarah could feel herself blushing. 'He's not like that – and neither am I.'

'They're all like that, pet. You mark my words.'

But Hartley was not like that, Sarah decided. Some folk might think he was soft, but really he was just gentle – a gentle man, whichever way you looked at it.

Cathy had ceased to expect another letter from Max. It was months since he had written, and he had said in that letter that he would not write again. That hadn't stopped her from watching the post, but it was foolish. That chapter of her life was closed, and she had better accept it.

In his playpen, Ben was clashing bricks together, sometimes putting them in his mouth and grating them against his emerging teeth. All the same, it would have been nice to know where Max was. Could he still be in Germany? The concentration camps had been emptied, the thousands of dead buried, and the rest restored to health, if health was possible after what they had endured. If he was no longer in Germany, would he have gone back to America and Miriam, or was he now in Israel?

She hoped he was back home. There was a bloody conflict in Israel now. It was almost a year since Jewish terrorists had blown up the King David Hotel, headquarters of the British forces in Palestine, and things were still no better. Jews were being jailed for terrorism right and left, and it was bound to end in tears. America was urging Britain to let more Jews enter Palestine, but it was British troops who were being murdered there, not Americans. Militant Jews were attacking British civilians now, and the Government had ordered women and children home. Catherine had always struggled to understand Max's concept of a Jewish state being planted in an Arab land. She knew a dangerous situation when she heard and read of one.

She turned her attention to the newspaper Sarah had left with the coffee tray, seeking something more cheerful. The woman's section was full of Dior, with pictures of the new nipped-in waists and long skirts that the Frenchman was producing, and details of how his designs were sweeping the world. For years women had scrimped on material to save coupons; now they wanted to wallow in yards of fabric, swishing skirts, and voluminous sleeves – and who could blame them? Materials were changing too. Rayon, corduroy, and nylon . . . little mention of wool and tweed.

All the same, the soft shoulder-line was flattering. She would talk to Sarah tonight, and work out whether or not they were capable of making a coat.

≈

'What are you going to do today?' Valerie spoke as she leaned to refill his cup.

David shrugged. 'Not a lot. It's strange. I used to loathe going to the pit, but now that I don't have to I rather miss the place.'

It was six months since flags had been hoisted at every colliery in Britain, proclaiming the birth of the National Coal Board. '*On behalf of the people*', the notice-boards had said; but if all the reports he was hearing were true, the people were a little disappointed in their new possession. Absenteeism at the pits was rife, and production was down. But it was no longer David's problem. Perhaps his new idleness was not as bad as it seemed.

He looked up as he heard Valerie chuckle. 'What's the joke?'

'It says here that the Church of England is worried about sexual temptation in the workplace. It's "exceptionally prevalent in offices, shops and factories".' She read on. 'Oh, and it says that marriage is proving a disappointment because we're all gripped by "false romanticism".'

'I'm not disappointed in marriage,' David said.

'I should think not, after little more than a year.' She was folding the paper and putting it aside. 'You are a very lucky man, Sir David, and don't you forget it.'

'I don't. I'm the only man in Durham whose wife can strip down an engine and reassemble it.'

'So that's why you married me?' He was rising to his feet as she spoke and moving to take her in his arms.

'I married you, Lady Callingham, because you are quite the nicest person I know. And now I'm going to tear myself away and go and find something to do with my time.'

He kissed her, and moved towards the hall as fast as his gammy leg would allow. Damned polio, still plaguing him after all these years, he thought – and then remembered the man he had talked with yesterday who had left both legs behind in France.

'It will be different when you're an MP,' Valerie called after him.

'If, dear wife! It's "if", not "when".'

He made his way down to the stables and asked the groom to saddle his new mare. There were at least three years before Attlee needed to call an election. What was he going to do between now and then?

———

India moved on to the landing, and listened. There was no sound from below, so Rupert must have left for the office. It was intolerable the way he treated her now, as though she didn't exist. But it was a very different story with Loelia. The child should have been called something sensible, like Margaret or Ann. Loelia! How she hated that name. She had rather liked it in the past, when it belonged to her friend, but once she knew it was a Lindsay-Hogg family name she had realised how ugly it was.

There was no sound from the nursery either, so Nanny must already have Loelia dressed and out. Good! With luck she needn't see them until tonight, when Rupert would no doubt wish to indulge in the horseplay that thoroughly unsettled the child and made bedtimes battlegrounds. The girl was 15 months old, and already a tyrant. That would have to be dealt with, and it would be.

She sat down at the dressing-table and regarded herself in the mirror. She was still handsome. She must bend a little, show a little guile, and get Rupert back into her bed. Not that she wanted him – his body repelled her now. But she wanted, needed, a son. And she meant to have one.

———

'A car makes a difference,' Sarah said as they turned into the drive. Nowadays they collected their shopping in the car – no more trudging home with bags of vegetables, or whatever meat or bread they'd been able to get. They unloaded the boot, collected the children from the back seat, installed them in their playpen with toys, and put on the kettle for tea.

'Did you see that church report?' Catherine asked when they were settled. 'It says work leads to sexual temptation.'

Sarah pursed her lips. 'I could resist, if I had a job.'

'You've got a job,' Catherine said, startled. 'I couldn't do without you, Sarah. You know that. Should I pay you more, is that it?'

Sarah held up her hands in horror. 'No, please, it's nothing like that. It's just that I think about the future and the bairns, and where we will all wind up.'

'I know.' Catherine put her elbows on to the table and rested her chin on her hands. 'I feel like that, too. At first we were just getting our breath back, but it's different now. If you look down the years, it's frightening. But you're happy here for now, aren't you? And once everything's settled with Hamish . . .'

'Settled? It'll never be settled. They can send the letters back and forth as much as they like, but he'll always be out there. Biding his time.'

'All the more reason for staying put, then,' Catherine said firmly. 'We're not the only ones who feel unsettled, Sarah. Two million women have lived on their own for six years of war. Now they've found men returning who they hardly know, because war has changed them. Divorce is sky-rocketing. And what about women who've held down jobs? Or served in the forces? Are they just going to go back to the kitchen? We're all unsettled. Let's just give it time. Now! Have you seen the new Dior coats? Could we manage to make one . . . one each?'

It was a relief to discuss hemlines and buttons, and forget, for a little while, the difficulties of life.

Pamela sipped her coffee and tried to concentrate on the figures in front of her. After a shaky start, her father's factory was doing well. Orders were up, and they had taken on four more workers. She had another five shillings in her pay-packet now, and her mother would only take the minimum from her for their keep. But she and Michael were still sleeping in her parents' home.

Since they had married, at least they could openly share a bed, but she felt constrained by the presence of her parents across the landing. It had been different during the war, with the prospect that each love-making could be the last. She hadn't cared, then, who knew that she and Mike were having sex. Now some of the old inhibitions had returned. And there was no hope of a home of their own – even if they had money, there were simply no houses available.

It was the same all over the country, and squatting was now rife. It had begun in Scunthorpe last year: 40 or 50 families had marched into a disused army camp and just taken it over, and moved in. That had started a tidal wave: Middlesbrough, Salisbury, a place called Seaham Harbour, Doncaster, Chalfont St Giles, Jarrow, Liverpool . . . The names were carved in her memory. In some places, desperate men and women had overpowered the guards at the gate of large empty premises before taking them over. Last autumn it had been estimated that 45,000 people had illegally housed themselves. That figure had had a dramatic effect – 1,000 young families had moved into empty properties in London, flats, mansions, anything with four walls and a roof.

'Let's do it,' she had urged Mike, but he was adamant.

'I couldn't sleep a night in a place I'd broken into. We'll wait, Pam. It's bound to end soon, and we're on the waiting list.' He had pointed out that Aneurin Bevan had condemned squatters as 'a confrontation', and promised action against 'organised lawlessness'. But it wasn't action against the squatters that was needed, it was more houses, more prefabs. Michael had given her all the figures: half a million homes had been destroyed or made uninhabitable by air-raids, three million had been badly damaged, and 12 million had needed repair. Coventry had lost a third of its housing stock in one night of raids. Clydebank had only seven houses undamaged out of 12,000. And men were still coming home and needing a place of their own to live and love and start families.

'I want a baby,' Pamela thought. But Michael controlled their love-making, and without doing away with the wretched French letters there would be no baby. 'It isn't fair,' she thought, trying not to think of Catherine in Mellows with rooms galore. But Catherine's man had not come home from the war, and hers had. 'I'm a lucky girl,' she thought and went back to her book-keeping.

———

'Steak! How did you manage that?' Catherine felt her mouth water at the sight of the meat on her plate.

David inclined his head and gave a knowing wink. 'Valerie's a witch, Catherine. She charms things out of tradesmen, and they never realise they've been bewitched.'

'Don't take any notice.' Valerie was laughing. 'I grovel. That's my secret. I abase myself and beg.'

'Well, however you did it, thank you for inviting me to dinner. I've almost forgotten what good food is like.'

David was suddenly grave. 'And it may be a while before you get it back. We're in the most awful mess, now. Rupert was explaining it all to me at lunch. We're totally dependent on the Yanks, in spite of Attlee's efforts to keep us independent. The fact is that Britain is broke. Truman ended Lend Lease one week after Japan surrendered. Some ally! And we depended on that ever-open door for aid. Rupert says we've had billions. Do you realise how much of our food comes from America? We were getting it for free, or on generous terms, and now we don't have the dollars to buy it. We've been importing what we need, because we were making weapons. Now we have to retool, start to be self-sufficient again. Only problem? We haven't the money to retool. Unless we get help from somewhere, our economic survival is in jeopardy.'

'Thank you, David,' Valerie said. 'That's quite killed my enjoyment of the steak.'

'Sorry!' He was so contrite that Catherine stepped in to save him.

'I can't believe the Americans won't realise what they've done. It can't be in their interests to see Britain fail. We're their closest ally. Surely they owe us something? We've beggared ourselves to save the world. I can't believe they'll let us down.'

'Perhaps they feel they've given enough.' Valerie's tone was serious. 'And in the end we have to solve our own problems. I don't want to be dependent on America for the rest of time.'

'All the same, it makes you think.' Catherine chewed on a piece of her meat before she spoke again. 'Sarah and I were talking about this earlier. About the future and what we want to do with our lives.'

'Do you mean a career?' David asked.

Catherine raised deprecating eyebrows. 'Nothing as grand as a career. What am I trained for?'

Before David could answer, Valerie spoke. 'I might have a job for you.' She put her napkin to her mouth and dabbed while they waited for her to continue. 'How would you feel about being a godmother?'

There was silence for a moment, and then David cleared his throat. 'Are you trying to tell us something?'

'I've been trying to tell you for days, David. We're going to have a baby. In January, according to the doctor.'

David was pushing back his chair and rising to go to his wife.

'I'm so pleased for you,' Catherine said, and felt her eyes fill with tears. 'Lucky, lucky baby. It's coming to the two nicest people in the world.'

⸺

India took one last look at her reflection in the mirror. She looked good. The apricot peignoir was a becoming colour for her, and her hair, unpinned and falling about her shoulders, was the way Rupert had liked it in the early weeks of their marriage. Men were so obsessed with silly details. All the same, if it helped it was worth pandering to his whims.

She got to her feet and tightened the sash at her waist. She was even slimmer than she had been before Loelia had temporarily ruined her figure. She had hated, hated pregnancy, that feeling of being trapped inside an alien bulk. And all for nothing. But next time would be different. She had made enquiries, and apparently alkaline douches before intercourse made the conception of a male more likely. She had carried out the messy procedure before her bath, and had hurried through that to maximise the alkaline content of her vagina. This time she had every chance of a success.

She took a deep breath and went out on to the landing. Rupert still occupied another bedroom, in spite of her repeated hints that he was welcome back in her bed. Tonight she would go to him, because the time for shilly-shallying was over. She tapped on the door and then opened it immediately. Rupert was sitting up in bed, reading by the light of a bedside lamp.

'India?'

She smiled, but didn't speak, moving across to sit on the side of his bed. The eiderdown was silky under her fingers, and she arched her back slightly so that her breasts jutted under the apricot silk.

'Did you want something, India?' He was gazing at her over the top of the book, and she resisted the impulse to size it from him and hurl it across the room.

'Nothing in particular. I just – well, I was lonely, if you want the truth. I miss you, Rupert. I want you to come back to our room. This is silly. I love you . . .'

He held up a hand. 'Enough, India. Don't perjure yourself. You don't love me, and I doubt you ever did. What's far more important is that you don't love our child.'

'I do! I take care of her . . .'

'Be careful, India, you're on shaky ground. The "care" you've taken is to engage an ex-naval nurse to run my daughter's nursery like a ship of the line. Every time I enter, I feel there should be a cat-o'-nine-tails hanging somewhere. I don't like the woman, and if you are really serious about our resuming some semblance of a relationship, you can start by giving her notice. Now, if you don't mind, I want to finish this chapter before I go to sleep.'

He was dismissing her. As though she were a servant. India's mouth was dry. She didn't know how to extract herself from the hell of embarrassment into which he had cast her. In the end she put up her hand to smooth the neck of her peignoir, and tightened the sash, and then she rose to her feet and made the long walk to the door on shaky legs. It was not until she was safe in her own room that she could give way to the fury that now possessed her.

Pamela still loved the feel of his body above her, smooth and strong. The thrust of him inside her was still as thrilling as it had been that first time, but now she could not relax. The love-making tonight had not been intended, and happened before Michael could take precautions. 'It'll be all right,' she had whispered. Now she must make sure it was. In a little while, while he slept, she must retrieve the douching equipment from the toilet bag hidden in her wardrobe, and tiptoe to the bathroom to make sure that no element of their love-making remained inside her. She mustn't, couldn't get pregnant now. She longed to hold his child in her arms, but not until they had a place . . . any place . . . that they could make into a home.

Chapter Twelve

July 1947

BEYOND THE WINDOW THERE WAS a formal garden. 'Someone knows their plants,' David said.

'My wife. She's the keen gardener. I potter, but she keeps the gardener in check. Sit down, David. It's good of you to make time for me.'

The summons to see the Lord Lieutenant had come yesterday. 'If you have time, David, there are one or two things I'd like to discuss. Come over for coffee.'

The coffee was on the sofa table in front of them, now, along with a plate of petit beurre biscuits.

'Good news about the Americans,' David said. It was a week since foreign ministers of the European countries had agreed the recovery plan proposed by George C. Marshall, the US Secretary of State, and which would be funded by America. He had warned the American government that without aid Europe would face an economic, social, and political decline that would eventually impact on the United States. Now the US was digging deep into its pockets to help its former allies out of the mess into which a world war had cast them.

The Lord Lieutenant was cautious. 'It's good news, yes, but seeing will be believing as far as I'm concerned. I'm still reeling with shock at the way they ended Lend Lease – abruptly, as though once we'd helped them beat the Axis, they didn't care whether we sank or swam.'

'Still, it's good news of a sort.'

'Yes, I mustn't be cynical. How is your sister, by the way? I've not seen India and Rupert lately. They seem to have gone into purdah.'

'They're both well. Rupert is immersed in politics, as you know. And India – well, India . . .'

'Quite,' the Lord Lieutenant said. 'When I read that a black man was to be the first Governor General of the new Pakistan – the first coloured man to govern a British dominion – I thought, "India Callingham won't much care for that."'

'Jinnah is a fine man,' David said. 'India and I don't see eye to eye on Partition, of course. She remembers India as it was – or says she does: she was only three when she came home with my parents. She hates the idea of Partition. I was born after my family returned to England, so I feel less involved. I do remember we had an Indian ayah, though. She and India were very close, so I suppose that accentuates the way India feels.'

'The Indians chose Louis Mountbatten to be the Governor General – a nice touch, not getting rid of the Viceroy. Still, I didn't bring you here to discuss the break-up of the British Empire, David. I've heard of your visits to men returned from service, and your concern for their welfare. I want you to take on SSAFA, here in the country. You're familiar with SSAFA?'

'The Soldiers, Sailors and Airmens Family Association? Yes. Papa used to give a reception every year to raise funds for them. I think I'd like to be associated with such an organisation.'

'Why not borrow my blue dress – the one you made me? And my suede courts. Oh, and those pearl earrings you like . . .'

'Cathy, stop it. The way you're going on, you'd think it was something important. I'm only meeting a friend for a bite to eat.'

'Not just any friend. A man friend. Besides, you're making these lovely things for Valerie's baby's layette. I'm grateful. And yes, I'm in a romantic mood. Ever since I read about Princess Elizabeth, I've felt positively euphoric.'

'A royal wedding. Bet she won't have to count her coupons and have a cardboard cake like I did.'

'Don't be mean, Sarah, it's not like you. Besides, it'll cheer everyone up. That's why you should get dressed up today. It's cheering me up.'

'Well, pity about you, Cathy. If I've got to make something out of nothing to keep you happy, it's a bad job.'

'You do like Hartley, though? I wouldn't tease you if I didn't think that. He's so good-looking, and he's clever, and he's nice,'

'He may be all those things, but he's just a friend. And, in case you've forgotten, I'm married, and in no rush to have more trouble in my life. I've had more than enough.'

They both fell silent, then, remembering the thing they usually tried to forget. After Catherine had gone in search of the children, Sarah sat back in her chair, musing. Once upon a time Cathy had been a remote figure from the posh houses in The Dene. And then Sarah had received a letter from her dead brother, Joe, enclosing a letter to be delivered to Catherine Allerton, and to her alone. She had gone under cover of darkness and put the letter in Catherine's hand – seeing, even by moonlight, the look on the girl's face that meant she and Joe had been lovers. Her from The Dene, and he a boy from the pit who had gone to be a soldier. Since then Cathy had watched over her, even coming up to Scotland to see to her. Which had made it natural for her to fly to Cathy when life with Hamish became intolerable. But she didn't want to think about that now. She got to her feet and fetched the dough she had left proving beside the stove. Pounding it into loaves and buns was just the therapy she needed at the moment.

'Look at that! Orders up ten per cent on last month, and a new product being made from scratch. One of our own.'

'One of our own!' Pamela echoed her father's words. It was only a chair, but they would make it from scratch on a new lathe. 'Our first piece of machinery,' her father had said when it was installed. Until now they had simply restored used furniture, or embellished the Spartan utility furniture available. Now they were manufacturing again. 'Daddy,' she said, twining her arms round his neck, 'I'm so very proud of you.'

'Well,' he said, dubiously, when she kissed him. She knew he was remembering that other factory that had hummed with 50 such machines, and had ended in disaster early in the war.

'No "well",' she said determinedly. 'You are going to make our fortunes, so hurry up and do it, then Michael and I can build a grand mansion somewhere and live happily ever after.'

'A house would mean a lot to you, Pammy, wouldn't it?'

'A room would mean a lot to me, Daddy, but I'm not going to think about that now. Not on a day like this.'

'Prince Philip is penniless, of course.'

'But so handsome. And a war hero, India. You've got to give credit for that.'

'The country is bristling with war-heroes, Angela. And handsome is as handsome does. Still, he does have a title of his own. We won't have to create one as we would have to do if he were a commoner.'

'Well, I hope they'll be happy,' Angela said defiantly. 'And we could do with a glittering spectacle. I'm sick of austerity. Quite sick of it.'

India looked at her old schoolfriend. She had been pretty

when they were at school, but now her face was positively puffy.

'It looks like the Princess has a lovely ring, India,' she was saying. 'A solitaire. Still, it'll have to be good to be better than that ring of yours. Emeralds and diamonds: I've always envied you that ring. And your lovely hands.'

India looked down. It was true. The ring was magnificent, and her hands were definitely her best feature. Around them the café buzzed with chatter like a beehive. Silly women. Silly conversations. She flexed her fingers. 'Are you ready for pudding?' she asked. They decided on apple pie.

'I hope there's cream,' Angela sighed. 'I do so miss those little luxuries we had before the war. Do you think they'll ever come back? Still, mustn't moan. How's your daughter, my lovely god-daughter? And Rupert? Still as handsome? You must come to dinner soon. Desmond was just saying we don't entertain as much as we should.'

Yesterday Loelia had clung her father when India had reached for her, and Rupert's bedroom door was still closed to her, but discretion was her watchword. 'Loelia is adorable,' she said brightly, 'and Rupert, well, Rupert is still good old Rupert. Never changes.'

'I know what you're going to say,' Valerie said.

'What? And stop laughing at me.' They were in the old nursery, making plans for its refurbishment.

'You're going to say, "Oh, I remember this." You've said it seven times already.'

'You tell such fibs, Lady Callingham. I might have said it once . . .' Her eyebrows were threatening to disappear into her hair. '. . . well, twice. Anyway, I do remember this. It was India's, but she never played with it.' David put the music-box aside. The horse had caught his eye and reminded him of that day, seven years ago, when Henry had sat astride it on the day he was to marry Catherine Allerton. He had had to bend his knees to accommodate his long legs, but his hand had been curled in the tangled mane. He had talked of the future. 'If I cop it, the estate'll be up to you, David.' He had begged his brother not to talk of death, but Henry had been insistent. 'Sorry, old son, but it's true . . . unless I live long enough to sire a sprog.' And then his face had flushed, and he had said, 'My God. I'm getting married today!'

'I begrudged him,' David thought. 'I loved Catherine so much that I begrudged him. I even thought of Catherine when he died. That she might be mine after all.'

'Why so glum all of a sudden?' And Valerie's arms were round him, the scent of her hair was in his nostrils and the darkness that sometimes threatened to engulf him was retreating as it always did when she was there.

'I'm not glum. I'm just being sentimental. You know what a fool I am. I am thinking how much I love you, Valerie. How lucky I am to have you in my life.'

～～～

Little Joe was playing with toy soldiers on the hearth rug. She would have to stop calling him Little Joe: he was seven now, a scholar and, by all accounts, a clever one. Alexander was supposedly helping, but in reality messing up Joe's careful planning. Catherine smiled to herself at the sight of such brotherly tolerance. Ben was asleep in his pram just outside, under a light covering to protect him from the sun. She sighed contentedly and opened the paper.

Mass murders in Palestine – two British soldiers hung from eucalyptus trees near Haifa. Surely the Jews had had enough of bloodshed in the war, and yet tensions were rising steadily.

British troops were keeping Jews out of their Promised Land – 5,000 had been detained on a ship called *Exodus*, and three Jews had died in the struggle. That would cause more reprisals. It was the paper that had numbered the people on board the *Exodus* at 5,000 – but surely that was impossible? You couldn't get 5,000 people on one ship.

And where was Max? Hopefully not trying to reach his promised land. He would never risk his children, but nor would he leave them behind. Except that he had left them behind before, when he came to England to use his skills to repair the burned faces of British pilots. Would he think that he could be useful in Palestine now? Sometimes she could remember life on the wards quite clearly, even smell remembered odours of antiseptic and raw, rotting flesh. At other times it seemed like a dream, something that happened to another girl, not her. How strange life was and how little use it was to plan. 'We are leaves,' she thought, remembering Max's words. 'Leaves blown this way and that by the winds of war.'

She had almost reached the back page when she heard the doorbell. She was humming as she crossed the hall. It might be David, calling in for coffee. But it was not David. 'Hello, Hamish,' she said.

He brushed past her and came into the hall. She felt her mouth dry. The children were in the morning-room. If he heard them, would he try to snatch Alexander – and if he did, how would she stop him? 'I'm afraid Sarah is not here at the moment,' she said, 'but do come through to the drawing-room.' That was as far from the children as they could get. If only a squabble did not break out, or one of them come in search of a drink.

'Do sit down.' Catherine meant to be polite, even regal, but Hamish did not allow her to control the situation. 'Where is she?' he said forcibly.

But he seemed calm enough, and Catherine motioned him to

a chair again as she sat down opposite him. 'She's gone to visit friends in Durham. With the children. They left early this morning.'

Hamish's face was impassive. Was he buying the lie? 'I want the wee'un,' he said. Suddenly his face quivered. He's going to cry, Catherine thought, and felt terror. What could she do if he broke down, even begged? He was holding out his hands, palms up in supplication. 'Why?' he said. 'Why?'

Suddenly she remembered what Sarah had told her – that '*Why?*' had always preceded an assault on her. She spoke quickly. 'You could catch them at the bus station, perhaps.' She consulted her watch. 'Yes, they were going into the village first, so they're probably going for the bus right now.'

Hamish was on his feet, and she rose too. He leaned forward until she could hear his breath rasp in his throat, smell the hot, animal smell of him. 'I won't be thwarted! Not now. Not after all I've suffered. Tell the bitch I mean to have my way.'

Catherine nodded. If one of the children broke cover now, he would know she had lied. What would he do to her? She felt a whimper start inside her chest, and quelled it. 'I'll tell her what you say – but I'd hurry, if I were you . . . if you want to catch them, that is.'

When he was out of the house, she bolted the front door, and then sank down on to the bottom step. 'He will kill someone before he's finished,' she thought, and shivered.

———

They met outside the Havelock Cinema, and made their way upstairs to the tea-room. 'You look well,' Sarah said, undoing the top button of her coat.

Hartley did look well, and healthier, without the pallor of a night-shift worker. 'But he looks so young,' she thought. 'Just a baby, really.'

They made conversation over tea and cakes that weren't a patch on the ones Sarah could make herself. 'How did you come to wind up in the pit?' she asked.

'When I left school, I knew I'd be called up. I'd been in the Air Training Corps for three years, so I was sure I'd get into the RAF. But then they told me my number had come up, and I was to be a Bevin boy.'

'They picked the numbers out of a hat didn't they?'

'Well, actually –' This was one of the things she loved – the scholar in him that meant he liked to get the facts just right. 'Actually, they picked a number each week between one and nine, and everyone called up that week whose number ended in the one picked went into coal-mining.'

Sarah shook her head. 'It seems crazy – you half-trained for the RAF, and then sent down the hole.'

He was smiling at her use of words. '"The hole". The first time I heard it called that was in your father's kitchen. Anyway, when they said "mining", I was sent a travel warrant and instructions to report to a training centre in Wales. Three weeks we spent there, mostly on safety, and then it was the real thing. The cage – that was scary! Thinking of the shaft beneath, and seeing how flimsy the cage was. I was billeted on Hannah Chaffey. And I had my first bath in front of the fire with Hannah topping up the water all the while.'

'Now, that *was* dangerous!' Sarah rolled her eyes as she spoke.

'She has a heart of gold, though. I learned a lot in Belgate, Sarah. I wouldn't have missed it. I minded it at first, not being a flyer, but the past few years have been an education. And I met you . . .'

There was no mistaking his meaning, and Sarah felt her cheeks flush. 'Drink your tea,' she said sternly, 'or we'll miss the start of the film.'

Rupert was trying, as he usually did, to make conversation. India would have been quite happy to eat in silence, and go their separate ways, but he always put on a show for the servants. 'This Marshall plan could be tremendously useful if it goes through.'

'Really?' she said.

'Yes. We need food, raw materials, and machinery, and the Yanks are the only people who have these to share.'

'They'll probably give them all to Germany. I sometimes wonder who won the war. Not us, it would appear.'

He was on to Palestine now, as if anyone cared. She endured two full minutes about Philip Mountbatten and his fitness to be a royal consort, and then she laid down her knife and fork. 'Rupert, I won't beat about the bush any longer. And I won't go on pretending. I want another child, and if you are not willing to give me one, I will leave you and take your precious Loelia with me.'

Pamela had sensed that something was wrong for days now, but that had not prepared her for hearing her husband sob. She was on the half-landing when she heard the sound, and she mounted the second flight.

'Michael?' She pushed open the bedroom door to find him sitting on the side of the bed. There was a cardboard box on the coverlet and papers strewn about it. He looked up at her, and she flinched at the misery on his face.

'What is it?' She sat down beside him and reached for his hand. 'What's the matter?

'I don't know, I don't know Pammy. That's what frightens me. I only know I have this ache inside me, a kind of void. I'm waiting for something to happen, and there's nothing there.'

He was clutching a piece of paper, and she took it gently from him. 'What's this?' Looking down she could see it was poetry.

'It's a poem. A pilot wrote it. A Yank. We all had a copy, everyone in the mess.'

Pamela looked at the paper. The poem was called 'High Flight'.

'Oh! I have slipped the surly bonds of earth
And danced the skies on laughter-silvered wings;
Sunward I've climbed, and joined the tumbling mirth
Of sun-split clouds – and done a hundred things
You have not dreamed of – wheeled and soared and swung
High in the sunlit silence. Hov'ring there
I've chased the shouting wind along, and flung
My eager craft through footless halls of air.
Up, up the long delirious, burning blue,
I've topped the windswept heights with easy grace
Where never lark, or even eagle flew –
And, while with silent lifting mind I've trod
The high untrespassed sanctity of space,
Put out my hand and touched the face of God.'

'It's beautiful, Michael." She put up a hand and wiped his cheek. 'It's a beautiful poem, but why does it make you so sad?'

'Because that's gone, Pammy. All of it is gone. I thought I would be glad when it was over, but the truth is – I miss flying. I miss it like hell.'

'What happened to the man who wrote this?'

'He bought it in 1941. Spitfire Squadron.'

'How old was he?' Pamela asked.

'Nineteen, I think. Nineteen or twenty. A kid.'

She reached out and took him into her arms. 'Well, you're

alive, Michael, and I thank God for that. We'll work this out. I don't know how, but we'll find a way.'

She smiled up at him, hoping he couldn't see the anxiety in her eyes. Her period was five days late. She mustn't worry him now.

＝＝＝

It was dark by the time Sarah and Hartley left the cinema. 'That Cary Grant is a gorgeous man,' Sarah said. They had seen Alfred Hitchcock's *Notorious*, starring Ingrid Bergman and Cary Grant.

'Hitchcock is a tremendous director,' Hartley said.

Sarah nodded. She'd never been sure what a director actually did, but it was obviously important. 'You needn't come all the way out to Mellows,' she urged him. 'I'll be fine on my own.'

But Hartley was having none of it. 'I'll not let you walk on your own. We could get a taxi . . .'

'Taxi!' The outrage in her voice made him chuckle.

'We'll walk,' she said firmly.

'I'm enjoying university.' They had left the lamplit streets of the town and moved into darkness.

'You're lucky you got out of the pit so soon. There's one or two of your lot fretting to get away, and they're making them stop. There's not enough coal, they say – the men that were down the hole and then called up don't want to come back into mining, most of them.'

'It was extraordinarily silly to call miners up and put them in the forces, and then send other men down the pit to take their place. But then, politicians are silly sometimes. My father dabbles in politics – the Conservative Party. I suspect he may have pulled a string or two to get me out so quickly, but he was anxious I should take up my university place. He says a lot of men will want a university education now that they've seen the world.'

Sarah thought of Michael. 'Cathy's brother-in-law's like that. Well, he will be her brother-in-law. He was a pilot. Ended up in the sea one time. He's at college to be a teacher. Is that what you'll do?'

'No. I don't think I have the courage to face a classroom. My father hopes I'll enter the Diplomatic Corps, but . . .'

She never got to know about the 'but'. They had reached the wall that ringed Mellows, and were skirting a huge tree when it happened. Afterwards she would remember a roar and a thud, and then Hartley was on the ground, and Hamish was holding her back from going to help him. 'Let me go!' That was her high voice – and then Hamish was letting go of her, but only so that he could send his boot into the man on the ground. Again and again. And that prone figure was not moving, but lying there for all the world like a corpse.

Someone was shouting 'Why? Why?' But Sarah didn't for the life of her know whether it was her voice, or the voice of the man she feared.

Chapter Thirteen

July 1947

'You must have been terrified.' Valerie had rung at 8.30 to make sure they were all right.

'The worst was over by the time I knew anything about it,' Catherine said, 'although I'd been frantic all day, knowing Hamish was in the neighbourhood, and not being able to get in touch with Sarah. It was such a comfort when David arrived. Thank you for sparing him.'

'Not at all. I'm just glad you know he's there for you. We both are. So where is this boy now?'

'Still in bed. We put him in the guest room when he got back from the hospital– he was too bruised and shaken to go back to the village. David called in on his landlady to explain why he hadn't come home.'

'Is that Hannah Chaffey?'

'Yes. Has David told you about her?'

'A little. He says she likes talking.' They both laughed, and then Valerie said, 'And what about the attacker – Hamish? Sarah's husband?'

'He's in jail. Well, at the police station.'

'Poor man,' Valerie said. 'David says he was injured in the war.'

'In France. He's recovered physically, but I can never work

out whether the war changed him, or whether he was always a violent man underneath.'

Catherine was still pondering that question after the phone call ended. If Hamish had been changed by war, how many other men had suffered the same fate?

She set about preparing two breakfast trays, one for Hartley and one for Sarah, who had been absolutely exhausted when she returned with him from the hospital. 'Nothing broken,' she had said, and then burst into tears.

But as she carried the first tray upstairs, Catherine was thinking of something else. David had taken her by surprise last night as they waited for the ambulance. 'I've been thinking of what you said the other day, Catherine – about the future, and wanting to do something with your life. If I go ahead with this election business, I'm going to need help. An agent, if you like. Would you consider it? Being my right-hand woman?'

At first the idea had not been attractive, but later Catherine had thought of how he had always been there when she needed him. How could she now refuse to be there to help him?

Pamela had ticked off three addresses already. Only two left. She pushed open the rickety gate and walked up the path. The windows were grimy, the net curtains an unprepossessing grey. A plant drooped in a pot on the window sill, and even from outside she could smell boiling cabbage. All the same . . . Pamela raised her fist and knocked.

The woman who answered was elderly and vague. Yes, there had been an upstairs flat. No, it wasn't there now. No, there was no chance of the tenant moving out, and no, she didn't know of anywhere else. 'I could've let this six times over,' was her comforting parting shot.

Pamela shut the gate carefully, trying not to be silly and cry.

There was one name and address left on the list. She hitched her bag on to her shoulder, lifted her chin, and set off in search of it.

——

Breakfast had been an uncomfortable meal. Not as uncomfortable as dinner last night: nothing could be as bad as that. But uncomfortable, nevertheless. Rupert hadn't grumbled that his boiled egg was overdone although he'd have been entitled to say so. All he had said was, 'Could you pass the butter, please?' and India had twice asked if he wanted another cup of tea and received a curt, 'No thank you.' Otherwise there had been silence.

He had insisted on bringing Loelia downstairs before he left for the office, getting her so excited with his schoolboy antics that she would be difficult and unruly for the rest of the day. If it wasn't for the need to have a male child, she would have a good mind to leave him now. And take Loelia. With Nanny on hand she could manage perfectly well for the year or two before Loelia went away to school.

Her name was already down at India's old school. It had shaped her; it could surely deal with what was becoming a very trying child. Defiant, even. Well, little spirits could be broken – and if a foolishly indulgent father wasn't there, broken even more quickly.

Still, Rupert was essential to her plans, which meant he would have to be around. She would just have to soldier on for the time being, as she had always done.

——

Catherine had brought Sarah a boiled egg and soldiers on a tray, and had taken the same to Hartley. 'He's much better for a night's sleep,' she had reported. 'Bruised – apparently Hamish kicked him while he was on the ground – but he'll live. And he's amazingly cheerful.'

'Thank goodness for the passers-by who came between them. Not that Hartley was retaliating.' Sarah shook her head. 'I don't think he could believe what was happening. I couldn't, and I should have known.'

'Well, don't fret. And eat up. It's turned out better than it might have done. And the police will deal with Hamish now.'

But after Catherine had gone off to see to the children, Sarah lay thinking of last night and its implications for the future. 'He will never give up,' she thought. 'Never be far away. And as Alexander grows, it will get worse, not better.' There must be no more men in her life. Not even innocent friendships, like her friendship with Hartley. It simply wouldn't be fair.

She dressed then, and went along to knock on the guest-room door. Hartley was sitting on the edge of the bed, trying to do up his buttons with his one good hand. The other was caught up in a sling.

'Let me,' Sarah said, and began buttoning his shirt with fingers that fumbled because her hands were trembling.

～～

'The trouble is that the new Labour members are inexperienced in the ways of the House. They actually sang "The Red Flag" in the Chamber. Thank God it was the temporary chamber, and not the proper, bomb-damaged one.' Rupert sipped his aperitif.

'They're certainly a mixed bunch. Fabian intellectuals, trade unionists, civil servants . . . and war heroes. But they're good men,' David said hopefully.

'Do you think so? There are probably quite a few Communists among them, sneaking in on the Labour ticket. Watch out for the podgy man with the moustache. Wilson, he's called Harold Wilson.'

'So he's a Communist?'

'Good Lord, no. The man's a civil servant. Grammar-school boy. Got to Oxford, so he's no fool. Entered the Civil Service during the war, but a political animal to his fingertips. They say he's wily, and worth watching.'

Around them the club buzzed with gossip and lunchtime chatter. 'Our man's tired, David,' Rupert went on. 'A lot of our people are long-standing members and, frankly, played out. George Harris will stand down at the next election, and that will be your opportunity. I hear they mean to get rid of Attlee when they have a chance. He's too moderate for them.'

'He's a good man. I'd be sorry to see that happen,' David said.

'Well, don't write him off yet. He appears quite nondescript, but he can stand his ground.'

'He was a great stalwart in the coalition. Churchill thought highly of him.'

Rupert nodded. 'Poor Winston, how will he bear it? The lion of the House and now a mere backbencher.'

'The world reaction to his losing the election was pretty amazing. At one moment he's at Potsdam negotiating with Stalin, and the next he's out. What happened to gratitude? Anyway, enough of politics. How's my sister, and what does she think of our news?'

'The baby? I'm sure she's delighted, as I am.' But a veil had descended over Rupert's features.

'He doesn't want to talk of India,' David thought. 'Something's up.'

Catherine turned away as soon as Hartley came out on to the step. He would want to take his farewell of Sarah, and she didn't want to embarrass them. She got into the driving seat, but didn't start the engine in case he thought she was in a hurry, and cut the farewells short. It was only a moment before he climbed into the seat beside her, shifting carefully, and wincing at certain movements. 'All right?' she said.

'I'm fine. This is awfully kind of you.'

They were well away from Mellows before he spoke. 'I'm very fond of Sarah.'

'I know,' Catherine said, keeping her eyes on the road ahead.

'Do you think she cares for me?'

That was difficult. First, Catherine didn't actually know the answer – only suspected. And, then, even if she had known, should she interfere?

'I think she likes you. But Sarah has had a lot to contend with. She still has, as you saw for yourself last night. She's not a free woman, and she fears for her children.'

'Which is why I want . . . why I mean to . . . protect her.'

Catherine smiled. He sounded 14 – an ardent 14, but 14 nevertheless. 'Well, give her time. What happened last night has brought things to a head. She must be thinking, now. Perhaps you should leave it to Fate.'

Sarah made herself tea, and then left it to yellow in the cup. Hartley had kissed her on the cheek, there on the step, bold as brass. And she had let him do it. She had known he would try. All the time she was helping him downstairs she had known what was coming, and she had done nothing to stop it.

Last night, when they had got him back from the hospital, she had wanted to take him in her arms and kiss away his pain. But it wouldn't do. 'We are miles apart,' she told herself. 'In age, in class, but most of all in experience.'

In the end, she was woken from her reverie by the sound of Alexander calling her. And in an hour or so Hartley would be safely on the train, back to university. With a bit of luck, he'd meet a nice girl and she would never hear from him again.

Catherine had been back for an hour, and the children had finished their tea, when David arrived.

'I've spoken to the Chief Constable. He says Hamish will be put on a northbound train in the morning, and warned not to come back.'

'Is that all?' Catherine was scandalised. 'He puts a man in hospital – well, sends him there – terrifies a woman, and all they can do is send him home?'

David shrugged. 'Apparently Hartley was adamant that he wouldn't press charges. And Hamish didn't actually lay a finger on Sarah. There's a limit to what they can do.'

'I'm glad,' Sarah said flatly. 'He's bitter enough already, without giving him something else to bear a grudge about.'

'She's probably right,' David said, when Sarah had shepherded the children away. 'All the same, I'd be careful, all of you. If it's the boy he cares about he could try to take him.'

'No.' Catherine was definite. 'It's Sarah he considers his property, Sarah he won't let go. I don't doubt he has feelings for his child; of course he has. But Sarah is the one he wants to dominate, to subdue.'

'Then she has a problem, Catherine.'

'I know.' There was silence for a moment, and then she asked: 'Were you serious about that job?'

'Yes, very serious, and it's a real job, Catherine. It will be hard work when the election nears, so you must accept a proper salary.'

'You really will make me work?'

'Like the proverbial dog.'

'Then I'll take it, but you'd better be a good employer!'

'I will be. I will.'

They had not exchanged two words over dinner, so it was a surprise when India answered a knock on the bedroom door to find Rupert on the landing. He came inside the room, and shut the door behind him. He was still dressed for dinner so he wasn't going to ravish her there and then.

'About your threat –' he said.

'Hardly a threat. I simply stated my terms.'

'Your ultimatum, then. God, you are vile, India. However did I deceive myself into thinking you were lovable?'

'We can trade insults all night, dear husband. How could I not see how unutterably boring you would turn out to be? But it would surely be better if we cut this conversation short. Will you, or won't you?'

'Fuck you? Oh, don't raise your eyebrows at the word, India. And let's not pretend that even if I can manage it – and in the circumstances I'm far from sure I can – it will not be anything else but farmyard rutting, without a single degree of sentiment involved.'

'I don't want or need sentiment, Rupert. You know what I want.'

'A son? In God's name why? You have a beautiful child, and I have never seen you show her the slightest affection . . .'

' . . . I do my duty,' she interrupted.

'Your duty! My God, what I have to decide is whether or not I should subject another child to your sense of motherly duty. Perhaps I feel guilty enough about what I have done to one already.'

'This is getting tiresome. I repeat, will you or won't you?'

'I'll try. Eventually. Because I want to keep a home for my daughter if I can. But it will take time. At the moment, the mere thought of touching you turns my stomach.'

She had told Michael she'd had no luck, and he had simply kissed her soundly and said, 'Better luck next time, Pammy.'

Her parents had been supportive too. 'You'll get somewhere eventually,' her mother had said consolingly, and her father had added, 'You're welcome here for as long as you like. You know that.' And she had smiled her gratitude and tried to put a good face on it for everyone's sake.

But fear was gnawing away at her. Michael had been adamant: no children until they had a place of their own. And there was a child growing inside her now, she was certain of it. Her breasts felt suddenly full and heavy against her dress, and the longed-for period had not arrived. Would he make her get rid of it? People did that. Girls at the factory had done it, and come in with red-rimmed eyes and waxy faces. And Michael had seemed so down lately, which she had put down to stress. What if this was the last straw?

When at last they were alone in their room, she could bear it no longer. 'Michael, I'm pregnant. I'm pregnant, or I think I am, and I can't get rid of it, so you'll have to leave me . . . I'm so sorry!'

For a moment she wanted to laugh, because his face was comical, one emotion chasing another across his features. And then he was taking her in his arms, and kissing her hair, her eyes, her mouth.

'I'm sorry,' she said again.

'Shut up' he said. 'You silly, silly goose. If you apologise again I'll put you across my knee. If there is a baby, I'm to blame for at least half of it . . . the brainy part . . . and it's about the most thrilling thing that's ever happened to me.'

'But you said . . .'

'I have said a lot of things, and most of it bullshit, as Chalky would say.'

'But we haven't got a place of . . .'

He cut off her words with a kiss, and then he said: 'Just one question?'

She nodded. 'Go on.'

'Does this mean we can't – you know?'

'I'm sure we can, if we're careful.'

He made love to her gently, and then cradled her in his arms. 'We're going to have everything, Pammy, you'll see. A home and a child and each other and a career – this even beats flying. There now, what more do you want?'

She twisted until she could look into his eyes. 'Do you have the slightest idea how much I love you?'

'A bit – but you can prove it to me if you like.'

'Again?'

'Again!

Chapter Fourteen

January 1948

CATHERINE TURNED TO THE NEXT page of the newspaper. At long last the royal wedding was passing from the headlines. She had enjoyed the spectacle of the beautiful bride in the fairy-tale coach as much as anyone, but page after page of detail had become wearing. All the same, the ivory satin dress with its pearl-and-bead embroidery had made the mouths of women starved of clothes for eight years water at the mere sight.

Today, the only mention was of the redecorating of Clarence House, where the Princess and her new husband would live. It was going to cost £50,000: more than a worker would make in a lifetime. She turned the page. The doctors' unrest about the new National Health Service was rumbling on. The chairman of the British Medical Association was claiming that if doctors entered the new service, 'we will be selling our heritage and things will get worse'. The news of fresh clashes in Palestine was on page six. There had been a massive explosion near the Wailing Wall, presumably caused by Arabs, and seven Arab children had died in a tit-for-tat explosion caused by Haganah, the Jewish Defence Force. Max had often spoken of Palestine, but he had called it Israel, a promised land. From this account the promise was not turning out as he had hoped. Perhaps things would be better now that the sad exodus from the camps was over, and fewer people were desperate to get into Israel.

The problem of displaced people had been a huge one, though. Catherine had read everything she could find in the press, because it had helped to think of Max doing something useful, even if he was a continent away. Estimates of numbers varied from 11 million to as many as 20 million, because some counts took in only concentration-camp inmates, whereas others included those people freed from Labour camps and prisoner-of-war camps by the Allied armies. Still others took in civilians and military personnel who had fled their native countries for fear of advancing Soviet armies. Everyone said the Red Army had enacted revenge by raping, looting, and murdering – and a surprising number of people seemed to think they were entitled to do so.

The simple solution would have been to return the displaced people to their homes, but Europe had been thrown into such turmoil that some countries hardly existed in their pre-war form. Besides, many of the people were malnourished, ill, even dying. She had seen the newsreels at the cinema, and it didn't bear thinking about.

She turned the page in search of something lighter, and was into the letters when she heard the soft plop of post on the mat. She waited for a second to hear whether Sarah's footsteps crossed the hall, but there was only silence. Putting aside the paper, she went to pick up the letters. It was there: flimsy and blue, an air-mail letter! She looked at the postmark – New York; and opened it with fingers she defied to tremble.

'*Dear Catherine,*
I wonder if this will find you. I have no way of knowing whether or not you are still at Mellows and whether the good David is still watching over you. The man is a mentsch, but I know you realise that. You will see from the postmark that I am back at home. I did my first clinic in New York today, but I

have to admit my heart wasn't in it. How can I go back to appeasing the vanity of rich and foolish women when I have seen what I have seen?'

She read on, relishing each word, exulting in the fact that he still cared enough to write to her. It was true what he said: how could any of them return to normal life after living through a war? Even with Ben to fill her every waking hour, she felt an emptiness, a lack of purpose.

If David won the next election, then it might be different. Already he was introducing her to the problems of people living around her, problems of which she had been totally unaware. Could that be enough to fill her life – acting as his eyes and ears back in the constituency? In any case, when would the next election come?

Labour was still riding high, though life, for most people, had not improved. There had been a raising of expectations that were proving hard to fulfil. Britain now felt confident that the country belonged to its people. The National Health Service would make sure that you were covered when illness struck; and soon railways, collieries, even the Bank of England, would be the people's. According to Hannah, one man had said: 'We are the masters now!' and she could see that sentiment on people's faces when she went into Belgate.

David's popularity was growing around the region, and when the sitting MP retired he would hand on a hefty majority. All the same, Catherine couldn't see an election coming in the next two years – and that seemed a lifetime away.

She put Max's letter back into its envelope and stowed it carefully away. Lucky Max – at least he had a skill, a profession. 'I am equipped for nothing,' Catherine thought, and felt ashamed.

David nodded sympathetically as the man opposite him outlined the difficulties of living with an artificial leg. He was suggesting possible sources of help when he heard a knocking at the door. The woman who entered looked at him almost fearfully, eyes wide in a flushed face. 'It's for you, Sir David. Your wife needs you. She's having the baby . . .'

A moment later he was on the road and gunning the car towards Kynaston. The baby was not due for another week at least. Had something gone wrong?

Valerie lay serene in the wide bed when at last he flung into the room. 'David, come here! Don't look so scared. Everything is under control.'

David felt tears prick his eyes. Even when in pain – and the sweat on her upper lip told him she was in pain – she was comforting him. He sat down at the bedside, and looked across to the midwife. The woman nodded. 'Doctor's on his way, and it's coming along nicely.'

He felt Valerie's grip tighten on his hand, and heard her breathing shorten and grow louder. 'Hang on!' he said. 'Hang on, darling, I'm here now.'

≈

'Snook, they call it. Snook? More like nasty pap. Protein? If that's protein they can keep it.' Hannah folded her arms across her overall and glared her contempt at the tin on the table.

Sarah had heard of snoek which, according to the papers, was being imported from South Africa in vast quantities to supply the lack of protein in the British diet. 'It's wonderful, according to David,' Catherine had said. 'Cheap and nutritious, and the best thing is it comes from South Africa, so we can pay for it in pounds and not in dollars, which we haven't got.'

'Catherine says it's nice with a bit of salad,' Sarah ventured now, but Hannah's disapproval was not to be assuaged. 'I wouldn't feed it to the cat.'

In the past few months housewives had seen horsemeat offered to them as steak, and even whale-meat, which, although it resembled beefsteak, tasted overwhelmingly of cod-liver oil. Powdered egg, that great standby of the war years, had now been withdrawn, and other rations cut. 'It's not good enough,' Hannah said bitterly. 'I'm only glad I haven't got that Hartley here now. He could eat like a horse, for all he looked consumptive.'

Suddenly her eyes narrowed. 'Is he still writing to you? Ooh, I can see from your face he is. Well, watch your step, that's all I say. He's a nice enough lad, Sarah, I never had a pick of bother with him. But he's not our class, and that always leads to trouble.'

Sarah sighed. 'I'm tired of telling you, Hannah. We're friends, nothing more. He's more like a son to me than anything else.'

'He may be a son to you, Sarah, but do you seem like a mother to him?'

Sarah had intended to tell her that Hartley would be visiting soon. Now she decided to keep her mouth shut. Whatever she said, Hannah would twist it, and then it would get back to her father and Jim – and once Molly got hold of it . . .

'Have you heard about Mary Donnison?' she asked instead. 'They say she's dyed her hair red. Wants to look like Rita Hayworth!'

That would divert Hannah. Mary Donnison's carryings-on were a lot more interesting than her own.

―――

Pamela rested her elbows on the desk and her chin on her cupped hands. Her belly was so big now that she had had to move her seat back at least six inches. Outside in the workshop she could hear the machines humming. Only second-hand, but it was still machinery. Her father was making furniture again – if only he could make houses! This lunchtime she had gone after a flat near the park: three rooms, perfect. Even a little garden for the pram. 'You're too late,' a neighbour had told her. 'It went this morning.'

Although he was not saying anything, she knew Michael had now given up hope, and was resigned to staying with her parents even after the baby was born. But she would never give up. She had a yearning for her own front door now, something she could close on the world with her and her man and their baby safe behind it. But more than 400,000 couples had married last year, and all of them wanting a place of their own. Everyone was having babies too: they were calling it the baby boom. The housing situation was hopeless.

The Temporary Housing Programme she had kept reading about was putting up prefabs all over the place, but there would never be enough of them. The 'Portal' came with a brand-new cooker, sink, bath, boiler, fitted cupboards, and even a fridge. No one she knew had had a fridge before the war. Only very rich people, and hotels, had them now. There were other prefab designs – the Arcon, the Spooner, the Phoenix. Some came with a porch. She would happily take any kind as long as it came with its own front door.

She was still dreaming about prefabs when her father came into the cubby-hole she called an office.

'Pamela.' He only called her that when it was serious.

'Daddy?'

'Now I don't want you to get excited – not in your condition. But I know how much it would mean to you to have a place of your own.'

In spite of herself her heart began to beat faster.

'Well . . .' he went on. She resisted the impulse to get up and thump him.

'Well,' he said again, 'Mummy doesn't think you should move now, with the baby so near, but if you'll promise to keep calm . . .'

He had found somewhere. He would never have told her if

it weren't definite. Pamela was on her feet and rushing to plaster kisses on him, and her father was looking sheepish but pleased with himself at one and the same time.

———

The long expanse of roofs outside the window still annoyed India but she had other things to think of today. She would have to do something about Loelia. 'Shan't!' she had said yesterday, when asked to do some perfectly reasonable task. She wouldn't say 'Shan't!' again to her mother, nor to nanny – the mark on her cheek had been testament to that.

Rupert was the weak link, pandering to the child at every opportunity. They had not had sex for a week so he would probably come to her tonight. India sat down at the dressing-table and began to brush her hair with long, calm strokes. Every day she was more and more convinced that David would never uphold the family name. He might have an heir when the silly little girl he had married finally delivered, but it would be weak, like he was. If only Henry had lived! He and she had argued sometimes, but that was because he had spirit. Still, what else could you expect from a cripple but weakness?

She leaned forward and looked searchingly into the mirror. She was wearing well. Yesterday she had looked at Angela and noticed signs of ageing, puffiness around the mouth and chin, and tiny little cracks around her lips. Which was probably explained by her dreadful smoking habit. She herself had no such lines. She was wearing well, and that was down to breeding. There was no substitute for it, in horses or in men.

———

Sometimes Valerie had been unable to suppress a moan, at others a half-cry. Pacing the dressing-room, David suffered with her, willing it all to end, and terrified that it might end in despair, as Catherine's pregnancy had ended in that same room seven years ago, in the early days of her marriage.

He was standing at the fireplace, holding on to the mantel, when he heard the crying – at first a long drawn-out wail from his wife, and then a lesser sound, a reedy cry that blossomed into a cry of protest. The baby was in the world!

From the doorway, the midwife said: 'You have a daughter. A beautiful little girl. Mother and baby are doing fine.'

Catherine drove over as soon as David telephoned. He met her in the hall and drew her, hurrying, up the wide staircase.

'She's beautiful Catherine. Amazing eyes. Turquoise, I think. And she's long. A very long baby, the nurse says.'

Catherine was smiling as she entered the room where Valerie lay propped up in the huge bed. 'Well done!' she said, advancing to kiss her. 'I've heard from the father that it's a nonesuch, perfect in every way.'

'He's going to be insufferable,' Valerie said. 'I was afraid of it, and now it's true.'

'Well, look at her,' David said, moving the blanket to show the puckered face. 'She is lovely.'

Suddenly Catherine thought of her own baby, Joe's baby, born in this same room. '*I want to see him,*' she had said to the nurse who was holding the towel-wrapped bundle. The doctor had shaken his head, but the nurse had stepped forward and placed the dead baby on her breast. '*One peep,*' she had said. '*One little peep.*'

'Oh Catherine,' Valerie said, leaning forward to touch her friend's arm, 'no need to cry now. She's safely here.'

'She's so lovely,' Catherine said. 'So perfect! It just touched me. But, yes – silly to cry over such a lovely event.'

Pamela sat down on the bottom step to wait for Michael's return. 'Go straight home when you've seen it,' her father had said. 'And don't tell your mother it was me. Say you found it for yourself.'

She heard Michael on the path and threw herself across the hall to open the door.

'Darling, darling! We have a house. A whole house – not a room, not a flat, a house with windows and doors and cupboards. It's got a greenhouse in the garden, Michael!'

He was looking at her in disbelief. 'Are you sure?' he said.

And suddenly they were both laughing, and then she was crying as she told him about the man, a friend of her father, who knew another man who knew someone . . .

And then Michael stilled her words with a kiss. The bulk of their baby was between them, and Pamela knew that this was what people meant when they talked about heaven on earth.

The letters had been waiting for Sarah when she got back from Belgate. She read the official-looking one first. '*My client, Mr Hamish Carlyle, hereby gives you warning of his intention to apply for full custody of his son, Alexander Carlyle.*' It was not the first time she had received such a letter but it still had power to terrify her. Catherine would give it to David, and David would tell her not to worry, but she knew Hamish better than either of them. There was a devil in him, and one way or another he would find a way to beat her.

She opened the other letter, and found it no less worrying.

'*Dear Sarah,*' it began. '*I've tried more than once to say these things, but I've never had the courage, so I'm writing them instead. I think I love you, Sarah. I've never loved before,*' *not in this way, so I don't quite know how one is expected to behave. I only know I think of you all the time. Of the children, too – and they like me, I think. You must know that. What I'm trying to tell you is that, even if I don't have the courage to say these things the next time we're together, you know them now. You know that I want us to be together for the rest of our lives.'*

She folded the letter, and put it away. Poor boy! He saw love as something that made things better. Life had taught her different.

─────

The sex had been more savage than usual. Once or twice India had almost cried out, but instead she had bitten her lip. Rupert had been passionate like this at the beginning of their marriage – perhaps he was seeing sense? She felt his final thrust, so forceful that she couldn't suppress a sharp intake of breath that was almost a moan. He was rolling off her now, with a gasp of exhaustion. She turned on her side and put a hand on his heaving chest. 'That was good,' she said, 'quite inspired. You're such a romantic, Rupert.'

'Romantic?' His words were almost a snort. 'Romantic? Can't you tell that I'm desperate to give you your precious son, so I never need to do this again?'

She withdrew her hand. 'There's no need to be like that,' she said calmly.

'There's every need.' He too was calm now. 'My dear India, are you blind to the fact that I can hardly bring myself to look at you, let alone couple with you? I have to talk myself into being able to do it – will myself, my body . . . and I do it for our daughter. For my daughter! She may mean little or nothing to you, but she's the only thing I have to love. Perhaps, if you have a boy to worship, you can leave me and my daughter in peace.'

Chapter Fifteen

May 1948

THE PAIN WOKE HER, SUDDEN and stabbing, and low down. Pamela shifted slowly on to her elbows, anxious not to disturb Michael. He had worked so hard putting the house to rights yesterday, and then had had to settle to his studies. Heaven only knew what time he had come to bed.

She tried to make out the face of the bedside clock. Was it 5.15 or 25 past 3? It must be 5.15, because light was coming in through the crack in the curtains.

The pain had subsided for a moment – perhaps it was wind? Pamela turned her mind to the curtains. The house had seemed a gift from the gods, and indeed it was. The thrill of shutting the front door that first time had been indescribable, but she had not thought properly ahead to what a house needed. They had rented it as furnished, but only the basics were there: bed, a table and chairs, two sagging easy chairs, and carpets and curtains that had seen better days. The deposit had used up most of her remaining savings, and what little Michael had saved was eaten into daily by the necessities of living.

Most of what they had ready for the baby had been gifts from family and friends, and the girls at the factory. In the half-darkness her eyes pricked with tears at the memory of how Joyce and Sheila had arrived bearing gifts. '*It's not much but it might come in useful.*' There had been matinée jackets and bootees in shades for either sex, a rattle in cellophane box, and even a potty. '*It's blue,*' Joyce had apologised. '*Well, it had to be pink or blue, so we did eeny meeny miney mo.*' And to think that if it had not been for the war she might never have known them.

She was saved from further tears by a pain so shattering that it left her in no doubt. 'Darling – Michael! I'm sorry to wake you, but I think the baby's coming early!'

In the half-darkness David heard the whimpering and felt Valerie rising from the bed. 'Is it time? I'll get her.'

'I'm up, darling. Stay still.'

She collected the baby from the crib and carried it back to the bed.

'Let me . . .' David settled the pillows behind her, and watched as she put his daughter to her breast. The baby moved its head desperately at first, in an attempt to find the nipple. Valerie guided it gently, and it sucked ferociously until it found there was milk there.

'That's it,' Valerie said softly. Though he could see her outline, he could not see her features, but he knew she was smiling. Madonna and child, he thought, and found his lips also curling in contentment at the thought.

Catherine sipped her morning tea as she read the papers. According to *The Times*, Arab forces were mustering on the borders of Palestine in preparation for the ending of the British Mandate in Palestine. Yesterday the Jews had proclaimed a new state, the Israel that Max had often spoken of. Its flag was to be blue and white, and bear two horizontal bars and a Star of David. They were revoking the British ban on immigration, and would welcome any Jew from anywhere in the world.

Catherine she sat contemplating this idea. The world was thronged with Jews, even after Hitler. How could one country hold them all? And which Jew would not want to be part of a Promised Land?

Max had always spoken of Israel as a Promised Land, and now Catherine read every scrap of news about it that she could find. President Truman had issued a shock statement from the White House, recognising the new provisional Israeli government. Apparently the news had stunned the rest of the United Nations, and outraged the Arab world. King Abdullah of Jordan was ordering in the Arab Legion, and the 30,000-strong Haganah, the official army of the Jews, was on standby. 'There's going to be war,' Catherine thought. 'They've hardly buried the dead of the last war, and they're ready to fight again.'

The Jews had already blown up the Arab quarters in Haifa, killing almost 20 and injuring dozens more. In return, the Arabs had mortar-bombed the Jewish business quarter – more death and injuries. David had explained to her that Haifa was important because it was the only deep sea-port. Whoever held it had the advantage. The Jews had taken it by force, hundreds had died in the battle, and 60,000 Arabs had been displaced. British forces had restored a kind of peace; but they were powerless now, and there would be no one to stem the bloodshed.

If there were to be war in the Promised Land, would Max feel he had to be part of it?

———

Sarah sat down at the kitchen table to open the letter from Scotland. There was something inside it, and she shook it on to the table – a ring, a plain gold wedding-band. She picked it up and examined it. It was thin and worn down on one side. She looked at it in bewilderment, and then turned to the folded sheet of paper still in the envelope.

The writing scrawled on it tapered out at the end. '*For my son*' it began. She closed her eyes. The ring must have belonged to Hamish's mother.

She read on. '*I am writing this letter to put an end to things between us,*' it began. 'Perhaps he's given up?' she thought, knowing in her heart that it would not be as easy as that. '*My son will never know his heritage. I know that now. The blame is not mine. I did not ask for this hell to come upon me. I thought you understood. I thought you knew, would understand, but . . .*' Sarah couldn't make out the next line, for the handwriting had degenerated into a scrawl, but the ending was clearer. '*I am damned through no fault of my own. You have worked against me, you are like all the rest.*' It ended there without a signature.

She could hear little Joe in the garden, shouting with laughter. Alexander must be there with him, and he was a little imp of mischief. He should have had a father to fling him into the air, and teach him wise things. And Hamish should have had the right to hold his child. Sarah picked up the ring and put it back into the envelope. She couldn't think about it now. She would think about it all tomorrow.

She put the letter in a drawer, and set about getting ready to go and meet Hartley when he arrived at Durham station. She had done everything in her power to put him off, had even told him directly not to come.

'You're wasting your time,' Catherine had told her. 'You might as well try to hold back the North Sea.' But she must find a way to discourage him, before he too was drawn into the mess her life had become.

India drove into Durham and parked in the Market Square. She had considered going to Kynaston, and then decided against it.

She couldn't forgive the way she had been treated at the christening of David's daughter – having to sit there while Catherine Allerton held David's child for her baptism. Godmother, indeed! The child might only be a girl, but the principle was the same.

She halted at the children's outfitters in Silver Street. Loelia would need new clothes for winter, something sensible. She knew it pleased Rupert to see their daughter dressed like a china doll, but it wasn't practical, as Nanny agreed. Hiring her had been the best thing she ever did. Nanny's service background meant she knew the meaning of discipline, and had given her a proper sense of status. Most servants nowadays seemed unaware of just who was serving whom.

She entered the shop and asked to see something in navy blue. When the assistant informed her that nothing for age three came in navy blue, she suggested grey, and a pleasing variety of grey clothes was laid before her. She was about to pay for her purchases when she saw Angela Bond outside. She managed to catch up with her at the silversmiths further up the street, and they repaired to the tea-room to catch up on gossip over coffee and buns.

They had covered almost all the county when the subject of Catherine Allerton surfaced. 'Well, of course, I know she's your sister-in-law, India . . .'

'Was my sister-in-law, Angela. Was! Poor Henry, if it hadn't been for the war the marriage would never have happened. He'd have come to his senses. But you remember how rushed everything was then? We're paying for it now.'

'Quite. Well, of course we've all wondered about her child – the father. Apparently it was some doctor she met when she was nursing. A married man, and American into the bargain. Flicky Devonshire got it from a cousin of hers who was in the RAMC. Everyone knew, they say. Quite a scandal – and then he went off and left her in the lurch.' Angela paused for effect. 'And he doesn't know about the boy. She's never told him.'

India was about to say she knew all about Max Detweiler, but something held her back. Angela didn't need to know everything. In the car, though, driving home, she fumed over the fact that people were gossiping. Catherine Allerton had never truly been a Callingham, but she still had the capacity to bring the family name into disrepute. It was something to file away for the day of reckoning that Catherine Allerton deserved.

Michael had stayed with Pamela throughout the journey and her admission to a bed in a side ward. She had been in the general ward at first, and then there had been muttering as they poked and prodded her, and then a move to this small room.

'All right?' Michael said.

'I'm fine, darling, except you're holding my hand so tightly you're stopping my circulation!'

His 'sorry' was so fervent that she chuckled. 'Relax. Women give birth under trees, and in the desert. There's nothing to worry about.'

'Not my woman! Of course I'm worried when I see you in pain. I can't bear the thought that I did this.'

'You didn't mind at the time,' she said.

'It's not a joke, Pamela. It doesn't seem fair that you have to go through this . . .'

'I'm not going through anything, silly boy.'

It was true she had not had a pain for a while now. Contractions were supposed to come regularly, and more frequently with time. The nurses were coming back now, putting a thing like a trumpet to her belly, listening to her heart, feeling for her pulse. And then the doctor was standing at the foot of her bed, looking solemn.

'It's terribly bad luck with a first baby, but I'm afraid we can't wait for nature to take its course . . .'

He was still talking, but she wasn't listening. She was watching the growing horror on Michael's face, and feeling a terrible fear that the baby she knew so well, the baby she had been carrying close to her heart, might be going to be denied her.

⁓

They went downstairs together, holding hands. 'You look very handsome tonight, Sir David.'

'Your Ladyship looks equally beautiful.'

'Thank you, kind sir. Well, I had to make the effort for your sister's sake.'

'Imagine India's face if we hadn't dressed! God, I wish I had the courage!'

'End of the world,' Valerie said, as they reached the hall. 'But I do wish Catherine could be here, too.'

'Yes. She can't leave the children because Sarah is off somewhere with her beau. Or perhaps you told her India would be here, and she took fright?'

'She wouldn't do that, not Catherine. No, apparently this boy is besotted with Sarah. Catherine likes him, so she's happy to help them along. And he and Sarah don't see one another often, as he's in Oxford.'

'He's a remarkable young man. I didn't think he'd survive the pit, but he was made of better stuff than I feared. How about an aperitif?'

They were finishing their sherry when India and Rupert arrived. The newcomers accepted a dry sherry also, and David refilled his wife's glass.

'I saw Angela Bond in Durham today,' said India. 'She sent her regards.'

'Do I know her?' Valerie asked.

'No,' said David, 'she was India's co-conspirator at school. Her husband's in marine insurance.'

'You make him sound like a clerk,' India said. 'He's an entrepreneur, Valerie, and insurance is one of his enterprises.'

'Not good news out of Berlin,' Rupert said.

David could tell that he wanted to close down India's mention of Angela Bond. 'Yes,' he said aloud. 'The Russians are being deliberately provocative. Virtually closing the borders to road and rail.'

'Can Berlin exist in that state of isolation?'

Valerie was sitting up now, interested. India was examining her nails in the ostentatious way she used to signal boredom.

'Not for any length of time.' Rupert pursed his lips. 'It's dependent on food and fuel being brought in every day. Stop that, and the city starves.'

'They could fly food in . . .' Valerie was interrupted in midspeech by India's interjection.

'Have you any idea of the size of Berlin, Valerie? Why should we fly stuff in? We owe them nothing. Let them fend for themselves. Anyway,' she went on, 'I'm bored with all this anxiety over Germany. Have you read about the new Rita Hayworth film? Apparently her hair is dyed blonde. They say her husband, Orson Welles, made her do it, out of spite. They're splitting up. There's a terrific sequence in the film, in a hall of mirrors. And she dies in the end. Angela told me all about it.'

'It sounds fascinating. We must make sure we don't miss it,' Valerie said, and winked at David.

≈

All evening, the memory of Hartley's letter had been lain between them. Sarah knew every line. '*I've tried more than once to say these things but I've never had the courage so I'm writing them instead.*' Now she smiled at him to show she was happy to be here. He had spoken of love in the letter. '*I think I love you, Sarah. I've never loved before, not in this way . . . I only know I think of you all the time.*' He had spoken of the children too, to reassure her that he knew she would not be parted from them. But it was the last line that mattered: '*You know that I want us to be together for the rest of our lives.*' And yet neither of them could find the courage to mention it.

They were in the Royal County Hotel, ordering steak-and-ale pie with seasonal vegetables, speaking of everything but what was on both their minds. Afterwards they sauntered along the riverbank in the gathering dusk.

'Sarah?'

She waited but he didn't continue. 'Yes, Hartley?'

'Did you get my letter?' It was out, and they both sighed with relief.

'Yes, I did.'

'And . . .?' There was such anxiety in his voice that there was only one thing to do. Sarah looked around her. The road was deserted, and alongside them a grassy bank sloped gently up into trees and shrub.

'Give me your hand.' She led him up the bank, and on until no one could see. Then she sat down amid the spring grasses and pulled him down beside her. 'Don't talk. Don't ask questions. Just kiss me.'

It was not what she had intended. It defied commonsense, but she could no more help herself than fly.

―――

'The meal was passable,' India said in the car on the way home.

'I thought it quite delicious.' Rupert kept his eyes on the road ahead.

'At least it was meat. What was it we had last time? Rissoles. Rissoles! So I suppose mince was an improvement.'

'I'm afraid I don't rate evenings spent with your brother by the standard of cuisine. I find his company and Valerie's so pleasant that the food is irrelevant.'

'Oh, how I wish I could be as high-minded as you, Rupert.'

'You could if you tried, India. It's called behaving decently.'

They were passing the crossroads now. She wanted to say something withering, but nothing came to mind. In fact, she didn't feel up to witty repartee. She felt quite odd: dyspeptic. Could it have been something in the meal? She certainly felt nauseous.

The feeling had subsided somewhat, and they were nearly home, when she remembered the date. May 15th. Her period had been due on the 14th. Only one day, but still, a day was a day. She felt excitement rising, and tried to quell it. Mustn't get excited yet.

She let Rupert help her out of the car. He always offered, and she usually brushed him aside but tonight was different.

The hall was in darkness when they let themselves in. Upstairs a child was crying. 'That's Loelia!' he said.

'Don't go in Rupert. Nanny says we can't run in every time she cries, and I agree.'

'She's afraid of the dark.' He was taking the stairs two at a time.

'Then she must get over it,' she called. But he was out of sight, and a moment later the crying ceased.

─≈─

'I'm so sorry!' Catherine was flustered, her coat buttoned up oddly, so that she looked almost comically dishevelled. She saw Michael looking at her oddly and glanced down. 'Oh, crumbs. I came out in such a hurry. How is Pamela? I had to wait for Sarah to get home.'

'They're operating now. She's having a Caesarean section. But they think it'll be all right.'

'I'm so sorry, Michael. Still, it doesn't mean she can't have a normal delivery next time.'

'Next time?' He looked grim. 'There'll be no next time, Catherine. She's not going through this again.'

Catherine didn't argue. He would feel differently once it was over. Sitting down with him to wait, she found herself thinking about Sarah, who had been distinctly odd tonight when she came in, half-wanting to talk and half-relieved that Catherine was hurrying away.

She was still thinking of Sarah, when the nurse poked her head through the door. 'You have a son, sir. Eight pounds four ounces.'

'And my wife?' Michael was up on his feet now.

'She's fine. Still asleep and in recovery, but she's fine.'

'I'm an aunt,' Catherine said, in wonderment. 'Good grief, I'm an aunt.'

Chapter Sixteen

July 1948

CATHERINE COULD HEAR SARAH IN the kitchen, where she was keeping an eye on the children, who were out in the garden. In a little while they were going upstairs to strip and change the beds together, but she had a few precious moments left in which to sip her tea and devour the paper. Nowadays, she was hungry for news – perhaps because so much change was taking place in Britain. Or, if she were truthful, because she wanted to see what was happening in Israel.

She took in the rest of the news first, deliberately keeping Israel to last. There was trouble in Malaya, where banned Communist rebels were fighting British troops near Kuala Lumpur. Several pages were filled with items about the new National Health Service and the forthcoming Olympic Games. The Berlin airlift had faded to the inside pages: planes were still flying in supplies round the clock to beat the Russian blockade, but, since the Berliners were no longer threatened with starvation, it was regarded as old news.

The item that interested Catherine was at the bottom of the front page. Egypt and Iraq had ended the month-long truce, and were attacking Israel. Wherever you looked there was war, or the threat of war.

She was folding the newspaper when Sarah came in, drying

her hands on a towel. 'I'm done in the kitchen. What are we doing with the bairns while we're upstairs?'

Catherine glanced out of the window. 'They're all right for the moment. Sit down and have a cup of this tea. We'll all go up later, when they've tired themselves out. Joe seems to have everything in hand at the moment.'

Both women smiled at this. Joe was not yet eight, but he had installed himself as protector-in-chief of the younger ones, and he took his role seriously.

'Now,' Catherine said, when Sarah's tea was poured, 'you had a letter from Hamish today. Any news?'

Sarah was opening her mouth to speak when the phone rang in the hall.

'I'll go.' Catherine went and picked up the receiver. 'Belgate 494.'

The voice at the other end was faint and unknown to her, but certainly Scottish. 'This is the Reverend Donald McLean. I am hoping to speak to Mrs Sarah Carlyle.'

'Mrs Carlyle is here. May I ask why you want to speak to her?' If this was more trouble with Hamish, she wasn't having Sarah distressed.

'I'm afraid I have some bad news for her. Are you a friend?'

Catherine assured him that she was indeed a friend, and listened as the voice continued.

When she put down the phone, she stood for a moment, composing herself, before she went back into the morning-room.

'Sarah, there's no easy way to tell you this. Hamish is dead. He committed suicide – they don't know when. It may have been a while ago.'

———

'Hey! That's my nose.' Six-month-old Natasha squealed with delight as her father dodged her tiny fists.

'She doesn't get that aggression from me,' Valerie said demurely.

'That's your story. Seriously, she's terribly strong – quite advanced for her age.'

'You're an expert?' Valerie teased.

'I helped a lot with Ben when he was young. Of course, he's . . .'

'. . . advanced, too,' Valerie finished for him. 'Are you by any chance biased, my love?'

'Terribly. Anyway, I can't stay here arguing with an intransigent wife. I have to go and do some work.'

'Making plans to beat the wicked Socialists, I expect.'

'I hope so.'

'Honestly, David, you mustn't get your hopes up. Look at what Attlee is doing. The new National Health Service should see them re-elected, if nothing else does.'

'Are you a closet Socialist?' David raised quizzical eyebrows.

'Would you mind if I were? You know I'm on your side, darling, but I have to admit I'm impressed with Labour.'

'Of course I don't mind. Hey, baby, not in your mouth.' He restrained his daughter, who had just found a key-ring within reach. 'You know I respect your views. I share some of them. I support Beveridge's new slogan – what was it: "*Slay five giants. Want, Disease, Ignorance, Squalor and Idleness.*" I'm just not sure it's all do-able, Valerie. Or affordable. Labour's much-vaunted Coal Board lost £23 million in its first year of operation. How long can that continue? And if it all goes wrong who will sweep up the mess?'

~~~

'Oh, yes, Mrs Lindsay-Hogg, you're definitely pregnant. We'll check for dates, but I'd say you are six to eight weeks.'

India rolled the words round and round in her head as she

walked from the obstetrician's consulting rooms to the restaurant where she was meeting Angela. '*Definitely pregnant. Definitely, definitely pregnant.*' And she just knew it was a boy this time. It was her turn to get something she wanted.

Angela was delighted at the news. 'You're so brave, India. I gave Desmond his precious heir, and that was it as far as I was concerned. This éclair is terribly good – real cream, not that horrid ersatz stuff. Not that I'd want to bring another child into the world as it is at the moment. Those awful dockers bringing the country to its knees when we're already half-starved. Sixpence worth of fresh meat a week – how can a man exist on that? If we couldn't eat out, we'd starve.'

'They should be told work or face arrest.' India shook her head as Angela proffered the cake plate. 'They need a firm hand – not that they'll get it from that funny little man in Downing Street. Apparently, he wants to abolish the death penalty. There seems no end to his do-gooding. All the same, Rupert says the money will run out shortly, and that will bring Labour down.'

'Will Churchill get back in then?' Angela wiped cream from her mouth with a red-tipped finger.

'Churchill or Anthony Eden. Rupert says Eden is shaping up well.'

'And David is sure to take this seat, isn't he?'

'Given my brother's capacity for failure, I wouldn't bank on it, Angela. Can you catch the waiter's eye? We need some hot water.'

David enjoyed the sessions in the estate office when Catherine joined him. They had set aside one room for his political endeavours, and Catherine had christened it 'the War Cabinet'. It operated quite separately from the estate, although David could always call in Alistair Groom or the typist if he needed something done.

He glanced at the clock. Catherine was usually here by now. He pulled out the file that held his SSAFA cases. So much misery, and so little official gratitude for men weary from war. Still, he enjoyed fighting officialdom on their behalf.

And he had come to love the misty land he had inherited so reluctantly. Yesterday he had ridden up to the top-most point and surveyed his acres, every inch of them now familiar to him. Would Henry agree with the way he was managing it all? India didn't, but then India seldom agreed with anything. 'I feel no kinship with her at all,' he thought – and turned as Catherine came in, Ben at her side.

'Uncle David,' the boy said, holding up his arms. David picked up the child, and smoothed the dark hair from his forehead. 'How wonderful to see you. Have you come to help your Mummy?'

Ben nodded energetically, but Catherine was shaking her head.

'Hamish has committed suicide, David. Last week, they think although it only came to light today. Sarah has to go to Scotland, and I can't let her go alone.'

'Of course you can't. Will you manage? I could get away, if it would help.'

'That's kind of you, David, but we'll cope. There'll be an inquest, and a funeral to arrange. And a house to dispose of. I believe he owned the croft – but we don't actually know.'

'Well, let me know if there's the least thing I can do, and, if you encounter difficulties up there, I'm on the end of a phone.'

⁓

Pamela had fed the baby and laid him in his crib. She was buttoning her dress when she heard Michael in the hall.

'Darling? Is that you?' She had meant to have his food ready, but there never seemed to be time when she got back from her father's factory, and she couldn't give up work altogether because they needed the money. If Daddy hadn't let her take the baby with her, they would have been in trouble.

Michael looked strained and tired, and she went to him. 'Come in and sit down, darling. John's down for a nap. I'll make some tea. Let me get your slippers . . .'

'Don't fuss Pam.'

She looked up into his face. 'What's wrong?'

He shook his head. 'Nothing, really. It's just that there's been a big air-crash, near London. Two craft in mid-air. No survivors.'

'I'm so sorry, Michael.'

'One was RAF. Transport Command. The other was a Scandinavian Cloudmaster. They were circling over Northolt, looking for an opportunity to land. I heard it on the wireless in the restroom. It brought a lot of things back.'

'I'm sure it did. Come here.' She wrapped her arms around him. 'I love you so much, darling. I can't bear you to be upset. We'll soon be able to make love again, and then I can show you how much I love you.'

But he was pushing her away. 'It's not as easy as that, Pamela. I don't want us to have more children. Ever. And I need some real help. I think I need to talk to a doctor.'

———

Sarah had been dropped by Catherine on the outskirts of Belgate, Alexander holding her hand. She was going to wait until Joe came back from tea at his schoolfriend's, so she had an hour or two in which to break the news to her father and Jim, and make some arrangements for the children while she was away in Scotland. She walked up the path to her father's door. It had always been on the latch but today it was locked.

She knocked. It was a minute or two before she heard steps behind it, and when the door opened it was her sister-in-law, Molly, who stood there.

'Oh, it's you,' Molly said. 'We're honoured. Well, you'd better come in.'

Sarah followed her. No need to mention Hamish until Jim or her father appeared.

'I'll make tea, if you like,' Molly said. 'Your dad should be in directly. He's down the club.'

'I'm all right, thank you. I had coffee before I left home. How's Jim? And the bairns?' Molly's two were seven and five now, and probably roaming the streets, as Belgate children did. 'I am growing away from them,' Sarah thought guiltily, and then realised Molly had not answered her.

'How is Jim?' she asked again.

'Full of hell.' Molly expected her words to shock, and they did.

'What's the matter?'

'It's your brother that's the matter. Never satisfied. Always going on. I've had enough, Sarah. Slaving after two men, no place of me own. Marriage – give me penal servitude. Well, it is penal servitude. The war opened my eyes. There are better ways to live.'

'It can't be as bad as that,' Sarah said defensively.

'It can and it is. Anyroad, here he is. You can ask him for yourself.'

Jim was stooping through the door. He was already, clean except for the black rims to his eyes. That meant the new pithead baths must be installed and working.

'Sarah!' He kissed her warmly. 'We don't see you often enough. Everything all right?' Without waiting for an answer he turned to his wife. 'Have you not offered Sal a cup of tea?'

'See?' Molly said, and went into the back kitchen.

'I've got some bad news, Jim. Hamish has committed suicide.'

He let his breath out in a slow whistle. 'Are you sure?'

'Yes. A vicar telephoned Catherine. She and I are going up there as soon as we can.' She had been hoping that he and Molly would offer to take the children, but she wouldn't want to leave them here now. Not with Molly the way she was.

'How's Dad?' she asked instead. Before Jim could answer, there was a 'Coo-ee' from the door, and Hannah Chaffey was entering.

'Her at Fourteen told me you were here, so I've popped up to save you popping down.'

There had been times when Hannah's stream of gossip had been unwelcome. This time, however, Sarah would have welcomed any kind of intervention at all. The atmosphere in the house was unwelcoming.

Catherine sat at the table, trying to work out what to do for the best. If Sarah's two children went to her brother, she could ask Pamela to take Ben, just for a day or two. Her mother would help, too – might even look after him herself, come to that. She was fond of her grandson, now that he was in the world. And Ben was sweet with Pamela's little John. He was a good boy, although she said it herself.

She remembered him today, holding out his arms to David. 'He loves David,' she thought. 'And that love is returned.'

She was still smiling at the thought when Sarah entered. 'Come in, I've just made tea. Joe's upstairs with his jigsaw. How did you get on in Belgate?'

'Hannah was there. Full of woe, as usual.'

'What is it this time?'

'The war's been over three years, and we're still being rationed. The dock strikes got her predicting everything from famine to plague. Oh, and the woman next door is getting mince on the black market. I told her it was probably horse, but according to Hannah it's best beef steak.'

'Did you manage to ask them about the children?'

Sarah shook her head. 'They can't go there, Cathy. I don't know what's wrong, but something's up, and I didn't like it. I'll just have to go to Scotland by myself, if you'll keep my two here.'

'Do you want me to go for you?'

'No. I owe him this much, Cathy, I can't see him buried without some family. By rights, I should take Alexander with us.'

'He's too young, Sarah. Besides, there'll be a lot to do up there. I don't think you realise . . .'

They were still deliberating when the phone rang.

'Catherine? It's Valerie. David's just told me about Hamish. Please tell Sarah I'm so sorry. David says you're going to Scotland with her, so what's happening to the children? We can have them here, you know. Natasha will love it, and you know my husband is besotted with your son. I don't know whether or not Sarah has other arrangements but we'd love to have all three of the children . . .'

When she came back into the kitchen, Catherine was shaking her head. 'Problem solved, Sarah. And my brother-in-law David is definitely married to the nicest woman in the world.'

'What did the doctor say?' Rupert asked politely. They sat at either end of the long table, dressed appropriately, eating from porcelain with silver cutlery. India couldn't help a little purr of satisfaction. Some standards held.

'Everything is fine.'

'Good.' Rupert raised his glass. 'Here's to a successful conclusion. And let's also drink to the end of our ghastly charade.

I won't be visiting you again, India, and for that I am most pro-
foundly grateful.'

———

Sarah lay wide awake long after the house had gone silent, and
traffic had ceased on the road outside. 'I'm a widow again,' she
thought. This time there was none of the searing grief of that
first time, but there was no elation either, no feeling of freedom.
She would never need to fear Hamish again, never expect him
to appear from round some corner, or be there when a door was
opened. She ought to feel relief.

Instead she felt guilt. 'I let him down,' she thought.
'Everyone let him down. But what else could I have done?'

Outside the window the moon seemed to glare accusingly. In
the end she turned on her side to block out the sight, and wept
silently into her pillow.

———

Pamela lay on her back, keeping very still in case she disturbed
Michael, sleeping beside her. He had not put a comforting arm
around her as he usually did. He had not kissed her on the
mouth, merely brushed her temple with his lips, before turning
his back on her.

'Is this what it comes to in the end?' she wondered. 'After all
the turmoil of war, and the stresses of peace, that it should become
like this – two people who loved each other, lying like strangers?'

Chapter Seventeen

August 1948

THE COUNTRYSIDE OUTSIDE THE WINDOW was changing. 'We must be near the border,' Catherine said.

Sarah didn't reply. Instead she seemed to stare more intently at the passing landscape. What must it feel like to be going back to a place where you had been so unhappy?

Catherine didn't speak again, concentrating on her newspaper instead. News of the coming Olympic Games was everywhere. She passed quickly over it, looking for something that interested her. There was an article about a new schools system. Comprehensive education. It would be years before Ben reached that stage. She read on. Australia was dominating the Test match, but Bradman, their great hero, was out for a duck on his last Test appearance.

She turned the page again. Foreign news. Jerusalem had been attacked, and two Jews killed. It was months since she had heard from Max. Perhaps there would never be another letter. He would grow old and rich in New York, putting tucks in the faces of vain women. She couldn't help thinking it was a waste, but on the other hand it was none of her business.

And never mind Max – where would she and Ben wind up? She sought here and there for an answer, but there was none.

'Are you sure you can manage?' David looked anxiously from his wife to the garden, which literally seemed alive with children.

'Very sure, Sarah's Joe is as good as a nursery-maid any day, and I have Becky if I get into trouble. Off you go, and sort out this poor man of yours.' She looked at the clock. 'Where will they be now?'

'Crossing the border, I should think. Perhaps even over it. I don't envy them. Still, I'll get going, and hurry back.'

'Don't hurry back. I'm fine. Now, off you go.' She kissed him on the cheek, and then propelled him towards the door. He climbed into the car, started the engine, and took the Belgate road.

Almost every day now he was called to one house or another where a family was experiencing difficulties in adjusting to peace-time. There was not a single thread to their woes. Some men, who had become accustomed to discipline and being told what to do every minute of the day, were simply unable to function in a world in which they must take responsibility for themselves. Others had come back coarsened, and almost drunk with the power of a fighting man. David pitied their wives and families. 'He wasn't like this when I married him,' one woman had told him with tears in her eyes. Sarah had found that, too.

'We got it wrong,' David thought as Belgate came in sight. 'We imagined soldiers returning to Britain as heroes, welcomed by their wives or girlfriends, and slotting into their old lives with ease.' The reality was different. Men who returned and found they had been betrayed were apt to take vengeance on adulterous wives, or cuckoos in the nest. Families that had existed happily with daddy only a photo on the mantelpiece resented the disruption to routines when the photo became solid flesh. Children resented sharing their mothers' attention with fathers they hardly knew; women found themselves with divided loyalties; and men often felt left out of a close-knit family circle. 'He even slept between us in the bed,' one man said bitterly of the son, news of whose birth had reduced him to tears on the battlefield.

And, quite apart from re-integrating into the home, men who had grappled with violence, and even death, in combat found it difficult to return to their old jobs in offices and factories. Some of them, David feared, might resort to crime in an effort to recapture some of the excitement of battle. And yet others had been broken by war: some suffered from insomnia, others developed a tremor, too many felt guilty about surviving.

'I must do my best for them,' David thought yet again, as he pulled in to the kerb and switched off the engine.

It felt strange to be back in her office at her father's factory. Pamela wondered constantly if her mother really was up to caring for a new baby. But in one way it was a relief to be out of the house. In spite of all her efforts, it was not a home.

'I looked forward to it too much,' she thought. 'No matter where we got, it could never have lived up to my expectations.' The furniture was old and shabby, the curtains threadbare, the carpets even worse. 'It's a dump,' she thought.

And there wasn't a hope of doing anything about it until Michael was earning. She had left him poring over sample exam papers, but he didn't now seem as keen on what he was doing as he had been at the beginning. 'We have everything we always said we wanted,' she thought, 'but somehow it isn't working out.' Here she was, behind a desk, when she would rather be home with her baby, and here she was for only one reason: she needed the money.

One day it would all come right. They would own a house, and furnish it in the way they wanted. Michael's exams would be behind him, and she would no longer need to work. 'It will be better then,' she told herself firmly.

But the memory of her husband's face, grey with fatigue, and with something else – a kind of hopelessness that she had never seen there before – lingered in her mind.

'No.' India kept her voice even. No need to display emotion: Loelia seemed to feed on that.

'No,' she said again, 'you're not going to feed the ducks, and you know why, Loelia.' The child looked up at her defiantly. For a child not yet three she was astonishingly insolent. She was shaking her head, the round curls wobbling for all the world like Topsy's.

India turned to the nanny. 'We must do something about her hair. It's too short for plaits, but it needs subduing.'

'It won't suit Mr Lindsay-Hogg. He's very proud of his daughter's hair.' The scorn in the nanny's tone was understandable. All the same, she was an employee, and shouldn't have opinions about her employer, good or bad.

'I want something doing, Nanny. And Loelia's not going out today – or any day, until she learns not to have horrid wet knickers.'

The nanny was not prepared to stay quiet. 'Mr Lindsay-Hogg says I'm not to train her, madam. He says she's too young, and there's plenty of time.'

Inwardly India fumed. She couldn't decry Rupert to a servant. All the same . . . 'Well, Nanny, I suggest we just concentrate on the hair. Bunches, please, and no ducks.'

She bent to her daughter, looking into the mutinous little face. 'I mean what I say, Loelia. No toys, no ducks, until you learn to behave like a big girl. Now run along.'

For a moment mother and daughter eyed one another,

neither giving way to the other. Then Loelia spoke. 'Dada,' she said. 'Where's Dada?'

'He's not here, and if you don't do as you're told, Loelia, he won't come. Ever again.'

≈

Sarah had forgotten how beautiful Scotland was. As they alighted from the taxi, she stood for a moment and stared at the encircling mountains. Below, the loch sparkled in the sunshine; green slopes were dotted with white sheep; birds circled above. How could it have happened here?

She put a hand to her head, remembering the blows, in spite of herself. '*Why do you shame me?*' he had screamed. '*Why do you remind me I'm a useless hulk?*'

'Are you all right?' Catherine sounded anxious.

'Yes,' Sarah said. 'Yes. I was just remembering.'

They walked together into the house. It was much as she remembered it, except that in her day the plates on the dresser had sparkled, the fire-irons had been burnished. There had been no opened cans and dirty dishes in the sink.

'Don't worry,' Catherine said briskly. 'We'll clean this up in no time. First, where will I find a kettle? We could do with some tea.'

They had cleared the sink and made a start on the rest of the room when the knock came at the door.

'Duncan McLean,' the minister said, stepping over the threshold. 'Poor Hamish. Well, he's away now, and in God's hands, and we have a funeral to arrange.'

'Have some tea?' Catherine said, putting a hand to the teapot. 'Quite warm, but I think we'll have a fresh pot, and then you can tell us what you need us to do.'

She glanced at Sarah, but her friend looked quite detached from what was going on.

'Aye,' Mr McLean said. 'Tea is a fine idea. And Hamish was a fine man. A fine boy, and a fine man.'

Catherine saw Sarah's lip quiver, and be caught by her lower teeth.

'I'm sure you're right, Vicar. Or is it Minister? Do sit down and tell us all about it.'

He cleared his throat. 'Who knows what drove him to it?' His tone implied that he had a good idea. 'But a man left on his own up here . . . it can get very lonely. And drink had been taken.'

'What exactly happened?' Sarah's voice was urgent.

'He went out on to the hillside and sat down . . . and cut his wrists. The poor man bled to death.'

———

'It's hard to categorise them,' Rupert said. Around the two men the club hummed with conversation and sounds of eating. 'My, this plaice is good,' he added. 'No, what I mean by "categorise" is that they're a mixed bunch. Take Attlee, typical suburban gent, nothing to say for himself, does good works, and becomes a Socialist.'

David looked quizzically at his brother-in-law. 'Do you think you might be underestimating him, Rupert?'

'Oh, make no mistake, Attlee is a force to be reckoned with. So is Cripps, although I think the man's fanatical. Half Communist, of course. But as Chancellor he'd keep control of the purse strings. Dalton I don't put much store by.'

'I admire Ernest Bevin,' David said firmly. He agreed with much of what Rupert was saying, had thought it for a long time, but his own opinion was less jaundiced.

'So do I, old boy. But it won't do to say that aloud, now that you're the Conservative candidate-in-waiting. He doesn't know a thing about geography, but he's a damned good Foreign

Minister. Learned his wiliness in the trade-union movement. Unlike that ranting Aneurin Bevan – a born agitator; or Morrison – self-serving, and obsessed with his image.'

'You make them sound a pretty poor bunch, but they're coping well in the circumstances, surely? They inherited a country on its beam ends. They're not doing badly.'

'That may or may not be true, but you can't be heard saying it, David. You do want to win an election, don't you? Don't give people the impression that you're half-hearted. You know how petty they can be.'

'I do know petty people,' David said, 'and speaking of my sister . . .' He had meant it as a joke, but one glance at Rupert's face told him he had got it wrong. 'How is India?' he ended, lamely.

'She's well.' Rupert's voice was flat.

'You don't sound too happy,' David ventured.

'We have differences over Loelia. It makes for strains.'

'Anything I can do?' David fervently hoped his offer would be turned down. To his relief it was.

'Thank you, but I have to sort it out myself.'

Afterwards David would see that 'I' as significant. Rupert didn't say, 'We have to sort it out,' which would have implied co-operation. Whatever he meant to do, he meant to do it alone.

'What are we going to do with all this?'

Catherine gazed around the room. Now that they had swept and dusted, and there was a peat fire in the grate, it looked less grim, but it was still cluttered.

'It's tidy now,' Sarah said. 'I didn't want to leave it shameful, but I just want to walk away from it, Cathy. Let's get tomorrow and the funeral over, and then go home. Mr McLean will know what to do with the furniture, and the house will be sold. That money's for Alexander.'

'You ought to keep one or two things, Sarah. Presumably these things were Hamish's mother's? Those china dogs, for instance? One day Alexander might like something from his father's home.'

They settled on keeping the china dogs, and a little chair, low to the floor with a seat no bigger than a frying pan and a long thin back. 'It's inlaid,' Catherine said, 'and rather nice.'

'It's a spinning-chair,' Sarah said. 'Hamish's mother used to spin. I think the wheel went long ago. Will we get it on the train?'

'Of course. Look, light as a feather.'

At Catherine's suggestion, Sarah sat down at the roll-top desk and began to sort through its contents. 'Better clear it out,' Catherine said. 'You never know what's in there. Keep anything important, and we'll burn the rest.'

She got on with cleaning the windows, each one encrusted with spider's webs. It must have been months, almost years, since Hamish had cared for the house. And yet it had once been a home, she could see that in the knick-knacks on every ledge, the hand-stitched cushions on the settle, the naïf paintings and religious texts on the walls.

She glanced across at Sarah, half-tempted to say what she was thinking. But Sarah was staring at scraps of paper in front of her. Fragments of a life, Catherine thought, and gave thanks that, a day from now, they would be on their way home.

~~~~~

'Who has done this?'

India turned at the sound of her husband's voice. 'I didn't hear you come in,' she said pointedly. It was a bone of contention that he came home and mounted the stairs to the nursery three at a time, without the slightest acknowledgement that he had a wife.

'I asked you who had done this?' In his arms Loelia was looking puzzled and apprehensive.

'What are you talking about?'

'I'm talking about this – this distortion of my daughter's hair.'

'Admittedly it looks a little odd at the moment, Rupert, because it's too short, but I won't have her looking like a gypsy.'

'She's still a baby, India. Two years old . . .'

'Almost three, and it's you who is upsetting her now. Look at her.'

She walked past him to open the door. As she suspected, the nanny was lurking outside. 'Can you take Loelia up to the nursery, please?'

'Certainly, Madam.' The woman was obviously enjoying the scene, flouncing past her, all starch and officiousness.

'Thank you, sir. I'll take Loelia now, if I may.' The nanny was holding out her arms, but the child had shrunk against her father, hiding her face in the folds of his neck.

'Come along, Rupert. Let's not make a scene. It isn't fair on Loelia. Give her to Nanny.'

'I'll see you both in hell first.' Rupert was walking past them, holding his daughter with one arm, the other hand disentangling the ribbons from her bunched hair as he moved.

Sarah let herself out of the door, moving quietly so as not to alert Catherine, who had fallen into a sleep of exhaustion on the settee. In a little while they would climb into the high bed, and try to sleep without thinking of the ordeal of the funeral tomorrow. What had the minister called it? '*A sad, sad affair.*'

Above her the night sky was thick with stars. The first night she had come here she had looked up at the stars and marvelled. There were no street lamps to dull the eye, only the vault of the sky above, studded with diamonds. It was cool outside after the fire-warmed room, and she shivered a little.

She had found mementos of the young Hamish in the old desk. '*A good boy,*' his school report had said. A card had given details of his baptism. There had been a picture of him as a child, the same age as Joe now, his arms twined round the neck of a collie. Another picture showed him with a woman, his mother presumably. And a third showed him in what was obviously his first pair of long trousers. In every picture, the face of the boy, the face of the youth, had been open and friendly.

Now, she was remembering, that was how he had been when she first knew him: a kind man. She had felt safe in the pub when he was there, shielding her from anyone who would annoy her. And then he had gone to war, and come back a monster.

'It changes men,' she thought. 'They see things no man should see, and they cannot ever be the same as the men they were.'

She stood for a long time trying to find solace in the stars, and then turned and went back into the house.

※

Pamela had fed John and shushed him to sleep. Now she went downstairs. Michael had been quiet tonight. Too quiet. He was sitting still, and as she walked into the room she saw the paper in his hand. It was that poem, the one about flying.

He looked up at her and smiled. 'Don't worry, I'm not wallowing. Just thinking.' He looked down at the paper and then lifted his eyes and spoke the poem aloud. '"Oh! I have slipped the surly bonds of earth, And danced the skies on laughter-silvered wings. . ." I did that, didn't I, Pam?'

He was quoting again. '"I've climbed, and joined the tumbling mirth of sun-split clouds – and done a hundred things

You have not dreamed of . . ."'

'I try to understand,' Pam said. 'When we were talking before – when you showed me the poem – you said you thought you would be glad when the war was over, but that you missed flying.'

'In some ways I still do. In other ways, I like what I've got. You and the sprog – nothing can compare with that.'

She couldn't think of anything to say. Instead she simply locked her arms around him, and locked them tight.

After a moment, he lifted his head and smiled at her. 'I'm all right, Pam. At least, I think I am.'

'I'm glad," Pamela said, curling into the crook of his arm. "I did wonder if you would be able to settle, darling, and I'm so glad you feel you can.'

Chapter Eighteen

March 1949

'THE CROFT HAS SOLD FOR £200!' Sarah's eyes were wide with shock.

'Two hundred and eighteen, actually– and he says there may be a bit more money to come when the estate is finally settled.'

'Two hundred pounds!' Sarah was still shaking her head. 'I thought £50, even £100. But this . . .' The solicitor's letter shook in her hand as Catherine handed it back to her.

'The sale has happened quickly, but remember the minister did mention there was a neighbour interested in buying it. What are you going to do with the money?' Catherine tried to keep her voice even and not let her impatience show. There was a letter from Max in her pocket, put there when she picked up the post from the front door. But Sarah's letter from the solicitor had to come first.

'I thought you would pay it into your bank for me?' Sarah said. Catherine began to nod, and then shook her head.

'No,' she said firmly, 'it's time you had your own bank account. We'll go in to Sunderland tomorrow and open one.'

Sarah's eyes widened even further. 'Don't look like that,' Catherine said firmly. 'It makes sense. Now, are the curtains ready?'

Sarah gestured towards a pile of new material. 'Just the rufflette tape to stitch on,' she said. 'They'll be ready in time.'

Catherine nodded approval, and took her leave before the letter burned a hole in her pocket.

'I'm just popping into the village,' Sarah called after her. 'I'll be back directly. Can I leave the bairns with you?'

'Yes,' Catherine called back. She sped up the stairs and into her room, and then she ripped open the envelope.

'*My dear Catherine,*

You will see from the postmark that I have moved again. We have come to Israel, yes, the Promised Land. I suppose I always knew this would be where I would wind up . . .'

She heard the door clash. Sarah was gone. She went to the window, but the children were playing happily, and Joe was on guard. She moved back to the bed, and smoothed out the letter. Before she could begin reading, there was a ring on the doorbell. She glanced at her watch. Ten o'clock. Who would be visiting at this time?

A man and woman stood on the step. 'Lady Callingham?'

'Yes?' They couldn't be Jehovah's Witnesses. Those were always men. Besides, these two people knew her name.

'We've come to speak to you about something urgent, Your Ladyship.'

'Then you'd better come in.'

They settled in the morning-room and she looked at them expectantly.

'It's about our son,' the man said.

'Hartley.' This was the woman.

'Oh,' Catherine smiled. 'You're Hartley's parents. He's a charming boy. You must be very proud of him.'

'We are. That's why we're here,' the woman said. 'The boy has told us he intends to marry one of your employees.'

'Do you mean Sarah?'

'Sarah Carlyle. Yes, her. We've had her checked out, Lady Callingham.' The woman's face quivered with indignation. 'A barmaid. A Catholic – and drove her last man to suicide. The bottom dropped out of my world, I can tell you, when I read that.'

Inside Catherine, fury mounted. She stood up.

'My friend Sarah is one of the most honourable and gentle women I know. If your son succeeds in winning her, he will be a very lucky man. And now, if you'll excuse me . . .'

They blustered all the way across the hall, and were still doing it when she armed them over the step.

<hr>

'Two hundred pounds!' Hannah was turning the teapot round and round so that the hot water inside would warm it. 'By gum! Well, it says in the paper they're taking clothing off coupons. You can buy yourself a fair few dresses with that kind of money.'

'It's to be put away for Alexander. Get that tea mashed. I can't stop long. I just had to tell somebody.'

Sarah had decided not to tell Hannah about the other letter that had come that morning. That she would keep to herself for a while. Perhaps forever.

'*Dearest Sarah,*' it had begun. And it had ended '*You might as well say yes because I shall keep on asking you till you do.*' Two hundred pounds and a proposal in one day! She hadn't seen Hartley since Christmas, but his letters had kept coming regularly.

'You're colouring up,' Hannah said, suddenly curious.

'It's nothing. I'm a bit flushed. It's news of the money, I suppose.'

'Have you heard from young Hartley? His exams'll be coming up, I suppose.'

'Yes,' Sarah said, composing herself. 'Yes, he finishes this summer. But, no, I haven't heard from him lately.'

On the way back to Mellows, she was remembering that last day in Scotland. 'O, love that will not let me go,' they had sung; and then, in the churchyard above the loch, she had watched the coffin go down into the earth, and had prayed that Hamish might find a peace in heaven which he had not known on earth.

'He didn't mean it,' she thought. 'It wasn't his fault.' And she had felt suddenly peaceful.

But she would never marry again. It was too much of a risk.

India could hear bustle in the corridor outside her room. Matron must be due. In a moment they would come in tidy the bed, and hide everything. Nothing, nothing must be on show to catch Matron's eagle eye.

India didn't give a fig for Matron. For anything, really. She glanced across to the crib, inside which her new daughter was sleeping. So much pain and effort to bring forth only a second girl. She turned on her side, disconsolate. Her whole life was a web of frustration. Everything she cared about came to nothing in the end.

Even Kynaston. Every day that Valerie was there it was becoming more like a suburban semi. If she had only had a boy . . . In the paper this morning there had been a picture of Princess Elizabeth, proudly holding her baby son. Other women had sons – women like Catherine Allerton.

The paper had also shown a picture of Nehru, grinning still over having thrown out the Raj. A man who had received a Harrow education, and still he could display base ingratitude! Her India, her namesake, had been a peaceful country, because everyone knew their place. Now it was in a ferment, police stations set on fire, the beating of anyone perceived to be British, telephone wires cut, and railway lines blown up. Anarchy. And all because of a weak Labour government.

She had overheard Rupert telling someone on the telephone that the true story was being kept out of the newspapers. Understandably, because people wouldn't stand for the abandonment of such a jewel in the crown, if they knew the truth. How many people realised that, for every Indian who had fought for Britain, another had joined the Japanese and fought against her? And when these traitors came home after Japan's defeat, Gandhi's Congress Party had welcomed them as heroes instead of hanging them as traitors! What else could you expect when, if rumours were true, the Congress Party's Nehru was bedding the wife of the Viceroy? Edwina Mountbatten had always had a penchant for black men. To think that a member of the royal family – by marriage, if not by birth – had handed over a part of the Empire.

But what did that matter in the face of her own disappointment? A girl! Another silly chit for Rupert to drool over. A boy would have been hers. 'Every part of my life is rotten,' India thought, and turned her face to the pillow.

'What did they say?'

Michael had not spoken since he came out of the clinic. Pamela had waited for him in the park, her heart in her mouth. 'I can't bear him to be unhappy,' she thought. 'Not after all he's been through.'

He'd been coming to the clinic for six months now. A week ago he had had a new treatment, with Pentothal. That was the truth drug – she'd looked it up. He hadn't said much since then, and today he had been seeing the psychiatrist once more.

'Let's walk,' she said now, and put her arm through his. Why didn't he say something?

They walked for a while in silence, and then she spoke herself. 'Is it the job, Michael? Have you gone off the idea of teaching? You can tell me. We can manage, whatever you do. After what you told me about nothing being the same as flying, I understand.'

'They said I wouldn't feel any better until we talked, and they were right.'

'What do you mean.'

'Today, when I was under that drug, we talked about what they discovered. What I'd been holding back. Apparently it was a feeling of loss. Extraordinary when you think how fervently I longed to be free of flying – and yet it seems that in the back of my mind, I went on hankering for it.'

'And?'

'It's strange, but in a way – I do feel different now. Lighter.'

'Good. Now, for a treat, we're going to have afternoon tea at the Grand! Catherine arranged it and Mummy has taken John, so we're free, just the two of us.'

———

Catherine had been reading Max's letter once more, and trying not to think about her visitors, when the phone rang. It was a relief to hear a friendly voice, and pour out the tale of Hartley's parents.

'It was dreadful, Valerie. They said they'd had Sarah investigated, and that she'd driven Hamish to suicide.'

'How awful. I hope you showed them the door?'

'Too right I did. Horrid people! But should I tell her, Valerie?'

'I wouldn't. Not now, anyway. I'll talk to David about it. Now, how long did you say we had before Pam and Michael get home?'

'They're out having tea somewhere, and coming back at 6 o'clock. The van's due here at 2. Sarah's overseeing the loading at Mellows, and she'll come with the van.'

'And bring the curtains?'

'Definitely, the curtains. They're beautiful. Sarah is so accomplished. That's what makes me angry. If Hartley's parents only knew . . .'

'They don't, and I doubt they'd believe you if you told them. I told the carpet-fitters to meet us there. We've got a lot of work to do. By the way, what do you think about clothes rationing ending? I've told David, I'm going to have dresses in every colour of the rainbow, and all with yards and yards of fabric in them. Still, enough of that. I'll just finish off here, and then we're ready.'

India heard her brother's voice in the corridor. He would come in and coo over the baby. He was a weakling. And Valerie Graham-Poole had made him worse. Impossible to think of her as a Callingham. Or her puny daughter.

'India?' He was bending to peck her cheek. 'And this is my niece, little Imogen? Oh, what a charmer she'll be. Rupert is besotted with her already.'

'Rupert is easily pleased, David. Come and sit down, if you're staying, that is. Tell me about Kynaston.'

'Oh, there's nothing to tell. It's much the same. Valerie is having the dining-room painted. Eau de nil, I think she said. And getting rid of some of the furniture. Have you heard that the King's had an operation? On his foot. And Larry Olivier has won an Oscar for *Hamlet*.'

'I can read the newspapers for myself, David. If I'm interested, which I seldom am. I hope Valerie isn't doing anything with the hall and staircase? That mustn't be touched. And what furniture is she getting rid of?'

'The house is Valerie's province, India. I simply pay the bills. Anyway, when are they letting you out of here?'

Pamela fumbled for her keys while Michael paid off the taxi. 'I still say we should have collected John tonight,' Michael said.

Pamela opened the front door, and felt for the light. 'Cathy said I should leave him with Mummy, in case you were tired. We'll get him in the morning.'

She found the switch and flicked it. 'Oh my God!' she said, and then again, 'Oh my God!'

They ran from room to room like children. 'Curtains!'

'This carpet's new.'

'Catherine's desk.'

'I've never seen those chairs before!'

When they had explored, they stood together in the hall, drunk with pleasure. 'Good friends,' Michael said. He put out a hand and touched her hair. 'I love you, Pammy.'

'I know. What exactly happened at the clinic this afternoon?'

'I'll tell you everything later. Right now I want to make love to you.' His arms were around her, and she struggled free. 'I must put my cap in.'

'Damn the cap.'

'I could get pregnant.'

'I know.'

'You said . . .'

'I said so many things – no more words, Pam.'

'It's going to be all right,' she thought. 'It's going to be all right.'

'What do you think India would say about this?' David and Valerie had decided against dining in state, and instead were curled up on the sofa with plates on their laps and Frank Sinatra on the gramophone.

David considered for a moment before he replied. 'First she'd say we hadn't dressed.' Valerie nodded agreement. 'Then she'd say we weren't using proper cutlery.'

'And the plates are pot, or whatever they call it. Not porcelain.'

'Wrong plates, and you just threw a napkin at me. No napkin ring. And then she'd say bubble-and-squeak is common.'

'She wouldn't say that, because she's never heard of bubble-and-squeak.'

'You're right.' David lifted a forkful to his mouth. 'She doesn't know what she's missing, does she?'

'Don't speak with your mouth full,' Valerie said. The notes of 'Dearly Beloved' faded away, and there was a plop as another record fell on to the turntable.

'"Blue Moon",' David said appreciatively. 'I like that one.'

'What did India have to say?'

'She was moaning about India – the country. And about herself, as usual. You know what she's like.'

'I do, and I know she irks you. But we ought to make more effort, darling. She's your sister, and besides, I think she's dreadfully unhappy.'

'Of course she's unhappy. She hates the human race. Always has.'

'No, but I mean more than that. I don't think her marriage is happy.'

'It's not, but whose fault is that? Not Rupert's.'

'Perhaps he's had too many demands on him to spend enough time at home. He's so into politics now, and down at Central Office half the time. We could take their girls, and let them go on holiday somewhere, couldn't we?'

'Don't you think we have children enough? You're like the old woman who lived in a shoe.'

'But I don't live in a shoe, my darling. I live in a huge house with plenty of room for babies. And if you think that's a hint, it is.'

'Do you mean . . .?'

'Yes, darling. October, I think. Now close your mouth, and go and fetch the pudding. It's on the kitchen table.'

≈

'It's late. I didn't think you'd ring so late.'

'I wanted to hear your voice, Sarah.'

'Well, you've heard it. Now go to bed, Hartley. You've got exams to study for. You don't want to fail.'

'I won't fail. Have you read my letter?'

'Yes.'

'Well, what's the answer?'

'I'll tell you at Easter. Now go to bed.'

Afterwards, Sarah kneeled beside the bed, fingering her rosary. She prayed for everyone she loved: Joe, Alexander, Catherine, Jim, her father, Hartley. She prayed for Gerard, who she had loved dearly. At last she put the beads to her lips and kissed them. 'And Hamish, Father. God rest his soul.'

≈

Catherine had read and reread the letter since this morning. Now she almost knew it by heart. Max's son Aaron was 13 and had just had his barmitzvah. Max was hoping to work in a hospital in Jerusalem, but things were still in a state of flux in the aftermath of the truce.

Catherine had read about the truce signed on the island of Rhodes after weeks of wrangling. As far as she had been able to make out from the newspapers, agreement had only been reached because the UN negotiator had given way to the Jewish side. Beersheba, the town on a strategic crossroads had been

Arab under the UN's plans, but Israel had taken it by force, and the UN was allowing them to keep it. But the Arab nations would not agree to recognise Israel as a country in its own right. 'There'll be trouble,' Catherine had thought as she read.

But there was no mention of that in Max's letter. It was full of optimism, almost joyful. '*I think often, Catherine, of how your presence in my life made those years of war bearable. If things had been different . . . but we were not the arbiters of our own fate. The winds of war blow without thought for whatever is in their path.*'

It was true, and they were still not free from war. It was everywhere. There was unrest in Palestine, in Kashmir, in China. She turned back to the letter. '*I hope you are well and happy, and that you are not alone. Think kindly of me, Catherine, and this new and imperilled country. And be sure I think fondly and often of you, Max.*'

She held the letter in her hand for a while, but she did not cry. There was a time when tears dried, and that time had come. Besides, she had the gift that Max had left with her. She put the letter away, and went in search of her son.

BOOK 3

Chapter Nineteen

December 1949

DAVID HAD SETTLED CATHERINE IN a seat by the window, and stationed himself opposite. 'Hopefully we'll have the carriage to ourselves all the way. Comfortable?'

'Very,' she said. 'In fact, I feel cherished.' He had brought her chocolates and Vichy water, and magazines were piled on the seat beside her.

'It's a long journey,' David said. 'I'm grateful to you for coming with me, so I want to make it as pain-free as possible. You won't miss Ben too much, will you? Valerie wanted to come as well, but Diana is still so young.'

'She couldn't leave an eight-week old baby,' Catherine said firmly. 'And you can't just cart it off to London.'

David shook a rueful head. 'I never realised babies needed such a mass of equipment. Still, I can't remember encountering a single baby before Ben, so my ignorance is understandable.'

They were silent for a while, gazing from the window as Durham gave way to North Yorkshire.

'Will I understand everything?' Catherine asked suddenly.

'In London?' He wasn't sure what she meant.

'When we go to Central Office? The political stuff.'

'You'll understand as much as I will. Remember, I'm a novice too. It should all be straightforward: what the

Conservative Party is planning, what will be in the manifesto, what they want us to concentrate on locally. That's why it's so good to have you with me.'

'I only hope I'm going to be a real help to you, David. You're insisting on paying me, and I'm completely unqualified. You could have found someone really knowledgeable.'

'I couldn't. Good agents don't come along very often, and, besides, I'd feel uncomfortable with someone who was just a mercenary. Not really sharing my views, just doing it for the money. You and I think alike, Catherine – or I think we do.'

She just smiled at that, and he lapsed into silence. How could he explain that just to have her near him gave him pleasure? 'I love Valerie,' he thought. 'I would never betray her, but I need Catherine in my life. In whatever way that can be managed.' If Max Detweiler had been a free man, he and Catherine would have married, and she would have crossed an ocean to live with him. Was it selfish to be glad that hadn't happened? If so, he was guilty of selfishness.

'We might go to a theatre,' he said as they pulled out of York station. 'They say Lesley Storm is wonderful in *Black Chiffon* at the Westminster – or there's the ballet. They're doing the *Nutcracker* at Sadler's Wells. Anyway, you'll enjoy tonight. I've known Howard and Vanessa for years. Howard was at Eton with Henry and me, and married Vanessa in 1943. I think it was '43. You'll like her, and they always have a mixed bunch of guests. Great fun.'

He was silent for a while, and then he grimaced. 'Sometimes I feel overcome at the thought of what I'm doing. Standing for Parliament, I mean. Am I up to it?'

'David!' He smiled at the indignation in her voice. 'Do you remember, before Henry died, or just afterwards, you said you weren't up to running the estate? And you've made a success of that, a great success. Everyone says so – the people you care about in the villages, Sarah has told me how they feel. Of course you'll make a wonderful MP.'

'I want to make a difference, Catherine. War has traumatised this country. Oh, we laugh and joke, and we're relieved to be at peace again, but there's an enormous amount of hurt underneath the bonhomie. Look at the tide of divorce that is sweeping the country. And housing . . . I was speaking to a couple yesterday: he lost a leg at Arnhem, so he can't go back to his trade. He was a haulage driver. So he's out of work on a pittance of a pension, living in with in-laws who don't want him. I watched the mother and daughter squeezing past one another in a kitchen the size of one of Kynaston's cupboards – 24, Catherine, I've counted them! – and I felt ashamed. Think of the struggle Pamela and Michael have had, after his efforts in the RAF. Even those who have houses are cold because of fuel shortages; women still have to queue to feed their families. There's certainly a job to be done.'

'And you're the man to do it. Now, shall we open these delicious chocolates? And I'm not going to ask where the sweet coupons came from in case you've committed a crime!'

'So she's dumped young Ben on you?'

Hannah was getting ready to criticise, but Sarah was having none of it. 'She's looked after my two plenty, Hannah, so don't begrudge her. Anyroad, what's going on in Belgate?' She was becoming an expert at diverting Hannah with the prospect of gossip.

'Everybody's putting their gardens back. The Andersons are all being dug up. Some are keeping them for sheds, but most want shot of them.'

'How can you make a shed out of an underground shelter?'

'Well, if you're daft enough you can do anything. And talking of daftness, Lady Muck's going on a foreign holiday. Foreign!'

Sarah knew who Lady Muck was. She was commonly called
Lady Muck of Vinegar Hill because she thought herself above
her neighbours – her husband was an overman.

'Where's she going?'

'God knows, she just keeps on about abroad. Anyroad,
catch me going up in an aeroplane. Did you see that in the
paper, last month I think it was, about 142 people killed in
plane crashes?'

'Not in this country, though,' Sarah objected.

'Exactly!' Hannah's tone was triumphant. 'Exactly. All them
crashes were foreign, and she's champing at the bit to get out
there.'

'Well, forget Lady Muck – what else is happening?'

Suddenly Hannah looked shifty. Sarah knew that look. It
meant she was working out how much to tell.

'What else?' she repeated.

'There's a lot of talk about the GIs.'

The GIs' camp that had mushroomed outside Belgate was
still in operation. The American soldiers could be seen in town
sometimes in their fancy uniforms.

'What talk?'

'Well – there's talk about one or two walking out with them.
Married ones, an' all.'

Inside Sarah a suspicion grew. 'Which ones, Hannah? Which
married ones? You might as well spit it out.'

'Well, I'm not saying it's true. I haven't seen them. But I have
heard that your Jim's Molly . . .' Her words tailed off at the
sight of Sarah's face.

＝＝＝

'So it's all there for the taking, Pammy. For years people have
been starved of stuff. Cups, plates, lights, soft furnishings . . .
and all you could get was utility. I mean, firms are still using

pre-war designs! Change the colour of the box, and it'll sell. But underneath there's a hunger for something new, and we're beginning to tap into it.'

Pamela looked at her father's face, alight with enthusiasm. They had been going over the order book, and it looked good. They had started to use aluminium, now, and laminated wood, which were cheaper than traditional materials, and suited the mood of the day for things that were light, and portable, and brightly coloured.

'The Scandinavians are catching on, Daddy. I've seen one or two good things from there. Still, we're ahead of the game.'

When he had left the office, she sat back in her chair and eased her neck and shoulders. She had been hunched over the books for too long. She looked at the clock. In an hour she would pack up and collect John from her mother, then be home in time to make Michael's tea.

'I'm happy,' she thought. 'Daddy is his old self again, Mummy has a grandchild to fuss over, Michael is almost well – and if I can get pregnant again soon I'll be the happiest woman in the world.'

They went straight to Central Office from King's Cross. Outside the windows of the cab, London was dressed for Christmas, and teemed with life. 'A lot of people are still in uniform,' Catherine said, surprised.

David nodded. 'It's a favourite place for leave. And if you look closely, many of them are GIs.'

They were turning into Smith Square now, and Catherine felt her heart beat faster. David squeezed her hand.

'Don't worry. If we have to, we can bluff our way through between us.'

They were shown into an office that was surprisingly

shabby, but the chairs they were ushered to were comfortable, the tea that was served came with biscuits and in china cups, and the man across the desk was eager to impart wisdom.

'The Tories won't win, of course. You can't reverse a landslide in one fell swoop. But we'll do well, and you'll be all right in your seat, Sir David, I'm sure.'

'I'll do my best.' To himself, David sounded nervous and uncertain, but the other man seemed satisfied.

'What's on our side? Well, devaluation, of course. People are still reeling from the pound almost halving in value. The financial world is still in shock, never mind the poor, bewildered man in the street. And the Chancellor, the holier-than-thou Sir Stafford Cripps, denied nine times that devaluation would happen. Nine times! So the message there is not only that they can't save the pound, but that you can't believe a word they say.

'We expect that they will soft-pedal on Socialism in their manifesto. The public have had enough of nationalisation. Aneurin Bevan is pushing for more, of course, and that's leading to dissension within the party, which is all to the good for us. We're continuing to push the groundnuts thing – nothing like a joke for capturing the public.'

He saw the incomprehension on Catherine's face, and she felt herself blush as he explained. 'The Labour Government ploughed money into a scheme to grow groundnuts in Tanganyika. An idea to supply vegetable oil when we were running out of it. Only trouble was, they failed to find out how to do it, or even if it could be done. Result – total failure.'

'I see,' Catherine said, although she only half-understood.

'What about the press?' David asked.

'Apart from the *Mirror* and the *Herald*, the big ones are with us. The *Manchester Guardian* and the *News Chronicle* will both stick with the Liberals, I expect, but we're all right in that quarter. And don't be too disheartened. Last time, Labour had the national mood on their side, but they can't count on that again. Besides, they're tired. Tired and not well, if rumour is to be believed.'

'Not well?' David had leaned forward.

'Morrison had a thrombosis last year. Nearly snuffed it, I'm told. Ellen Wilkinson, who was besotted with him, died of an overdose of barbiturates while he was in hospital. They say she was depressed because Labour hadn't achieved more. Attlee has, or had, a bleeding ulcer, and Bevin and Cripps both look like ailing men.' The man chuckled macabrely. 'One through over-indulgence, and the other through denying himself almost everything.

'We intend to go after them over food. We're planning posters showing horse and whale, and saying: "*That's what Socialists have to offer.*" That suggests we can offer them fillet steak – which, of course, we can't. But they'd do the same to us.'

~~~~~

India had come to enjoy her sessions in the beauty salon. At first she had come for something to do, because she was bored. Now she enjoyed the feeling of being pampered. It reminded her of pre-war days when you had people fussing over you. Servants might now be too conscious of their rights to give a fig for making comfortable the people who paid their wages, but in the beauty salon the client reigned supreme.

Today she was having a manicure, and Angela was in the next chair having the same.

'So apparently it's coming out next month in *Ladies' Home Journal*, which has a huge circulation.'

'I can hardly believe it,' India said. 'She always seemed so devoted.' She was digesting the news that Crawfie, Marion Crawford, governess to the Princesses Elizabeth and Margaret Rose, was telling all in an American magazine.

'They say she's leaving nothing out.'

'Are you sure?' India asked.

'Positive. My cousin works for a publisher in New York. He says the market's agog for it.'

They were still consumed by this latest treachery when India's sister-in-law, Valerie, entered the salon.

'India!'

'Valerie.' She allowed the other woman's lips to brush her cheek. 'Are the children well? And my brother – is he still in the land of the living? I never see him nowadays.'

Valerie was smiling that ever-present, stupid smile of hers. 'He's in London, India. He went off with Catherine today. You know she's helping him with his campaign. They're there till the weekend.'

'How nice. But he left you behind. Too bad!'

'David wanted me to go with them, but Diana is too small and too precious to leave, at the moment.'

After Valerie had been ushered to a cubicle, India fumed. She couldn't care less about Valerie – if she was too stupid to see what was going on under her nose, she deserved all she got. But Catherine Allerton was another matter. Not content with killing Henry, she had obviously got her claws into another Callingham. Something would have to be done.

<hr />

'That's right, Daddy. Just trickle the water over.' The baby was kicking his legs, enjoying making the water churn. 'I must stop thinking of John as a baby,' Pam thought. 'He's almost a toddler, now.' Aloud she said, 'Lift him out now. That's it, on to the towel.'

She loved bath-time, seeing Michael relaxed and happy as he always was when around his beloved son. And the little boy was pure joy. Perhaps one was enough, because there could never be another as perfect.

They carried the sweet-smelling child up to bed, settled him down, lit the nightlight, and tip-toed from the room.

'How did your day go?' she asked as they sat down to supper.

'Pretty well. There's a boy in my class with a real future, if he gets his chance. They're promising such wonderful things for Britain's schools, Pamela. Can they keep their word?'

'Probably not all their words, darling. Politicians always overreach themselves when it comes to promises. But I'm sure they'll try.'

'Anyway, what about you?'

'My day was rather splendid. Daddy is like a child with a new toy. Business is expanding; he's got a new machine that isn't second-hand. He says the sky's the limit.'

'So you'll all be filthy rich, and this poor old penniless schoolmaster will be surplus to requirements?'

To her surprise Pamela felt her eyes fill with tears. 'Have you any idea, any idea at all, how much I love you?'

He was round the table in a moment. 'You silly, silly goose. I know you'd never leave me, because if you did I'd track you down and drag you home by the hair.'

When their embrace ended, she wiped her eyes and got up to fetch the pudding. All in all, it had been an absolutely perfect day.

'Do come and meet everyone, Catherine.' The room seemed full of terribly sophisticated people all engaged in enthusiastic conversation.

'This is Cassandra Cassell,' said her hostess Vanessa, 'and this is her husband Eliot who writes *the* most penetrating column in Fleet Street.'

Catherine murmured a greeting, and was then whisked away to meet the next pair. Across the room she could see David deep in conversation with Howard, their host. He looked up, caught her eye, and raised interrogative eyebrows. 'I'm all right,' she mouthed back, and smiled to show it was true.

'And this is Will Devine, who wrote the most marvellous book about the demise of the man about town,' her hostess said. 'He is a very bad boy, but I must leave you with him because I see the Caulfields have arrived. Will, meet Lady Callingham – Catherine.'

The man in front of her was thin and pale, with floppy hair that he pushed back now with one hand. The other hand grasped hers. 'So you're David Callingham's wife.'

'I'm not, I'm honestly not. His wife is Valerie. I'm just a friend – well, actually his sister-in-law.'

The writer was laughing now, and suddenly more attractive. 'All right, you don't need to protest so much. I'm relieved that you're not married to David. Now tell me you're not married to anyone else, and my cup of happiness will overflow.'

⁓

Sarah had settled the children, and was sitting down to listen to the wireless. She loved *Monday Night at Eight,* so the knock at the door was an irritation. Who could be calling at this hour? Not Hannah. Was something wrong at home? Since Hannah had hinted about Molly, Sarah she had been worried. Trouble of that kind would break Jim's heart, and what it would do to her father, if it were true, did not bear thinking about.

It was neither Hannah nor Jim on the step. It was Hartley.

'What are you doing here?' she said, but she drew him over the step just the same.

And she knew in that moment how the night would end. She could sense the need in him, had sensed it almost from the start; and now there was a need in her that matched it.

They made love in the dark. She saw relief in his face when she asked him to put out the light. In the end it was she who undressed him, gently as she might have done with a child. Then she folded him into the bed, and stood to divest herself of clothes. When skin touched skin, he was trembling, and she soothed him. 'It's going to be all right.'

'I've never . . .'

She shut off his words with her fingertips.

'I know,' she said. 'I know.' And then she was guiding him into her, and they were rocking together, gently at first and then faster and faster until, as she felt the breath go out of him and his full weight descend on her, a miracle took place inside her, and she cried out, 'God Almighty!' at the wonder of the feeling.

They ate in silence nowadays, except for 'Do you want more bread?' Or, 'Could you pass the salt?' Tonight, though, India needed to know how much Rupert knew. 'I saw Valerie at the salon today. She says David has gone to London on election business – did you know that?'

'I did.'

'You might have told me.'

'I didn't think it was anything to do with you.'

'Did you know he's taken Catherine Allerton with him?'

'If you mean Catherine Callingham, yes, I know. As she's acting as his agent, I took it for granted she'd go too.'

'Will he win at the election with an agent who knows nothing about politics . . . and very little about anything else?'

'There's every chance. Now, I know the purpose of this inter-rogation: you're digging for dirt. Well, there is none. Not a speck. So, if you're determined on a discourse, can we discuss an important topic . . . that concentration-camp guard you've seen fit to engage to care for my daughters?'

Catherine's bedroom in David's town house looked out on a quiet Westminster street. She stood by the window, for a while, gazing at London. It was one o'clock in the morning, but there were still cruising cabs passing by, and the odd person on foot hurrying somewhere. 'London never sleeps,' she thought, which probably explained why she couldn't sleep – or, at least, had no desire to.

She thought of the glittering dinner-table tonight. Everyone so very sure of themselves. And Will Devine. He had insisted on knowing where she was staying, and, when she was leaving, had lifted her hand to his lips and kept it there until, embarrassed, she snatched it away. He had laughed, then, and whispered in her ear, 'You are delicious, Catherine Callingham.' Silly.

The whole evening had been silly – all that talk of Juan les Pins, and nicknames flying about, and then terribly serious talk about the Chinese civil war, which had almost escaped her notice entirely but was obviously of enormous importance. 'I'll soon be home,' she thought, consolingly. She wanted to go home to everything that was familiar and safe.

But something had happened tonight. She wasn't sure quite what, but it was but something . . . When at last she climbed into bed, she lay for a long while looking out at the night sky. There were no stars – only one or two so faint that she could hardly make them out. At home, the stars were always clear, but here, in London, the stars seemed to have paled in contrast with the city's brilliance.

Chapter Twenty

February 1950

DAVID WOKE BEFORE DAYLIGHT. ELECTION Day had come at last, and by midnight he would know whether or not he was the new MP for Belgate. The retiring Conservative member, George Harris, had had a majority of 16,000 before the war, but the 1945 election had seen it cut to 5,400. Another drop like that, and Labour would carry the day.

There had been smiling faces as he canvassed, but, since many of the men worked on the estate, they could hardly afford to scowl at him. How they might vote was a different matter. Their wives, for the most part, had stayed silent. 'What do they really think of me?' he wondered, and then he remembered Catherine's words last night: *'They couldn't do better than vote for you, David. You're a good man.'*

Beside him, Valerie stirred. 'Is it time to get up?'

He turned on his side and kissed her tenderly. 'Not yet. Go back to sleep. It's going to be a long day.'

Sarah woke as light began to filter through the curtains. She listened for a moment: no children crying or getting up to mischief. She snuggled down for a few minutes of peace.

Catherine would be with David all day, so the care of the children would be up to her. She didn't mind. Ben and Alexander played happily enough together, and Joe . . . she smiled foolishly into the darkness . . . Joe was a good bairn, a bairn in a thousand, even if she said it herself.

A picture came into her mind: the day he had flinched as his stepfather Hamish approached him. That had given her the courage to run away. She could scarcely believe she had made that trip, on her own with two small children. But she had done it, and all that sadness was behind them now. She had tried hard not to feel relief that Hamish had died, but it had been a relief and no mistake. 'It was the war,' she reminded herself. The war might be over, but it was still wreaking havoc in people's lives.

Today she was going to walk the children to the village, record her vote, and then see how the land lay at her father's house. She knew now that what Hannah had hinted at last Christmas was true: Molly was carrying on with a GI. Catherine had seen her with him in Durham, and said that he looked Italian – a pleasant face, and black curly hair. But he couldn't be as handsome or half as kind as Jim. What made women want another man? Their eyes must be too big for their bellies, and that was a fact.

Except that with GIs it was pure greed, mostly. Women had ever-open hands for what was unobtainable elsewhere: chocolate, and chewing gum, and nylon stockings – though what was so special about a stocking the wind could blow through Sarah couldn't work out. The Yanks were generous, you couldn't deny that. They didn't just lure women for their own satisfaction, trails of children followed them everywhere and seldom went away empty-handed. A GI had given Joe a candy bar once, when she was in Sunderland. And he'd blushed, and said, 'Shucks, it's nothing, Ma'am,' when she thanked him.

But it wasn't all sweets and kind words. They drove like

crazy men in their jeeps and on their motorcycles, tearing up and down country lanes. And she didn't like tales she heard of the way they treated the black men among them, even holding separate dances for whites and blacks, as though the blacks were scum.

How had it started with Molly? With a candy bar for her children, or a pair of nylon stockings?

As she got washed and dressed, Sarah she was still reflecting on the strangeness of human beings. What made Hartley want her, for instance? She was not particularly pretty, and certainly not half as clever as he was.

Suddenly, outside the window, she heard a booming voice. Someone was drumming up support for one candidate or another. She herself had decided to vote for David Callingham. She would once never have dreamed of voting Tory – what person of mining stock would? But David was a good man, who would do his best for everyone. Besides, a vote against him would be hurtful for Catherine, and she owed Catherine everything.

She buttoned up her cardigan, and got ready to set about breakfast. She would have to keep quiet about voting when she got to her father's, though. He was red-hot Labour, and Jim was worse. Sarah was thinking over what she would say if they asked her outright how she'd voted, when she remembered that her period was due about now. A glance at the calendar confirmed it. It should have come yesterday.

Still, no need to panic over 24 hours.

———

An astonishing number of people had turned out to help with David's campaign. Some of them Catherine had met when she went to London, others were strangers. All morning they had ferried voters to and from the polls, and now they were assembling for refreshments.

'How is it going?' she asked, looking up from the sheets she was attempting to keep up to date.

One driver shook his head. 'You can't tell. If they accept a lift, you assume they're yours, but you can't be sure. Secret ballot – they can please themselves.'

A woman chimed in, then. 'I'm optimistic. One or two of them were mentioning Fuchs.'

Catherine was surprised. Klaus Fuchs was the scientist charged with giving the secrets of the atom bomb to Russia. Now he was on trial for treachery – but what had he to do with the election?

'These voters don't particularly care for the Tories, but the Russians really scare them,' the woman explained.

'And they think the Tories are anti-Russian?'

There was all-round muttering. 'You can't tell how voters' minds work,' one man said at last. 'Elections are lotteries. Look at the last one, with poor old Churchill tossed aside after he'd won the war. But that wasn't as unexpected as people said. Twenty-two sitting MPs were killed during the war, 21 of them Tories. And when that caused by-elections, who took the seats? Not the Tories, but a rag-bag of Left-wingers and crazies. Tom Driberg, as Left-wing as they come, but standing as an independent, walked in in Maldon. Some of the candidates were pacifists – and they still won.'

The woman spoke up again. 'If you mean Ernest Millington, he was a pacifist before the war, but he served in the RAF. So he'd changed his mind.'

'Well, he still took a Tory seat for the Commonwealth Party, whatever that means. And had "This is a fight between Christ and Churchill" as his slogan.'

'I can't believe that.' Catherine was aghast.

'It's true,' the woman insisted. 'He had a banner saying just that put up in the Market Square, as though Winston were the Devil.'

Catherine was still trying to take this in when they went back to their duties. She was ticking off the names on the electoral roll, when she heard someone clear their throat. She looked up to see a huge bunch of chrysanthemums and a head slowly emerging from behind it.

'Hello, Catherine.'

'Will!'

'It is me. I couldn't stay away. Besides, I'm a loyal friend of the candidate, and dedicated to the cause. I had to come.'

She was laughing at him. He made her laugh ever since their first meeting. He had taken her to see *The Third Man* in London, and then played 'The Harry Lime Theme' to her on a comb and paper, in the middle of a London street – not giving a fig for what people might think.

All the same, David hadn't given the impression that he and Will were friends. She'd got the distinct impression that David didn't care for him; and he'd dismissed the book that had made Will's name as a 'one-day wonder'.

'I didn't expect to see you here,' she said weakly.

'Well, if you won't come to me, I have to come to you. I'm hoping David will give me a roof. He jolly well should, when I've come all this way to help his campaign.'

'I thought you'd come to see me.'

'I have. But I'm multi-talented. I can woo you and shove him into Parliament at the same time.'

Catherine tried to look composed, even nonchalant, but it wasn't easy because her heart was thumping fiercely in her chest.

———

India had offered to help at the election. 'I can take one of the cars, and drive people to the polling booths.'

But Rupert had been adamant. 'I don't want you there, India. Neither would David, if he had any sense. You've done your level best to undermine him from the outset. Whatever makes you think you have anything to offer now?'

'He's my brother,' she said heatedly.

'How I wish you'd remembered that earlier, India. Sooner or later you will have to learn that actions have consequences. You share a trait with many of the people who come before me when I'm on the bench: a chronic inability to understand that chickens come home to roost.'

'You are a pompous, silly little man,' she had replied, but only under her breath.

Rupert had gone off at first light to fuss over his wretched polling booths. 'God, I will be glad when this is over,' India thought. Nanny had the children out somewhere, and the house was quiet. Not that she wanted elephant feet thundering everywhere, and shrill little voices making demands. Rupert had ruined Loelia, in spite of her efforts.

She walked to the window, and then remembered that she would see only those wretched roofs. Nothing for it but to have a drink, even if it was still breakfast-time. One drink . . . a small one . . . would make the whole thing more bearable.

━━━

Pamela drove carefully. She was still not at ease behind the wheel, and the old Ford wasn't easy to drive. All the same, she and Michael had agreed it was important to back David up. Look at what he had done for her father – that alone deserved a favour.

'We need men like him in Parliament,' Michael had said. 'I don't like the way things are going, Pam. We're too dependent on America; we stagger from one financial crisis to another. This government is dismantling the Royal Navy – up and down the country they're destroying perfectly good warships. Over 800 have been dismantled already, and more than 700 cancelled on the stocks. It's the Navy today; will it be the RAF tomorrow? And all the while, Russia is building up its armed forces to more than their wartime strength.'

'There couldn't be another war?' Pamela had asked. But the vehement denial she had hoped for did not come in reply. So today she was driving for David. What he could do, single-handed, she wasn't sure, but if she hadn't been doing this today, she'd just be sitting wondering whether or not she was pregnant.

She slowed down to read the numbers: 36, 34, 32 . . . that was the one.

'Mrs Fossett? I've come to take you to the polling booth.'

'What time will you be back?'

'The polls close at 9. David says I needn't stay for the count, which could go on into the early hours. So I should be home by 9.30. Will you be all right until then?'

Sarah reassured Catherine, and put down the phone. It was 3 o'clock, and Hannah had promised to bring the children back in time for tea. They liked spending time with Hannah, who had no rules at all and fed them dolly mixtures, but she and Catherine had agreed that once in a while it couldn't do harm.

She scalded a pot of tea, and carried it through to the morning-room. The fire was low, and she built it up with coal from the scuttle. She liked this house, the house that had always given her shelter, but one day she would have to leave it. She took Hartley's latest letter from her pocket, and began to read it again.

'Sometimes the work overwhelms me, but then I remember what I'm doing it for – so that I can care for you and Joe and Alexander – and then I work like a fiend. Only a few more months, Sarah, and we can be together. It will be a struggle at

first, because I don't expect much help from my parents. But we don't need anyone else, now that we have one another.'

He went on to write of his love for her, a love he swore had come instantly when she had walked into Hannah's kitchen years ago. Could you fall in love like that? She never had: love had always crept up on her slowly, even with Gerard. Did she love Hartley? She did, but at the same time she was afraid of loving him. 'We are chalk and cheese,' she thought.

When he had the posh job he was working towards, she would have to be a proper wife and not let him down. Panic came and went. Catherine would help her; she would know how it should be done. Besides, she made him happy.

Sarah closed her eyes, remembering how he loved her. That first time he had been nervous, and she had needed to guide him. Now he was an adventurous lover, seeming never to get enough of her. She felt her mouth go dry, thinking of him above her and around her, his flesh warm and firm against hers, his voice urgent in her ear. *'Is that good, Sarah. Is it good, good, good . . .'* She felt a sudden wetness between her legs. It must be the tardy period.

Relief overcame her. She wanted Hartley, but she did not want to trap him. A baby on the way would make it impossible for him to leave her. But when she went upstairs to check her underwear, there was no sign of the longed-for blood. She splashed her face with cold water, and closed her eyes in a prayer that God would make it all come right.

———

They had been counting for hours, now, and still the piles of votes cast for Labour and Conservative were even.

'Relax,' Valerie whispered in David's ear.

But it was impossible to relax. 'It's going to be close,' the man from the regional office said. 'I rang Roger a few moments ago. Same thing in his constituency. It's going to be tight.'

The returning officer was approaching them, looking solemn. 'We expect the result by 2.30, or 3 a. m. at the latest, Sir David.'

Three more hours. 'Can I last that long?' David murmured.

'Of course you can, darling.' Valerie squeezed his hand. 'You're wonderful – you can do anything you put your mind to.'

He smiled down at her. 'You're a terrible liar, Lady Callingham, but I do love you.'

———

Catherine was home by 9.15, tired but happy.

'Sit down,' Sarah said. 'You look all in. The kettle's on. What do you want to eat?'

'Nothing.' Catherine was easing off her shoes. 'We've nibbled on things all day. But tea would be Heaven. Children OK?'

'Out like lights, all three of them.'

Sarah made tea and put some shortbread on the tray, just in case. She was carrying it in, eager to hear the doings of the day, when the phone rang in the hall.

'I'll get it.' Catherine was lifting the receiver, and Sarah halted in the doorway, seeing her face pale. 'All right,' she was saying. 'Yes, straight away.' She put down the receiver. 'That was Hannah. You're needed at home, Sarah. Some trouble with Jim. Hannah was ringing from the pub.'

'No one's died, have they? It's not me Dad?'

'No, no one has died. But there's been a fracas between Jim and Molly. The police are at the house.' Catherine hesitated, and then picked up the phone again. 'I want a taxi to come to Mellows, on the Belgate road. Double fare if you get here quickly.'

She put down the receiver. 'I can't drive you there, because someone has to stay with the children. But the cab'll be here in five minutes. Stay there as long as you're needed, and get a taxi back. Unless you're still there in the morning, in which case I'll come for you. And don't worry . . . well, try not to. Now, let me get you some money.'

⸻

The journey to the village seemed to Sarah to last forever. What had happened? Had Jim attacked the American? Would he go to prison?

The sight of the house, with all the lights blazing, was both a relief and a shock. At this time of night there was usually only a chink of light from the living-room.

Hannah opened the door to her, looking shocked. 'By, I'm glad you're here, Sarah. What a carry-on!'

Sarah pushed past her. There were two policemen in the room, one standing by the fireplace, the other seated at the kitchen table. Jim was seated opposite. Of Molly there was no sign.

Sarah crossed to her father's side. 'Dad? What's going on?'

'You might well ask.'

She turned to the policeman. 'Will someone tell me what's going on?'

'And you are . . .?'

'I'm Sarah Carlyle, Jim's sister. Is he under arrest?'

'Not yet, Miss. We're taking a statement. The inspector will be here shortly.'

'Where's Molly . . . where's his wife?'

It was her father who answered. 'She's upstairs with an eye out on her cheek, and a split lip. She's asked for it, but I cannot believe a son of mine hit a woman.'

His words roused Jim to fury. 'She betrayed me, Dad! Betrayed all of us – you, me, and her bairns.'

'You shouldn't have hit her, Jim.' Sarah was thinking of her own face when a blow had landed on it. As if he read her thoughts, Jim turned on her.

'Men get the blame, but mebbe it's women who bring it on

themselves. I took your side against Hamish – of course I did. But now, it makes me wonder . . .'

Sarah heard him with mounting horror. Was he saying she had deserved what Hamish had done to her?

She felt Hannah's arm come round her, and then the older woman was speaking. 'It's the war has done this, Jim. Turned half the men into spivs and scroungers, and the rest into cuckolds. Women have been ground down by years of shortages and making do, and that's why yon Yanks have got away with it. They're glamour, Jim, and the likes of Molly are craving it.'

When Sarah was safely away to Belgate, Catherine sat down to drink her tea. It was still hot, and she sipped it gratefully, thinking back over the night's events. It had been a night of tensions, but no one could have expected it to end like this.

She still thought David would win, but there was no denying that there was opposition to him. 'He's a toff,' Will Devine had said. 'That's against him for a start. They're preaching Red revolution out there, these Socialists. At their conference there was this man called Dennis Healey, still in uniform, and breathing fire. According to him, the upper classes are selfish, depraved, dissolute and decadent. An impudent oaf – but terrific fun.'

Catherine had chided Will for thinking that something so unpleasant could be classed as fun. 'I thought the war would put an end to class division,' she had said, but he'd only laughed further. 'He thinks everything is funny,' she thought. 'It's part of his charm, but it's frightening, too.' He earned his living as a writer – 'Only the best periodicals, darling' – and it was pretty obvious David didn't care for him. But she would probably never see him again.

She was rinsing her cup in the kitchen when the doorbell rang. Sarah surely had a key? She ran across the hall, anxious that the caller shouldn't ring again and wake the children. But it was not Sarah on the step, it was Will Devine.

She stood looking at him, and he shrugged and held up his palms in supplication. 'If the mountain won't come to Muhammad, Muhammad must come to the mountain.'

———

It was after midnight when the whisper came. 'You're in, David. Majority's well down, but you're safely home. They'll announce it in a moment or two, so get ready.' David felt his heart stutter in its beat. Had he done the right thing? Was he up to this? And then Valerie was squeezing his hand and smiling up at him, and he knew it was going to be all right.

'What about the rest of the country?' he asked. The answer was a rueful shake of the head. So Labour were back in, and he would be with the Tories on the Opposition benches.

'That doesn't matter, darling.' Valerie was still smiling. 'You never wanted to be part of the ruling élite. You simply wanted to change things, and now you'll have that chance. I'm so very, very proud of you.'

'I couldn't have done it without you, Valerie.'

'I did my bit . . . and so did Catherine. As soon as it's over, find a telephone and tell her the good news.'

Around them a sudden silence fell, as the returning officer mounted the platform. David felt a buzzing in his ears as the announcements began – and then came the words that mattered . . . 'I hereby declare that the aforementioned David Callingham is duly elected for the constituency of Belgate in the County of Durham.'

People were cheering, and David felt a sudden relief that no one was booing. 'I will do my best,' he told himself; and any doubts he felt at his ability to fulfil the task faded as he looked down into his wife's trusting face.

Chapter Twenty One

June 1950

'WELL, SHE DOESN'T GO SHORT, I can tell you,' Hannah said. 'They're all walking round looking at their legs as though they were gold-plated.'

Sarah smiled, although talk of the current obsession with nylon stockings was a painful reminder of her sister-in-law, Molly. That had begun with the gift of a pair of nylons, and look where it had ended.

'Yes,' she said, 'women have gone crazy for them, all right.' A few weeks earlier, customs men had seized a liner in Liverpool and found it stuffed with illegally imported nylons, more than £80,000-worth. Every woman wanted them, or so it seemed. Personally, she was happy with lisle, or silk for special occasions. If nylons hadn't laddered in the same way silk stockings, did she might have been more bothered. As it was, she was indifferent.

'Anyroad,' Hannah said, pushing forward her cup, 'your Jim's making a good fist of looking after his kids. She was always flighty, that Molly. I could've told him.'

'It's a pity you didn't,' sprang to Sarah's lips, but she bit back the words. Molly was gone, and Jim had not wound up in prison, so that was a blessing – but she herself no longer felt welcome in her father's house, and that was a curse. She smiled and chatted to Hannah, but her heart wasn't in it. The look that Jim had given her that night, his sudden realisation that women might bring on their own misfortune, had hurt Sarah badly. And his bitterness was terrible to witness. '*I didn't have the glamour of a fancy uniform, I just went down the hole for her and her bairn*s.'

Aloud she said now: 'Catherine's gone to London today. Just till the weekend.' She shifted in her seat, anxious that Hannah's sharp eyes should not detect the gentle mound of her belly. But even as she did so she knew it was futile. She couldn't keep a baby quiet forever.

As if Hannah read her mind, she raised the subject. 'How's that Hartley? And don't crack on like you don't know who I'm talking about. When are you two going to stop waffling on? Are you going to get wed, or not? I've been thinking for a bit of having a perm – well, everyone seems to, nowadays. But if there's a wedding coming up, I'll hang on.'

'India.'

'David.'

Their acknowledgement of one another was civil, and David had to smile at the relief on the solicitor's face.

'Do sit down,' he said, and began to put papers requiring their signature in front of them. It took only a few moments; and then they both declined an offer of coffee, and made for the door. They had very few assets in common now, so their business was easily done, and that suited them both.

'Have you got the car?' David asked. 'If not, I'm going your way.'

'I'm driving, David. It's such a relief to have petrol back. I hate being dependent.' Petrol-rationing had ended after a decade, to universal rejoicing. At some garages, drivers had torn up coupons and danced round their cars.

'Yes,' David said, 'ten years is a long time. You and Rupert must come to dinner soon. Valerie was just saying we see too little of you.'

'One day we will, but life is so hectic at the moment. How are you enjoying the House?'

David murmured something about Parliament's being rather intimidating to a new boy. He had momentarily considered trying to explain the emotion he had felt on his first day in the House of Commons, but India wouldn't have understood the wonder of suddenly finding yourself part of the fabric of history.

As they walked back to the car, he could see that something was welling up inside her. At last the temptation to speak became too much.

'Valerie has certainly changed Kynaston.'

'Yes,' David said. 'She's made it a happy place.'

Mercifully, they were at her car, and she could fold herself into the seat without delivering the reply he could see bubbling on her lips.

———

'Yes, Mrs Hamilton, you're definitely pregnant. Now take it easy – no mountain-climbing.'

As she came out into the street, Pamela felt she didn't need a mountain to climb. She was walking on air. A baby! A brother or sister for John! Another proof of their happiness.

She would have to give up work once there were two children to care for, but she and Michael could manage. He was earning, and she was getting tiny dividends from the factory now. Besides, she could deal with anything when they were together.

She couldn't wait until tea-time to tell Michael. He was

never keen on her interrupting him at school, but today was a special occasion. She stood in the corridor outside the class-room for a while, watching him with the class. He smiled a lot, and so did the children. 'He's a good teacher,' Pamela thought – but then she had always known he would be.

She waited until one child, more perceptive than the rest, spotted her lurking there. She could see a buzz going round the class, and eventually Michael sensed it. He looked up, and their eyes met. At first, he looked alarmed but her beam told him all was well. He said something to the class then, and came to the door.

'We're going to have a baby,' she said, and saw from his face how pleased he was.

≈

'It's no use arguing, India. It's done.' Rupert had met her in the hall and given her the news. He had dismissed the nanny while she had been with the solicitor and David. Just like that, without a by-your-leave.

'You can't go over my head like this, Rupert. I won't stand for it.'

'Then sit down, my dear, because it's done. That woman is going. Handsomely compensated, you'll be glad to hear, but definitely gone. The house can breathe at last.'

'Nanny's been wonderful with the children.' Even to her own ears, India's words sounded weak. Behind him, on the mantel, were Rupert's prized Meissen figures. She thought of moving forward and smashing one of them into the hearth, but something stayed her. This was a new Rupert, no longer bitter, but almost triumphant in his certainty.

'I won't look after them,' she said, turning away. 'You can run after them, because I shan't.'

'God forbid I should ask you to act like a mother, India. I know my limitations. The role is beyond you. But there'll be no need for either you or me to "run after" the children, as you put it. I've hired a new nanny, Norland-trained. Even you will be hard put to find fault with her. She should be here in an hour.'

He was upstairs checking on the children when the woman he had so shamefully dismissed came into the morning-room, buttoning her leather gloves as she spoke.

'I'm leaving now, Mrs Lindsay-Hogg. I've given my keys to Cook, and I've said goodbye to the children. They'll need feeding at 1 o'clock.' She turned to go, and then turned back. 'I pity you, Madam, I really do.'

India lifted her head. She would not accept pity from a servant. 'I'm sure I don't know what you mean. Don't let me detain you. And don't hesitate to ask if you need a letter of recommendation.'

She stood proudly erect until the woman exited, then she turned and moved to the sideboard. She wanted a drink, and sherry wouldn't do. The whisky burned her mouth, but was strangely comforting. She lifted the decanter and poured herself another.

Catherine had travelled more by train in the past few months than in the whole of the rest of her life, she reflected. Well, almost. She enjoyed watching the Cleveland Hills fall away, and the change from open country to industrial landscape as the train neared Doncaster. She liked train journeys, with their curious feeling of being cut-off. No one could get to you; there was nothing you could do about anything; all you could do was sit back and relax.

But she missed Ben while she was in London, missed Joe and Alexander, too. Ben was so like Max, dark-haired, determined, dexterous even at four years old. Alexander was an imp of mischief, and Joe – Joe was a little father, too caring and sensitive for so young a child. So like that other Joe, his uncle, her first love. 'I love little Joe as though he were my own,' Catherine realised, and smiled to herself.

She thought ahead to London, then. And Will. Did she love him? She couldn't be sure. She only knew that life with him was never boring.

———

'I think that's about it.' Alistair Groom closed the books they had been examining, and shuffled the loose papers. 'Nothing much to worry about with the estate, so you can concentrate on the nation's ailments.'

David smiled. 'They're beyond me, I'm afraid. But at least I attend debates, which is more than can be said for some honourable members.'

'Do you enjoy it?'

'I'm still in awe, if I'm honest. There's so much to learn, so many hidden protocols. I live in fear of treading on someone's toes. But it can be enthralling, especially when one of the great orators is on his feet.'

'They say Aneurin Bevan is mesmerising.'

'Yes, like most Welshman. But I admire Attlee.'

'Barrister, wasn't he, before politics?'

'In the beginning. I believe he taught at the LSE before the First War. He served in that, of course, and was badly wounded. Became Mayor of Stepney not long after.'

'You've studied him!' Alistair sounded surprised.

'Yes,' David said, 'I respect him. Don't look so surprised – all possible good does not reside within the bastions of the Tory Party.'

They were about to take leave of one another when a clerk knocked and put his head round the door. 'They're saying North Korea's invaded the South. Early this morning.'

'Are you sure?'

'It's been on the BBC.'

'I must get back to London, then,' David said. 'There'll be shock waves from this, if it's true.'

'Can I do anything? Catherine will take care of things this end while you're gone, no doubt?'

'Yes. She's a huge help in the constituency office, as you know, but she's in London herself at the moment. Still, we'll manage.' He held out a hand. 'Thank you for keeping such a watchful eye on the estate.'

The other man looked rueful. 'Half the job's gone, along with the pit and the colliery houses. Still, as you were fond of saying, those are better their worry than ours. I hear the colliery lost a man last week. Fall of stone.'

David turned the car towards Kynaston, and put down his foot. He had been looking forward to an evening with Valerie and the children, but if there was a war somewhere, the House would probably hold an emergency debate. His duty lay there.

⸻

'India, this is Nurse Adams. Nurse Adams, my wife.'

India ignored the proffered hand. The girl looked about 17. Wide-eyed and stupid.

'Do you have your qualifications with you?'

Norland College had been founded more than half a century ago, and Norland nurses considered themselves a cut above the average nanny. The Norland motto was 'Love Never Faileth', which, as India had observed to Angela, sounded very wishy-washy. But, since Norland's curriculum was based on some strange German ideas, it would be.

She took the folder the nurse was holding out. 'Thank you, Nurse.'

'My name's Polly, if you'd prefer.'

'I prefer you to be Nurse Adams. To everyone, please.'

'I'll show you the nursery,' Rupert said, putting an arm round the girl's shoulders. 'The children are longing to meet you . . .'

'Liar,' India said, but she said it under her breath. She would have to deal with this situation before the children were ruined, but she wouldn't brawl in front of the servants. She needed to think.

She poured herself a drink. Whisky always seemed to clear her head, organise her thoughts. She was still regretting not being honest with David earlier, and telling him the truth – that she couldn't stand what Valerie Graham-Poole had done to Kynaston, turning it into something resembling a suburban semi, full of servants who didn't know their place. And now Rupert had landed her with a half-wit for a nanny.

Yes, she would think it all through, and then she would make something happen. That's what she always did.

———

They ate from plates on their knee, anxious to be closer to each other than the dining-table would have allowed. David was catching the sleeper at Durham, so they had only an hour left.

'Will there be a war – for us, I mean?' Valerie asked.

'It depends on the United Nations. The Security Council is meeting again tomorrow, and meanwhile they've called for a withdrawal by the North Koreans to the 38th Parallel.'

'I'm not sure what that means, but I hope it works. I couldn't bear another war, David. We've hardly tasted peace yet.'

'I wouldn't worry. I can't believe the world would be foolish enough to plunge back into war. Besides, if you want to worry, there are things closer to home.'

'What? I knew you were anxious about something.'

'It's Will Devine. I've always tolerated him as an amiable idiot, but now I'm not so sure. And I think – I fear – that

Catherine is becoming besotted with him.'

'Is she seeing him when she's in London?'

'Yes. Staying with him, for all I know. He has a place in Half Moon Street.'

'He's not a bad man, is he? I know you're fond of Catherine – do you want me to speak to her?'

'Not yet. But keep your eyes and ears open when you talk to her. She trusts you, my darling. We all do.' He took her hand and raised it to his mouth. 'Especially your husband.'

———

'So you see how it could work out, Sarah? We wouldn't be rich, but I'd work hard at teaching. We'd have to rent at first, but then we'd buy a place. A teacher can get a mortgage. We'd find a house with a garden for the children –'

'You've got it all worked out,' Sarah interrupted, 'but you go too fast for me. You said you didn't want to teach. It's not what your parents want for you . . .'

He cut her short. 'It's my life, Sarah, so it's what I want. It won't pay as much as the other job, but now I think I'll enjoy it more.'

What would he say if he knew there'd be one more mouth to feed than he had bargained for?

After she had put down the phone, she thought about what he'd said. He was going to settle for teaching, and he was doing it because of her. If it hadn't been for the war, his life would have gone on uninterrupted, and he might have become a great man. Would have done, no doubt about it.

Thinking of war reminded her of what she had heard on the wireless about Korea. If there war were to break out again, there would be more turmoil, more lives swept up and carried along like chaff. If there had been no war, she and Gerard would be old marrieds by now, probably with a houseful. She would never have met Hamish, never have set foot in Scotland, and certainly would not be carrying the child of a future schoolteacher. Hartley's life was going to be changed through no fault of his own, and that was problem enough, without a war thrown in.

═══

'Say goodnight to Mummy, Loelia.' Nurse Adams was urging Loelia forward, but the wretched child was hanging back.

'Come along.' India held out a hand, but the girl had buried her face in the nurse's apron. 'Loelia!' The word came out more sharply than she had intended, but it still had no effect.

India heard Rupert's step in the hall, and then he was in the room, taking Imogen from Nurse Adams's arms, and holding her aloft.

'Daddy!'

Loelia would have run to him, but the nurse, freed from the burden of the baby, kept firm hold of the child's hand. 'Give Mummy a kiss and say goodnight.'

'No!' With a wrench, Loelia was free and running to twine herself around her father's legs.

'Loelia!' This time it was Nurse Adams who spoke, her cheeks scarlet with embarrassment.

'I don't want to kiss Mummy. She smells nasty.'

'Loelia,' Rupert was handing the baby back to the nurse and picking up his elder daughter, 'don't be unkind. Say goodnight, like a good girl.'

As usual, the little brat was going to do everything her father wanted. They came towards India, and she turned her cheek for a kiss – but also so that Rupert would not smell the whisky on her breath.

═══

Will had been waiting for Catherine when she arrived at King's Cross, carrying an idiotically large bunch of daisies. 'Stolen from Highgate Cemetery,' he said, holding them out.

'You're quite mad,' she had said, but loving the gesture, just the same.

Now they were seated in a dimly lit club, a bottle of wine on the table between them, a candle glittering in a bottle encrusted with candle grease.

'Penny for them?' Will asked.

Catherine smiled. 'I was wondering about Ben. Has he gone to bed like a good boy, or is he giving Sarah trouble?'

'He'll be sound asleep by now. He's a good boy. Like his mother, who is a little nun.'

'I'm not in the least nun-like. I'm a working woman, and don't you forget it.'

'Heaven forfend. You're up there in coal-land dishing out gruel to the poor and afflicted, while David puts the House to sleep with one of his dreary speeches.'

'That's cruel. As yet he's only made his maiden speech, and I thought it was wonderful.'

'Of course it was. I'm only being beastly because I'm wildly jealous of him.'

'Jealous? Because he's an MP?'

'No – and you know that very well. I'm jealous of any man who has your attention for a single second.'

In the background, the pianist was playing 'In the Still of the Night'.

'Do you want to dance?' Will asked. 'Or shall we go home and make love until we drop from exhaustion?'

She didn't answer. Instead she got to her feet, collected her wrap and evening bag, and let him take her hand and lead her out into the evening air.

Chapter Twenty Two

September 1950

'WAKE UP, HARTLEY. WAKE UP!' Beside her he stirred, groaned, and turned away.

'It's time to get up.' Sarah's anguished whisper at last brought him awake.

'What time is it?'

'Time you weren't in this bed! Joe'll be up in a minute, and he can't see you in here.'

Hartley had long accepted that Sarah's children came first. He groaned again, but dragged himself obediently out of bed and began to fumble into his clothes.

'Go back to your own bed, and you can have another half-hour.'

He shook his head. 'I'm up now. I'm taking the children to Hannah's this morning, if that's all right. She's promised them gingerbread men.'

Inside Sarah, pleasure stirred. He was good with the children, and boys needed a man in their lives. In the past few weeks she had seen the clouds lift for her elder son. He was more forthcoming, even cheeky sometimes, though never in a nasty way. That was Hartley's doing. Alexander had been too young to suffer under Hamish as Joe had done, and he was a Mammy's boy, anyway. But this man was good for him, too. As he would be good for the child growing inside her.

'I'll be down in a minute,' she said. Even now she didn't like him to see her naked. But when she was dressed she would make him a good breakfast. They would sit on either side of the table and talk about Butlins, as they had done last night.

She had heard of Butlins before the war, but never dreamed she would go there. Billy Butlin was a barrow-boy, according to Jim – although Hartley had told her last night that the Butlin fortune came from amusement parks. There'd been three Butlins camps when war broke out, at Skegness, Clacton, and Filey – although that one had been only half built. The army had taken them over during the war, but now they were holiday camps again.

Hartley had suggested honeymooning, there because the children would love it and, according to him, it cost no more than a week's pay. Well, she would believe that when she saw it. All the same, it was a thought. Except that it would never happen – something was sure to go wrong.

Pamela made an effort to read the front page, although she knew it would be doom and gloom. More about the Russian bomber the Americans had shot down; and the thing Daddy had been chuntering on about – Attlee refusing to allow Quintin Hogg to stay in Parliament now that he'd inherited a peerage, which seemed a bit mean. Some miners were trapped in a pit in Scotland – she shuddered at the thought, and turned the page.

There was a lovely picture of Princess Elizabeth with her new baby, Princess Anne. Anne was a nice name for a girl, Pamela thought. If she had a girl, she might consider it. Her mind jumped to the ordeal of childbirth that lay just ahead of her. Funny to think of the Princess going through that just like any other woman. Would she shout out, like the women in the maternity hospital? Calling on God, and swearing at the man who had landed her in the labour ward?

Pamela was chuckling at the memory when the first little niggle of pain started, low down in her abdomen.

<hr>

'We ought to get up,' Catherine said.

Will remained prone, eyes shut. 'Why?'

'Because we're only in Paris for two days. You may have been here umpteen times, and seen everything, and be utterly blasé about it, but I haven't. So get up and show me round.'

'For a price,' he said.

'What price?' But she knew very well what he meant. He was a wonderful lover, tender, passionate, sometimes a little cruel, but always unexpected. 'I love him,' she thought when it was over, and they lay, exhausted, looking at the ornate ceiling. 'Or is it that I just love being with him?'

That was the thing about love: it was multi-faceted. She had thought she loved Joe completely, and indeed she had felt both passion and affection for him. With Max, it had been almost a compulsion. She hadn't been able not to love him, although she knew it would end in tears. Then, she loved David, too. She felt better whenever he appeared. But what did she feel for Will?

In the end, she abandoned the puzzle and leaped out of bed. 'Get up, lazybones. I want to see Montmartre and the Trocadéro and the Louvre and Versailles . . .'

He was up and catching her round the waist. 'We'll need a magic carpet to see that lot in two days. But your wish is my command. One more kiss!'

It wouldn't end there, and she knew it, but what could you do when it was so delicious?

<hr>

It was nine years since that night in 1941, during the Blitz, when the House of Commons Chamber had been destroyed by a German bomb. Five hundred and fifty German planes had dropped bombs indiscriminately, along with thousands of incendiaries. And they had struck lucky. For a moment, the country had rocked. If the seat of democracy was demolished, what hope for democracy? David could remember thinking that.

Now he was looking at the carefully recreated chamber. The rebuilding work had taken a long time, but it had preserved the essential features of Barry's original building. He gazed around him, feeling his eyes prick and his throat constrict. Next month, the King would officially open the restored building. The chamber would be packed that day. As he looked at the deserted benches, he thought again of the wonder of being part of it all.

All the same, he couldn't stop thoughts of Catherine intruding. What was she up to with Devine? All he wanted for her was a happy ending, the same contentment he had found with Valerie, but he couldn't see that happening with Devine. 'He is a clever wastrel,' David thought – but people in love never saw things as they truly were. Catherine would be no exception.

India closed her eyes and let the therapist's clever fingers soothe her tensions. People were so beastly. She had greeted Angela warmly when they met at the salon entrance, but Angela had looked uncomfortable. 'She would have cut me if she'd dared,' India thought. They had been friends since schooldays: why would anyone behave like that?

She bundled aside uncomfortable thoughts, and focused instead on clothes. Not the overblown designs inspired by Christian Dior – the 'New Look', with its profusion of petticoats billowing out from an unnaturally reined-in waist, was not her style. What she did want was sumptuous material, good cut, wonderful buttons. Under the therapist's ministrations, she relaxed, and began to plan spending Rupert's money. When it was time to leave, she felt positively rejuvenated.

She could hear a lot of laughter as she came into the house. Rupert getting the children excited again, no doubt. He had never come home early from the office before the children, not even in the first days of their marriage. Now it was an almost daily occurrence, and the so-called nurse was actively encouraging it.

She crossed to the playroom and flung wide the door. Loelia stood in the middle of the room, looking for all the world like an urchin, dirty, dishevelled, a ribbon hanging from her hair, and something that looked suspiciously like jam round her mouth. Rupert was on his hands and knees on the floor, making growling noises, and Nurse Adams, consumed with laughter, was holding Imogen in a precarious grasp.

'Loelia, come here at once. You look a fright.'

'Shan't!'

'I said, come here.'

The 'shan't' had been bad enough but now the child was ignoring her, urging on her father to begin the game again. Insolence! India moved across the room, ready to strike the defiant little face, but Nurse Adams was too quick for her, stepping between them.

Their faces were only inches apart, and India saw the girl's lip curl in distaste. She must smell the drink. India's hand had crept unbidden to cover her mouth before she remembered who she was.

'Get out of my way!'

The girl was looking not at her, but at Rupert, and he was rising to his feet.

'Take the children upstairs, Nurse Adams. I'll tidy up the mess.'

Sarah crossed the hall as the doorbell rang for a second time. It couldn't be Hartley and the children back – not so soon.

She knew who the couple were, even as she first looked at them. The man was like Hartley, older and greyer but recognisably his father. But it was the woman who spoke first.

'Mrs Carlyle?' The tone was hostile. So that was how it was going to be!

'Yes,' Sarah said, as evenly as she could.

'Our name is Walters.'

'Yes?' She asked it as a question, and then thought it foolish. 'You'd better come in,' she said.

They sat down in the morning-room and refused her offer of tea or coffee. If only Catherine were here! But she was too far away to be of help now.

'We've come about our son, Hartley.' The woman was doing all the talking. 'We understand you say you're carrying his child.' The emphasis on 'say' was almost laughable.

'I am carrying his child.'

'We only have your word for that . . .'

Before Sarah could reply, Mr Walters said: 'My dear!' It was meant to be a warning not to go too far, but it was too late. Mrs Walters was continuing. 'How do we know . . .'

Inside Sarah something snapped. 'I neither know nor care what you know or don't know, Mrs Walters. Your son knows. That's all that matters to me.'

'If it is his child . . . and I say if . . . you've trapped him. Oh, he was a lamb to the slaughter, no doubt. It will be a nice sitting-down for you, compared to what you've been used to. Don't you realise that marriages between different classes never work? And I'm saying that as much for your sake as for my son's – you'd be hopelessly out of your depth in Hartley's world. You'd be moving in circles you couldn't even begin to understand.'

So he hadn't yet faced them with the fact that he was going to be a teacher, Sarah thought, and felt a sudden anger at his weakness.

'Don't you realise what marriage to you would do to him? If you love him you won't drag him down like this – besmirch his good name. You've had a chequered career as far as men are concerned, and people will talk.'

Her husband was laying a hand on her arm, but it was useless. She was into her stride and nothing was going to stop her. 'This war has a lot to answer for, uprooting innocent boys and sending them into dens of vice. As if he couldn't have gone into a decent service like the RAF.'

'So you'd rather he'd been killed, as he likely would have been, than wind up happy, with a child of his own?'

The woman struggled for words. 'She's tempted to say yes,' Sarah thought, and was appalled.

Any moment now, Hartley would be back with the children. She couldn't let them witness this. Joe was young, but he was quick on the uptake. 'I think I've heard enough,' she said, getting to her feet.

'You may have heard enough but I'm not finished. Not nearly finished. Do you think I'm going to stand by and let some harpy dragged up in a pit village ruin my son? Do you think I like having to descend to this level, and use this language . . .?'

'I'm sorry,' Mr Walters said, rising to his feet. 'But you have to understand our anxiety. Hartley is our only child.'

Sarah smiled. 'I do understand, Mr Walters. I have children of my own, so I understand anxiety. What I don't understand is venom. And venom based, for the most part, on what is very far from the truth.'

She was proud of herself as she ushered them out of the house, but when the door was closed she leaned against it, suddenly drained of strength.

David rang Valerie as soon as he got back from the House, but the line was engaged. He listened anxiously to the news on the wireless. UN troops were pouring ashore at the port of Inchon, on the west coast of Korea. General MacArthur was in command, and 260 ships were involved. The war over there was certainly escalating. Once more he wished his brother were alive. Henry had been so good in times of crisis, national or domestic.

If only Catherine were at Mellows, or, better still, in London with him. He had smiled at her excitement about going to Paris, but he felt a sense of foreboding too. He had known Will Devine for years, and never really looked at him until now. 'I don't like him,' David thought again.

Was it jealousy? A little, perhaps. He would have liked to be there on the Champs-Elysées himself, sniffing the air of Paris, redolent of wine and food and good cigars. At least, it had been before the war. If he were there now, he would take Catherine on a boat down the Seine, under the bridges. They would walk hand-in-hand down from Trocadéro towards the Tour Eiffel, and pause to look at the art displayed along the riverside. He would buy her a watercolour, of Montmartre, perhaps, or Montparnasse. . . .

The phone cut through his daydream.

'David?' It was Valerie.

'Darling, I've been trying to ring you.'

———

'She is taking my child's love away from me, Rupert. I won't stand for it. I want her dismissed.'

At the other end of the table, his face was stony above the glint of crystal and silver. 'Nurse Adams is taking nothing from you, India. There's nothing to take. Your daughter gives you what you have given her: anger at worst, and at best indifference.'

'You're good with words, Rupert, but you don't mislead me. I want her out of this house. My house.'

He leaned forward and for a moment his expression made her afraid. 'My house, India. And if anyone is leaving, it isn't the nurse.'

———

'It doesn't matter, darling,' Michael was saying. 'There'll be other times. And it's great fun trying.' Pamela had miscarried that morning, and the doctor and nurse had now cleaned her up and installed her in bed, propped up on pillows.

'I wanted that baby, Michael.'

'So did I, but it wasn't to be. It'll always be loved, because it was ours, but we can't be sad forever. Life isn't like that.'

'I love you,' she said, putting her hand on his arm.

'I know you do, and it's mutual. Now lie still and I'll bring John in to say goodnight.'

Pamela lay after Michael left the room, trying not to let misery overtake her. But she couldn't help a tear escaping, and trickling slowly down her cheek. 'I mustn't cry,' she thought. 'Not when I have so much.'

By the time Michael came back with John, she was smiling a welcome.

———

They had come home full of choux buns and crêpes and wine. 'I'm full to bursting,' Catherine said, puffing out her cheeks and rounding her belly.

'I won't love you if you get fat.' Will curled his lip in mock-disgust.

'Then stop feeding me such scrumptious things. Those crêpes from that stall near the Eiffel Tower . . . I thought I'd

246

died and gone to heaven.'

'If you'd eaten another one, you might have done. We can go back there tomorrow, before we leave.'

'Could we? Oh, Will, that would be wonderful.' She leaped on to the bed, and sat cross-legged.

'What are you up to now?' he said.

'I'm cogitating.'

'About what?'

'About everything, what I liked best, what I want to see again. Paris makes you feel . . .'

'Young?' he suggested.

It was true. She did feel as though the years had slipped away, that she was a girl again, and that there was no war, nor ever would be.

He was regarding her solemnly. Then he pursed his lips, and twisted his mouth, before he spoke.

'Will you marry me, you funny little thing?'

Chapter Twenty Three

November 1950

'YOU LOOK LOVELY.' SARAH STOOD back and surveyed her handiwork.

They had looked at dresses in the shops, and seen nothing that Catherine liked, so the wedding dress had been fashioned from a piece of pale-blue cloque that Catherine's mother had unearthed from a chest. The little bridesmaids were David's Natasha and India's Loelia. Ben and Joe would be their escorts, and Pamela's John would present a lucky horseshoe.

'I still wish Pammy had agreed to be a matron of honour, but she was adamant. Once is enough, she said.'

'And it's not long since she lost the baby. She's maybe still a bit emotional.'

'Yes.' Catherine turned to the side and regarded herself again. 'There is that, and at least John will give me a horse-shoe.' She turned to the other side. 'Sarah, it's wonderful. You're so clever. It'll be your turn next, but I won't be able to return the favour. I can't sew for toffee.'

'You designed it. You can do the same for me.'

Sarah was silent for a moment, and then she said, 'If it ever happens.'

'Are things no better?' Catherine was full of sympathy.

'No. Hartley keeps saying he'll speak to his parents, but he'll have to be quick or this bairn'll be born a bastard.'

⟨⟨⟨≡⟩⟩⟩

David and Valerie breakfasted early, anxious that nothing should go wrong. But they were still finishing their toast when the nursemaid appeared. 'Diana's red hot, m'Lady. I don't think you can take her out today.'

Valerie looked at David in despair. 'It's OK.' he said. 'It's Natasha who has a part to play at the wedding. Diana can stay here in the nursery. Nurse, you can ring us at Mellows if you need to.'

Will Devine wiped his mouth with his napkin. 'You've got to be there, Valerie. If I don't have back-up, I may chicken out, and then where will we all be?'

Valerie laughed half-heartedly, but David's doubts deepened. The man could make a joke of anything, it seemed.

Valerie had gone up to the nursery to check on Diana, and get Natasha dressed in her finery, when the maid appeared.

'There's a message for you, Sir David. From the Barracloughs. He's worse, and she says can you come?'

Will looked alarmed. 'You can't go now,' he told David.

'I have to, I'm afraid. He's one of my SSAFA men. Ex-Changi, and suicidal, I'm afraid. I'll be back in plenty of time for the wedding.'

'Well, no best man, no bridegroom,' Will said, and went back to *The Times*. David resisted the urge to say, 'Don't tempt me.' He would like nothing better than to stop this wedding. However, it wasn't up to him.

As he drove towards the village, he asked himself how he had been trapped into being Will's best man. Surely Will had other friends? Except that his crowd were a strange lot, all of them very taken up with themselves, and full of witty repartee. 'They profess undying friendship for one another,' he thought, 'but actually it's all talk. I'm doing this for Catherine, but whether or not I am doing her a favour, I'm not sure.'

The doctor had arrived at the house by the time he got there, and the man was calmer. 'What do you think?' he asked the doctor as they came down the stairs.

'I think it might be kinder if we let him take his life,' the doctor said ruefully. 'Look at his children, shivering there. What life is this for them?'

When eventually David could tear himself away, promising to return, he realised he was going to be late. If he was, Valerie would be furious. She had the most even of temperaments unless she was pushed too far.

'Thank God,' Will said, as David got out of the car. He was standing in the portico, obviously ready to leave. 'Valerie's gone on ahead with Natasha. She wanted us to go in style.' A bridal car was waiting on the gravel.

'Who has she gone with?' David asked, already sprinting up the steps as fast as his gammy leg would take him.

'She's taken her own car. She said she might want to nip back later to see to the sprog, and that you were to come to the church with me. Get a move on, old chap!'

But David was already crossing the great hall, and did not bother to reply.

＊＊＊

'Have we got everything?' Pamela was looking round as though certain she would see something forgotten.

'I have one wife, one son, one silver horseshoe . . . what else should there be?'

Michael was being indulgent, knowing Pamela was tense.

'I don't like going to church any more, Michael. It just makes me sad.' Now she checked her handbag. Two hankies, a comb for John's few curls, and cough sweets in case either of them got a tickle at a vital moment.

'Can we go now?' Michael was beginning to be impatient, but Pamela couldn't cast off a feeling of doom.

'Do you think she's doing the right thing, Mike? I mean, she hasn't known this man five minutes.'

'She has, Pamela. I distinctly remember him being here months ago.'

'Well, if you're going to be literal, I give up.'

They began to walk out to the car. 'Do you know,' she said, slipping her arm through his, 'do you know I used to loathe my sister before the war? Positively detest her. And now all I want is for her to be as happy as we are.'

<hr>

'Have you got the ring?'

'You've already asked me that, but I'll check again.' It was there in David's waistcoat pocket. 'Satisfied?'

'Yes. Sorry. But a chap doesn't do this every day.'

'I should hope not. Let's talk about something else.'

But even as they made inconsequential chatter, David was thinking about what Devine had said last night. They had been sharing a nightcap together – several nightcaps, in fact. Will had suddenly looked up, and grinned. 'Well, it's all a farce, isn't it? This marriage talk. Till death do us part, and all that. Still, if that's what the lady wants . . .'

He had leaned forward, and refilled his glass, and David had not attempted a reply. For him, marriage had been a solemn, even awesome, occasion. Wasn't there something in the order of service which said not to be entered into lightly?

Now he looked out of the car window as the hedgerows gave way to the grey church wall, and hoped again that Catherine wasn't making a terrible mistake.

<hr>

India tried not to allow irritation to overcome her, but it wasn't easy. Loelia was sitting in the crook of her father's arm, looking smug in her wedding finery. When Catherine had asked if she could be a bridesmaid, India had said, 'No, she's too young.' But in this, as in so many other things, Rupert had overruled her. And the child knew it. An expression of 'I won't' was written on her pert little face.

'I wish this day were over,' India said at last, unable to refrain from giving vent.

'Don't worry, my dear. Just think of the alcohol you'll be able to consume quite openly. That has to be good for something, surely?'

'I don't know what you mean.'

'I think you do. I can smell it, India, and it's not yet noon. How much longer do you think I can stand being pitied by our friends?'

'Pitied? How dare you say that? If our friends have pity, it's reserved for me. I married beneath me, and I'm paying the price.'

It was out, and she didn't care. Rupert had never been good enough, even at the beginning. And he could not even give her that thing she craved above all else: a son.

Sarah turned as 'The Bridal March' pealed out. Catherine looked like a queen as she came down the aisle on her father's arm. The dress was perfect, and Sarah felt a little glow of pride. Everyone looked nice, considering clothes were still hard to get. Pamela was pale from the miscarriage, but her dark-blue suit brought out her colouring. And Valerie Callingham wore pale grey with lace panels backed in pink. That must have cost a pretty penny.

Will and Catherine were at the altar now, and Sarah looked at Joe, solemn as a judge, shepherding the tiny bridesmaids, taking Catherine's bouquet and handing it to her mother, as he had been instructed to do. The Vicar was welcoming the congregation. 'In the presence of God, Father, Son and Holy Spirit, we have come together to witness the marriage of Will and Catherine, to pray for God's blessing on them. The grace of our Lord Jesus Christ, the love of God, and the fellowship of the Holy Spirit be with you.'

Sarah felt her eyes prick. You started out with such dreams, but life was cruel. 'Keep Catherine safe,' she prayed, and tried not to think about the risk she herself would be taking if she stood before the altar with Hartley.

The service was continuing and the Vicar was talking about joyful commitment. Except that sometimes there was no joyful commitment, there was only pain. Suddenly Sarah was remembering her own two weddings, with candles flickering at the feet of the saints, and all of Belgate there. Beside her, Hartley was standing, mesmerised by the scene at the altar steps. Would he and she ever stand together and be pronounced man and wife? Not if his parents could help it.

When she had told Hartley of their visit, he had simply shaken his head in sorrow. As a response, that was not enough. There would be no wedding for the two of them, unless he found some backbone and fought his parents for the bairn she was carrying.

Catherine kept her eyes fixed on the rose window and tried not to let memories intrude.

'All right?' Will was whispering in her ear, and squeezing her hand.

'I never wanted to be married twice,' she thought, but she smiled reassurance at him.

This morning the papers had reported on what was happening in Korea. War, war, and the rumour of war. There was no escape from it. It had taken two men from her: three if you counted Max who was dead to her, to all intents and purposes.

She tried to concentrate on the words of the service, but the Vicar was asking if anyone knew of any just impediment to the wedding. That question had been asked when she married Henry, and she had held her breath, sure that someone would stand up and brand her a liar. Guilt swept over her now, all-consuming and yet undefined. Why did she feel this way? Surely it was time to forgive her old sins?

The Vicar was speaking to Will now. 'Wilt thou have this woman to thy wedded wife, to live together after God's ordinance in the holy estate of matrimony? Wilt thou love her, comfort her, honour, and keep her, in sickness and in health; and, forsaking all other, keep thee only unto her, so long as ye both shall live?'

Will's voice was firm: 'I will.'

Her turn now. 'Catherine, wilt thou have this man to thy wedded husband, to live together after God's ordinance in the holy estate of Matrimony? Wilt thou obey him, and serve him, love, honour, and keep him, in sickness and in health; and, forsaking all other, keep thee only unto him, so long as ye both shall live?'

And her own voice, not wavering – 'I, Catherine, take thee, Will, to my wedded husband, to have and to hold from this day forward, for better for worse, for richer for poorer, in sickness and in health, to love, cherish, and to obey, till death us do part, according to God's holy ordinance; and thereto I give thee my troth.'

The ring was on her finger. When it was time, Catherine lifted her face for the kiss, and vowed that this was a marriage that would last.

Every room at Mellows had been decorated with flowers, so that the whole house was a bower. 'It's gone off really well,'

Sarah whispered, when she and Catherine found themselves alone for a few seconds in the hall. The speeches and the feasting were over, and now everyone was mingling.

'Yes,' Catherine said. She was looking through the door to the dining-room, where David had Ben on his shoulders. The boy was literally holding on by the hair, David's hair. 'He loves his Uncle David,' Sarah said indulgently, following Catherine's gaze. 'Like a father, he's been to him.'

'Yes,' Catherine said, trying to sound at ease. But yesterday morning, Will had said, 'Can't you shut that child up?' in quite peremptory tones. She had told herself he just wasn't used to children – but then David had had no experience of children when Ben was born, and he had been wonderful from the start.

She was roused from painful thinking by the sight of a waitress, clearly agitated, bobbing up and down in the doorway.

'Don't worry,' Sarah said, 'I'll see to her. You go back to your guests.' Obeying this instruction, Catherine was moving from group to group in search of her bridegroom when she felt a tug on her arm. One look at Sarah's face told her something was dreadfully wrong.

'You'd better come, Cathy. He's in the lobby, I told him to wait there.'

The policeman was young and fresh-faced, and obviously in awe of his surroundings.

'It's Lady Callingham, Mrs . . . Madam. Her car's in a layby at the Hall Bend. It looks like she's been taken ill. They've sent for an ambulance . . .'

Catherine interrupted him. 'There must be some mistake. Lady Callingham is here, in the drawing-room, I think. Someone must have stolen her car . . .'

Her words tailed off, as she saw Sarah's face. 'Valerie went to check on the young bairn. She said not to say anything to you, and she'd be back directly. "I'll drive like the wind," she said. "They'll never know I was gone."'

There was silence in the side-ward except for the occasional beep of the machinery that was keeping Valerie alive.

David sat holding her hand, and Catherine sought for words of comfort. 'She may be able to hear us, David. Speak to her.'

But his eyes were on the inert figure in the bed and he merely shook his head.

'I loved her, Catherine.'

'I know you did.'

'I loved her, but never enough. I never said it enough.' Catherine was taken aback by the vehemence of his tone. 'Did she know I loved her. Catherine?'

'Of course she knew! But you're talking as though you've lost her. You mustn't give up hope, David. The doctors think it's an aneurysm, and if they can pull her round a little they can operate.'

There was silence for a while, and then David spoke again. 'She gave me all her love, Catherine, and I gave her – I didn't give her enough. I kept something back.'

It was time for stern measures. 'You're a fool, David. Of course you loved her enough, and Valerie, being wise, knew it. Knows it. Do you think you could have fooled her all these years? She is, I think, the happiest woman I have ever known. Are you telling me she was a dupe, someone who could be fobbed off with less than a whole?'

David was looking at her with such entreaty that she went to him and took him in her arms.

'Are you sure?' he asked.

'Very sure,' she said.

She left him, then, and went in search of Will, who was waiting outside the ward with Rupert.

'I suppose,' he said, 'this means the honeymoon's off?'

Chapter Twenty Four

December 1950

WHEN SHE WOKE, CATHERINE THOUGHT she was at Mellows. It was a moment before she realised she was at Kynaston – the first time she had slept there since she left it to go to do war work.

She was alone in the wide bed. Will had been honest when she told him they were going to stay at Kynaston with David: 'We can't leave him alone there, Will. Not until the funeral is over.'

He had looked at her with that apologetic smile of his. 'I was going to speak to you about that, darling. I don't do funerals. Never have been able to. Couldn't even go to my own. I thought I should just nip up to town and check on things. I would come with you if I could, but . . . it's just one of those things.'

Catherine had been hurt, outraged even. Not for herself, but for David. And for Valerie, too. But all she had said was, 'If that's the way you feel.'

Now she got out of bed, shivering a little in the December air, and began to get ready to face the day.

Sarah dreaded getting up, these mornings. She felt so huge, much bigger than she had with Joe or Alexander. This would be the last baby, so please let it be a girl! Anyroad, no use lying here like a beached whale. She had a houseful of people and children to care for – her own two, Cathy's Ben, and David's two poor little loves. They'd be lost without their mother – and what a mother she had been. 'She was a really good woman,' Sarah thought, 'straight as a die, and with not a ha'porth of side, for all the money.'

She liked people who were straightforward. That thought brought her to Hartley, asleep now in the offshot bedroom to which she had consigned him when Pamela had insisted on coming to stay at Mellows. *'You can't be on your own, Sarah, while Catherine is at Kynaston – and she has to be with David. Mike says he and John will be fine on their own, so I'm moving in for a bit. You're too near your time for there not to be a woman in the house.'*

Sarah would have replied that she had Hartley, but she had run out of patience with him, if she was to face the truth. *'I'll speak to my parents, I'll speak to them.'* He said it plenty, but he never did it. And she wouldn't wed him till he did. If he didn't care enough for her to stand up to his family, he wasn't man enough to stand up at the altar. But a bairn coming into the world as a bastard was a terrible thing.

Horrified afresh at the thought, she was struggling upright when there was a knock at the bedroom door. 'I've made you some breakfast. You lie still. We've plenty of time.'

Pamela was halfway out through the door again, when Sarah spoke. 'You'll be like this one day, Pammy, and I'll do the same for you!' She knew how much Pamela longed to be pregnant again, and it raised the expected smile.

What did you talk about on the day you were burying your wife, David wondered, as he looked at Catherine across the breakfast table. 'The Korean situation is getting shocking. Have you seen *The Times*?' Even to his own ears, the words sounded bizarre.

'Yes,' Catherine said eagerly. He could see she too had been worried about what to say. The Korean War was safe ground.

'The Chinese are swarming over the Allied lines – 200,000 of them, according to Reuters.'

'I can't believe we're at war again, can you?'

David grimaced. 'Sadly, I can believe it.'

She was smiling, and he felt his own lips curl in response. This was awkward for them both. He knew now that he had loved Valerie, loved her deeply. It had not been the confusion of desire that he had felt for Catherine, but it had been real love. He would never have left her.

If he had not gone out that morning, if she had not taken the car, she might not have gone back to check on Diana, and might still be alive. For him and for the children.

But even as he thought this, he knew it was nonsense. It had been a congenital defect in an artery in her head that had killed her. It had held out long enough for her to become a wife and a mother, and then it had given way.

'It could have happened at any time. I'm really sorry,' the doctor had said, and David had seen compassion in his eyes.

'What am I going to do about Christmas?' he asked aloud now, and saw the confusion on Catherine's face as she sought for an answer.

———

Sarah was eyeing the clock and thinking about when she would have to get changed for the funeral, when the doorbell rang. 'I'll go,' Hartley called. She would have called out, 'Leave it to me,' but it was too late. She had got as far as the kitchen door when she heard the front door creak open and then the mutter of conversation. Putting aside the tea-towel she was holding, she emerged into the hall. Hartley was ushering in his parents, and Sarah felt her heart begin to thump.

'I won't beat about the bush . . . ' the woman began. 'This is important, Hartley, so don't look at me like that. Your father hasn't succeeded in deterring me, and neither will you. We need this settled.'

Hartley was standing there, looking as though death would be a preferable alternative, and his father appeared no more cheerful.

'You'd better come in,' Sarah said firmly. 'At least we can sit down in a civilised way, not stand in the hall like this.' She felt a sudden glow of pride in herself. Her voice hadn't wobbled once.

They sat down in the morning-room, two couples ranged opposite one another. 'But it's really her and me,' Sarah thought. The men would do their level best to stay out of the fray.

'I've come to plead with you,' Mrs Walters began. 'My husband seems to think you're a decent woman. If you are, you'll do the decent thing and let my son go.'

Sarah waited for Hartley to speak, but he was looking at his feet. It was truly going to be up to her.

'You seem to be under the impression that I'm holding Hartley against his will, Mrs Walters. I can assure you I'm not. He's free to walk out of here with you now, if that's what he wants.' She looked directly at Hartley to see if he would pick up the challenge.

'Don't be silly,' he said weakly. 'Of course I'm here of my own free will. I want to be here, Mother. I've told you that.'

His mother was shaking her head. 'You don't know what you want, silly boy. Living here, surrounded by all this . . . of course you think it's all going to be rosy. But what happens when it's you and her alone, Hartley? When she can't work, and she's lost her place here, and you've destroyed your career? Don't think we'll help! Tell me what you'll do then?'

Under her breath, Sarah was imploring one of the men to speak out, but they were both still staring at the floor.

She was about to put an end to the whole confrontation when Hartley cleared his throat. 'It won't be like that, Mother – the disaster you envisage. We have plans . . .'

His mother erupted. 'We have plans? She has plans, you mean, and we all know what they are. To saddle you with three children, parentage unknown . . .'

'Mother!' Mr Walton's expostulation came as Hartley rose to his feet.

'You've got it all wrong,' Hartley said desperately. 'Let me explain.'

It was Sarah's turn to rise. 'If you'll excuse me,' she said, 'I have better things to do than listen to this.'

She managed a dignified exit, but the tears came once she was out of the room. She was still sobbing when the front door closed, and Hartley came into the kitchen.

'Don't let it upset you,' he said, holding out his arms. 'She doesn't mean it, Sarah. She gets anxious about things. Dad will talk her round in the end.'

'Talk her round?' Sarah said. '*Talk her round?* Get out of here, Hartley Walters, before I do something we'll both regret.'

'We'll need to leave here at 11 sharp, India,' Rupert had said. 'I'll come back to change for the funeral. Please don't be late and, above all, stay away from alcohol. For one morning at least, surely you can manage that?'

She hadn't answered, hadn't spoken at all. She was tired of his constant nagging, his permanent expression of disapproval.

A phrase she had heard during the war sprang into her mind: 'As though he had a poker up his bum.' It was apt. Very apt. And so funny. Hilarious!

She was still giggling as she uncorked the bottle and poured herself a glass of port.

'It makes you put everything into perspective, Mike. I know you won't take this the wrong way, but I've felt better since Valerie died. Less sorry for myself. I lost a baby that I dearly wanted, but we still have each other and we have John. If there's never another baby, that's enough. Poor David, he loved Valerie so much. I used to think he was keen on Catherine, at one time, but he and Valerie were sublimely happy.'

'David and Catherine are just good friends, Pam. Brother and sister, really. She's his sister-in-law after all. But I'm glad you've cheered up a bit. Could you pass the marmalade, please?'

'It's not wrong of me to feel like that, is it? I mean I'm very, very sad about Valerie.'

'We all are. Is Sarah OK?'

'Yes, she was just getting up when I came out.'

'You needn't have rushed over here. I'm perfectly capable of making my own breakfast, you know.'

'And of bathing John, and getting yourself ready, and getting to the church on time?'

'All right, all right, you're indispensable. Now, do you think I could have another cup of tea?'

'The church is full,' Catherine whispered. David didn't answer, but she could see that he was pleased. It mattered that people came to funerals. It was a sign that the person who had died had left a hole in the world. And Valerie had left one hell of a hole.

The Americanism reminded her of Max. There had been no more letters. Was he still in Israel, or back in New York, the darling of all the empty women with cash to spend and lines to erase? She had seen Max in Ben when she had explained to him that Aunty Valerie was gone.

'Does that mean I won't see her again?' he'd asked.

'I'm afraid so. We have photographs and memories of her, though. You had happy times with her, didn't you?'

He was nodding in the solemn way small children have. 'Will I see Natasha and Diana again?'

'Of course you will. More often probably, because they'll miss their Mummy.'

'We must be very kind to them,' he said solemnly. That was when she had seen Max peeking out from his son's face.

But Valerie's death had been so sudden, so unexpected, that it had made her realise that anyone, anyone at all, could vanish from your life at any moment.

Now she opened her hymn book and sang. It was lucky she knew the hymn by heart because tears had blurred her vision.

＝＝＝

'It was a lovely service.' Hannah spoke with the certainty of someone who had never missed a funeral in her life if she could help it. 'Very suitable, and none of that bobbing about you get at some places.'

That was a dig at Roman Catholicism, but Sarah wasn't rising to the bait. 'She'll be missed.'

'Aye.' Hannah's fur hat had obviously over-heated her head, and sweat was glistening among the strands of hair that straddled her brow. 'And talking of missing,' she went on, her eyes raking the crowded room, 'where's that fancy lad Cathy wed? I don't see him here.'

For a moment Sarah was tempted to lie. Hannah would be after a rumour like a ferret up a drainpipe. 'He had business in London,' she said at last.

Hannah snorted. 'Fancy business, if I'm any judge. I never liked the cut of his jib from the start.'

'Hannah, don't start looking for trouble where there is none. Now, I've got to go and make sure everything's all right out back. Behave yourself while I'm gone.'

'Bring some of them fishy things when you come back. They've cleared the plate with them on. The chicken bits are sticking, though, so don't bother bringing them.'

Across the room, Sarah could see David, head bent, talking to a man with a goatee beard. But Catherine was there with him, so he'd be all right. 'She married the wrong man,' Sarah said to herself, and then felt ashamed. What a way to think before a good woman was cold in the ground!

It was a relief when the last person had gone over the step, and they could shut and bolt the huge Kynaston doors.

'Everyone's been very kind,' Catherine said, 'but I expect you're glad it's over.'

David nodded. 'Shall we use the library?' He could see that Catherine knew he didn't want to use the morning-room. That was where he and Valerie had spent most of their days. 'I won't ever want to use that room,' he thought.

As they crossed the hall, he looked around him. This house seemed to have known nothing but death for years: his father, Henry, and now Valerie.

'Here.' Catherine was holding out a brandy glass and clutching another for herself.

'Valerie was so young, Catherine. It seems so wrong.'

She was nodding – 'I know,' – and fishing a paper from her

pocket. She held it out. 'Someone sent me this when Henry died. It was written 400 years ago about a young man who'd died. It helped me. I hope it helps you.'

He looked down at the poem.

> 'It is not growing like a tree
>   In bulk, doth make man better be;
> Or standing long an oak, three hundred year,
>   To fall a log at last, dry, bald, and sere:
>   A lily of a day
>   Is fairer far in May,
>   Although it fall and die that night;
>   It was the plant and flower of light.
>   In small proportions we just beauties see;
>   And in short measures, life may perfect be.'

Before David could clear his throat, the phone rang, and he got to his feet. 'I'll answer it.'

But the call was not for him, it was Will Devine telephoning for Catherine.

'How did it go, old chap?' he said when he realised it was David on the other end. He might have been asking how a party had gone – and, if the background noise was any indication, he was having a party himself.

'I'd've been there if I could, David,' he was saying. 'You know I would. But in my game you have to keep in the swim. You do understand, don't you?'

'I do understand, Will. I understand perfectly. Now, I'll get Catherine for you.'

'Loelia is getting out of hand, Rupert. I have warned and warned. I went upstairs when we came back, and there was chaos in the nursery.'

'What do you expect of a little one, India? *Good Housekeeping* magazine standards? She's a child – weren't you ever one? Why can't you be nicer to her, woo her a little? She's your daughter. As she grows up, she's going to need you more and more.'

'I thought we employed people to keep up standards, Rupert. I see I was wrong in that, as well as everything else. Forgive me. Just what would you like me to do?'

He was wilfully refusing to acknowledge the sarcasm she had thought biting. Instead he was answering her literally, knowing it would annoy. 'Read to Loelia, take her for walks occasionally. Put her to bed sometimes. I love that moment when she's sleepy, and struggling to stay awake.'

'I'm not as sentimental as you, Rupert. However, I will try. I'll put her to bed tonight. Right now, in fact. It's bed-time.'

She took the stairs two at a time, so anxious was she to put her idea into practice. So he wanted her to be a model mother. Well, she would be. But with a difference.

'You can go now, Nurse Adams. I'll put Miss Loelia to bed myself.'

And, when the nurse demurred, she said: 'Run along, now, I won't take no for an answer.'

She kept smiling while the little chit bathed, and then helped her into a clean nightgown. 'Now, into bed.'

'I always have a story.' The child's voice was a whine. But a defiant whine.

'You're going to get a story. It's about a little girl who lived in a big house just like this one. She was called Loelia, just like you. Now what Loelia didn't know was that this was not an ordinary house.'

The child's eyes were wide. She's expecting magic, India thought, with a glow of satisfaction. 'All the rooms had secret doors in them, and behind those doors there were monsters.

Green monsters whose skin was like iron. They had long claws on their hands, and they came out at night and ate up all the little children.'

'I don't like this story.' Not so defiant now. Good!

'You will. Just listen hard. You couldn't see the doors that had the monsters behind them. You could only see the wall. Can you see that door in this room, Loelia? It's there, you know. Is it on that wall? Or that one? Can you hear anything? Could it be the monster's claws scraping on the ground as he gets ready . . .'

'Thank you, Mrs Lindsay-Hogg.' Nurse Adams was in the room, minus her apron, and with her hair, usually neatly coiled, tumbling round her shoulders. 'I'll take over now.'

There was such menace in her tone that India was taken aback. Before she could retaliate she found herself in the doorway, and heard the girl's voice, clear and firm. 'There are no monsters, Loelia. Not in this house, or anywhere else.'

———

'Pamela?'

'Yes, it's me.' Pamela was letting herself in at the door. 'What are you doing here, Catherine? I said I'd be back at 9. Is Sarah all right?'

'Sarah's labour has started. I rang to check on her, and when she told me we came straight over. David is in the drawing-room with the doctor. The midwife's upstairs with Sarah, and the children are all asleep, worn out. Come in and get a drink. You look frozen.'

'I'm glad it's started. Sarah has found the last few days difficult. She's so enormous.'

'You've been very good. She told me how kind you've been. We both know how you must be feeling.'

Pamela shrugged. 'I'm not jealous. I would have been once,

but I'm older and wiser now.'

'You're still my little sister, I hope.'

'Always will be, Sis. You're stuck with me.'

They joined the men, and made conversation, until a voice called down to the doctor from upstairs.

'That sounds like this is it,' the doctor said, putting down his glass.

But it was an hour later before they heard the first cry.

'Thank God,' David said. He raised his glass. 'To the newcomer.'

'The newcomer!' they both said, and drank.

'It's odd, isn't it?' David said quietly now. 'A life goes out and a life comes in.'

They sat in silence until they heard a second cry.

'It's a vocal little thing,' David said. 'Well, not a thing – but we don't know yet whether it's a boy or a girl.'

But Pamela was standing still, her head cocked on one side, listening. 'That's not the same baby,' she said.

Chapter Twenty Five

April 1951

CATHERINE COULD SEE DAVID ON the benches below. Any moment he would speak. He had risen twice, but had had to sit down when the Speaker signalled to someone else.

'The House is in a ferment,' he had told her last night. 'Some of our lot say the Labour Party is finished. Aneurin Bevan resigned, and Harold Wilson is following they say. Not that he's so damaging – they call him "Nye's little dog".

'What no one can understand is why Attlee has let it happen. The economy has picked up since the dark days of '47. National income has risen. The Festival of Britain is opening soon, to cheer everyone up. So why provoke a row within the party now? No one can work out why Gaitskell decided to impose charges for false teeth and spectacles – charges he knew would cause this rumpus. Bevan called Gaitskell "a desiccated calculating machine", apparently, but the truth is that Labour are increasingly seen as having has lost the will to live. They were defeated in the House last month, don't forget, on the raw materials debate.'

David was up on his feet again, and now the Speaker was naming him.

'Mr Speaker, I feel I must speak out on behalf of my constituents and the many other people who will be harmed by these proposals . . .'

It was obvious that not everyone on the Conservative benches agreed with him, but Catherine glowed with pride. David was his own man, just as she had told him long ago. That was why she had fought against his resigning his seat after Valerie died.

It had been hard: '*How will I manage, Catherine? The girls must come first.*' But they had solved all his problems. Rupert Lindsay-Hogg had found a perfect nanny, and had masterminded the children's move to live with him in London for the time being. David had called Rupert a godsend, but Catherine thought he must be an angel if he could live with India. Even now she shuddered at memories of her own time spent living with India at Kynaston.

David was sitting down now, and she relaxed. This was what she had come for – that he should take his stand. He had not let her down.

'If anyone had told me that meat would still be rationed six years after the war's end, I'd have laughed in their face,' Sarah said.

'Not just rationed, Sally. They cut it last January, don't forget that. It amounts to four ounces per person, or five if you'll take New Zealand lamb. Mind you, with rump steak at two and eightpence a pound, it's a wonder we can eat at all. Are the Jerries still rationed, that's what I want to know. Who won the bloody war? It doesn't feel like we did.'

'I know what you mean.' Sarah shifted the baby to her other breast. Like every other woman in Britain, she was tired of the struggle to provide varied meals.

'Freddy's a good little feeder,' Hannah said complacently. 'Is his dad pleased with him?'

'I think he is, but it's the girl he's gone loopy over. "Daddy's little Princess", he calls her. I tell him it's daft, but they never listen, do they?'

'Men? Cloth ears, the lot of them. Talking of men, have you heard anything about yon Yank, the one your Molly got mixed up with?'

'I wish they would all go home. Jim says he's over it now she's gone, but if he ever came face to face with them . . .'

'She's not still with him, you know? Wherever he is, it's not with her.' Hannah always perked up when she had fresh news to impart. 'I thought you knew. The Americans had him shifted to another camp at the other end of the country as soon as they got wind of it.'

'So where's Molly?'

'Back with her dad, and he's none too pleased about it. Hoping your Jim'll take her back, no doubt.'

Sarah shook a rueful head. 'Our Jim's never been the forgiving sort.' She detached the now sleeping baby from her breast, and buttoned her blouse. 'I'll just put this one back in his crib, and see if Catherine Rose is awake.'

She checked on both babies, and then returned to her seat.

'Speaking of Catherine,' Hannah was leaning forward in the hope of a titbit, 'how's she getting on with that fancy man of hers?'

'All right,' said Sarah, 'and he's not her fancy man, as you put it. They're married, as you well know. She likes living in London – and Sir David's there, too. You know how well they get on.'

'Well, she saw him through tragedy, didn't she? They're not a lucky family, that lot.'

'No,' Sarah said, thinking of what she had heard about India Lindsay-Hogg's drinking. But she didn't say anything to Hannah. Catherine had told her in confidence, so her lips were sealed.

＝＝＝

'You did well today,' Catherine said warmly, when she and David were seated in the dining-room. Around them, MPs wined and dined – very well, from what Catherine could see.

'I still don't enjoy speaking, but sometimes it has to be done. Anyway, it's over. Now, what about you?'

'Things are going well, touch wood. Will's enjoying writing his column.'

'It's good!' David's tone was deliberately vehement. Catherine was proud of Will, so why tell her he privately thought the column a conceited flim-flam of name-dropping?

'Don't sound so surprised.' Catherine was laughing. 'Anyway, as I said, Will's doing well, and Ben likes his new school.'

'Does he like his new stepfather?'

There was a pause before she answered. 'They get on well enough. I don't think Will quite understands children, but it's early days. They co-exist.'

'Yes, it is early days. Give it time.'

'I will. And I enjoy living in London. I wondered if I would, but I do.'

'What did the poet say? Well, someone said it. "The man who is tired of London is tired of life?"'

'I like it best at dusk, when the parks have emptied and are all misty in the lamplight. What about you? Are you happy – well, as happy as you can be? How is your agent, my replacement, doing? The girls seem to be getting along fine.'

'They're blooming. Nanny Grace is a wonder. She creates the same mood – a kind of ease about everything – that Valerie created. But I've been doing some thinking.'

'The way you said that sounds ominous.'

'I'm going to get rid of Kynaston.' He sat back, knowing she would register shock.

'But how can you? Isn't it entailed?'

'I wouldn't be allowed to sell it, but I think I can give it away, or lease it, or something. I've got people looking into that now. It can become a school, or a rest centre for invalids, or any damn thing they like. But I can't face living there, Catherine, not without Valerie.'

'I can't say I blame you,' Catherine said at last. Privately, she was resolving to be well away from County Durham when David told India.

———

Pamela had folded the ironing, and put away the ironing-board. Now she made herself a cup of tea and carried it through to the living-room. John was with his grandmother, so she had the house to herself. She picked up her copy of *Woman and Home*, and was sipping her first hot cup when she heard a key in the front door.

'Mike?'

He came through the door, stooping as he always did for fear his head was near the lintel.

'Darling, you're early.'

'I felt a little off colour, so Briggs offered to take my last class for me. Is that tea fresh?'

She fetched a cup and poured him one. 'Do you think you have a temperature?'

'No. It's nothing like that. I don't feel fluey.'

'You don't think –?' She hesitated to say the dread word 'depression'.

'No, I'm not depressed.' He had read her mind. 'There are times when I still miss the old life – the excitement, the danger, the triumph. You don't get that in civvy street. But I'm over that now, Pammy. When I go to the RAF Association, I see lots of chaps who aren't over it. They cling on to old bits of uniform, flying jackets, that sort of thing. That's not for me.

'No, the truth is my tummy's been upset lately. I've had pints of milk of magnesia but it hasn't helped.'

'Well, drink your tea. You're home now.' She said it cheerfully, but doubt was nibbling at her mind. He couldn't have anything seriously wrong with him. Not now, not when everything was coming right at last.

⸺

Catherine could hear laughter as she let herself into the house. Will must be home – but it was a woman's laughter. She walked through to the room they shared as a study to find him perched on a desk, one leg tucked under him, the other dangling down to the floor. In the desk chair a woman was lolling, looking up at him.

'Hello Jacqui,' Catherine said. The woman in the chair was a radio presenter, quite famous for her deep, melodious voice and abundant red hair. Jacqui Currie, that was her name. Will had introduced them at a party, but the woman was regarding her now as though she were an intruder. She gave Catherine a languid smile, but didn't speak. Her eyes switched back to Will.

'Darling,' Will said, but he didn't get down from the desk. 'I didn't think you'd be back so early.'

The word 'obviously' trembled on Catherine's tongue, but she bit it back. 'Can I get you some tea, Jacqui?

The woman smiled, revealing white, slightly buck, teeth. 'Tea? I don't think so. But thank you, just the same. Will has already given me some scrumptious Chablis.' For the first time Catherine noticed the open bottle and the glasses, one tinged with lipstick.

'There's a letter for you on the hall table,' Will said. 'Airmail.'

Catherine was glad of the chance to get out of the room. 'Ta,' she said as airily as she could, and turned on her heel.

The letter was from Max.

'*I expect you will be surprised to hear from me, after such a long time. I'm still here, in Israel. I hope you are well and happy. Perhaps you have married again? Quite a few years have gone by now, and I hope your life has opened out as you deserve. If so I wish you joy, and I consider him a lucky man.*

'But the reason I write this letter is that I have heard from David Edelman. Remember him? He was the anaesthetist towards the end– he replaced Maurice Gee? Apparently, a McIndoe reunion for those who worked with him, and the patients, is planned for next year. Miriam says I must go. Will you be there?'

Long after she had finished the letter, Catherine sat, thinking. Did she want to see Max again? Would old wounds be reopened? And if she did see him again, should she tell him he had a seven-year-old son whom he did not know existed?

———

They had bathed the boys and tucked them in bed, Joe with a book and Alexander with his new Lego. Now they were settled either side of the fire, each with a baby on their knee.

'Happy?' Hartley looked slightly apprehensive as he asked the question.

'Very,' Sarah said firmly. 'Watch Catherine Rose's head. She's a right little wriggler.'

There was a ring at the door and they both jumped. 'What can it be, at this time?' Sarah said. It was only 7 o'clock, but when Catherine was away, Hannah was their only visitor. Unless there was trouble at home? Jim and Molly, perhaps? Her heart began to thump as Hartley got up to go to the door.

It wasn't trouble at home. It was worse. It was Hartley's parents who followed him into the room.

'We waited till now to make sure you were here, Hartley.' His mother's tone was laden with doom.

'Sit down,' Sarah said. She had regained her composure now. This was a chance to build bridges, and she intended to take it. For Hartley's sake, and for the twins' sake, too. These were their grandparents, whether or not she liked it.

'We haven't come to make trouble.' This was Mr Walters, who looked thoroughly miserable.

'We've come to beg you to see sense, and come home, Hartley.' Mrs Walters looked at Sarah for the first time. 'This woman has you mesmerised, and now there's two children to consider. I've talked to a solicitor, and he says that, if you're sure the children are yours, you can apply for custody . . .'

'You've done what?' Suddenly Hartley's voice was a roar.

'I warned you, Mother,' Mr Walters said, ruefully.

'You've consulted a solicitor about my taking my children away from their mother? What are you, Mother – though I hesitate to call you that now – a monster? And more important, what do you think I am?'

'I think you've been a silly boy, Hartley, but it's not your fault. You weren't equipped to deal with the situation.'

Hartley's voice had returned to normal but there was a new authority in it. 'I'm not a boy, Mother, I'm a man. If you can't accept that, you and I can have no relationship. I love Sarah, and I want to marry her – if she'll have me.'

A few moments later, he was ushering them out. But his father turned in the doorway.

'I'm sorry,' he said to Sarah. And then, looking at the baby in her arms, 'Take care of them.'

'I will,' she said, and smiled at him.

Hartley came back into the room. There was colour in his cheeks, and it made him look more boyish than ever.

'I think you've got a question to ask me,' Sarah said, 'and before you do, the answer's yes.'

———

'Are you home for ever, Daddy?' Natasha was climbing on his knee. Nanny Grace had placed Diana on a rug in the centre of the floor, where she sat placidly playing with coloured bricks.

'Not for ever, darling. But for the rest of the evening.'

'Does that mean you won't have to go out to vote?'

'No, there'll be no division tonight, and even if there is I'll pretend I don't hear.'

Natasha giggled. 'That's naughty.'

'Very naughty. But then I am naughty, sometimes. Now, is it stories, or shall we play Ludo?'

Natasha plumped for Ludo, and they sat in a pleasant haze of dice and moves and whoops of glee when one or the other of them got a counter home. 'I'm happy,' David thought. 'Not perfectly happy – that can never be – but as happy as is possible.'

Even as contentment overcame him, though, the outside world intruded on his thoughts. There was serious unrest in Persia, where British citizens had been killed; and men were still dying in Korea. President Truman had been forced to sack the revered General MacArthur for his escalating threats against China, which was pouring men in to inflame the conflict there. When he and Valerie had married, he had envisaged them growing old together, raising their children in a peaceful world. Now he doubted whether the world would ever be peaceful.

He was called away from the Ludo board by the ringing of the telephone, but the call did nothing to cheer him. Ernest Bevin, that mixture of shrewdness, humanity, and, when it was needed, brutality, was dead.

'Surely you can spare an hour?' India was aware she was pleading but she couldn't help it.

At the other end of the line, yet another friend was making more excuses. 'It's the children, India. And then Archie says I gad about too much.'

When she put the phone down, she saw that Rupert's eyes were fixed on her. 'Have you no pride at all, India? That's the third call you've made tonight, and each time you got the same answer. When will the penny drop?'

'I don't know what you mean?'

'I think you do. You just won't admit it, even to yourself. No one wants to be seen with you, or to be with you. You're a drunk, India, and a particularly unpleasant one, at that. I've offered to get you help, but until you face the fact, nothing will work.'

India felt fury bubble up inside her. 'How dare you? How dare you speak to me like that, you malformed pygmy. You're nothing without me. You were lucky to marry into my family, to be associated with the Callingham name. You're a whipper-snapper, Rupert, and this house says it all. This is what you brought me to – little better than a semi-detached, when I had been used to the splendour of Kynaston. I lowered myself –'

Suddenly Rupert was fighting back. 'The splendour of Kynaston? That place you love more than flesh and blood? Well, you'd better get used to living without it, India, because your brother is giving it away!'

~~~

'Jacqui? You're surely not jealous of Jacqui? She's just a good sport – we have a laugh.'

'I don't like her,' Catherine said stubbornly. 'She's – well, there's a kind of insolence about her. As though . . . as though . . .'

'Oh, Jacqui's too clever by half, I'll give you that, poppet. But she's useful to me. Now come here and let me show you who I really care about.'

'No,' Catherine said, but they both knew she didn't mean it.

'Come on,' he said. 'Come to daddy, or the big bad wolf will come and gobble you up!'

'Aren't you ever serious?'

'Not if I can help it.' And then he was kissing her, his lips moving down her throat and into the cleft between her breasts, and nothing seemed to matter any more except becoming one with him.

Chapter Twenty Six

October 1951

'IT'S A NARROW WIN,' DAVID said, 'but we're back in government!'

He and Catherine were listening to the BBC's summing up of yesterday's election. There were still one or two results to come in, but it looked as though the Tories were assured of a 17-seat overall majority. 'The Liberals have virtually collapsed. They polled two million fewer votes than last time.'

'The voters have obviously turned to the Conservatives,' Catherine added.

'I feel sorry for Attlee.' David was frowning as he spoke. 'The Left-wingers are already accusing him of having betrayed Socialism.'

'But the country is rejecting Socialism, can't they see that?'

'They're not rejecting it entirely, Catherine. I don't think that will ever happen. But they're tired of being lectured, and they're tired of austerity. That's why they reacted as positively as they did to the Festival of Britain – they want fun and froth, and a general feeling that everything is going to be better. Overnight, if possible. It can't be done, of course, but Attlee is blamed for it, all the same. We've all known that Labour was done for. Not even the Festival could save them.'

'At least you're back in, David. That's a relief.'

'With a decreased majority, but, yes, I'm back. And the electioneering is over, thank God. Now I can concentrate on clearing out Kynaston ready for the handover.'

'No regrets about that?'

'A few. Memories. Tradition. But do I want to change my mind? No.'

'What about India?'

'What about India? She's her own worst enemy, beyond any doubt. She has used every legal manoeuvre, every form of blackmail, threat and skulduggery. She even suggested I should just deed it to her. Can you see that – India in Kynaston waging war on the peasantry.'

'Don't be cruel. I don't think she's happy at the moment . . .' Something stopped her from telling him about the rumours sweeping Belgate, that the Lindsay-Hogg marriage was on the rocks.

'If that were true, Catherine, I would feel pity for her. But the truth is that my sister was never happy. Never in her entire life. She came into the world cursing the midwife; and she'll leave it saying the doctors let her down! I'd be feeding all her fantasies, her delusions of power, if I let her get her hands on Kynaston. I've done the best thing all round, Catherine. I don't doubt that for a second.'

~~~

Most days now, India drove to Kynaston and sat drinking in the beauty of the place, but today she couldn't summon up the energy. Instead she stood at her bedroom window looking out at the roofs that seemed to move nearer their house every day. 'I am suffocating here,' she thought. It was all David's fault. If Henry had lived, Kynaston would once more have become the focus of all eyes, the epicentre of the county, indeed of the North, and she would have been there at his side, the perfect mistress of a great house.

She heard feet pounding along the landing. That would be Loelia, who was already a hoyden. She needed thrashing. If Rupert weren't so lily-livered, he would do something about it. But he was besotted with Loelia, and in the clutches of little Miss Butter Wouldn't Melt. No doubt Imogen was cast in the same mould . . . or would be once Rupert and Nurse Adams had done with her.

That nurse had become the chief focus of India's animus, second only to David. Sooner or later, she would deal with her, but her brother was another matter. Thinking of David brought her back to Kynaston. What did anything that happened in this horrid suburban house matter when compared with the loss of Kynaston?

She sank on to the dressing-table stool, uncertain whether or not to cry. Instead she opened the bottom drawer in the dressing-table and felt for the bottle hidden under her silk hand-kerchiefs. Rupert had removed drink from downstairs – only the tantalus was left, and even that was locked. So now she was forced to hide her supply, like some guilty, thieving servant.

She would have a drink to pull herself together, and then she would work out how to sort it all out. She could surely still make things go her way, if she worked at it.

⁓

'Well, I reckon he's dying. There was a photo of him in *Picture Post* last week, and he looked ghastly.' Hannah pulled her face into a grimace. 'Like this, as though he had strings in his face.'

The King did indeed look gaunt, Sarah thought, but Hannah always looked on the black side. As far as the papers were concerned, George VI had had a satisfactory operation last month. Everyone was saying he had cancer, but they could do wonders for that nowadays.

'Time will tell,' she said to Hannah, and tried to turn the conversation to things other than imminent death. 'How do you feel about Churchill getting back?'

Hannah's face was a picture, a mixture of pain and satisfaction. 'Well, on the one hand I'm sorry, because he's a bloody Tory. On the other hand, we'd all be in concentration camps if it wasn't for him. I never voted for him, mind.' But her guilty face told a different story.

'You did!' Sarah accused her.

Hannah pondered her chances of brazening it out, and then gave way. 'Well, they should never have chucked him out when they did. Not with the war still on. It was ungrateful.'

'So you evened it up this time? Well, just don't tell our Jim. He'll be beside himself this morning. And speaking of Jim, how's it going with Molly since she moved back in? They're polite enough with one another, when I go down there, but one swallow doesn't make a summer.'

'She's learned her lesson. Well, she has if she's got any sense. Those bloody Yanks, they'll still be here next year, you mark my words. It's occupation, that's what it is. I mean, what do we need their men for now we've got National Service? And that's another thing – they're shipping young lads off round the world for two years, getting them into all sorts of trouble, getting daft ideas. They'll be bringing slitty-eyed brides and all sorts back, if we're not careful.'

'Hannah, half of them never get beyond Catterick Camp, and that's just up the road. Anyway, I'm all for folk moving around, seeing a bit of the world.'

Hannah chuckled.

'Folk moving around didn't do you any harm, did it? Sending you yon fancy man you're wedding the morn.'

This morning Pamela had felt a slight tug when she buttoned her coat. She was three months pregnant, and already showing. She turned her head and smiled at Michael. 'It won't be long, darling.'

He nodded. The waiting-room was painted green, and Pamela tried to work out the exact shade. Not pea, certainly; not jade. Apple, perhaps? A nurse appeared in the doorway, a folder in her hand, calling, 'Mrs Godber?' A woman stood up and followed her through the door.

'Shall I see if I can get a cup of tea somewhere?' Pam suggested.

Michael shook his head. 'No, let's get it over, and then we can get back home.'

They were waiting for him to have an X-ray of his chest. He had been seen in another department, and the X-ray had been decreed. 'Upper and lower torso,' the doctor had told the secretary, who wrote it down and them a form.

'Please God, let him be all right.' Inside her head, Pamela was praying. He had come through a world war; she couldn't lose him now – not with a longed-for baby on the way at last.

***

'Why are we going to Belgate?' Beside Catherine in the passenger seat, Ben was looking to her for an answer.

'To collect something for Aunty Sarah. She's getting married tomorrow. You know that.'

'Will I be her pageboy? Like I was for you? With Alex and Joe?'

'Not this time, darling. Aunty Sarah isn't having bridesmaids or pages. But I'm going to be her Matron of Honour.'

'Like hospitals?' Ben was looking confused, and slightly alarmed.

'Nothing like hospitals. It's not that kind of matron, it's more like a helper. We're going to have a lovely time.'

'Will Uncle David be there?'

'Yes. He certainly will. He's staying on specially.'

'I like Uncle David.'

'I know you do. And he likes you.'

'He says I'm Number One Boy. Better than girls.'

'I bet he said no such thing. That's a fib.'

'Well, only a little fib. He does think I'm the best boy.'

'Little fibs count. They make your nose grow.'

'Like Pinocchio?'

'Exactly like Pinocchio.' She had taken him and Joe to see Disney's film at the cinema, and it had made a great impression.

There was silence for a moment, and then Ben spoke again. 'I don't like Will.'

Catherine knew it was important not to react, so she kept her voice even.

'Why not?'

'Because he doesn't like me.'

'I'm sure that's not true.'

''Tis. He says I'm a damn nuisance.'

Catherine felt her mouth dry. Did she reprove Ben for using a naughty word, or ignore what he had just said, or do what she wanted to do – stop the car and hug him tight?

'Well, we're nearly there, so get ready to help me with Aunty Sarah's things,' she said at last. She was fobbing him off, and they both knew it; but what else could she do?

Last night she had tackled Will about money. 'When we bought this house, you said we'd share the expenses. But I've paid them all up to now. If you could just . . .'

He had thrown up his hands in mock horror. 'Of course. Why didn't you say? It's just that you're so loaded, it never occurred to me you'd need my little pittance. But I'll see to it right away.'

'The knives will be out for Attlee now. A pity. He's a good man.'
David looked around the constituency office. 'God, I feel as
though I've lived here these past few weeks.'

'We almost have.' The agent had taken his pipe from his
mouth, and waved it to illustrate his point. 'It's the Liberal
collapse that's let the Tories in, but Attlee will get the blame.
Morrison will see to that. And Bevin, who was his greatest ally,
is gone, which hasn't helped.'

'I was saying much the same to Catherine earlier.'

'We miss her in the office. A dab hand with constituents, she
was.'

'She's still a big help to me when I need it,' David said. 'But
yes, she was a wonder here. I hope Attlee won't decide to retire
from the fray. I admire him immensely. He took on a country
whose stamina had been sapped by six years of war, and tried
to make it whole again. The trouble is, America is like a vast,
suffocating mogul, stifling all competition. Attlee wanted to
build Jerusalem, and to some extent he has. But it wasn't
enough.'

'It's poetic justice in a way. He came in because of the
nation's ingratitude to Churchill, and he's going out because of
its ingratitude to him. Perhaps history will vindicate them
both.'

As he drove back to Kynaston, David thought about the
attempts to build a Socialist Utopia. That had been the dream
at the end of the war, but the old class system had proved
harder to shift than the Socialists had expected. People still, on
the whole, went into jobs according to their class. The aristoc-
racy flourished, waited on by people born to service and rigid
laws and rules. 'They cling to what they know,' David thought.
'They don't realise that their vote has power . . . and with that
power goes the responsibility to build a better society.' Capital
punishment, the ostracising of homosexuals, physical punishment of young offenders – all emblems of a bygone age . . .

there was a long way to go.

But as he neared Kynaston, he turned his attention from the worries of his country to a worry closer to home. In last week's gossip columns there had been a frisson about a certain male writer and a certain female radio presenter. It had been obvious to him who was meant, and discreet enquiries had confirmed it. According to rumour, Will Devine and some minor BBC figure called Jackie, or some such, were having an affair.

India managed to turn on the new television that Rupert had installed in the sitting room. Privately she thought the wretched things common, but when you were bored you turned to anything.

It was showing pictures of Churchill re-entering Downing Street, and she felt a little glow of satisfaction. Served those Red usurpers right! But the satisfaction didn't last. She had hoped for some music or fashion, even laughter, but all she got was politics.

She was wondering whether or not to turn it off, when Rupert entered the room and pre-empted her.

'Why have you turned it off Rupert? I was watching that.'

'I need to talk to you, India, and I must have your full attention.'

She turned what she hoped was a languid gaze on him. 'Well?'

'I'm going to divorce you, India. I'm sorry it's come to this, but it has. We'll both be happier apart.'

A wave of fury rose up in her. How dare he dictate the future? If there were to be any leaving, she would do it. 'If you leave me, you'll never see the girls again,' she said.

'If you think I'd leave my daughters with you, India, you misjudge me. The girls go with me.'

'You can't do that. No court in the land would take young girls away from their mother.'

'I think they would when I showed them this.'

He was handing her a paper, and she took it with a shaking hand. Something in his voice frightened her.

The paper was a notarised statement, in fact a dossier, complete with dates and detail.

'*On 13th October I observed Mrs Lindsay-Hogg the worse for drink. This was the first of many such occasions. She made Loelia cry by saying she was going to cut off her hair for being naughty.*

'*On 17th December, I came into the bedroom to hear Mrs Lindsay-Hogg frightening Loelia by telling her there were monsters in the walls who would come out at night when she was asleep.*

'*On 14th February I had to intervene when Mrs Lindsay-Hogg . . .*' India couldn't read on, and the paper fell from her hand.

'You will turn up at the church, won't you?' Hartley sounded really anxious, and Sarah looked up at him, laughing.

'I might. Anyroad, it's you who'll get cold feet.'

'Never. I've even written a speech.'

'What does it say?'

'It tells everyone what a witch you are. How you got a poor Bevin boy under your spell so he couldn't think straight any more.'

'I'll tell them different!'

'Brides don't get to say anything, so you won't be able to.'

They went on teasing one another, but pictures were whirring through Sarah's mind: Gerard going off to war; his face when she told him she had fallen wrong. Hamish gentle; and then the returned warrior she had come to fear. Last of all, the shy young man in the Belgate High Street, and the day he had grown up. She smiled at him.

'Time you went. I've things to do.'

He picked up the case he was taking to Hannah's, where he would spend the wedding eve. 'I'll see you in church, then,' he said, and suddenly his voice was thickened with emotion.

'Not if I see you first. Now be off with you.' She kissed him tenderly, and led him to the door.

———

They had opened a bottle of wine, a rare extravagance. 'Cheers,' Mike said as they clinked glasses.

'I'm looking forward to tomorrow,' Pamela said. 'It's not going to be a grand wedding, but you know they'll be happy.'

'It'll be pretty grand. Catherine has pulled out the stops, hasn't she?'

'Oh yes, there'll be all the trimmings. But there won't be a huge crowd. No one at all from his side, they say.'

'Which is sad. Still, Hartley and Sarah are well matched. They shouldn't be – they're different ages, classes, education. But they fit together.'

'Like us?'

'Not like us, we have everything in common. Pass that bottle. You shouldn't drink too much in your condition, so I'd better drink yours as well.'

'It's going to be all right,' Pamela thought. 'It's going to be all right.'

———

'Right. Five minutes of peace and then we're both for bed.'

They clutched mugs of cocoa, and sat on either side of the fire, old friends in perfect harmony.

'I'll miss this place when I go, Cathy,' Sarah said. 'It's been like a sanctuary to me. Remember that night I came back from Scotland?'

'I do remember. The three of you came up the drive like orphans of the storm.'

'That's what we were. And you took us in without a word.'

'I was glad to see you, Sarah. I was on my own too, remember – pregnant, and without a husband.'

'How did we become friends? I mean, we were chalk and cheese.'

'It was Joe. Big Joe. He brought us together with that letter.'

'Do you think he meant to do that? Intended that we should be friends? I mean, why ask me to deliver a letter to a girl I didn't know?'

Catherine shook her head. 'I don't know whether he deliberately set out to make us friends, but I think he'd be glad that we are.'

'If our Joe hadn't been killed, what would've happened?'

'He'd've come back after the war, and we'd have married, eventually.'

'Your parents would never have let you. You living in The Dene, all posh, and him a squaddie. A miner he'd've been, when the war ended.'

'I like to think we'd have been brave enough to stand up to them.'

'In a way,' Sarah said thoughtfully, 'in a way, Hartley's parents are a bit like that . . . trying to keep us apart because of class.'

'And equally wrong,' Catherine said firmly.

'What will we be like when our own kids are grown up? Will we try to make them do as we tell them?'

Catherine groaned and put down her cup. 'I can't look that far ahead, but I can see as far as tomorrow, and if we don't shut up and get to bed we'll be a pretty sight in church in the morning.'

They carried their cups to the kitchen and then, arms round one another, they climbed the stairs to bed.

Chapter Twenty Seven

February 1952

INDIA SCANNED THE MORNING PAPER, but there was nothing of interest. This was a local paper, so she had expected only rubbish, but there had been nothing that mattered in *The Times* either. Her tea had grown cold, and she rang the bell. 'Make me another pot,' she commanded the woman who shuffled in. The woman picked up the pot, but she didn't speak. They were all insolent nowadays.

The world had gone mad, India thought. No point in dismissing staff, as the replacements were often worse. Those servants she had trained to a semblance of good behaviour in this house had now gone off with Rupert and the children.

She looked round the room. She had some pieces from Kynaston now, but even their lustre seemed dimmed in this utterly suburban house. Quality needed a proper setting. She and that Louis Quinze cabinet had a lot in common: they had both been wrenched from their natural habitat, and stuck down here.

The fresh tea, when it arrived, was little improved, but she made the best of it, and picked up the local paper again.

She was skimming over the announcements when a name jumped out at her. Kynaston! She read avidly. A custodian was wanted for Kynaston, the magnificent stately home that was to be an education centre for the County Council. Gifted to the people of Durham on a 99-year lease by Sir David Callingham, the house would be used by school groups and adult-education classes. The custodian would be in full charge . . .

Suddenly a heavenly vision opened up to India. At 5 o'clock on Fridays . . . or maybe even earlier . . . strangers would depart, and the house would belong to the custodian. She pushed away her half-eaten toast, and leaned back in her chair to think.

Pamela sat with her knees pressed together and her gloved hands folded on the top of her handbag in front of her swollen belly. Michael had been in with the consultant for 20 minutes. He must come out soon. It was now nearly five months since his operation for cancer. They said they had got the tumour out, but you could never be sure. She would know by his expression now whether the news was good or bad. She had always been able to read his face.

He had cried on the night they had heard the diagnosis. 'I'm frightened, Pammy. I could take Jerry on, but I can't take this.'

'You can,' she had told him firmly. 'You can and you will, because John and I need you.' But inside her, fear had boiled, and gone on boiling.

If the news today were bad, she would still smile, still fight – but inside her something would die. She had loved Michael since that first day when she had come out of the factory and seen the bus pulling away. She was running without much hope of catching it when a blue-clad arm had come out from the platform, and half-lifted her up beside him. The conductor had said, *'That's dangerous, Miss, what you just done!'* and she and Mike had looked at one another and grinned. She had thought him the handsomest man she had ever seen, and cursed the smell of machine oil that always hung around her clothes and hair when she left the factory. But it hadn't put him off. '*You look all right to me,*' he had said, when she apologised for her headscarf and her grimy face.

She realised she was smiling foolishly and looked around guiltily, in case people were looking at her. But they were all sunk in their own troubles, just as she was. She would know the minute he walked down the ramp towards her . . . She swallowed hard, and set about composing her face.

And then a figure was appearing and striding towards her, and she could see that he was grinning like an idiot. 'It's tickety-boo, Pammy, tickety-boo.'

David settled back in his chair in the committee room, and listened. The situation in Egypt was getting worse. In January, Cairo had been rocked by rioting in which 17 British citizens had perished. King Farouk was trying to keep a lid on the unrest, and British troops in the Canal Zone were on full alert, but the situation was sticky. The speaker was a member who had served in Egypt for years, and knew the Egyptian temperament, and this early-morning meeting was to allow him to impart his expertise.

He was a good speaker, so it surprised David when a whisper started to go round the room. It grew and grew, until the speaker halted and looked towards the noise.

'Sorry.' Another member was half-rising to his feet. 'It's just that the King has died – in his sleep last night. At Sandringham.'

There was genuine sorrow on people's faces. And shock – although the King was known to have been ill for six months. 'He looked ghastly when he saw Princess Elizabeth off to Australia,' David said to his neighbour.

'And when he opened the Festival,' the man replied.

'A bit sticky when the heir to the throne isn't on British soil. Princess Elizabeth's in Kenya now, isn't she? Who's actually at the helm till she gets back?' No one knew.

The meeting broke up, then. Everyone had their tale to tell, their opinion, their view of what should happen. David passed groups in the corridors, or glimpsed them through half-open doors. The Palace of Westminster was like a beehive, he thought, buzzing with gossip and industry, sometimes producing honey and at others venom. But on a day such as this – a momentous day, since the man who had died had been an anchor for his people in time of war – on a day such as this, it truly was the hub of the nation.

Catherine was ready to go shopping when the telephone jangled.

'Pammy! I'm glad you rang. What's the news?'

At the other end of the line, Pamela was upbeat. Michael had had a promising result. 'He's not out of the wood yet, but so far so good. Really good! However – have you heard, Cath? The King's dead?'

When Catherine put down the phone she reached into her pocket for a hanky. He had been a good man, who had overcome that terrible speech impediment to lead his people in war. Will was upstairs in his study: he might not know. She put down her bag and gloves, and sprinted up two flights.

'Will? Have you been listening to the wireless?'

'Hardly, poppet. I'm in the middle of writing what is rapidly becoming London's leading comment column. It does need a smidgen of concentration.'

She hated it when he treated her as though she were silly. 'I only asked because the King's dead. Pammy just telephoned.'

Will did not raise his eyes from his typewriter. 'Well, he did have cancer – and he's 50-something, and hardly the brightest star in the firmament. Sad for his family, of course. Can I get on now?'

Catherine backed out, without answering. Did Will care about anything? Last month she had suspected she was pregnant. '*God, I hope not,*' he had said. And then, seeing her face, had added: '*I'm sorry, old thing, but I can't stand children . . . never could. And you have Ben.*' And finally, seeing her expression again: '*One day, maybe, when I'm old. When there isn't so much to do.*'

Now she turned back and looked in at the door. 'You haven't forgotten I'm going out to a dinner with David tonight?'

'No, I've remembered. What time will you be back?' His eyes were still on the typewriter.

'Late,' she said. 'Not before midnight. Don't wait up.'

In the beginning they had not wanted to be apart. He would have been waiting up with a nightcap, and kisses, and wonderful, wonderful love-making. She went downstairs and let herself out on to the street.

She had come to love London, even its ordinary terraced streets with their wrought-iron railings and extravagant window-boxes. But today the sky above was leaden, the pavement beneath her feet uninviting.

≈

India had telephoned the council offices, sure that the mere mention of the Callingham name would be enough. But the girl on the other end of the phone had been ignorant. 'You'll have to apply,' she kept insisting. 'Write in to the Chairman.' His name was Councillor Rewcastle, and it was c/o County Hall.

'Rewcastle.' The name rang a faint bell. She'd heard it before, but nowhere important. She tipped the pen nib carefully against the inkwell, and began to write. Once she explained who she was, they would know that she, and only she, was the person to care for Kynaston.

———

Sarah and Hartley had been in their little house for six weeks, but she still couldn't get over the fact that they actually owned it. When Hartley had mentioned the word 'mortgage', her eyes had flared alarm.

'We'd never get a mortgage,' she had said. Mortgages were for other people.

But he had smiled away her fears. 'It'll pay off in the end, Sarah. Yes, it'll be a struggle, but worth it. And what else would we do with Cathy's money but use it for a deposit?'

Privately, Sarah had been able to think of 101 things she could do with the £100 that Cathy had given them as a wedding present, but in the end they had put it down on No 57 Meadow Close. It was a semi-detached with three bedrooms, two reception rooms, a kitchen, and a bathroom. 'And there's a space for a garage,' Hartley had said, as if they would ever have a car of their own.

But what had entranced Sarah were the leaded windows. She had never dreamed of having a house with leaded windows. She looked at them now, and thought, quite seriously, that she might die of pleasure.

But that wasn't funny, not on the day the King had actually died, and a sad young Princess was having to come all the way home from Africa.

She thought about the new Queen as she made tea. It was strange not to have the wireless on, but nothing was being broadcast except things like weather forecasts and news bulletins, and they were all about the poor, dead King. The boys would be home from school, soon. If the twins stayed asleep until Hartley got home, that would be perfect. He and she could explain to the boys about the King – unless they'd been told at school – and then they could all have a nice time together until bath-time and bed-time.

She smiled, thinking of the boys' faces as they 'helped' to bath the twins, making an unholy mess but warming her heart just the same. Sometimes she would look up and catch Hartley's eye and know he was thinking what she was thinking, and that was so nice.

'I'm home!' Hartley was calling from the hall, and she was drying her hands to go and greet him when he came into the kitchen, an open letter in his hand, the letter she had put aside for him this morning. He went on reading, without giving her his usual kiss, so she knew it was serious.

'It's from my father,' he said at last, meeting her eye. 'They want to come and visit. It's quite a conciliatory letter. It seems they've climbed down. The question is – should we let them?'

Sarah felt her heart pounding, but she kept her voice steady. 'Of course we should. They're your parents. They've got a right to come.'

Catherine had settled Ben for the night as soon as she was dressed. 'I wish you weren't going out,' he said, but in tones of resignation, not real misery.

'So do I,' she said, kissing him. 'But I have to back Uncle David up, you know that.'

He nodded, and then his face brightened hopefully. 'Is he coming to pick you up? Will he come up and see me?'

She shook her head. 'I'm going over in a taxi, so that he can have more time with the girls. He'll bring me home after dinner, but you'll be sound asleep then – or else! But we might see Uncle David and the girls at the weekend. Will's downstairs, if you need anything. Now, lights out at eight. Big day at school tomorrow.'

'OK,' he said resignedly, and then: 'It's sad about the King, isn't it?'

'Yes. Yes, it is sad. He was a good man.'

'But at least his children are grown up. I mean, they knew him. It's not as if they were babies, like Diana. I expect she misses Aunty Valerie a lot.'

He's trying to tell me something, Catherine thought. He's using Valerie's children, but he's really talking about not knowing his own father. Fear clutched at her. Sooner or later there would have to be a confession. Aloud she said, 'I expect she does, but she has Uncle David. Now, only read for a little while, and then go to sleep.'

'Is that a promise about the weekend?' he asked, and when she nodded, he smiled, and went back to his book.

Will was in the hall when she got downstairs. 'Umm,' he said, 'someone looks good enough to eat. Why not stay in and let me gobble you up?'

She smiled at him but the hurt over the pregnancy false alarm was still there. 'I won't be back till midnight, I should think.'

He kissed her, then, and she felt the old stirring. But the cab was at the door, so there was no time to dally.

＝

'I don't know, I'm sure, Sir David. She's been clingy all day, poor lamb, but I didn't think it was more than just a little cold.'

'She looks flushed,' David said. Natasha looked small in the bed, and the face looking up at him was Valerie's. 'What do you think we should do?'

Before Nanny Grace could answer, there was a ring at the door. 'That will be Mrs Devine,' he said, and catapulted down the stairs.

'Don't panic,' Catherine said firmly, as he poured out his fears. 'Let's go up, and see what's going on.'

In spite of his anxiety, David could still register the fact that Catherine looked beautiful tonight, the fur collar of her coat thrown back to show the aquamarine dress underneath. But there were shadows under her eyes, and she looked strained. 'I'm sorry,' he said. 'I shouldn't be bothering you with this.'

'Who else would you bother? I am Natasha's godmother, David, in case you've forgotten.' She put a hand on the little girl's brow, and a finger on her pulse. 'Poor Natasha, I expect you feel dreadful. Well, we'll soon put you right. Shall Nanny Grace get you a nice drink?'

The child was nodding, but Catherine was turning away and beckoning David to follow her out of the room. 'I think we should have the doctor, David. I'm sure it's not serious, but better be safe than sorry.'

'What shall we do about the dinner?' he asked, when he had telephoned the doctor.

'Give me the details,' she said. 'I'll ring with apologies.'

'But you were looking forward to it, Catherine. Why don't you go alone? You'll know everyone there.'

'I wouldn't dream of it. And to be totally truthful, I'll be glad of an early night.' She didn't say her heart had quickened at the prospect of going home to Will.

They went back upstairs, and toasted the dead King in a good dry wine. 'Yes, he'll be missed. I remember those wartime broadcasts – everyone holding their breath, hoping he'd get the words out.' David was smiling as he remembered.

'And knowing the Queen was there, willing him on.' They were still reminiscing when the doctor arrived, and diagnosed a mild case of measles. He gave them strict instructions, and together they saw him back out to his car.

'There,' Catherine said. 'It's not serious, but you needed to know. I'd keep her away from Diana, but it's probably too late.

Anyway, better they have it now; it's only serious when you're older. I suppose you've had it?'

'Yes, when I was away at school. Miserable in the san till Papa came to get me. What about you? You couldn't take it back to Ben, could you?'

'Both had it. Now, I'll run up and talk to Nanny Grace. You pour us two more glasses of that nice wine, and then we'll both be good and go early to bed.'

In the cab on the way home, Catherine felt relieved. She really would appreciate an early night. Perhaps she and Will could share a nightcap? If he hadn't eaten, she'd rustle something up, and then – in bed, there was still no barrier between them. She felt desire well up in her as she paid off the cab and fumbled for her key.

There was a light on in the hall to welcome her, and lights in the kitchen and living-room beyond. She took off her shoes, which were pinching her toes, and padded through. But the downstairs rooms were empty. Will must be in his study.

She took the stairs two at a time, not calling out for fear of waking Ben. But the study door was ajar, and the room in darkness. He must have gone to bed, but he'd still be awake. He never usually went to bed as early as this. There was light under the door and she was smiling as she opened it.

It was Will's back she saw, his naked back, rising above the bed – and the woman who lay beneath him had red hair that was fanning out on the pillow. There was no mistaking who she was. It was Jacqui Currie.

Chapter Twenty Eight

April 1952

INDIA DRESSED WITH CARE. MUSTN'T look too regal. These were little people, after all, and used to simple things. She would simply explain why she understood Kynaston as no one else did, and that would be that. There would be other candidates there – they had to do that for appearance's sake. But the job was obviously hers. The clerk had said as much: 'Councillor Rewcastle specially wanted you included, Mrs Lindsay-Hogg.'

It was annoying that they were using Rupert's name, when she had taken care to put 'Callingham' on the application form, but it didn't really matter. So there it was, a *fait accompli*.

She unlocked the door of the Wolseley Rupert had left for her, and got behind the wheel.

At first it had been a relief to be back at Mellows, and know that she need never again set eyes on Will. But Catherine missed the hustle and bustle of London; and Mellows without Sarah and the boys was not the same. If only David had still been here, not at Kynaston but safely installed in the Dower House, his new home. However, he was 270 miles away, and it was no good fretting. At least she had Pamela and her parents, and Ben, not yet at his new school, was there beside her.

She heard the post plop on to the mat, and went to collect it. Bills, what looked like an Easter card, and another letter. The stamp was foreign, but she recognised the handwriting before she opened it.

Max was still in Israel although the security situation was making life difficult there. '*I hope you are well and happy, Catherine. I know we agreed that what was between us had to end, but you know that I care for you. I hope I, too, have a small place in your heart. Could we meet as friends? I have often asked myself that question. Now, the reunion I wrote of is happening. I shall be in London in late October. It would be good if we could meet then, for old times' sake – but of course I understand if you think this is out of the question.*'

She sat with the letter in her hand, trying to imagine how it would be. He would walk towards her. 'Hello,' he would say, and she would answer. Would she see disappointment in his face? Would he see undiminished love in hers?

For a moment she probed her feelings gently. Did she still love him? Would seeing him again reawaken the old longing?

She was still pondering when the phone call came. 'I think this is it, Catherine. Can you get here?'

'I'm on my way, Pammy! Just hang on until I get there.'

'They say Mountbatten is literally climbing the walls,' the Whip said cheerfully. The Queen had just announced that she was retaining Windsor as her family name. Her descendants would be called Windsor, rather than by their father's name, Mountbatten. This was, apparently, much to the annoyance of Louis Mountbatten, Prince Philip's uncle, who had openly exulted over the fact that future kings would bear his family name.

They turned to parliamentary business, then, and the demands that the forthcoming coronation would make on resources. 'A huge morale-booster, though. What do they say: give the people bread and circuses? Keep them happy. Of course, we're doing well out of the disarray within the opposition.'

Last month, Bevanite MPs had defied a three-line whip on a defence vote. David nodded. 'Yes, you can't help feeling sorry for Attlee and some of his lot. They've worn themselves out for their beliefs, and now they're being tossed aside.'

'Happens to us all, old boy, in time. But don't expect me to be sorry for Socialists. Ruination of the country. Ruination!'

David contented himself with smiling. His own opinions were not nearly so trenchant.

———

David had felt uneasy ever since Churchill's announcement to the House that an atomic bomb 'will be tested this year'. The test would happen in Australia. The old man had previously denounced the Labour government for secretly building a plant capable of developing an atomic weapon while decrying those same atomic weapons. 'Machiavellian,' Churchill had called it, which was one way of describing downright hypocrisy.

'But where do I stand on this?' David wondered. 'Do we stay armed, for fear of attack, or set a good example to the world – which might turn on us at any moment? According to Americans, the forthcoming test was a peace move, since it would add to the world's deterrents. That was fine – but what about fall-out, radio-activity? They were all new words that had entered everyday vocabulary.

Still . . . he put his worries aside, and went to make sure Natasha got off to school.

On his way to the House, he thought about Catherine. She

was safely installed back at Mellows now, and he missed her company in London. But she had come to him the night she had discovered Devine's infidelity. 'To me,' he thought, and felt exultation well up in him. He would never possess her, but he would always be there for her.

〜〜〜

'Well, it's like they're brushing Philip under the carpet, Sally. And him a war hero. She should have stood up for him. "I'm Mrs Mountbatten," she should've said. There's a picture in the *Daily Express* today – Philip's got a face on him like a wet weekend, and who could blame him?'

Sarah nodded wearily. She had endured a full 20 minutes of the state of the monarchy, interrupted mid-flow only by a furious protest that the cheese ration had been cut again. As if Hannah had read her thoughts, she reverted to the cheese scandal.

'One ounce! You couldn't bait a mousetrap with that, let alone make a decent sandwich. And while I'm on about sand-wiches, have you seen the advert for *Singing in the Rain*? Supposed to be the best musical to come out of Hollywood. Mind you, it'll take months to get to the Regent. We might as well be on a desert island here.'

She paused for breath, and Sarah seized her chance. 'I was wondering how things were at me Dad's? I'm going there when I leave here.'

'Jim and Molly are still together, if that's what you mean. But your Jim's changed, Sal. He was a nice, open-hearted kind of man, but that's all gone. Cold he is now, picking people up on the least little thing. I was telling him about Cathy being back at Mellows, because that fancy lad she married had been acting up. Went up in a blue light, he did. All about men always getting the blame, when really it was the woman that caused the trouble. By, he's changed!'

'Blame the war, Hannah. It's changed everyone, men and women – for better or worse.'

―――――

When India's name was called she went forward into the room. Eight or ten people, men and women, were ranged behind a table, and she was directed to a chair in front of them, for all the world like an inquisition.

The man in the middle introduced himself as Alderman Hoy, the chairman of the sub-committee, and then asked the other members of the panel if they had any questions to put to her.

India looked along the line. Where was Rewcastle, who had wanted her for the job? The sub-committee chairman was saying, 'Councillor Leithead?' And an elderly woman was shaking her head to show she had nothing to say.

'Councillor Rewcastle?' This was it. The woman outside had told her this Rewcastle was the chairman of the Council, but was only here as a committee member, not as chair, which was a pity. Never mind, he could still be an ally.

A man two seats from the end was leaning forward – he must be Rewcastle. 'You were in the WVS in the war, Mrs Lindsay-Hogg?'

'Yes,' she said. 'Throughout the war. I was in charge of this area.'

'And you were there to supply people's needs?'

'Within reason. We had to be firm sometimes.'

'My wife came to you once. When I was in hospital, and we had children, and another on the way. She turned to you. The hospital had told her you would help.'

Inside India, a little knot of unease formed. 'There were so many applicants,' she said, 'that I can't remember them all.' She gave him quite a warm smile.

'I think you might remember my wife. She was eight months pregnant, and alone and desperate.'

Suddenly an image came into India's mind. A woman in a shabby raincoat that strained over her swollen stomach. She had mocked her – she could now remember that. But what exactly had she said? More important, what had she done?'

'Do you remember, Mrs Lindsay-Hogg?' Rewcastle was smiling now, but it wasn't a pleasant smile. The woman had asked for things she needed for her confinement, and India had answered, '*What an earth made you think we could supply things?*'

'You asked her how many children she had,' Rewcastle went on.

India sought for words. 'I probably did. I would need to know a lot of things if I were to be in a position to help.' Perhaps the man didn't know everything. She could still make this work.

'But you didn't help her, did you? You suggested her child might be a bastard, and that even if it wasn't, she'd been careless to get pregnant at all.'

'I hardly think I'd have said that.' Even to her own ears she sounded guilty.

'You did, I can assure you. Your words are imprinted on my wife's memory. I wasn't there to fend for her because I had been wounded in a V2 raid down south. Where I was on war work, Mrs Lindsay-Hogg. War work. You told her you'd see what you could do, but in the end you couldn't . . . or wouldn't . . . do anything.'

India knew then that it was hopeless. The faces opposite her had turned to stone. It was a mercy when the chairman said she could go. 'You'll hear from us later,' he finished, and she felt hysteria bubble up in her. They were such silly little people. What did they know about great houses . . . about anything?

In the car she lifted the bottle from the glove compartment

and took a swig. It burned her throat, but it also empowered her. She would show them! For a moment in there she had been afraid, but that had been foolish. They would need her eventually. No one understood Kynaston and its little foibles as she did.

She let out the clutch and moved off, taking another drink, and wiping her mouth with the back of her hand. She would show them – she knew every stone, every pane, every nook and cranny.

She was still listing the reasons why she and Kynaston were destined to be together, when the blue car came round the bend and roared towards her.

⁓⁓⁓

On the opposite bench, David could see Nye Bevan looking smug and bellicose at the same time, his usual expression – except when he scored a hit, at which time the beam almost split his face. 'I don't like him,' David thought. 'I instinctively don't like him, and yet I know he has done good things in his time.'

Perhaps that dislike grew from his own admiration for Clement Attlee? Last month, sickened by the personal vendettas and endless warring within his party, Attlee had denounced Bevan and his gang as wreckers. They were, he had said, running a party within a party. David looked along the benches opposite at Bevan's acolytes, Harold Wilson and Richard Crossman. They were on Labour's National Executive now, so the Left were winning. Like Churchill, Attlee would be dumped. But Churchill had come back. Never the same man, David inwardly conceded, but back in office, nevertheless. Perhaps Attlee could do it, too?

I'm not cut out for this place, David thought. Or perhaps I want to live in a fantasy world where no one is ever disloyal or unpleasant? The word 'unpleasant' pricked his conscience. That was how he had found visits to India lately – unpleasant, if not unbearable. If Valerie had still been here, she would have known what to do. Perhaps she might even have kept India on the right track.

As it was, he had simply avoided her, and now, by all accounts, it was too late – her drinking had taken over. I am no better than the people I condemn, he thought, and felt ashamed. He would seek India out the next time he went north, and see what he could do. Perhaps if he talked it over with Catherine . . . or Rupert? He must do something.

≈≈

'It's a very nice cake.'

Sarah could see that Mrs Walters was trying to make conversation.

'Thank you,' she said, 'I haven't got a recipe for it. My Mam used to make it. I just copied her.'

'Well, it's good,' Mr Walters said, helping himself to another piece.

'Hartley says you used to make him lovely cakes when he was at home.' He had actually told Sarah that his mother's ginger cake was dry as sawdust, but today was a day for building bridges, so what did a little white lie matter? A small smile crossed her mother-in-law's face. So far so good. It was heavy going, but it would be worth it in the end.

This morning, Hartley had looked up from the paper and lamented the death of Ernest Bevin. 'I had a lot to thank that man for, Sarah. At first I cursed him for sending me down a pit, but if he hadn't . . .' He had smiled at her then, a lover's smile, '. . . if he hadn't, I'd never have had all this. So I wish him well, wherever he is.'

'The twins are coming along no end.' This was Mr Walters,

giving Sarah a cautious smile. Catherine Rose and Freddy were cooing on the rug in front of them.

'Hartley is really good with them,' Sarah said. 'You'll see when he gets here. He shouldn't be long. Still, while you're waiting . . .' She bent and picked up her daughter from the floor. 'This one's a Daddy's girl, so we'll give her to Grandma, shall we?'

The older woman's eyes were on her as she hugged the baby, and they were misty. They were also ashamed.

'Babies need grandmas,' Sarah said. 'And my Mam's gone, God rest her soul, so Catherine Rose is lucky to have you.'

I feel generous, Sarah thought. I feel I want to draw them in, stop the hurting. There's enough war in the world, God knows, without us fighting at home.

———

Catherine left Pamela serene in her bed, the toil of childbirth over. The new baby, to be called after his father, was sleeping like a top. Michael himself was still thin. In fact, his collar stood away from his neck and the bones of his wrists were prominent when they protruded from his cuffs. But his joy at seeing his son was heartwarming, and when Pammy had looked up at him there had been no trace of fear in her face, so it must be true that the doctors were pleased with his progress. One less thing to worry about!

She was back to brooding about whether or not she ought to see Max again as she drove up to Mellows, but as she put her key in the door she could hear the phone ringing.

'Rupert?' What was Rupert Lindsay-Hogg doing ringing her at this late hour?

She listened with mounting horror, hardly able to take it in. India was dead. Killed in an accident on the Kynaston road. 'I tried to telephone David,' Rupert was saying, 'but the number was engaged – and I have to go out now to see to things.'

'Of course, I will tell David, Rupert. What about your girls? I'll come and help you with them if you need me. I'm so terribly sorry.'

When she put down the phone she was shaking as she dialled David's number.

'David, I'm so very, very sorry, but I have something terrible to tell you.'

When he put down the phone, David sat staring into space. She was gone, the woman who had dominated his childhood far more than his mother had done. He tried to imagine India dead, inanimate, silent. He couldn't. If ever anyone had been alive it was India.

He thought of her now, striding along the landing at Kynaston, her arms heaped with bed linen. The house had been full of guests for Henry's wedding to Catherine, and she had coped with everything. We never backed her up, he thought. We were never grateful to her. She had been hard, brutal sometimes, but she had cared about the family. He had even taken Kynaston from her, the only thing she had really loved – except for Henry.

'I'm alone,' he thought suddenly. 'They've all gone: Papa, Mother, Henry, India . . . I am the Callinghams, now.' He had not loved India – she had made that impossible. But while she had been there he had been part of the whole. Now he was the whole. There was no fall-back, apart from children too young to understand.

Do I pick up the torch, he wondered. Or do I let it go, in this new England? Perhaps there is no longer a place for the family we were.

Chapter Twenty Nine

November 1952

CATHERINE COULD HEAR THE CHILDREN chattering as she came down the stairs, Ben's voice louder than those of the two little girls. He liked being here in David's London house so much that she felt guilty to be returning with him to Mellows, as soon as the McIndoe reunion had taken place. She had talked with David's solicitor in Durham before she came away. Soon her divorce proceedings would begin, and the further she was away from Will the better – so Mellows it must be.

David was entertaining the children at the dining-table with his oink-oink pig imitation.

'Honestly,' she said as she took her place, 'I didn't think I had four children to look after.' David gave an enthusiastic 'oink', and the children collapsed into gales of laughter. The laughter continued until Nanny Grace appeared to whisk them all away for a walk in the park. Ben ran towards the door, and then, seeing the girls kiss their father, ran back and held up his face to hers. A second later he went and repeated the gesture with David. It was entirely natural, and Catherine felt her lip quiver. She had deprived him of a father of his own. Had she been selfish? Was it too late to tell him now?

'Penny for them?' David said, when the children were gone and peace restored.

'Ooh, there's more than a pennyworth.'

'Worried about this evening?'

She nodded. 'But don't mollycoddle me, David, or I'll cry.' At 7 o'clock tonight she would enter a crowded room at the Connaught Hotel and come face to face with Max – her lover, Ben's father, a man she had not seen since a few months after D-Day when his American superiors had transferred him from the hospital where they worked together, to the battle-front.

'You can always back out, Catherine.'

'I know. Don't think I haven't thought of that. But sooner or later I have to face up to things. The burning question is, do I or don't I?'

'Tell him he has a son?'

'Yes. Do you think I should tell him?'

David shook his head. 'Catherine, I would do most things for you – but settle a momentous question like that? I couldn't do it. Whatever decision you make, you will have to live with it.'

'So will Ben,' she said. 'So will Ben.'

The wind caught Sarah as she turned in at the cemetery gates. Today would have been her brother Joe's birthday. If he had had a grave here, instead of somewhere in France, she would have been carrying flowers for him from Catherine, and a posy of her own. There would have been flowers, too, for Gerard Foxton, her first husband, if he had not, like Joe, been buried near where he fell. One day she hoped to go to the war cemetery in Brittany, with its neat rows of crosses. Hartley had told her it could be done.

Now she picked her way to her mother's grave, and refilled the vase, doing away with dead flowers and replacing them with chrysanths she had cut from the garden that morning. Her mother had been dead for 15 years now, and Sarah still thought she caught sight of her sometimes, in the street or, increasingly, in the mirror. 'I'm growing old,' she thought and smiled to herself at the thought.

She was on her way out of the cemetery when she saw the black marble stone. '*India Lindsay-Hogg. A loving wife and mother.*' She remembered, now, that India had not been buried in the Callingham vault in the private chapel, because Kynaston was no longer in Callingham hands. There was a biblical quotation on the stone, but that was all. They had stretched things a bit to say 'loving', if all accounts were true, but they had to put something.

There were no flowers on the grave, and the black stone and surround were stark against the bare earth. On an impulse Sarah went back to her mother's grave and took a single bloom from the vase. She laid it on India's grave and crossed herself. 'Have pity on her, Holy Mother, and grant her eternal rest.'

David valued his time on the benches of the House. There was a comfortable security about those green leather seats, an anonymity about being one among many. He had sought to catch the Speaker's eye sparingly since his maiden speech, but when he went into the voting lobby he felt as though he was making a difference. Sometimes he worried about what would happen if there was ever a three-line whip on what he considered to be a matter of conscience. Was he man enough to vote with the opposition? He wouldn't do it lightly, but he hoped he would go through with it if the occasion warranted it.

Yesterday he had watched the new Queen, looking ethereally beautiful under the heavy crown, declare open her first Parliament, and felt a lump in his throat as he watched. 'I am turning into a sentimentalist,' he told himself, and looked guiltily around in case members were watching him smile foolishly into space.

Opposite him, Attlee was listening intently to the debate. He looked tired, almost shrunken. Last month he had lashed out at Bevan and his Left-wing supporters, accusing them of wrecking the Labour Party. They, in turn, had accused him of 'dithering and doodling' while the party tore itself apart. As the Bevanite portion of the National Executive became stronger, David's own party were rubbing their hands in glee at their opponents' disarray. He himself was less amused: the state of the world demanded that politicians in every democracy should concentrate on what they were doing, not indulge in silly spats.

Trouble rumbled on in Korea. In Kenya more than 40 people had been murdered by Mau Mau terrorists, using pangas to hack to death any European they came across. There was a new president in America, the former General Dwight D. Eisenhower, and rumours that a weapon was being developed which was more powerful even than the atom bomb. Sometimes it seemed that war had not been defeated, it had merely retreated underground, ready to emerge at any time. So children like his daughters, like Ben, might one day also find themselves at war. It didn't bear thinking about.

Across the chamber Harold Wilson was whispering in Bevan's ear, and the Welshman was grinning. What were they up to? But thinking of Ben had brought thoughts of Catherine to spoil his concentration. What would happen when Max Detweiler was ready to leave the reunion? Had it perhaps happened already?

'Have I lost her?' David asked himself, and then accepted the harsh reality that she was not his to lose.

Pamela tried to concentrate on the figures in front of her, but she couldn't stop thinking about what they were going to eat tonight. Mercifully the baby was sound asleep in the carrycot by her side, and at least she could supply his needs. Not that it would be long before he was toddling, and she would not be able to tote him round so easily. Still, he was a joy, so she would cope somehow. She smiled at the thought of Michael's face when he had first seen his new son, and then returned to the serious business of tonight's meal. Since she had returned to work for her father, shopping had been a problem; and now, with the meat ration reduced and their coupons used, it would have to be eggs or cheese – and little enough cheese at that. It was 1952, seven years since the war's end, and still no end to rationing.

In the workshop, a wireless was playing the *Limelight* theme from the latest Charlie Chaplin film. Apparently the girl in it, Claire Bloom, was ravishingly beautiful. Michael had offered to take her to see it when Catherine came to baby-sit, and she had pulled his leg about lusting after a film star. But a trip to the pictures wouldn't solve the problem of tonight's meal. She was still racking her brains when her father came into the office.

'Catherine's big reunion, today,' he said.

'Yes. After all these years. She's hoping to see some of the pilots she nursed, and hear how they've got on.' She didn't mention that Max Detweiler would be there, too. She and Catherine had agreed there was no need to trouble their parents. '*They'll only hope for a happy ending*,' Catherine had said. 'And there isn't one,' Pamela thought now. Well, not in that direction, anyway.

She turned her thoughts back to her meatless plight. It was true what the British Medical Press had said a few years ago: everyone in Britain was suffering from malnutrition, whatever the Government might say to the contrary.

'Order book's looking good,' her father said, looking up from a ledger. 'Fifteen per cent up on last year at this time.'

It was true. Slowly but surely things were improving. Eventually, even meat would come off ration.

Catherine had tried on and discarded one jacket already, and the clothes she had brought to London with her were limited. Downstairs she could hear the *Limelight* theme: Nanny must have the wireless on in the morning-room. Funny how film music took the world by storm. It seemed only yesterday there had been that zither tune, 'The Harry Lime Theme'. Now it was Chaplin – they said he'd composed the *Limelight* theme music himself. She hummed it, remembering the words that went with it: '*I'll be loving you eternally, With a love that's true, eternally.*'

The words seemed apt for today. Except that she wasn't at all sure whether she still loved Max. Sometimes she could hardly remember his face.

She was still humming when she heard the doorbell ring. A moment later, a maid appeared. 'There's a gentleman downstairs, Madam.'

'Have you told him Sir David's out?'

The girl looked distinctly uneasy. 'It's for you, Madam. It's Mr Devine.'

Catherine's heart sank. What could he want? She was tempted to tell the maid to send him away, but that would cause gossip. 'I'll be down directly,' she said.

Will was lounging at the fireplace, one arm on the mantel, an elegant foot on the fender. 'Catherine!' He was smiling, until he took in her expression.

'Oh, don't worry, old girl. I don't want to try again. It's the divorce court for you and me, I know, and I won't make waves. I've got this huge assignment coming up with the Spectator, but the truth is I'm a bit strapped for cash at the moment. So if you could see your way clear . . .'

———

'It was awful, Hartley, just bare. No loving words, no flowers, just bleak. "*India Lindsay-Hogg. A loving wife and mother*".'

'I'm tempted to say you reap what you sow, Sarah, but I know you wouldn't like it if I did.'

'I can't deny she hated the world, Hartley.'

'Which means she hated herself.' He smiled at her as he said it, and then moved to put his arm around her in a consoling hug.

Afterwards, as Sarah dished up the meal, she found herself still thinking about India. How could two people born of the same parents be so different? David was as kind as India had, by all accounts, been cruel. Hannah had been full of a tale of India's being humiliated at a Council meeting, and crashing her car deliberately, but the inquest had ruled that it was an accident.

'They covered it up,' Hannah had said afterwards, 'like their sort always do. But it's true, I had it off her that cleans at the Council. She said it was all round the offices. I pity her bairns, but she got what she deserved, that's all I can say.'

Did anyone deserve a lonely grave, and no one to mourn them? One day, Sarah thought, when money's not tight, I'll go back to Scotland and see to Hamish's grave. I could plant a bush there.'

'Penny for them?' Hartley said, coming up behind her.

'I was thinking about holidays,' she said. 'Butlin's.'

Around Catherine the room was thronged with men, most of them young, most with pretty girls at their side.

'Nurse Callingham?'

The last time she had seen him, the scars had been red and angry. Now they had faded to silvery lines, except for the odd place where the skin was puckered and tucked. 'Garrett? It is you!'

He was smiling down at her, and then a girl had appeared at

his side, a baby in her arms. 'This is my wife,' he said proudly, 'and this is Georgie Garrett Junior.'

Catherine cooed over the baby, and heard about Garrett's marriage and his place at a college where he was learning microbiology; and then another man was taking his place. It was Stephen Baker, the boy who had once come in to visit the badly burned Spender. He had had a girl by his side then, a pretty girl with a sparkling engagement ring on her finger.

'Are you here alone?' she asked him now, and he nodded. She saw that the eyes in the tight eyelids were sad. 'You're remembering Daphne,' he said. 'She . . . it didn't last. Still, there's better fish in the sea.'

After that it was a whirl of meeting and remembering, but all the while she kept thinking of Spender. 'You're my star patient,' she had told him once – and then he had killed himself because of a 'Dear John' letter.

She felt tears prick her eyes at the memory, and looked around the room. Where was Max? Perhaps he hadn't come after all. She had almost run away herself at the last minute. She could see Sir Archie McIndoe at the head of the room, the great man who looked not great at all, but had worked miracles of plastic surgery. He was surrounded by men, patients mostly, but she recognised also one or two members of staff.

She was raking the group for a sight of Max, when suddenly he was there at her elbow.

'Hello, Catherine. I was watching the door for you, wondering if you'd come. But when I found you, you were surrounded by young men.'

There were lines around Max's eyes that had not been there before, and the hair at his temples was grey, even white. 'It's been a long time,' she said, holding out her hand.

'It's eight years. You haven't changed at all. I want to know all about your life now.' He reached for her other hand. 'A ring?'

She shook her head. 'A ring. I'm Catherine Devine, but I'm no longer married.' It wasn't strictly true, but with luck it soon would be. She felt strange standing here with the man who had been her lover, her only real love. As if he sensed her thoughts he smiled ruefully.

'This is . . . kind of strange. I have often imagined this moment. Coming face to face with you again – '

'Me, too, but . . .'

'No crowds, in those imaginings?' he said, and she nodded. 'We have to stay at the party, for a while at least, but then maybe we can get away . . . if you're free? There's so much I want to know. You're still living at Mellows? I used to wonder if my letters ever reached you.'

'You never gave me a return address,' she said. She knew her eyes were fixed on his face, but she couldn't look away. People would notice but what did it matter?

'I was moving around.' They both knew that was an excuse. 'Have you been happy?' Max reached for her hand again, and she gave it willingly. Let people talk.

'Sometimes,' she said.

Around them, the room heaved with emotion. Acquaintances re-met, memories re-lived. Sometimes the laughter was uproarious, at other times a hush would fall. All their lives have moved on, Catherine thought, and so have ours.

And yet, standing there with Max, it was as though time had rolled back. 'It is 1944, again,' she thought, 'and we have never been apart.'

'What's this? Is this a wolf in my daughter's bedroom?'

Ben had left his own room and joined the girls. Their laughter had penetrated downstairs until David had thrown aside his speculation over how Catherine's reunion with Max was going, and had come to seek company upstairs. Now he advanced on the boy, fangs bared, claws extended, until all three children screamed mock terror.

'That's enough, now,' he said at last, 'or I'll be in trouble for getting you excited at bedtime.'

'Don't go,' Ben said. 'Not yet, anyway'.

'No, Daddy, please.' Natasha was giving him the smile that could not be resisted.

'Well, just a few minutes, and then it's lights out. But no more wolves. It's bedtime.'

'Tell us about Uncle Henry,' Diana said. 'I like it when you talk about when you were a little boy.'

'Well –' David sat on the edge of his daughter's bed and pulled Ben to him, 'I had a big brother called Henry . . .'

' . . . who was very brave, and was killed in the war. My Mummy told me about him.' Ben said, suddenly grave.

'Yes, he was brave. Even when we were young.'

'You used to be knights on the staircase!'

'That's right. Henry was King Arthur and I was his knight.'

'Did my Mummy play with you then?'

'No, Ben – she came later.'

'And you had a sister too. My Aunt India.' That was Natasha.

'Why was she called India?' Ben asked. 'It seems a funny name for a girl.'

'She was born in India. My father – your grandfather, Natasha and Diana – was out in India helping people, and that's where Aunt India was born. And then they came home, and Uncle Henry and I were born. At Kynaston. India loved Kynaston.'

'She died in a car crash, and I have two cousins, Loelia and Imogen, and an Uncle Rupert.' Diana recited these details proudly.

'Yes, you have,' David said.

But when he and Nanny Grace had settled the children, he made his way downstairs with his conscience pricking him. He couldn't pretend to have fond memories of India as he did of Henry, but she had been family, after all. Did Rupert tend her grave? He couldn't blame him if he didn't – but surely her children should be reminded of their mother?

He thought of the many times he and the girls talked of Valerie. They hurt like hell, but at the same time they were balm. He would have to see what he could do.

He looked at the clock. Ten minutes to nine. How was Catherine faring – and would she come in with eyes aglow at having met Max again? He poured himself a whisky, and switched on the 9 o'clock news in an effort to block out dangerous thoughts.

It was 10 o'clock before the speeches had been made, the tributes paid, and Max and Catherine could retreat. It was cold when they got outside, and he took her arm and pulled her closer to protect her from the wind. She hoped he could not sense that she was trembling, and began to chatter fiercely. 'So, are you permanently based in Tel Aviv?'

'Yes. Miriam works at a clinic there, and soon Aaron will go to university. But he must do military service first, which is a worry.'

'Are you afraid he'll be killed? Israel is not at war?'

'We're not at war, but we're not at peace either. Once upon a time the dream was of Jerusalem. "Next year in Jerusalem," we used to say. "We'll make the desert bloom," we said. Now we're in Jerusalem, but our coming has driven so many Arabs away. I ask myself how it can be right that we, who were always refugees, have created so many more.'

A side street was looming up, and they turned down it, away

from the street lamps.

'There are camps, now, Catherine. No cruelty there, except the cruelty of being displaced from the land you thought was yours by right. One day perhaps Aaron will have defend his land against other young men who think it is theirs.'

Their pace slowed, and he looked down at her and smiled. 'Don't look so downcast. It is not all gloom. We are a melting-pot there – doctors, lawyers, professors, and the odd *shlemil* – all working together. And sometimes . . .' He shrugged. 'We dance, we drink a little wine . . .'

A pub sign glowed in the darkness. 'Let's go in here,' he said.

It was quiet, and they found a corner alcove away from the few customers. When they were settled, drinks between them, coat collars loosened, he took her hand. 'I've wanted to see you so much, Catherine. To make sure I hadn't damaged your life with my selfishness.'

She wanted badly to reach out and touch his face, but she knew that physical contact would be too much for both of them. Knew that he was thinking the same thing. It was there in his every gesture – the yearning to touch and hold that, once allowed, would not be denied.

Instead she smiled, to banish the anxious look from his face. 'No,' she said, 'you haven't damaged my life. We loved each other, but we were right to part. We'd have lived in guilt if you had stayed, because we'd have been hurting innocent people. But you didn't harm me, Max – quite the contrary.

'What we had was wonderful, and I have a little part of it still. I always will. I have wondered whether or not to tell you this, and I still wonder if it's right . . . but now I think, perhaps, you should know.'

'THERE,' SARAH SAID, PINNING THE poppy firmly into place on Alexander's jacket. He was looking down at it, and she could see that he was still uncertain about its significance. Joe, on the other hand, had puffed out his chest the moment the poppy was placed on it. 'He knows his father was a hero,' she thought. And yet, in his own way, Hamish had lain down his life for his country, too.

'You should both be proud,' she told them. 'You both had dads who went to war. This is the day when we say thank you to everyone who did that.' She did not add, 'and died in the attempt'. Time enough for that. They had each accepted the one death. The thought of all those crosses, row on row, would be beyond them.

'That was Dad on the phone,' Hartley said, coming back into the room.

'Everything OK?'

'Fine.' He smiled at her. She hadn't come to love Hartley's parents – and in the case of his mother, she probably never would. But she understood them. 'I'd fight for my sons, too,' she reflected, 'if I thought someone was threatening their happiness.'

'Anything we need to do for the twins?'

She shook her head. 'No. I think we're about ready to go.'

They collected the pram from the lobby, installed the twins in it, gave the older boys a final inspection, and set off down the road to the Cenotaph. It stood on the green that marked the centre of Belgate, the place where, at the 11th hour of the 11th day of the 11th month, this small part of the nation would pause to remember.

'So you're going to have the most lovely day with Nanny Grace, and when you come home, Ben and I will be here, and we'll all have supper together.' Two little faces looked up at Catherine: Valerie's face, each one. Hannah Chaffey had had a saying, *'She'll never be dead while that bairn's alive.'* It was true: you did live on in your children.

One day she would talk to them of their mother. For now, she contented herself with making sure they were buttoned and gloved against the cold, and sent them downstairs to say goodbye to their father.

David had read *The Times* from cover to cover, although it was only 7.30. He had been waiting for it when it plopped through the letter-box. Sleep had evaded him last night, and when he had slept, he was tormented by dreams of Catherine and, curiously, of Valerie too.

He could understand why he was disturbed about Catherine. Today was the last day of Max Detweiler's stay. He had remained in London so that he could attend the Remembrance service and parade at the Cenotaph in Whitehall. David had secured places for himself, Catherine, Ben and Max, where they would have a good view of the proceedings. Afterwards they would all lunch here, and then he would go off briefly with Ben so that Max and Catherine could take their leave of one another.

Except that they might not take leave of one another – they might decide to leave London together. And yet Max talked freely of his wife and family back in Israel – would a man do that in front of a woman, if he was contemplating asking her to share his life? Perhaps he was worrying unnecessarily.

His cogitating was interrupted by the arrival of his daughters to say goodbye, and hold up their faces to be kissed. 'Aunt Catherine says we can stay up for supper tonight,' Natasha said carefully, watching his face for signs of rebuttal.

'If Aunt Catherine says it, it must be true.' David rose, and went to the window to watch them down the steps and into the car.

He went back to his paper, but looked up as Ben entered the room. 'I'm very hungry,' the boy announced.

'It's only an hour since breakfast,' David said, but he rang the bell to summon some food.

Ben looked squarely back at him. 'I'm a growing boy. Mummy says so.'

David smiled, but he was struck by a new and terrible thought. If Catherine went away with Max, Ben would go, too.

'Are you looking forward to today?' he asked, as Ben tucked into hot milk and biscuits.

The boy nodded. 'Will I be with you?'

David smiled. 'Yes, you will.'

Ben's 'Good!' was emphatic.

'Max will be there too, as well as your mother.' That elicited only a shrug, and David felt a surge of pleasure. 'I matter to Ben,' he thought, 'more than Detweiler does.' But when had a boy's liking ever swayed a woman's heart? 'You're a fool,' David told himself firmly, and went back to the paper.

'Mummy says the Queen will be there to lay a wreath.'

'Yes. It'll be the first time she does it as Queen.'

'It must be scary for her, being a woman.' Ben's tone implied a degree of pity for the Queen's female state, and David felt his lips twitch.

'Oh, I expect she'll manage, Ben. Women are quite strong, you know.'

'You're not taking Natasha and Diana to the Cenotaph!' Ben said accusingly.

'That's because they're too young. They wouldn't understand. But you will, young man. It's the day when we remember very brave men and women, so off you go when you've finished your second breakfast, and come down here smart as a new pin.'

'Uncle Max was in the war. Mummy says he was pretty brave.'

'And I wasn't. I just stayed at home because of this leg of mine. That was a bit grim for me.'

'Mummy says you did a very important job, holding everything together and running the Home Guard in case the Germans came. She says there's a pillbox near your old house. Did you have a gun?'

'Yes, I had a gun.' David thought of the Home Guard. They had been brave, but how long could old men and boys have held out if the Germans had actually come?

'I'll show you the pillbox one day. Now, run along and get ready. I sent a tray up to your Mummy, but I expect she'll be down directly.'

Michael had gone ahead to join the RAFA contingent at the Sunderland Cenotaph. When first he joined the RAF Association, Pamela had worried. There would be endless reminiscing there, a rekindling of the memory of old, dangerous times. Would it reawaken the feelings of loss that had plagued him? But no, Michael came back from his club nights looking relaxed and boyish.

Today he was the standard-bearer. She would hold John up, baby Michael too, if he was awake, and let them see their father perform his task. There was still a stretch of years ahead of them before they could be sure his cancer was cured, but she had faith that it was. Fighting cancer was a battle fiercer than war, but they had seen war through together. This would be no different.

Pamela pinned her poppy in place, and went in search of her children. Today she would bow her head and give thanks for Michael's safe return. And she would say another prayer for the women, thousands of them, who had not been so lucky.

A fine mist of rain had been falling as the ranks marched towards Whitehall. Now it had cleared, and the marchers could lift their heads. They were all proud – serving men and women immaculate in their uniforms.

But all eyes were drawn to the veterans, some of them seeming to totter but all pressing forward. If Henry had lived, David thought, he would now have been 33 years old. But he had died in combat, and the mantle of Kynaston had fallen on himself. 'I never wanted it,' David thought now, 'but I have come to love the land and its people.' It had been worth defending. Henry had known that – and now he knew it, too.

They were playing 'The RAF March Past', and David turned to find Catherine's eyes on him. She remembers too, he thought.

Catherine knew David was thinking of Henry. So was she, but she was thinking too of Spender, and Joe, and Sarah's Gerard. And those men – boys, really – who had turned to her for comfort when they were afraid. It was almost incomprehensible now, the notion that she had gone to bed with strangers simply to banish their pre-battle fears for a little while. 'I'm not proud of it,' she thought, 'but neither am I ashamed.' You did what you had to do in war, and didn't ask for quarter.

'It's impressive,' Max whispered in her ear. 'You Brits do these things well.'

She turned and saw that his eyes were on the young Queen, ramrod-straight, the red poppy on her breast vivid against the black she was wearing. This was the royal act of remembrance in Whitehall, but all over the country, in city or town or on village green, there would be the same reverence, the same acknowledgement of the nation's debt.

She felt Ben tugging at her sleeve. 'Is this the best parade in England, Mummy?'

She shook her head. 'They're all the best ones. Aunty Sarah will be a Belgate with Joe and Alexander, and Aunty Pamela in Sunderland with Uncle Michael and John. Perhaps little Michael, too.'

'And we're here.' He sounded satisfied, but then another question occurred to him. 'Will they have the same hymns and prayers?'

'The words are always the same, wherever you are on this day, so we're all together in a way.'

Across the boy's head her eyes met Max's, and she saw approval in them. He had met his son for only the second time today, and she could see that he was proud of him. She remembered his face when he had learned of Ben's existence – incredulity, and then a dawning satisfaction. 'I was right to tell him,' she thought, and was glad.

Hartley had lifted Alexander on to his shoulders for the march past. The child's hands were placed gently on either side of his stepfather's head. The last marchers were passing now, the sound of the colliery band dying away. Sarah was straightening Joe's coat and tucking pram rugs around the twins. 'Time to go.'

'It's a wonderful occasion,' Hartley said as they walked home. 'One day in the year when class does not exist, when no man is more exalted than another . . . we honour them all the same.'

He sounded pleased, so Sarah didn't tell him what she was thinking – that men had had to die before they could be treated as equals. The war had broken down some barriers, but others remained. It was still his lordship in his castle, the peasant at his gate.

They ate lunch around David's table: cold salmon and salad, with a fine crisp Sauvignon to wash it down. David had wondered if the conversation might be awkward, but in fact it flowed.

'I was thinking about a friend of mine today,' Max said. 'A man called Cohen, Chuck Cohen. He was in London at the Embassy.' He smiled at Catherine. 'Remember the tinned peaches and the cookies? They came from Chuck. I was going to meet him in a pub in London, when a flying bomb took the pub out. Right out!'

'It must have been towards the end of the war, then?' David said.

Max nodded. 'Yes, Hitler's dying act.'

The conversation moved to the new President, General Eisenhower, and whether or not he would be as good a president as he had been a general. Afterwards they listened as Max talked with obvious enthusiasm about Israel.

'So you fly out tonight, and you're in Tel Aviv for the morning?'

Max nodded. 'Given the time difference, I'll be home in a

few hours. It's my daughter's batmitzvah soon, and I must be there for that.'

He's thinking of his wife, David thought, and felt a sudden anger. He had not thought of her seven years ago, when he fell in love with Catherine. Or perhaps he had still thought of her – you could love two people. He knew now he had not cheated Valerie by never stopping loving Catherine.

Under cover of sipping his wine he looked closely at Max Detweiler. Did Catherine still love him? Max was talking to Ben, telling him about America. 'You'd like New York. Maybe you'll go there one day. I grew up in a place called Manhattan . . . an island, although you'd never know it.'

David looked now at Catherine. She had a half smile on her face, but he guessed she was deeply aware of Max's departure, and counting the remaining moments. 'Ben,' he said aloud, 'I want to show you the new birdhouse. Let's go into the garden.'

'What will you tell the boy?' Max asked, when he and Catherine were alone. 'Or *will* you tell him?'

'I must tell him one day, unless you'd rather I didn't. He'll ask questions before long.'

Max shook his head. 'I'd be proud for him to know I'm his father. Perhaps when he's a bit older, and can understand.'

'Will you tell Miriam about him?'

'I don't know. I don't want to make her unhappy.'

'Ben has a right to know he's your son,' Catherine said defensively.

But Max was shaking his head, and gesturing towards the window. In the garden David's head was close to Ben's, the two of them deep in conversation. 'My seed,' Max said. 'But David's son.'

She stared at him as he continued. 'David loves that boy, Catherine, and he also loves you. I've known that since the

Christmas when he first brought me to Mellows. I saw his face when you opened the door to us. He loves you, and I think you love him – though perhaps you don't know it yet.'

David saw Max coming down the garden towards him. Beyond the high walls of the garden, the hum of London had replaced the military hubbub of the morning. The American halted in front of his son, and held out a hand. 'I guess I'm on my way now, Ben. It's been great to meet you.'

He looked at David, then, and the two men exchanged a glance of understanding. 'This is hard for Max,' David thought, and wondered whether he should leave man and boy alone for a while.

But Max forestalled any action. 'I think you should go see to your mother now, Ben. Remember what I said about New York. Maybe we'll meet there one day.'

'He's a fine boy,' David said, as Ben raced towards the house.

'He is,' Max said, not taking his eyes off Ben until he disappeared into the house. 'Thank you for all you've done for him. For Catherine, too.'

David was about to say that it had been a pleasure, but Max's next words took him by surprise. 'I know you love her, David. I've known that from the beginning. Catherine has told me how much you loved Valerie, but it is possible to love twice. I know – because I've done it. Catherine loved me, and I hope a part of her still does. But you are her real love, David.

'You can tell me to butt out, and you'd be entitled, but I have to say one thing before I go – don't waste any more time.'

He held out his hand. 'Goodbye, and thank you.'

David could find no words, but he covered their clasped hands with his free hand, and hoped that conveyed his feelings.

As the American walked quickly back into the house, David wondered quite what he should do next. Was Max right? Could Catherine love him? He knew she already loved his children, as he loved hers.

He shook his head, as though trying to shake his jumbled thoughts into some kind of sense. She had called him a fool, once, because he couldn't see love when it was staring him in the face. And she had been right. He had loved Valerie, and always would. But how could it be possible, after all the years, that Catherine could love him?

And then he saw that she was coming towards him.

'David?' She sounded young and scared. He wondered what to say, and then he dispensed with words and held out his arms. She came into them willingly, and he held her as he had held her in a thousand dreams.

They stood for a while, not speaking, and then Ben was calling from the step. 'Uncle Max has gone. He said to say "Shalom".'

'That means peace,' Catherine said.

'I know.' They stood together as the boy came down the garden towards them. David gathered him into the crook of his free arm, and together they went back into the house.

If you've enjoyed this book and would like to find out more about Denise and her novels, why not join the **Denise Robertson Book Club**. Members will receive special offers, early notification of new titles, information on author events and lots more. Membership is free and there is no commitment to buy.

To join, simply send your name and address to **info@deniserobertsonbooks.co.uk** or post your details to The Denise Robertson Book Club, PO Box 58514, Barnes, London SW13 3AE

Other novels by Denise Robertson

All Denise's novels are available from good bookshops price £7.99 Alternatively you can order direct from the publisher with FREE postage and packing by calling the credit card hotline 01903 828503 and quoting DR10TP1.